Sun Dance

by

Iain R Thomson

**Grosvenor House
Publishing Limited**

This book is published by
Grosvenor House Publishing Ltd
28-30 High Street, Guildford, Surrey, GU1 3EL.
www.grosvenorhousepublishing.co.uk

A CIP record for this book
is available from the British Library

ISBN 978-1-908105-59-2

By the same author,

Isolation Shepherd

The Long Horizon

The Endless Tide

The Raven's Wing (poetry)

Achnowledgement

Who better than a Gaelic speaking, retired headmistress with her family roots in Skye to gather the drift of this yarn and moreover, fathom my style of spelling. For many years Roddy MacKenzie and I have played for the annual Hogmanay dinner dance at the Lovat Arms Hotel in Beauly. Auld Lang Syne, a 2am. last waltz and we all drew breath, I raised my glass to a couple whom I noticed knew all the dances; Morag Foster and husband, Peter. During the course of conversation I admitted to the intention of writing a novel. In the spirit of the occasion the lady offered to proof read it. Fortunately I didn't forget. Years passed. On making a hesitant phone call, greatly to my surprise and now my sincere appreciation, she took up the challenge. Her expertise was applied and much encouragement has followed, hence the decision to publish. Thank you, Morag.

To Robbie Fraser Thomson for the front cover design and by no means least to Jane for providing my writing den with the odd bottle of Highland Park.

PRELUDE

The Skylark's Song

Hand turned coilacks of hay, cured by sun and the faintest breeze, dotted a small field beside the sea. Meadow grass and wild flower lay brown and gathered. Hay fork and wooden rake stood propped. The air's merest breath came and went as if the long gentle swell which spread without a sound on the curving sands was the lung of the great ocean itself. And here, under the sun's burning orb, the sheep's fescue and honeyed clover, poppy and trefoil in the fragrance of their wilting yielded the scent of days wholesome and forgotten; for over the scatter of tiny crofting fields there hung the blueness of immense time and distance.

Generation upon generation had built each field's fertility by the toil of the foot plough and the seaweed fills of woven creel. Crop of the seabed, harvest of an ocean cycle, it was cast at the foot of shifting dunes by the curl of winter's gale; long, dark lines of nature's bounty, gathered and spread by hand, dried by the summer's warmth. Bent shoulders carried its wealth to fields that tasted the salt spray and trembled to the thud of a winter sea. Living fields, alive, nurtured as though of the family they looked towards an ocean rim which lay so wide and vast it curved before them as the arc of the earth mirrors the tip of a setting sun.

Land, sea, and livelihood, man and beast; century upon century; slow the steps of change. Since times of hut circle and stone arrowhead what happenings had truly broken the bond twixt man and his natural habitat? Sunshine or storm, each season brought its trials, demands of self reliance, be they of the hearth, of birth, or of death; yet in turn they gave a quiet joy to the spring fields of plough and sow, filled a harvest barn with happiness.

Rhythms of the natural world reached to the heart of a simple life. Set amidst the shore borne cries of another's existence it held the satisfaction of caring for the living soil, and an abiding love and respect for the sea. Always about their daily work was the beat of the tide; and of a night, be it a sliver of crescent above mainland hills or queen of the harvest the moon lay golden on the western horizon, then deepest of all the union of moon and tide brought an unspoken awareness of the endless circle of being within the cusp of space.

That summer's day wild blooms covered a sheep cropped machair which gave margin to the land. Purple violets, a swath of buttercup yellow and here and there in clusters of blue petals flecked with white the little speedwells hugged the soil. Young skylark crouched speckled backed beneath tussocks of maram grass and where winter gales had stripped the dunes ring plover chicks hid panting in nests of shingle. Amongst the winding trails of orange dulse and bladder wrack whose tangled lines marked the tides of spring, listless the gulls stood hunched and silent.

Down on the beach cattle idled away the heat of the day flicking sand on their backs and cudding. By and by the imperceptible swell of an Atlantic at rest would spread cooling ripples about their feet and as far as a horizon could draw the eye each meandering current was etched on the surface of an ocean in different shades of blue; few the strangers that came the way to intrude on the peace, or leave the footprint of progress.

Eachan MacKenzie had passed several days turning and coiling his hay. As the field lay just beyond sight of the kitchen window, not a few moments were spent 'in meditation' on the sunny side of his largest coilack. Leaning hay rake against pitch fork he allowed sun and the merest breeze the privilege of his afternoon's work. Through a dip in the dunes he watched a making tide, and turning his head looked down the field to the tufts of grass where he'd stopped the mower to save a skylark's nest. He closed his eyes, and overhead the skylark sang.

CHAPTER ONE

Fag ends

Last on, the exhaling breath of tube doors squeezed rubber to rubber, squeezed commuters, body to body. Contacts unnatural and indifferent, stranger to stranger, two million on the move, rarely a nod of recognition. I forced my way, the last aboard.

A jolt. The rising note of acceleration. The flow of electro-magnetic particles. The smell of energy turned to motion. The rumble of speed, a pack of faces left to wait quickly blurred. Flitting particles of humanity on a speeding platform, a nebulous streak, waiting.

We are children of the sun, energy transmuted, wavelength into particle, atom into molecule, inorganic to organic; from the kinetic fields of space, the sun's rays condensed into consciousness, became the seeking wavelength of imagination, prying into the unknown, unwrapping the layers of fresh understanding. Will this body of knowledge evaporate with the death of the human species, be crushed to a singularity by the swirling blackness of gravity; or will it escape, pass through the orifice, emerge and remain the corpus of our thoughts, a wavelength in the realms of space, to wait?

Ten past five, flight at seven. A lean forty-six year old physicist, I led a research team at Geneva's Fast Particle Reactor. Our work lay at the heart of the search for the ultimate relationship between mass and energy. By creating an immensely strong magnetic field and smashing together fundamental particles we sought to penetrate the fabric of a universe controlled by the ghostly hand of gravity; a force so weak, yet its effect all powerful. Standing before a screen watching the pattern created by disintegrating atoms dreamlike I'd wondered, could an understanding of particle entanglement be the key which would unlock the secret of time, the vital knowledge which could gain entry to dimensions beyond the grip of gravity, the circle of a reality where past and future are as one; for within the universe of entangled particles, though light years may set them apart, the force that binds them is mysterious as the nature of existence itself.

I was heading home to Switzerland having had what I'd expected to be a private interview in Downing Street with the U.K.'s Chief Scientific Advisor, Sir Joshua Goldberg. The fact of being called to Number 10 had surprised me. No matter, they checked identity and showed me into an ante-room; thick damask curtains, two leather topped desks, three solid mahogany doors, and in keeping with the nation's peck order, an un-smiling portrait of the Queen hung on a richly panelled wall.

Sir Joshua padded in, his Hong-Kong pin-stripe suit perfectly tailored to fit a squat barrel on legs. His large round balding head, its dome burnished by high living, sat hunched on shoulders without any obvious neck. Nor was there a jaw line, rather two pouches which boasted crinkly grey sideburns. A flaccid handshake drew my attention to hands soft and exquisitely manicured. From under thick black eyebrows, small dark eyes gave an impression of not wishing to expose the thinking behind their unfocused greeting. As the interview developed they matched his evasive demeanor. I was addressing a man whose judgment influenced political thinking at the highest level, an awareness which, on reflection perhaps accounted for my starchy delivery.

In a perfunctory manner Goldberg flicked to the summary of my research paper, "I can read, so please be brief. Carry on."

His eyes remained on the desk. I began a broad outline of its content.

"I'm sure, Sir Joshua you are alert to the fact that during the past thirty years of nuclear production the operators of these facilities have been steadily enriching their uranium fuel to increase what they call the 'burn up' factor. Indeed during this period they have improved the daily gigawatt output of power per ton of uranium used by about fifty percent."

Head to one side, elbow on the desk, with an air of impatience he drummed elegant fingers on its rich maroon leather surface. Looking sideways at the carpet he gave a non-committal grunt. I hurried to the main thrust of my paper, "Much higher temperatures are generated in the radio-active waste from this high 'burn up' residue." I repeated, "in fact, much, much higher,"

He shrugged his heavy shoulders but said nothing. I drove home my point. "Enriched uranium with this level of efficiency can create a waste which is fifty percent more radio-active. Indeed this highly corrosive material is of considerable danger to the cladding of existing reactors. Any loss of their cooling water could trigger rapid oxidation and a possible explosive spillage of plutonium into the facility itself. As you will be aware Sir Joshua, the lifespan of these radio-active materials far exceeds the timescale of the unpredictable environmental changes we face. Even some of today's nuclear plants may be under threat from climate change, rising sea levels, pressures on rock formations and so forth. Waste storage definitely faces the same problems. Should these unstable environmental conditions occasion wider leakage, then most certainly it would lead to widespread......"

Without looking up, the Chief Scientist interrupted me in a rasping tone. "The wider environmental issue is not the concern of your report. Kindly confine your comment to what it has to tell me. Please give me its specifics."

I blushed at this rebuff, heart beating, anger rising. "Well, Sir Joshua, let me tell you, if the proposed extra nuclear plants go ahead in UK then the storage facilities you propose, on current design, are totally inadequate. I consider it to be unacceptable risk taking which I must say smacks of cost cutting."

His eyes remained on the desk, the bald dome in front of me reddened.

Time to make an impact, drive home my second concern. "Frankly, these mini-nuclear plants, these encapsulated units, may be no more than 10 mega watt output, but I understand they are currently under construction by American and Japanese manufactures and are set to come on stream in the next few years. They will be sold worldwide. Nuclear packages, shipped round the world."

The man's shoulders stiffened. I carried on. "Developing countries may well lack handling expertise, and as for security, won't you consider the global proliferation of radio active material could be a Godsend to insurgents?"

Goldberg looked up. For the first time, our eyes met. A second- no more. I looked into dark rimmed, black orbs filled with venom. They slid to one side. He penned a note and tossed it towards a secretary, who hurried from the room.

Resorting to insolence, if not intellectual arrogance I went on, "Anyway, back to waste storage. This is not sardines you're dealing with, Sir Joshua, this stuff doesn't pack easily. The underground storage you have in mind may not cope with the heat engendered and containers will be in danger of rupture. At the very least any break down would leak into surrounding rock strata and I'm sure I don't need to remind you it remains dangerous for tens of thousands of years. However as a physicist, involved in the behavior of particles subjected to the pressures of intense radio-activity, I must warn you that under certain conditions the release of energy is, to put it mildly, dramatic."

I continued with the details from my paper highlighting the disastrous contamination which might result due to underestimating the potential of the material involved.

Tapping the ends of his fingers together, Sir Joshua listened without comment. I became conscious that he watched me as I read from my notes. Each time I looked up his eyes darted away. The odd question or two indicated a shrewd brain. The secretary reappeared and with an unctuous stoop placed a note at Goldberg's elbow He rose abruptly, eyes swivelling to the door, "The P.M. wishes a word with you." Maybe this was not the favourable consultancy report they required.

The secretary stepped forward. "This way, sir." I followed him up a wide stairway flanked by studio portraits of Number 10's past incumbents. All looked sincere but high office rather than nature granted dignity. I was ushered into a large Georgian drawing room warmed by the cheerful blaze in the wrought iron grate of an Adam fireplace. A magnificent secretaire bookcase, satinwood side tables, a walnut grandfather clock, all the trappings of gentility somehow gave the room an atmosphere of a Hollywood movie ripe for a cheap plot. A guitar slung on the carved shoulder of an elegant Chippendale chair suggested a relaxed attitude on the part of the musician.

Whilst waiting, my attention focused on a magnificent Dutch seascape. Rocks loomed ahead of a sailing ship in danger of foundering. Storm and action, a bearded skipper gripped the spokes of her wheel, sails shredded before a gale. Barefooted men strained at her ropes, obviously not in the same league as the talkers and manipulators I'd passed on the stairs, guiding the Ship of State

The P.M. breezed in, a welcoming grin and a hand with a resolute grip.

Motioning me to the large Chesterfield he beamed, "Do sit down. Care for a coffee?" Flinging an arm along its back casually, he sat himself at the other end. The effect of his manner was immediate. I marvelled at the approach, his controlling eye, the voice. Charm, charisma, an infectious mix of attributes difficult to quantify, but as history tells us, when applied to a world stage, their impact on the direction of events has often proved calamitous.

Sir Joshua slipped in quietly and stood uneasily at the casement window contemplating a garden bathed in March sunshine. Throughout our discussion, there'd been only fleeting eye contact. An unappealing man, and I suspected, he'd an agenda equally unattractive. Without doubt he regarded my paper as important, even dangerous. I'd exposed major issues which could undermine the government's surreptitious programme for nuclear expansion.

The merest click and a side door opened. A tall, lean faced individual stalked into the room. He placed himself at the end of the couch behind the P.M., a baleful presence perhaps due to his hawkish nose. Eyeing me intently, his stare conveyed a challenging intellect. "Now, what's this Josh has been telling me?" the P.M. began. His eyes appeared direct and friendly complimenting a gushing manner and school-boy grin.

"How can I help? Tell me about your work." It had been an easy start. I began to outline my understanding of the problems faced by a growing nuclear industry. "My basic research, Prime Minister, is with the energy transfer between fast moving particles within the most intense magnetic fields we have so far produced, but my work for the consultancy paper which your government asked me to prepare has thrown up results with serious implications for the long term storage of nuclear waste. Preliminary findings highlight the possibility of conditions arising which could bring about a situation of the most critical nature. Depending on location and volume, the mix of various degrees of radio activity might......"

He cut in brusquely, launching into his usual theme of nuclear power being the clean energy alternative to our dependence on fossil fuels. Looking me straight in the eye he spoke at length. I listened with increasing surprise as it became clear how little appreciation existed for the long term consequences of the major changes which lay ahead. "Nuclear expansion is vital, a socially responsible undertaking. I intend to pursue the case with the utmost vigour. Naturally, we shall continue to support other forms of renewable power, but they can't compete financially." He smiled, a shade less friendly. "Budgets have a nasty habit of dictating limits and as you'll know, one has to prioritize."

Cash- the politicians yard stick. I watched his eyes. In unguarded moments they became just a jot unfocused, the merest glazing, a look which suggested the zeal of a man on a mission. "Our duty is to future generations," he concluded emphatically. Long pause. His eyes met mine. "By the way, I know we provide a considerable amount towards funding your work. It's under review at the moment." Another pause. His eyes became hard and calculating. "You realise there's considerable call on the national budget. Our welfare programmes are very demanding and to be honest I have to say, the Chancellor must allocate according to the greatest need."

No smile. The inference was clear. My colour rose. I countered, aware of condescension in my tone, perhaps a hint of intellectual superiority. "In view of my research findings, Prime Minister, I feel my duty as a scientist is also to consider the safety of future generations, and I warn you due to the worldwide proliferation of nuclear facilities their safety is much in jeopardy."

Hatchet Face moved forward and put his hand on the back of the couch. I ignored him. "That danger apart, on the wider issue of energy supplies, Prime Minister, wind and wave are folly, environmentally disastrous, geo-thermal maybe, but already there are solar energy farms in operation using mirror and lens enhancement to drive steam turbines. It may sound outlandish, the possibility exists for harvesting sunshine from the troposphere, never mind what could be dramatically achieved at house top level, if funds were diverted from, shall we say, military operations."

My tirade reached fresh heights, "You all fail to realise it's too late. The planet will continue warming at an accelerating rate in spite of your feeble attempts to reduce carbon emissions. Even if we could stabilise CO_2 levels tomorrow overall temperatures will rise by two degrees at least, much more in some areas."

I glared round the group, "Emission rates are accelerating gentlemen, up by thirty percent already in this decade. You fail to understand that the projected effect of any carbon cutting will be more than offset by the fast declining ability of our natural environment to absorb carbon and by no means an insignificant factor, world societies' ever escalating consumption of energy,"

I repeated, doubtless in a supercilious manner, "The world's ever escalating use."

Silence. I'd struck home! Eyes fixed me with rapt attention. No holding back angry words from a racing mind. "Wind power, wave power! Look, gentlemen, you are harnessing two of the planets greatest natural forces, largely benign as a present function of the overall global system. Exploit their latent power and apply it to our form of energy usage and you'll turn what are the earth's natural features into substantial emitters of heat."

Not a move. Were they stunned by my outburst? Goldberg, gazing out of the window had his back to me. Was I beginning to shout? "Emitters, dissipaters of heat, simple first form physics by turning wind power into radiant energy you're adding to what the sun already supplies. It's concentrating a cool breeze into electricity and running it through a two bar fire and putting it back into the atmosphere as heat escaping through the window. Never mind turning the tide into air conditioning systems for the wealthy whilst the poor swelter. You fools, nuclear power is the worst of all. Even forgetting the dangers I've outlined, you're releasing into the environment the cosmic energy which was locked in uranium when the planet was formed."

I let that sink in. Hatchet Face cleared his throat. I kept on regardless. "Anyway, I believe that major U.S. industrial business interests are bent on a rapid expansion of nuclear energy generation, both here and abroad, but within forty years mineral uranium will become a dwindling stock, not dissimilar to the current oil situation. So carry on, gentlemen, but if you want a future for your families then throw taxpayers money at photosynthesis and solar power, and make it fast."

The P.M.'s eyes narrowed, pupils shrank to dots. His face twisted into a fixed smile. Before he could stop me, I began again, without doubt in a loud arrogant tone,

"Can't you understand, methane is the real menace, twenty-five times more potent than CO_2 at producing warming. Today's escalating CO_2 emissions are leading to the unleashing of the earth's vast store of methane. It's under the

9

permafrost. We're at the mercy of melting permafrost, and perhaps you aren't aware that trillions and trillions of cubic meters of methane exists in ice clathrate deposits right across the globe, even below the sea bed. Extraction of this new type of fossil fuel is about to start. Make no mistake, this sort of disturbance could trigger a run away release of methane from the clathrate beds. The balance is delicate. Add in the melting effects of ocean warming on seabed reserves and you could get an uncontrollable chain reaction with disastrous consequences. Mark my words, the methane clathrates will be the planet's next energy gold mine."

Sir Joshua spun round, startled. I leaned closer to the P.M. almost shouting in his face, "It's your inability to see beyond the flashy world of high finance. It's your myopic economic policies versus the environment and moreover, Prime Minister, I question your political mandate from the electorate for any such expansion of the nuclear industry. Had you spent a fraction of our taxes on researching low frequency photovoltaic cells, instead of vast sums creating the misery of your illegal attack on Iraq, the menace of nuclear generation could be avoided."

I raged on without drawing breath, "And by the way, all nuclear facilities are to a certain degree under micro-chip control, don't forget the manufacture of these components is vital to much of today's modern living and it's passing out of U.S. control, moving to cheaper labour out East. Your so called terrorists will quickly learn that by infiltrating the design and manufacturing processes of the micro-chip industry they can create mayhem in far wider zones than the battlefield. Nuclear plants, aircraft, air traffic control, early warning systems, banking affairs, health, innumerable areas of our complex societies could be vulnerable. It'll make the type of wars you're presently spending billions on fighting seem as outdated as armoured knights on a medieval crusade."

They sat back. Stunned at my outburst nobody spoke. In an attempt to recover my composure I ended by saying in a more moderate pitch, "as far as climate change is concerned the challenge is even greater. We're passing the tipping point of runaway temperatures and we'll need intelligence to survive, not ideology."

Hatchet Face made to speak. The P.M.'s raised hand stopped him and glaring at me his eyes narrowed to venomous black dots. I heard Goldberg draw a sharp breath. The silence turned icy. The clock ticked loudly. "I think these wider issues are really not part of your specialised field," with considerable self-control, his words were delivered in a measured tone.

Immediately we all stood up. Smiling thinly, mouth only, he squeezed my arm. "The industry is confident the matters which concern you are well in hand. There's always a lunatic fringe opposing us, constant danger from extremists, religious fanatics and so forth, but have no fear, we will control these issues."

His head lifted a fraction; his eyes glittered with an arrogant hardness, "I know I'm doing what is right. It's for the great mass of honest people, their future, their homes and their jobs. Thank you none the less for coming over but if you don't mind my saying so, I think your views are both highly offensive and irrelevant."

The atmosphere became frigid. He dropped my arm. Hatchet Face exchanged glances with Goldberg and moved from his listening post behind the Chesterfield to stand at the Prime Minister's elbow. We moved to the door. With a piercing glance, as though it could be an afterthought, the P.M. continued,

"I understand your consultancy paper is not yet up for discussion elsewhere." He became unpleasantly insinuating.

"I'm sure you know what I mean. Sections of the press can be so disruptive when it comes to the interests and wellbeing of our Nation." His eyes drilled into mine. "Nor would a lack of discretion of any kind be in your own interests."

From now on had I to fear surveillance?

Turning abruptly he nodded to Hatchet Face who without a word showed me out. Un-noticed, Sir Joshua had already slipped from the room.

That was it, another wasted day. I loathed meetings and the paper shuffling types who cultivated them into a profession. Two hours in the H.Q. of power; cloak and dagger tactics behind the curtains of influence and preferment. Northing what it seemed, sleight of tongue replaced straight forward exchange, expediency before honesty. Throughout my ill chosen outburst, Hatchet Face studied me, heard all, said nothing, but contributed to the atmosphere of side glancing suspicion. Two hours in the shadowy corridors of talkers and plotters, two hours too long.

As I'd left, lens- eyed vultures waited at the front gates hoping to pick over some object of degraded 'officialdom', maybe a politician who fiddled with his expenses, his secretary, or both.

The fag ends of a fading democracy.

I came away disgusted.

CHAPTER TWO

Eyes

The tube gathered speed. Passengers leant against me. Suddenly the day's tension snapped. Enough of politicians and their bogus altruism, to hell with Heathrow! I'll get off - but where? After five years buried in the abstraction of particle physics, why miss a chance to dive into this honking-bonking, kiss my wallet world of aspiring millionaire-dom?

Wealth, lovely wealth, its scent followed every glamorous hairdo, clung to elegant suits stepping out of taxis. Sophistication romped along a neon runway of brittle, soul devouring fun. Excitement zipped. Covent Garden and a dose of opera? Tube adverts proclaimed, 'Lucia di Lammermoor.' A new production, a heart ripping tragedy. Too staid. I needed to compensate for the afternoon with a jazz club sweating out Dixie-land. Supper in Chinatown at two in the morning, then where, Soho?

Downhill all the way. I fancied a spot of decadence. Yes boy. From attempting to track the illusive nature of existence surely I could wallow in its spin off; an outbreak of dissipation threatened. Time to step aboard London life, balance on its gloriously undulating surface, ride its exuberant peaks, be carefree in the troughs, be as irreverent as stuffing a whoopee cushion under the Archbishop of Canterbury at a hypocrite's funeral.

After dealing with that pack of jokers a malt beckoned. A large one plus a reflection point. I needed a spot of relaxing debauchery, a high stool and a barmaid with a sympathetic eye, maybe lap dancers, anything to remove the taste of politicians, even a 40 inch TV filling its plasma face with the inanity of snake eating celebrities. Tube stations came and went, Hyde Park, Kensington.

Try as I might the evening's prospects yielded to cynicism. I retraced a meeting which had left me stunned. Political careerists fiddling their expenses, directorships in companies receiving government grants. My despair at their lack of foresight and honesty was matched only by loathing. Self-seeking men, mere soft handed talkers with little experience in a commonsense life of practical skills, nor with any obvious courage to face a bullet, could by manipulating words inflict the carnage of Iraq, send soldiers to their grave, unleash the horror of killing and maiming untold innocent women and children and sitting at a desk they could think up the obscene mockery of calling their actions, 'shock and awe'. From the haze of cigar smoke curling from dens of nepotism and religious dogma came the smoke of depleted uranium shells, and leukemia.

The tube train journeyed through a conduit of bitter thoughts. I looked out of the carriage window. Platform after platform still thronged with faces, many far from exuberant. White faces, grayed by the fluorescence of office hours, wooden faces, blank and indifferent, yellow faces, green under the glare, brown faces, sensitive and thin, black faces with shining skin and egg white eyes; what feelings did they register? Aspiration, despair, love, sorrow, greed? Hardly- more a dullness of eye which reflected the linear graph of a living that awaited the impact of some spike of circumstance, good or bad.

East bound, west bound, a red circle round Piccadilly, shiny tiles mirroring adverts. Toothpaste and the perfect grinning teeth, the rosy glow of an outdoor existence courtesy of liver pills, a week's sunshine care of Thomas Cook. Hurrying days, scurrying people grasping at media- hyped expectations, the superficial creating the superfluous in a mirage of wealth and happiness. A hurly-burly of feasting on the planet's diminishing resources. Rolling out the powder keg of economic growth whilst champion of freedom and democracy, the American Dream wearing ear plugs locks the masses in a chamber of their own making and lights the touch paper.

Did nobody sense a trap?

Unsure of where to alight, I stayed aboard the rush hour medley of clanking acceration and the whoosh of air rank with electric discgharge. A trickle of sweat hovered on the edge of a collar too tight for its wearer. It occurred to me that city suits and their umbrellas required extra space. Meeting a fellow traveller eye to eye seemed rare. Too disturbing, maybe suggestive? Certainly eyes didn't linger, a momentary glance, perhaps; instead they studied the red artery of the Central Line or some futile exhortation, a latter day version of the High Street sandwich board, 'Repent, the End is Nigh.' Few appeared convinced, nor were following the advice.

Being several inches above average height I looked across swaying heads, felt the press of bodies dependent upon a stranger's hand holding a strap or clutching the corner pole. Tubby flesh leant on me, a dog collar in a grey 'mac' with the vacant eyes of righteousness. Hoping not to give offence, I shuffled aside. A briefcase, discretely strapped to my left wrist contained the unwelcome research paper. My right hand was free in case of trouble.

Several shoulders down the compartment the woman's head caught my attention. Her hair tumbled shoulder length in a natural mass of gentle waves, thick and golden. Far from affectation she held her head with a natural pride which appealed to such an extent that had I been beside her I could not have helped but speak. The instant attraction caught me by surprise. She had the long slender head of a Nordic woman. At no more than a first glimpse I knew this woman belonged to latitudes of the fiord lands, larch clad and silent.

Train lights flicked along tunnel walls snaked with cables, bodies lurched at each bend. I remained gazing at her proudly shaped head with a fixed intensity. The press of strangers went un-noticed, clatter and smell faded from any awareness. A dark cliff formed before me, sea pinks bloomed on ledges above an empty shore from which came the tang of salt air. Rippled by the tide, sand shone white beneath limpid water. Beyond the gable of a house, fields long abandoned sloped to hill and moor, forsaken by time and remoteness; the lost freedom of a people.

A small boat lay beached on the edge of a bay. The woman stood bare foot, tall and easy, a hand on the boats gunnel. Her hair shone as wavelets tipped with sunlight. Warm and downy it slipped golden through my fingers. She turned towards me, tossing her beautiful head. Her eyes held the blueness of a day where sea and sky were one.

My image could only have been momentary; the crowded train returned. Staring at the woman's averted head became obsessive. Alarmed she might alight at the next station, vanish amongst the mass of commuters, I determined to reach her side. "Excuse me, excuse me please." No response from the passenger jammed against me. Good manners failed. I must speak with her. Drawn, it almost seemed by the intensity of my attraction the woman turned and our eyes met.

The impact drained all other thought. Steadfast and deep set, sparkling as the first of a morning sun will dance on crumbling waves. Her eyes were those of my vision, the eyes of the woman beside a boat. The bay, the boat and the eyes of this woman became a single imprint, for their blueness was of the sea which flowed in the blood of the Viking.

She gazed at me unwaveringly. It was no passing glance; on her face I saw the expression of a person focused somewhere distant from the crush of a tube train, in her eyes a look of inexplicable searching. In return I made no effort to hide the appeal of their beauty.

At last she smiled, her eyes moist and shining.

Orange white, the world erupted in a flash of searing brilliance; it shattered the carriage; laser blinding, instantly engulfing everything in a split-second. Steel ripped into steel, screeching, screeching, ear splitting screeching. The carriage tipped into blackness, dragged along the tunnel wall, a contorting mass of twisting metal. Glass flew in lethal shards, seats buckled. Electric wires fizzed and crackled. Throat gripping smoke poured through the compartment, acid thick in a choking blanket of terror.

Bodies crushed against me. I fought for breath. Cordite filled my lungs. Screaming, screaming surrounded me, the agony of mutilation. Body parts splattered the seat that pressed into my back. Above was the hideous rattle of a person trying to breathe through a windpipe cut by splintered glass. He grappled with me, pouring blood from his neck and fighting death. I wrenched one arm free, felt my face. Blood, warm, horribly slippery, trickled down my neck. Mine or his? Both of my legs, immobile. I gave up attempting to free them, conscious only of groaning.

Time is but the measure of movement in space. It slowed------ became slower. I was falling,---- falling. Its passing bore no relevance, except as the medium by which to dwell on those whom I loved. They flooded into being, beside me, looking down, in tears. I tried to speak to them. This was death; a futile death, no purpose, no glory, no sacrifice for fellow man.

Amidst fading thoughts came a voice; it trailed away, drew me towards a distant blueness, the intensity of sunlight through the prism of life.

"We shall meet, we ...," I watched the woman become fainter and fainter, till alone her eyes remained, smiling out of a gathering blackness, comforting as the warmth of an entwining body. Deep within the cloisters of some wave sculptured cave soaring voices sang a requiem to beauty, the sole expression of truth. Strongly, then faint as an ebbing life, it echoed amongst the hollow chambers of a dying consciousness.

Masked faces under yellow helmets gently eased out another mangled form. Was it me?

Voices, muffled voices, "Cut that bloody briefcase off his wrist, that's what's holding him, I'm pretty sure he's dead. Get him on the stretcher anyway. Pass that mask, Joe. We'll give him oxygen, yes the pure stuff. Switch it up. Now boys, lift. Steady, he's a big lad."

A moments awareness rushed through me. I floated on the sensation of breathing. My eyes were open. Sirens wailed, lights flashed, stretchers and urgency. I fought a terrifying dread.

The ambulance driver leaned back. His words floated on a cacophony of wailing sirens.

"Which way Chief, hospital, or the morgue?"

CHAPTER THREE

The Coffin

As a newborn child on the edge of sleep is aware of breathing, so a mind without awareness of any other self, concentrates upon the rhythm by which some hidden urge demands survival. Slowly, though it need not have been, for time had no meaning, only a dim sense of un-ending space seemed present. It beat with the pulse of waves that fall endless after a storm.

No bodily sensation intruded, merely a lightness suspended amidst flickering colours. They grew then faded, to re-appear with the brilliance of a rainbow on thunder black clouds. The air took on a pureness, a freshness known to the heady cartwheels of childhood when limbs stretched to grasp the joy of living. Each breath stirred scenes which hovered on the brink of an awakening to a horror embedded in the sub-conscious. All paled into a crimson haze, through which the first barbs of dawn pierced the fog that hung over a torpid sea.

I opened my eyes, green- was everything green? Light bored into aching sockets, garish lines of fluorescence. Serious eyes looked down out of masked faces, their voices muted. Without moving my head I glanced to one side. Tubes dangled. Blood red shone above me. It seemed bright as the first tip of sunrise streams across still, mauve waters, and breathing the pureness of sea air, gradually the ocean took me, closed over my head, green and drifting, green and drifting as the lightness of a sail on the motion of a long, long swell.

Over the stern of a gently swaying boat the white haired old man hauled in a line. Gasping fish filled the boxes on the bottom boards of his boat. Great cod with round expressionless eyes fought against asphyxiation; each gasp became slower, their mouths opened and closed less frequently. Gnarled fingers held the fish by a gill, drew a hook and slipped the silver body to flap its tail amongst the rest. A dark brown sail lay across the thwarts. An island fell away to starboard. It stretched untamed like some ultramarine creature under vast marble clouds. White sculptured columns they rested upon an advancing streak of grey.

The fisherman lashed his tiller and stepped to the mast. A lug sail clawed aloft, barely filling its canvas in the fitful puffs of wind that beset man and boat. He glanced astern. A black line split the sky over the white of a frothing sea. The air hot, then cold. The canvas shivered. Without warning the sail cracked, belly full. Jabbing waves surrounded the boat. Pointed crests broke over the gunnels.

A white head crouched, one hand to free the tiller, the other struggling to loose the main sheet. Stern lifting, heeling hard, he fought a broach. Fish boxes slid. The wind from howling turned to screeching. Mast stays, old tarred rope, rod taut. A hissing sea began to lift and spiral. Crack, crack, the sail backed. Devil's violence, the mast crashed onto a gunnel. She broached. Beam to sea, she rolled. Boxes slid, dead fish poured into a tumult of lashing spray. Crooked hands grasped the gunnel, their grip was torn away. A face looked up. The face of a Viking.

A shock of white hair, a bobbing head amongst seething wave tops in a green, green world. One light above, dimming, dimming, until only eyes of understanding held the horizon in their blueness, and stared out of a long box.

Consciousness came to me as great white sheets swirling about a floating form. My eyes opened. I struggled to focus on the green figures. Bent and hovering forms against a halo of light. And again, the smell of blood, warm as though oozing from a dying form. I clawed wildly. Escape, escape.

Blackness was closing, I felt neither fear nor bodily pain, only the mental ache of a profound regret, the sadness at an unfathomable loss. Slipping away- the gleam of light at the edge of understanding was slipping away. My mind struggled, grasping ever more feebly to reach the truth my work had been about to reveal. The light dimmed, began to flicker, as though the energy of my innermost soul was being transmuted into dimensions without physical form.

"No, no. Not now, not now, I need to know." I heard a disembodied croaking. Great black wings spread on a billowing canvas. The Raven had put to sea.

Wavering light played on a dark ceiling, candlelit shapes weaved in and out of being. A sharp face stared out of a long box. Its white hair had been neatly combed above a broad, smooth forehead. Strong features, narrow nose and jutting jaw, no face of smooth living, but carved by Atlantic gale.

Worn hands of sinew and vein, lank and finished, flanked the sides of a coarse grey smock. Crooked hands, clenched by the grip of toil. Thumbs and fingers made cups, each held a spray of the first little blue speedwell. The head tried to rise, hands straining at the rough sides of a long box, eyes burnt with the brightness of a warning, an ardent plea. Gradually the old face sank back into a salt stained pillow, and slowly its flesh dissolved. Bit by bit bones protruded, cheeks became craters below a tall forehead, until only teeth and skull remained.

Last to fade from black round sockets were imploring blue eyes, blue and deep. In their distant focus were horizons of space and freedom.

Vague stooping figures bore a coffin of rough hewn planks along the grooves of a sand blown track. Spring had come to the dunes, the machair sparkled, fresh from the showers which fell like dust on the lambing pastures. The thin bleating of the new born was on a breeze that held the warmth of southern latitudes. Down by the tidal wrack a flock of dark backed curlew were resting before a journey long and far; and occasionally their ascending trill was on the soft rhythm of an ebbing tide.

Above the beach, the green of sheep cropped turf was smothered by yellow primroses. In a burying ground of low stone dyke were simple wooden crosses, their bleached arms and worn spines ground smooth by drifting sand, the wood hardened by salt. They leant against each winter gale, unpretentious symbols, worthy by their toughness of those below. And amongst their number the long box was lowered.

'Earth to earth, dust to dust.' I heard the music of the geese rising from Atlantic's edge, and on their northbound wings went all meaning of death.

Thoughtful heads were bowed; by turn each figure bent, took sand. In solemn thuds it fell, dull, hollow thuds, a beating drum in the caverns of eternity.

Slowly as the coffin covered, I looked down.

Letters were burned upon its lid.

Hector MacKenzie of Sandray, drowned 30th April, 1846, aged 84.

In utter horror, I looked upon my name.

CHAPTER FOUR

A Sundial without a sunset

Ten days, ten years, a thousand, nothing marked their passing. There is no judge of time beyond a conscious form, nor for a mind separated from bodily sensation. I merely lay, inert and staring; the white ceiling, sometimes clear and bright, often a fog wavering with dark shapes. Yet my thoughts remained surprisingly lucid. The hallucinations, if that's what they were, I relived clearly and strongly. Had they any meaning beyond the ravings of a brain wrestling on the edge of some great journey, defending itself against death?

Mysteries of the occult, flickering candles and an esoteric cloak of preying shadows, the black art of necromancy, communications from the grave, warning or portent; what factor, what force, totally unknown to present science could bridge the gap, exist outwith time and space?

Nothing in my research on particle interchange so far led me to believe that images sprang from the cosmic void. Exchanges in the energy flow of charged particles I understood, to a degree. Electro-chemical reactions become memories, are stored, forgotten, and await recall; dormant yet existing; but in what form? Could the charged heights of human emotion be transmitted? A psychic wavelength imprinted on some unfathomable dimension of the heavens? There to wait, holistic and impervious to the particle decay which destroys a universe, only to build again.

Beyond all my attempts to frame some logical understanding, her eyes had appeared in my vision, appeared to me moments before we'd gazed at each other; that much I knew. The eyes of the vision and those of the woman were identical. I'd looked into them in a waking dream, only to meet them again in the seconds before a suicide bomber almost took my life and limb.

Moreover, dramatic scenes and faces had arisen as I hovered on the brink of death. Happenings totally unrelated to anything of which I was aware; not in my daily work, certainly not in memories, yet still they possessed an inexplicable familiarity. Was I subconsciously reaching for a wholesomeness, the caress of a breeze untainted by progress, its healing touch, the freedom to work at pace of each tide? An incessant calling filled the corridors of my mind, played like a torch flame on the cave paintings of survival, became rays of sunlight on shallow water that lit the union of radiation with the grains of being. The sun, the sun, I longed for the sun on my aching body.

Yellow and bright on a white counterpane, sunlight poured through a tall window drawing a line across my bed. Three o'clock, one minute past, two, three, then five past, the long hand on the wall clock moved in jerks. My eye flitted between its hand and a shadow moving on the bed. The grandeur of a skyscraper opposite the hospital became the pointer of a sundial which crept across my counterpane until its dying shaft gave way to the glitter of a thousand office windows. The shadow of the skyscraper fell across the bed, a sundial without a sunset. I raised myself on an elbow and gazed at towers of concrete. Street lighting replaced sunsets.

I lay back on the pillows, immobility had revalued attitudes. Behind glass rows of office workers sat at computer systems; by raising my head I could see them, the epitome of an imprisoned population dependent on a surfeit of cheap food produced by artificial means and adulterated by chemicals. The previous year I'd watched a colleague in Geneva die at fifty with stomach cancer.

Another bout of fear gripped me. Forty flights up and an escalator, buildings leaned into my mind, half my life spent cooped in concrete, the prison walls of a system controlling my existence. Walls were crushing me, entombing me in the terror of claustrophobia. I panicked, "Nurse, is it possible to open my window, please?" I asked as steadily as possible.

She smiled and shook her head. "Maybe tomorrow, if you're a good boy," and trying to restrain me, "don't get up."

Though kindness surrounded me and treatment had been faultless, I pushed her arm to one side. Coughing and wheezing for the first time I swung my legs over the edge of the bed. Shaking her head, the nurse helped me to stand tottering at the window ledge.

Forty stories below car lights probed a haze of diesel fumes and weaved amongst bus roofs, a torrent of civilisation swept along the motorway, a species under pressure, threshing erratically in the quick-sands of a modern lifestyle. A planet killed by coal and the motorcar, the supreme irony of sunshine buried for three hundred million years being in released in three hundred. Death by diesel. I struggled to stop a frenzied train of thoughts from controlling my mind?

Pavements jostled with earnest people, hurrying minions under constant surveillance, their private affairs stolen by hidden computers. It reflected my own hustling days, flagging a taxi to meetings, drinking coffee with pompous chairmen heading for the knighthoods nudged by political donations. I suffered research budgets cut by top brass civil servants retiring to index linked pensions paid for by the nation's masses. Talk, talk, a facility for jargon in a safe pair of hands. Invited to fancy bow tie Geneva parties because I'd been introduced to some of the faceless Bond Market and currency manipulators. It didn't take long to realize their interest was limited to speculating on how quickly scientific results could be turned into cash. From the safety of exclusive bunkers they viewed the world, natural or otherwise, as a giant bank vault. It left me in no doubt that financial fanatics controlled international affairs.

Narrowly escaping death at the hands of another breed of fanatic had overwhelmingly altered my perceptions of modern society. My view that evening from a hospital window took on a strangely objective detachment. A massive unstoppable charade played out on the street below; civilization walked blindfold towards a precipice and the yawning chasm of planetary collapse. The certitude of the peril we faced struck me with the power of a revelation.

Momentous decisions are straight from the gut. From that moment the direction of my life would be changed totally. My head ached, my heart pounded. I was being driven, unmercifully driven by the calling of some other place, the challenge of finding some another way to achieve a purpose for existing. *Geneva no more* sounded melodramatic. But to where, to what? That didn't matter. Sick or not I'd break out of here.

The nurse helped me from the window. I sank back on the bed, panting from the effort. Good god, my arms were thin, I held up the left one and studied an ugly red weal on my wrist? Of course, the briefcase, yes, where was it now and its politically damning contents?

Confused thoughts were clearing. I found it possible to recall my appointment with the swivel eyed Goldberg and the soft handshake of a scientist putting a front on politician designs. Sitting beside the PM., a man of gushing bonhomie brimming with altruism, his nuclear intentions held with a messianic certainty.

More particularly, I recalled the unspoken pressure to gag my research paper hid a certain menace. Would I be followed? My research results could impact adversely on the whole nuclear industry, the weapons' industry and definitely the wider field of international treaties. The problem of the safe long term storage of lethal material lay at the crux of all these issues.

I knew the Non-Proliferation Treatise was in limbo, had failed to halt the spread of nuclear weapons. Any agreement based on 'we have weapons, and won't give them up, you haven't and are not allowed them, was bound to fail. The fact of America not signing the Treaty amounted to defying any ban. Some countries were even withdrawing from current arrangements and weapon testing was suspected.

Worse still, turning a blind eye on Israel's secret nuclear bombs by a main player in negotiations, the U.S.A., had made diplomacy a fraught business. Other nations clambering to develop civilian nuclear plants with potential for producing the fissile material required in bomb making would become a dire threat. Back in 1995 the U.N. had proposed a treaty which aimed to outlaw the making of weapons grade material. Nothing came of it, mainly due to America's refusal to accept the required inspection.

Depression always followed a high. I knew at first hand the dangers of radiation and I'd picture the mushroom cloud which obliterated Hiroshima. Suddenly the flash would strike, back on the tube train, I'd smell cordite, see the blood, hear the tortured screams, the hideous screaming. Arms flailing, an unstoppable groaning would seize me, until gradually the scene faded and I'd look into beckoning blue eyes and feel a surge of relief.

I'd turned the key of my two bed-roomed Geneva flat on the morning of the tube train attack and flown into London. Colleagues at the research establishment had wished me success. A single chap, none left to worry about me nor expect any contact until my return. None at all, not even the shreds of a broken love affair, two years past and a regret rather than the anguish of separation.

Long days at the research establishment, do they mean more to you than me? She'd said this again as we walked that night along the shores of Lake Geneva. How could I explain I'd embarked on a quest that burnt in my mind by day, lit fresh insights on wakening. I was climbing, slipping, climbing again, striving to grasp The Holy Grail of science, the unravelling of particle behaviour at the birth of the universe, perhaps even the mystery of dark matter.

How often I'd tried to explain. She'd walked a little ahead. The meal had lacked conversation, no mention of the of the film we'd seen that evening, but its background music lingered. The sadness of 'Watership Down,' played through my head. "Bright eyes, burning in like fire. How could eyes that burned so brightly suddenly burn so dim, bright eyes?" Perhaps the tune set my mood. I had caught up with her and put an arm round her waist. "I'm sorry," was the best I could muster. Across the lake in the bitter sharp night of an Alpine winter the great giants had their peaks under snow and slept on the lake. She followed my eyes and guessed my meaning. We clung, sobbing, and then, without a kiss, we walked in opposite directions.

I phoned a line which rang and rang.

My father, the chief analytical chemist with Imperial Tobacco in New York, and a forty a day man, died relatively young with lung cancer. Mother, as a beautiful young widow, stayed on in America and eventually married again. For all I knew there could be half brothers and sisters somewhere in the States. Although she was a first generation American, the mark of Highland blood showed in her strong, handsome face. I recall her expressive playing of the old Scots fiddle tunes. To childish amazement I'd watch a tear trickling down her cheek. Possibly because I was still quite young when they packed me off to boarding school, neither of my parents featured greatly in my affections. Was she still alive? I didn't know.

A week before Dad's death she'd flown me out from school to see him. I stood beside his hospital cot. Sunlight through the window fell across a crumpled, yellow faced old man, all that remained of the virile father I'd known. I see yet the form of his face; broad, high forehead, a hooked nose, predacious in profile, but most strikingly, the clear blue eyes. That afternoon they shone out of his gaunt features with a peculiar light which penetrated through and beyond me.

We had never been familiar but he caught my hand and the smile which always lurked behind his eyes appeared as he spoke, "All my life has been a search, a quest for that ultimate equation, the key to unlocking a mathematical pattern which is the pure and glorious template of infinity. Understand infinity and you strike the anvil upon which every force and particle of this universe and all other universes, past and future are forged. It's the music of unending beauty."

His voice became a cough; he turned aside for some minutes, until, with a spark of the vigour which I remembered from childhood, he said, "I never found that equation. If you ever do, guard it with your life. It's the key which unlocks the secret haven of eternal consciousness."

I looked out of his window. Sunlight played on the leaves of the aspen trees. They shivered in a breeze which highlighted their paleness. And in their yellow fluttering, the sun danced.

He stirred a little, "Hector boy, I lie here dying. Tonight, tomorrow? The music is soaring, filling my head, taking away fear. I'm young again. There is no void, only these soaring notes of beauty. I hear them, as though from the heart of all creation. There is no death. Believe in beauty. Its melody is the key to eternity."

I was twelve. Those were his last words.

The blue eyes remained staring.

He was reaching for that key.

CHAPTER FIVE

Escape

How long had I been in this single ward? Had I been identified? So far I hadn't been asked to put any details on a form. That struck me as strange. No visitors, but then there was nobody I knew in London. Would my colleagues trace me? Unease continually affected my thinking. Never mind the contents of my briefcase. If the damn thing still existed, maybe I'd shown my contempt for the politicians too openly. So far no police to see me, but I was getting increasingly alarmed. Concern over being detained erupted. God, I must get out of this place.

Weakness kept me chained. The horror of the tunnel burst again and again. Its roaring crash and splinter brought panic attacks clawing my sinews. Escape, escape, it screamed. I'd cast wildly round the bedroom, gripping the frame of the bed and sweating profusely. Only when her eyes looked down at me, blue and intense, would each attack pass away. Shining with inner laughter they smiled, and I would sleep, as though rocking in a warm sea.

The sundial re-appeared each day, a yellow slash on my bedcover. Its spring light drove a reviving spirit. After one fierce bout of the recurrent trauma, never mind limb and lung, I knew a mental recovery to be just as urgent. I needed to deal firmly with my revulsion for city smells whether stale air or recycled water. No more tranquilizers. Confidence, self discipline, I needed to regain control of my thoughts, quell these ridiculous manias. Action was needed now, the action I'd determined upon weeks ago.

Restless beyond endurance, beyond the rational, I threw sheets aside. Damn medication, a breath of the ocean, salt air would cleanse burnt lungs, the power of the sun would give me back strength. I knew it, I knew it. I rose.

Cash, clothes, I needed both. Ask the nurse to help? No, she might be implicated in my disappearance, lose her job. The wardrobe, check the wardrobe. Why? I crossed to it unsteadily. Staring me in the face, clothes on hangers; not the grey suit and smart meeting tie I'd worn, that would be impossible; no, a check shirt, Harris tweed jacket, flannels, socks, heavy brogues. Incredulous, who the mischief? At the bottom of the wardrobe, a leather portmanteau!

No sight of my briefcase. Some person could be privy to its contents, deliberately or otherwise. That wouldn't stop me. It had gone, with any luck in smithereens. Putting the portmanteau on the bed, I opened it gingerly. Shaving kit, more clothes. I snapped it shut, sat a moment. None of it mine.

Morning round had been and gone, "What the hell," I was being recklessly driven by the voice hammering in my head, "Get out of here, boy, out, get out!" Pants, shirt, trousers, socks, I fell back on the bed to pull them on, "Boy, boy, am I weak." Struggling to dress, I grunted with pain as I bent.

"Good God, this lot fits me." Whose? Hollow cheeks and lantern-jaw watched from a mirror over the sink. I touched the face with a skinny hand, noted the actions, not a man I recognised, surely I was alive? I attempted a grin, it's me O.K.

Tweed jacket, an amazing fit. Hurriedly, automatically my hand went to the inside pocket. A blood stained wallet. I stared at it in disbelief. "Mine. How in the name of creation did it get into this outfit?" Fumbling through each pouch, cash, bank cards, "of course it's mine."

In disbelief I checked the contents again. A small card slipped onto the floor. I picked it up. Just a handwritten phone number. No time to think that one out.

Visitors thronged the passage, chattering, clutching grapes and flowers. None ever opened my door. Joining the stream was easy. Corridors, lifts, more corridors with pictures. Past reception. Front door, don't look back. I was outside, goodbye hospital, and thank you.

I leant against a taxi rank pillar. A coughing fit overtook me, "You OK, guv?" The cab driver took my elbow, "Yes thanks, I'll be fine in a moment," and after a pause, "Euston station, please." Why in the world should I pick Euston?

The cabbie helped me to a seat in the station.

Amongst the throng of everyday city life I sat thinking.

A small card, hand written phone number, I turned it over.

Blank.

CHAPTER SIX

Semi-detached

Clack-arty, clack, clack-arty, clack, it hammered through an aching head, a drumbeat pounding from Euston to Glasgow, rolling into bends, roaring through stations, the route of 'The Royal Scot' since days of glowing firebox and the hiss of steam. Silver tracks and clattering points, the train swaying in lively tempo. Hurrying north, driven by some wild urge, it might be a ridiculous whim but there was no denying my shiver of expectation. Ten years cooped in a physics lab testing theories, exploring new concepts, here was the same nerve jangling sensation I experienced when my research stood on the edge of fresh insight.

Perhaps I'd venture to some hazardous retreat, elemental and remote which could ignite a spark of imagination, lift my mind beyond mundane thoughts into a torrid zone of inspired dimensions where ideas emerge or equations present themselves. Unravel the enigma of 'Dark Energy', prove it the force driving the expansion of the universe. Deduce the nature of 'Dark Matter', invisible, yet thought to be the overwhelming mass of this universe. Research which occupied past work haunted my brain, torturing me with ideas just out of reach. I was far from well.

Was this headlong stampede northwards the trick of a fevered mind, the first symptoms of insanity, maybe schizophrenia, had I lost contact with reality? The injury to my head in the explosion might explain the violent swings of a mind in the grip of disjointed thinking which I found impossible to stem.

Abruptly a fresh mental turmoil erupted as I began to consider the widespread indifference and gross ignorance that could be driving our species towards extinction when the potential evolution of intelligence might set the waves of imagination on a journey through the orifice of singularity towards a comprehension of infinity?

I heard myself lecturing the carriage, "An age of enlightenment awaits us, knowledge yet untapped. Ninety-six percent of this universe remains virgin to our understanding. All that we are, all the stuff that constitutes everything we touch, all we experience as reality, all we see about us as though it were totality, is a mere four per cent of a supreme mystery. Let me tell you...."

I became aware of standing and shouting. The woman beside me got up in some alarm, snatched her case off the rack and moved down the compartment. In mortifying embarrassment I sank back on my seat. Hands sweating and twitching, I looked out of the carriage window. The need for treatment was becoming obvious. Could a practical life help me recover?

We rattled through mundane countryside. Copse and hedgerow dovetailed into bow fronted homes, red brick and mowed lawns. Their uniformity fed into factory gates surrounded by bumper to bumper car parks. Skylines puffed away. Brickworks' chimneys, slender and elegant, hour glass energy towers topped with steam carried away in twisting spirals on a blustery day.

Streets followed the contours of forgotten valleys. End on houses formed serrated rows of tiled roofs and castellated chimney pots, each tiny back garden proudly walled from its neighbour. Ariel forests gave viewers access to the disappearing jungles, or maybe the ritual of sexy soaps and violence. Squeezed between graffiti and washing lines I spotted the odd decrepit residence; pillared doorways, shading beech, the remnants of an unassailable feudal divide. As we banked through industrial estates, gigantic multinational signs presided over factory parking lots and used car dumps. Sickly trees waved plastic bags. Pub signs, potting sheds and greenhouses, a conglomeration of human bolt holes, temporary shelters before the onslaught of compulsory identification and draconian measures are brought to control the anarchy which will engulf these same streets as the fallout from a growing wealth gap.

City overspill and rolling countryside, the conurbations of modern housing stretched their tentacles into fields trimmed white with hawthorn blossom. Here and there red tiled farmsteads evoked an era of squire and lady, fox covets and hunting horn, whilst squat farm cottages with perhaps a dry lavatory down the garden caught the mellowness of a rural culture with Morris Dancing beside the duck pond. Spacious undulating countryside, its hollows of leafy lane and thatched roofed village suggested more the stockbroker hideaway rather than any rural deprivation. On a rise of ground a dark oaken glade, pagan in its seclusion, skirted the tower of a Norman church Square and solid the bastion of a cherished age, the hands of its gold faced clock stood at twelve, slow or maybe stopped?

The rail tracks climbed into the Lake District, grassy fells and grey homesteads clinging to primitive hillsides. Stone dykes wound over the skyline, hand built monuments to bygone skill and the hardiness of a people. National Park territory, few cattle, but plenty of bed and breakfast signs, a rural culture providing scenic amenity. Out on a ridge windmills facing a day of heavy showers and a blustering wind turned their energy to offsetting the activities of an expanding species. Ten billion humans set to require the resources of two planets? The sun hid behind clouds of stupidity.

Rain drove across the carriage windows in diagonal streaks. Crewe, Preston, Carlisle had passed my window. Soon we'd be crossing the Solway Firth. Utterly weary as I was, I raised my head and watched intently the last of Jerusalem's green and pleasant land. Louring cloud brought gloom to the flat expanse of the last miles of England. The steel struts of a bridge carried the train over mud flats and a tidal creek. Showers of angled desolation appeared slate grey and bone cutting. Was this the miserable crossing which divided two cultures?

Its empty dejection became the echo of my mother's mother, the sadness of her voice. Looking out I remembered. I heard her talking to a child at knee; a soft voice, distant in its telling of the Jacobite's retreat to the Highlands. I saw stumbling men who came home to death by Redcoat bayonet, the sacrifice of a people to the aspirations of royal vanity. "Well boy, back through Carlisle came the Highlanders, ragged and hungry, cheering and victorious they'd been, just months before, loyal to the fatal Bonnie Prince Charlie." The old grandmother paused with a sigh of reflection, "Now they wanted only hill and high ground, the sanctuary of wild places with its winter snow and hidden pride. We didn't ever recover from the slaughter on Drumossie Moor,"

She never stooped to calling the defeat of her people, the Battle of Culloden. That was the name the English put on it, she said and speaking as though it were yesterday, she put a hand on my head, "My great, great grandfather's elder brother fell on the field, east wind and sleet in his face, a musket ball through the chest, so they told. And fat, gloating Cumberland standing on a high stone at the back, waving and cheering. The Butcher they called him. The younger brother of that dead relation and some of the boys from the Ross-shire crofts took to the hill, hunted down like foxes, den to den."

It was my childhood lesson in lingering Highland bitterness, "A friend from Wester Ross had a fishing boat and put that relation ashore in the Outer Hebrides. Over the side at night and swim. It was on a lonely island, I don't remember the name. Anyway, the people hid and fed him. They took a great risk. They could have been shot too, a gunboat was cruising and stopping and searching every boat they came upon. Plenty that were shot out of hand."

Oblivious of train and surroundings, I remembered so clearly her long silence and the childhood tension of awaiting a stories ending. Eventually she whispered, "Well, a'bhalaich, that man was your great, great, great, grandfather." How little it meant to me then, how precious now.

I'd viewed the plodding tameness of feudal class divisions and its reverential bowing to superiors; how different from the voices which sprang into a sudden craving. Words came flowing, song and poetry, long forgotten lines arose in my head, 'Scots wha hae, Sound the Pibroch,' great songs, melodies that wept tears in the lost tides of defeat, bold words that waved the banners of victory, and sang the tunes of glory.

My father came strongly to me; 'A Man's a Man for a' that,' the line he stressed in a poem he loved. I heard him again, playing the piano, the songs of Old Scotia, he called them, melodies that lived in haunting times, stirring times, the poetry of a nation with the undying emotions of love, battle, and sacrifice in its soul. Out of lament for the old ways I learnt at granny's knee, there came a lift in my heart.

Exaltation sang to the vaulted generations of awaiting spirits. Scotland. For the first time in my life, I was in Scotland. And beating a pulse in my head, my father's deep voice;

'From the lone shieling of the misty island,
   Mountains divide us, and the wastes of seas,
   Yet still the blood is strong, the heart is Highland,

And we in dreams behold the Hebrides.'

My eyes filled with the tears of joy and sadness.

Nobody in the compartment looked up from their magazines. Crossing the border- no more than crossing a street. Apart from that humiliating outburst of shouting, I had not spoken to anybody, nor anybody to me. The seat beside me remained vacant, Maybe my hollow, wet cough sounded like T.B. or cancer? Not that I wanted company, conversations raged in my head.

Crossing the border, I felt conscious of the stirrings of an ethnic divide.

Where was I going, and why?

The rail line twisted amongst soft and rounded contours. Border hills, grass to their tops and dotted like daisies with sheep. Sheep! I'd never before seen so many ranging the open hills, subject to wind, weather and a shepherd's skill. The empathy between a man with his working foot on the hill and the animals which daily depended on its pasture occurred to me.

Out of the shadows of evening light the burns overflowed, white and creamy from gullies cut by ten thousand storms. Here was I, a scientist grappling with the calculations of the sub-atomic particles which govern existence and there on a passing hillside a system dealing with a purpose, tangible and simple. A distant flock of sheep appeared as an undulating white canopy flowing down the hill. I spotted a striding man and with a stab of pleasure I caught sight of two dogs.

An image of busy city millions superimposed itself, the trap of civilisation hurtled into my picture. Taxis, tube trains and forced body contact became the cannibalistic screaming of rats fighting in a cage. How to heal with this erratic mind racing, stop these bouts of recurring horror? I wrung my hands and groaned aloud, aware passengers were glancing at me. Gradually my thoughts steadied, became lucid as hills gave way to ploughed land and fields of dairy cattle. On the horizon I glimpsed the skyscraper tenements of Glasgow and again I was assailed by this morbid dread of confinement.

Access to land as the basic requirement of survival was denied to countless by force, yet to millions of western consumers it was discounted by choice and certainly had no bearing on their daily activities. Perhaps I was being too simplistic in believing the sun and soil to be the fundamental requirements if civilization began to crack. What else counted in a final reckoning?

From fields and hillsides to high rise flats my I saw the land in a totally different context. No longer just a weekend playground, I wanted land sufficient to live on, to live by, to care for, be part of its cycles with the intimacy of belonging; hold my head high with the pride and satisfaction of working in harness with its natural forces. I needed the solace of the elements, and happiness.

Ideas and inspiration churned with the fury of a riptide. My head throbbed, bursting to be released from a body weak and sick, be able to stride like the shepherd I'd watched on that Border hillside. I must find health, land, and independence.

Why in the world had I traveled north, any direction, but north? Yet I felt drawn as if by a magnet, a helpless compass needle swinging true. Some force seemed in control of this diabolically stupid breakout. Barely fit to walk fifty yards without a coughing fit, I groaned aloud. Was I ditching a field of research which might break the stranglehold of Einstein's lordly equation? Fool, you fool! What madness drove me?

A phone sat on the bedside table of a Glasgow Hotel.

For the first time since 'escaping' from the hospital, an incident I preferred to regard as leaving of my own accord, I stared at the card with a handwritten phone number. Never mind clothes, money, how or why had it all happened? Somebody must have slipped this card into my wallet. The number meant nothing to me.

I lifted the receiver. Should I dial? It could be a ridiculous folly.

"This is reception, how can I help you, Sir?" I relayed the number to a thick Scottish accent, "It's ringing for you now, Sir."

It rang and rang, would I put down the receiver?

"Hello, hello," a mellow voice answered, relaxed, no practiced, 'How may I help you?'. I waited, until eventually, "I'm in the bar just now, hang on." I heard him speak to someone, but not in English. The clink of a glass followed by, "That's for yourself, Iain," then back to me, "Who's calling please?"

"Is that the, the, er, er," Taken aback to hear the strains of energetic fiddle playing, I faltered. Should I hang up? After all, I hadn't the least idea whom I might be contacting. Lively music, laughter and voices, my hand stopped in mid-air.

"It's the Castleton Hotel you've got," the man had raised his voice above conversations which were certainly not in English. The strains of an accordion joined the fiddler. "Sorry about the noise. Are you hearing me.?"

"Yes, I'm hearing you. Er mm," I cleared my throat, "is there any possibility of accommodation please. Have you a single room, I, er, maybe tomorrow?" This is ridiculous, tomorrow? I was in Glasgow, could be speaking to John o'Groats or Lands

End. The code said it must be somewhere in U.K. "By the way," I tried to sound casual, "where exactly are you?"

"Well now, you've reached the Isle of Halasay. If you're coming over, just jump on the ferry from Oban. There's plenty room here, no problem. In case you're late, what name is it?"

The situation was gaining a compelling momentum, but did I want to give away any details? The implied threat at the Goldberg meeting concerned me. All too vividly I was aware of the case of scientist whose assessment perhaps didn't fit the conclusion desired by his political masters, who as a prominent advisor to the Government on the issue of weapons of mass destruction in Iraq was found dead and some doctors were questioning the suicide verdict. Given the highly suspicious convenience of the hospital arrangements, clothes, wallet and cash but no briefcase, was I being set up? In spells of rational thought I'd planned to remain incognito and disappear.

I hesitated. John Smith sounded foolish. The background noise settled the matter and my name fitted the music. I plunged on, "This is, er, Hector MacKenzie."

There was something of a pause, I guessed he relayed the information down a bar counter. I heard my name at the end of a sentence before the voice came again,

"No problem Mr.MacKenzie, just come across when it suits you. Don't you be worrying, there's plenty Mackenzies on this island already, another one won't make any difference."

CHAPTER SEVEN

A Thousand Years

Untwine the double helix,
Decode its formulae,
It will tell you home,
Explain affinity.

I winced at the lungfulls of salt air. They stung, sharp as iodine, tender lungs crackled like brown paper, smarting with each greedy breath. Sunlight reflected off the sea, burnt a face pale as a hot plant reared in an office. Wasted muscles, no better than a newly born kitten, weak eyes narrowed, overpowered by the brightness and though the spring hinted summer's warmth I shivered. Clinging to the ship's rail, swaying to each roll, I learnt what it was to be truly soft and I hated it. Somehow I'd beat it.

Trains or planes are dull, but putting to sea! Any ship, great or small, casting her ropes and pulling away from land has aboard the thrill of setting out, anticipation, perhaps adventure, leaving an old world, seeking a new. It coursed through me. Glorying to prospects I knew not, I stood on the upper deck and let a driving wind whipping my face carve the future.

Our dipping bows cut through the oncoming swell, hurled aside rhythmic sheets in fascinating cascades of light. The great sea, the ferocious sea, drowning, playing, pounding, singing. Don't say it had no thought, nor its motion lacked an embracing feel. Rainbows shone in its spray, children of the sun, yellow red and green, in splendour the dark marine. Beside us sailed masters of the gale, gliding along each trough, tipping the surface, banking with the ease of upward sweep until they crossed the breaking tops of a world so dangerous and immense.

Away to the north a fishing boat was flinging spray, her bows gleaming broke each crest. Men on the winches handling nets, skipper at helm judging wind and weather, real men. Watching turned into craving. I'll be part of this world of 'doing' Find a practical life, outdoors each day, live with the sun, the healing sun.

Hilltops grew from the sea, turned to islands, long and sleek, dark as a seal's back. Travel the world here the tendrils that bound me were imprinted in the blood. How else their power to sway? Tears came, blinding and unashamed. Why, why? What were these shores to me?

Wave tops flecked with white, rocks and breaking swell. Ancient limbs reached into the sea, primal land to sky without bounds. No insipid shades- sounds and colour, strong and pure, vibrant as the energy of places wild which face the rolling sea. No weakness now would hold me back.

All doubts fled, a rough existence would be the making of me. Away with security, no conformity, my own master come what may, trim sail to gale, the fickle moods of sea, ride storm and danger; face the doom of Nordic myth, *what will be, will be.* The spirit of Viking days gripped my imagination, a psychic force driving my actions; the fatal power that bends us to its ends.

The island closed, ahead the pillard light. Skerries dark, white edged with the rising tide. A wild bird's flight.black winged against the sea. The helm swung sharp a-starboard, turned the headland close. Beaches shelved to turquoise, a bay, a castle, sea girt on a rock and straggled crofts beneath a snaring peak. I stared in disbelief.

One island hill stood clear against the blue. Sunshine faded into night. I heard a new born cry upon an ice moon hill. A shadowed crone sat amid the frozen needles beneath a winter larch, till smiling through her dying groan she watched the raven galley sail to seek a freedom home.

What force unravelled time and place, stirred imprinted memory?

Though a thousand years had passed,

Yet beat the pulse of true affinity.

CHAPTER EIGHT

Hilda

The image faded as the ferry manoeuvered alongside. It left me deeply concerned by these repeated glimpses of past events. Did they somehow emerge from a cosmic interface where past, present and future exist locked together as an indestructible wavelength imprinted on the process of particle annihilation and recreation. After all wavelengths form our reality, must reach into the neural connections between our brain cells. The hypothesis of parallel universes has been suggested, why not a form of parallel consciousness?

Outlandish speculation, I shook it off by concentrating on first impressions. Some of the folk in the saloon had conversed in Gaelic, their rising and falling voices reminding me of the few Irish I knew. A surprising contrast to the strident tones I'd left behind fighting the decibels of a different culture often harsh and loud with assertive conversation. Other contrasts stood out voices apart, facial and in their manner, the gulf appeared vastly wider than that dividing the revolving mix of people on a London bus.

Unsteady and exhausted, I was last down the gang plank. One of the young men working on the pier smiled a greeting. Tall with deep straight eyes, the face tanned and relaxed, I was aware of a like kind. He spoke to me, his voice soft and expressive, "How are you tonight?" I took it as more of a pleasantry towards a stranger than a question.

"Fine, fine," I forced a grin, aware I must appear a poor wretch, "a lovely evening."

His eyes went to the horizon, "Yes, it's set fair," He reached for the ships bow rope, then paused, and turning back to me without curiosity, "Are you needing a hand?"

"No, no thanks, I, I'll find, er, go to the hotel shortly, the Castleton, but thanks again."

"No problem, just head up the street," and grinning to me he watched for a signal from the ships bridge. "The boys up there'll look after you all right, there's a few characters amongst them."

The gang plank rattled clear and ropes were slipped. I envied hands that could coil and handle the heavy mooring ropes so deftly without any hurry. Greetings had come, farewells gone with the last wave from deck to pier. The few people and cars had left. Loading ramps clanged shut, water churned and the ship drew away. Engines throbbed into the approach of evening quiet. Cabin lights wove amongst departing ripples and into the mauve of an easterly headland the dot of her red port light vanished.

I couldn't leave the sunset. Although my legs still felt the motion of the ship I swayed unsteadily to the end of the pier and on the point of collapse, sat on a bollard. Lights dotted a single row of houses curving up from the harbour. A shop front shone onto the road. High above the bay, a steeple clock reflected the hour of sunset. The fresh breeze of a Minch crossing died to nothing. Somewhere above me on a hillside lost to sunlight, a sheep called. A single bleat. Its clarity surprised me, the only sound to encroach on the stillness. Drained of energy, I sat alone. The sun grew large. Its orange strands fell across the bay and slowly they darkened.

Outlines fell into sharp detail imparting form and feeling to the glimmer of transient light. On a blood red sea a boat lay motionless, perfect to the curve of her anchor rope. I saw her, a maiden long and slim, shapely on the water. In her lines was the beauty of youth, born by the freedom of tide and shore.

The bonniest girl, she came running and laughing, sunshine streaming through flaxen curls.

A reverie of infinite sadness engulfed me, the weeping of a dying melody.

The last roundness of the sun was taken by the sea.

Varnished planking shone in a moment of crimson.

I read her name, and spoke it softly,

'Hilda'.

CHAPTER NINE

Stone on stone

Sturdy feet brown with sun, no shoes that summer day.
Hardship, poverty, a child deprived?
Those children of the tide had a wealth abounding,
Countless as the grains of sand,
On the beaches of their childhood.

Heading towards eighty, tall and angular, Eachan MacKenzie's features carried the distinction of his forebears. Passing generations reduced the hooked nose to a degree, but his genes had not relinquished the penetrating blueness of deep set eyes, judge of man and oncoming wave alike. Physical and facial hardiness marked an outdoor man. His pink cheeks, though furrowed by a lifetime of drawing his eyes against the light, still carried the freshness of spring. Hands without flesh were shaped and bent by the tools of crofting. Old by the measure of years, hardened by the elements whose power and vagaries he'd good reason to respect, MacKenzie had the wisdom to work in tandem with their moods.

A life spent in an open landscape, land, sea and weather, space and distance always the setting. Westwards the curving earth vanished over Atlantic's rim, eastwards on days of sharp light were the low outlines of mainland peaks; how often he looked south across a narrow sound to the headland of an island empty of people, the isle of Sandray, for it was from there his grandfather had moved family and the chattels of subsistence to make a home here on the Halasay croft of Ach-na-Mara, the 'Field of the Sea.' Upper most in MacKenzie's make up was an abiding reverence for the hardiness of his distant forebears. "They came by the sea, on a wind from the north. Chancers of the first order," and looking at his wife, Ella, he would laugh, "in search of women."

Instinct told Eachan the weather. A glance at the clouds, a shift in the wind, the feel of the air on his face, they formed the barometer by which he read the signs that shaped each day's work. His intimacy with land, livestock and the producing of food imparted a sense of values beyond the jargon of modern living. In keeping with a fierce independence which bowed only to the demands of weather and season, he treated all people equally. To strangers who met Eachan working about the croft, his easy manner and sparse appearance seemed part of the landscape, almost as though he were moulded by his surroundings. Quiet spoken, unhurrying and practical, about him was a manner which merged without effort into the attraction of the island. Time was not his master, he'd never possessed a watch. Instead the immutable rhythms which govern places of solitude were his timepiece and the sedateness of passing hours allowed for a spread of thoughts wide as the circle of his daily horizon.

Confidence comes to those who know their origins. Eachan knew his roots, they spread through many, many island generations. Moreover the old man well appreciated the toil of his ancestors. When the grey lines of winter sea had tops blown to the clouds and waves trembled the shore, frothing torrents surged into the dunes, rolling massive stones, grinding them storm after storm until clean and round they lay awaiting the labour of carting. Heavy hammer and skill had cracked them and built what was now Eachan's barn and byre. Hand on its wall he was given to saying, "Only those with the knack to split a stone and know the aching bones can give credit to the art of placing stone on stone."

The original homestead had been a Viking longhouse, its gable towards the mild sou-westerlies a byre whose connecting door had brought warmth from wintering cattle. At the farthest end the gable facing the chill of nor-east winds kept freshness to the hay barn. Between byre and barn the house was snug from the elements. Salt brown and weathered, low of eve and squat, defying the onslaughts of January longer than memory could extend, nature tucked the buildings with little effort into the vast empty scenery, nor did the house which Eachan's father added to the old Norse design encroach on the harmony of a wind carved scenery.

Each day the old man saw a need for a job about the croft as befitted his years. That day he'd worked down at the shore, re-stringing lobster creels in the lee of his boat. Ninety-one seasons of sowing, fishing and harvest. The March wind was from the east. It sought him out. He came back to the house, ice in his bones. No, nor hot stones from the fire wrapped in towels could warm him. A young doctor stood beside his bed, hesitating. After a little the old man turned his eyes, "I've never known the need of a doctor in my life, and I won't be needing you now, but thank you for troubling to come." He made to shake the doctor's hand but the pain took him. In his eyes were summer days, terns fishing the bay and with his children's laughter he crossed the sea. At the bedside his son Eachan bent and closed the lids.

A cold spring it was. With more years to count than his appearance belied, Eachan took on the croft of Ach na Mara and put his father's plough to work. The land still lay under the bleakness of winter, its stubbles gleaned bare by the passing geese. Harness and traces, his pony put her head down and leaned shoulders to the collar. Callused hands gave a lift of the shafts and the plough point slid into sandy ground. Eachan strode the furrows of another season.

Steady and straight, light the touch of reins on his pony's neck. His white pony, one ear forward, one ear back, the digging of her hooves marked the plough's next round. Sunrise fell obliquely across the land. Brown crests glistened, new made, damp and fresh. In the quiet of morning the man, a stooping figure, watched the living soil curl away from the plough board, heard the crackle of their turning as they broke over in countless tiny veins. On the clean air, fulsome with the smell of his pony, a tilt of the shafts, a click of the tongue and Eachan turned his plough on the end rig. A polished mouldboard would shine, bright as the early sun that warmed the backs of man and beast. Gulls circled from the banks of winter seaweed to strut and squabble at his heel. Lapwing left their tumbling flight to settle on the new turned crests, the lustre of their dark wings green and bronze in the brittle light. Soon hollows scraped in the fresh soil would hold three mottled brown eggs. And far out, thin lines of geese marked the edge of the Atlantic, northbound to retreating snows their voices clamorous on a young morning.

Out of respect for the old ways Eachan sowed the corn with the slender moon of a Good Friday. A canvas sowing sheet hung across his shoulders, each handful of oats flew through his fingers in a curve of seeds at every measured stride. Ella, his wife, carried pails of grain to fill the sheet whenever he paused. By nightfall the field was sown and at first light his white pony would drag the harrows to cover the seed. Crying lapwing stooped, flapping wings beat about their heads. Sharp eyed as he walked the sowing, Eachan marked each clutch of eggs with a stick. A touch of the reins at the harrowing and each nest was safe. A month and green shoots of corn sheltered tiny, black legged chicks. Handfuls of crouching fluff, mottled as the shells from which they had broken.

When the golden heads of grain crackled with ripeness, mower blades were sharpened and with her ears back, the white pony pulled Eachan's chattering iron reaper. Standing corn fell in thick rows. Ella bent and gathered. Her deft hands took a few straws and heads and with a quick twist which made the harvest knot, she bound each sheaf. Their children ran home from school, threw satchels into the kitchen and set up the stooks. If an evening breeze held off the dampness Eachan would cut on until the great round moon fell golden on the sheaves and laughing children would hide in stook huts and long to sleep the night in the smell of fresh straw.

By the moon of the returning geese, corn sheaves filled a neatly trimmed stackyard and hungry bills gleaned the stubbles. There was no grudging the feeding of other life about the croft whose worlds knew different bounds. Their arrival was greeted as naturally as the seasons. On a still February nights, Eachan, out at the byre to tend a calving cow, might catch the whistle of a dog otter. By May his cubs would be playing in the rock pools. By June, amongst the half grown oats the plover chicks could feed in safety. Seldom the loom of summer's night without the grating notes of a corncrake, secretive bird, she hid amongst the beds of yellow iris and threw her voice with such skill few found her nest. The croft land reared many families, not least that of Eachan and his wife. They and their children in turn saw other life no differently.

The cobblestone byre remained little changed since Viking times. It wintered the croft's eight cows. Each knew its own stall and they appeared at the door always in the same order. A fondness for cattle came naturally to Eachan, he enjoyed their smell, gave each a scratch as he worked about them and in the way of animals, they knew it. A wooden pen, snug below the hay loft, kept the calves in the warmth of the byre. Before and after school whilst Ella milked the house cow, the children let out calves bawling to suckle their mothers. Eachan shovelled out the dung, swept the cobbles and come April, he carted the winter midden to each field in turn. The yearly cycle put natural fertility on the land, gave back what had been taken out. Worms throve, bird life throve and his family ate an untainted diet. On occasion and in the right company, Eachan, always a master of the pithy statement, was wont to pronounce, "The folly of chemical farming is killing the mouths it feeds. Destroy the diversity of the living soil and you'll destroy mankind and much else." Needless to say, such observation called for a further libation.

A white-washed home of red tin roof and attic windows, the days of summer shone through tiny windows into 'the good room' with its heavy winter curtains and faded photos sitting atop a walnut upright piano. Across the hallway was a wood lined kitchen of deep stone sinks that had bathed each child in turn. Against the gable wall a peat hungry stove warmed the towels which wrapped healthy infants. Outside of the hall, a front porch laden with pegs full of oilskins and wellies, served as the headquarters of their collie dog, 'Rab'. Nose on paws, eyes alert, nothing moved on the croft without requiring his attention.

The crofthouse of Ach-na-Mara had known love and birth, ceilidh nights and the anguish of death. Once the focal point of an island community, Eachan and Ella, his young wife, held open house to fiddle and dancing feet and even now, seldom was its lum without a trail of smoke or the welcoming reek of peat at a flagstone step had been worn by the tramp of calling feet. Eachan found a head looking in the door an excuse for a dram. Their brood of children were overseas and the ever patient Ella felt the house quiet. The kettle steamed gently on the stove and always her morning's baking found a ready uptake. Ella, broad and placid, her forehead unwrinkled, had been the beauty of village dances before the days of face cream and mascara. By many years she was the junior of Eachan, indeed a generation existed between them and for a strange reason.

A young and handsome Eachan had the fashion of walking the miles across the hill to the east side of the island. Saturday nights, without fail, he would be at a fireside talking to an old crofting couple. Sheep conversations apart, his mind was on their daughter who sat quietly, awaiting a tap on the door which would take her to the local dance. The light of the Tilley lamp shone on a lustre of flaxen curls, made her eyes liquid pools of deep attraction. Eachan was in love, unashamedly and distractedly. He attended her wedding, dancing, drinking, and longing.

Out of affection for her folks he kept up his visits to their crofting fireside. One night with a gale out of the west hastening his walk he arrived to find the village midwife busy heating towels. As always a welcoming dram from the 'bodach' and they sat to the fire, talking. The night drew on, women's work went on. In the wee hours the midwife brought through a crying bundle to wash at the warmth of the hearth. The birth of a daughter to the girl he had lost to another man. By and by he tiptoed through to the back bedroom. The girl he loved looked up from feeding her baby. He kissed her tenderly and went out to walk, long, long, miles.

Full twenty years were to pass, hard work alone on the croft of Ach-na-Mara. And one night when the hillside lay in soft velvet light, he proposed to the girl he had seen washed, a new born baby by the fire. And the light of the moon fell with the eyes of her mother, and she said 'Yes.'

Graying a little, but handsome still, fresh air and soft rain had kept Ella young. A powerful woman, she'd helped at the digging of the peats, the sowing and harvest. She rolled wool at the clippings, kept corn to the hens and fed collie dogs, cooking stove and family alike. A busy woman, trained from childhood in the ways of a crofting household. When a 'nor-wester' tuned the slates and the boom of breakers kept it time, all would feel snug in their tiny kitchen, then the warmth of the peat fire helped produce a sizeable brood of children. The frequency of winter gales was to fill a home of scrubtop table and bunk beds beneath the wood lined eaves. Ella presided over her man and brood with the eyes of kindness.

Evenly featured offspring, blue eyed and willing. Dependent on age, work about the croft was part of their upbringing. A bottle and teat to feed the pet lambs fell to the youngest. The oldest by ten, would be digging the 'tatties' they'd helped to plant and perhaps before bedtime, peeping into the byre with the hurricane lantern on a nail above the stall throwing its yellow light on the pressing cow, until out came a wet, spluttering calf.

Round the fields on a spring morning they followed their father to see him draw the front legs, then a head, and gently bring out a living lamb from a ewe in difficulty. With school pals at communal sheep clippings when neighbours gathered, they carried fleeces to pack the wool bags, all the time working and learning the skills which made possible an island life. Jobs were given to all the children, simple disciplines without question or pay and happiness ruled.

Patched-hand-me-downs, their barefoot children ran the summer long, lively expeditions to the hill, building stone and heather shelters, or down to the beach when the white sand burnt their feet and only the beady-eyed gulls dozing one- legged amongst the seaweed complained at the intrusion. Green edged rock pools filled with treasure, open razor shells and mauve pebbles were spread to dry. Heedless of time, driftwood games and homespun adventures by the light off the sea filled their childhood days

Below 'The Field of the Sea', a double ended sailing boat lay winched on its launching track, clear of the tide. Headlands enfolded the bay, green topped and fertile. Spring and autumn alike, the passing geese would rest and feed. Tapering headlands fell away to creviced rocks where the cormorant stood holding their outstretched wings to the sun, a safe haven to all when plumes of spray burst in crannied gullies and the booming Atlantic was in voice.

As the high days of summer waned and moon put her harvest light upon the sea Eachan would run out his sturdy little boat and take the children fishing. The brown lug sail would pull them clear of the headlands on a faint breeze that followed the sun to the west. The herring would be running and the net would fill, and the lithe silver bodies would pour about their feet. A last haul and the moons orange path, broad and dappled reached from a darkening horizon. By her dying beam he would steer his boat for their rock bound haven, the breeze just a ghostly hand.

Each spring when the great wild flocks calling in the night steered north by the stars, there came a restlessness for the stravaiging days, it tightened the sinews and coursed through the man whose ancestors had fought on the high seas of adventure. By way of easing the yearning Eachan would sail his children across the Sound to Sandray. They'd sit about him at the old house, scones and buttermilk, and the mood would be on him to tell of his people's coming to the island a thousand years before. And he would drift to sleep and they would take off to play.

One of the girls with a sprawling mop of the curliest flaxen hair, perhaps the most daring of their family, had fallen. The children came running to tell him. Out on the headland she'd climbed the cliff where the fulmar nested. There on a ledge at its foot, he found her, and in his boat they sailed her home.

Careless of things that winter, a storm had splintered his boat. Without a boat he was a man without a hand. His family built him another, the finest of Norway larch and double ended, she had the sturdy lines of the galleys that came to Sandray in the stories he'd told.

She was all he wanted of a boat, sleek and beautiful, truly a maid of the sea,

In memory of the girl they'd lost, he called her 'Hilda'.

The light was failing, yet its dimness drew radiance from the sea. The luminous gleam of the sun remained a dying presence beneath the surface of the glowing sheet of water. The air, the atmosphere, every particle of existence became tinged in a delicate suffusion of the palest lemon.

Time's passage slowed to a total fixation. As the changing light told me of a turning world, so my life was turning beyond recognition. Nothing mattered but to watch the transforming glimmer, its reflection on the sea, the land, a clock spire of worship oblivious to the puniness of an earth that spun in obedience to the dancing waves of space; a revolving, trivial dot in the mysterious grip of the sun's gravity, a planet at the mercy of the Sun God, radiation.

The boat turned gradually, its mast a silhouette against the horizon. She epitomised all I needed. A boat, instantly determined, I needed a boat, a journey, follow the elements. Sail by the wind, taste the sea. Shaking with excitement, I tried to rise. A coughing bout raked through me. I bent, hand on the bollard, a rope tripped my foot and I stumbled.

Somebody caught me.

"Steady, steady, too late for a swim tonight." Hard hands lifted me to my feet. I stood swaying. The man remained holding me firmly. The coughing subsided, and turning, "Thanks, thanks," I managed to say.

"You're not too well boy," the deep ring of his voice startled me. I looked up. My head spun, thoughts twisted, I grasped at memory. Where before, where had I seen this face, those eyes?

After the pause, "Yes, I ..er.. I was.. my lungs were damaged by an explosion."

Minutes elapsed. We looked at each other, no fleeting glance but a searching intensity. His eyes shone, clear as the horizon. A strange bonding. Without ceremony he shook my hand.

"Sit there just now," a quiet command. Seated again on the bollard I watched as he rowed a tiny dingy out to the boat. An outboard engine broke the silence of the bay, the ripple of his boat its calm waters. She came alongside. The man climbed the short iron ladder and made fast.

"Now," the voice brooked no dissention, "I'll go aboard. You'll come down, step by step."

He caught me on the last rung, "Sit at the mast, a'bhalaich, I'll get your case." Too exhausted to protest or enquire, I said nothing. Casting off, sure footed at every move, he sat in the stern. A man, strong faced, old and white haired.

The engine rattled into life. We swung away from the pier. An island beyond the bay tapered into the darkness, slim and faint, beyond comprehension.

Was I touching this boat? I looked into the night, was I touching the boat which drugged my thoughts with both sadness and a longing?

Had she risen out of that dream which creeps without warning into dimensions of fantasy and desire? Had I descended into a sleep which had opened the portals of fate, where all tomorrow is a refection yesterday's hope and tragedy?

At the first roll of the swell she rose gently and dipped gracefully.

I held her mast. My head reeled.

Was I at sea, aboard the 'Hilda?'

CHAPTER TEN

Shadows on the Sun

"Josh, how splendid to see you," the P.M. turned from studying papers on a large leather topped desk and rose to a cordial handshake with his Chief Scientific Advisor. "Do sit down. My jove you're looking so well. Been on holiday?" he queried, smiling warmly.

Sir Joshua Goldberg, tanned and urbane, sat heavily on one of the three armchairs, "Well yes, I have as a matter of fact, no, not quite a holiday, I nipped over to Geneva for a few days but as it happened, the weather was magnificent." His eye flitted over to the brightly lit operations panel which covered the end wall. Large scale, Middle East, he noted, Israel to Iran.

The P.M. returned to his swivel chair. The strong light from behind him left his face in shadow and focused on Goldberg. A longish, narrow room without windows, blanching and airless, one of a complex of nuclear proof bunkers below Downing Street, it served for strictly private conversations, un-minuted, totally un- recorded. An extractor fan whirred softy from the low oppressive ceiling.

"Geneva, mm, that's interesting," a non-committal remark, yet it evoked a thoughtful look. "Anyway," the P.M. continued, "we've had all the fall out." He checked himself with a boyish grin, "I'll re-phrase that. We've had to deal with all the complications from that hellish tube bombing. This is the first chance I've had to talk to you about the nuclear issue. You remember we discussed it after that bloody ignorant scientist had to be more or less thrown out."

His face reddened and smacking a fist on the desk, "How the hell he had the cheek to mouth all that stuff at me, right in my face! I've never had that kind of impudence before. Don't worry, Josh, I'll see his project clipped," ..adding in a grinding tone, "maybe his wings too."

Steadying himself with a deep breath, "More to the point, I'm sure you'll know the U.S. manufacturers are already tooling up for these mini nuclear power plants. I was furious that the bugger seemed to know about that as well. We can't risk any hitch which might frighten the financiers. Is there any truth in what he said about the storage of nuclear waste?"

The Chief Advisor studied his finger nails aware he'd been responsible for the debacle of their meeting the scientist. "That was the purpose of my little Euro trip and yes, there will need to be certain modifications, but deep burial is definitely on, given, as I say, a bit of attention to some of the details MacKenzie raised. However," he looked up, "I'm in close contact with the Japanese and U.S. designers and operators. The matter can be handled but," his eyes flickered slightly, "it would be extremely unfortunate if the points he raised were to be passed, for example to the green press."

"I know that too damn well, leave that bit to me, I have a bully boy who can bring that shower to heel," came the P.M.'s impatient reply, and then more carefully, "The political side is difficult, but with care we'll get a nuclear debate through the Commons on a quiet day. The economy will be is such shit state, thanks to Mr. Prudence and his banking pals, they'll be screaming for Government spending and what better way than building nuclear plants to cut this f-ing CO_2 millstone and more importantly, the punters' power bills. Well, maybe.

Anyway the bloody 'Greens' will scream blue murder but they're no more effective than a fart in a blanket. The Tories will lap it up, behind the scenes shareholders and all that stuff. Three years from now and three million unemployed! Just wait for it, Josh, the students, the lefties- they'll only be howling about their jobs and student fees."

The pause was deliberate, before he remarked slowly, "Yes, it can be handled," and then with a laugh, "Of course, Josh, I may not be in office. There's a man who's just beside himself to take over the reins," his eyes hooded slightly, "I don't need to mention its not meat for those yapping media hounds, they have their uses when required but certainly not on that issue."

"Oh no, no, they're the last people we need in on such topics," Sir Joshua spoke smoothly. "Like yourself, Prime Minister, I may not be in this post much longer. I would like to resign, if you find that to be in order. Quietly please, very quietly, on a day when there's plenty of news; nothing beats bad news as a smoke screen. As it happens, I've been approached to advise an American consortium, rather attractive, a place on the board, so I'd be able to concentrate a little more on my business activities. I hope you understand Prime Minister?"

"Of course, of course, Josh, I greatly appreciate all you've done, any change you may wish will be dealt with appropriately," and perhaps a little coyly, he enquired, "Er, not Nuen by any chance?" The P.M. mentioned the largest U.S. Company in the nuclear business.

"Oh, nothing definite," Goldberg waved a podgy hand, "but a friend in Nuen did suggest that a U.K. contract would be greatly appreciated." For the first time he looked directly at the P.M. "Maybe there's also a space on their board." The comment hung between them in mutual understanding. Their eyes locked for several moments.

"By the way, Josh, strictly across this table, the deal to sell UK's shares in our Atomic Weapons Establishment at Aldermaston to that Californian crowd, Harris Engineering, is just about through. You may know, they're doing a lot of research into the next generation of nuclear warheads. The M.O.D. seems quiet relaxed about it and of course the Chancellor's delighted. Any way, it'll tie together quite neatly with any development that Nuen has in mind. We've had to keep this little arrangement out of earshot of The House, otherwise there'd be one hell of a hullabaloo."

During this disclosure, Sir Joshua's eyes had fallen to looking at the carpet before he commented, "I must admit, I did get an inkling of the deal."

Drawing a sharp breath, the P.M. looked suspiciously at his advisor.

"Very, very discreetly," the Chief Scientist continued smoothly, cursing inwardly for admitting as much, "through a friend, as it happens. I do assure you, P.M. this Californian Group, quite apart from their vital work on nuclear weaponry and starting production on the latest airborne megawatt laser guns, are well to the fore in several fields, advanced physics, super computing, and that's just two areas." Pausing a moment, he looked up, "More particularly, so far as this waste storage question is concerned, they are into the science of creating the exotic materials which may well be required for casing these underground facilities."

The meeting had gone on long enough, too open for the comfort of both. "Look Josh, I can see we must get this storage question sorted out," the P.M. mused aloud. "Underground you say, well maybe somewhere with a low population density. An agreeable landowner is always better than compulsory acquisition; less fuss, then there's planning, public enquires, all that damn nonsense."

"Leave it with me, P.M." Sir Joshua lifted his considerable weight out of the chair.

A cordial handshake brought further discussion to a close. "You have my full confidence, Josh," The P.M. held onto the man's hand. "By the way, I can't just recall who's the chairperson of Nuen." His smile settled warmly on Sir Joshua, "Do pass on my best regards for their Company's future."

"Naturally I shall do so, as soon as a suitable opening arises." He disengaged his hand.

A green light flashed on the desk. The P.M. reached and touched it. Without any sound, a large steel door slid open. Goldberg left equally silently.

Whistling the latest pop tune, the P.M. drew a diary from his inside pocket and wrote a few careful notes before sitting back at the desk and drumming his fingers. He swivelled his chair, stared at the operations map and checked his watch. A red light flashed. He touched it. The room's only door opened silently. A tall man stood at the end of the room without speaking. Dark city clothes emphasized the pallor of a face seldom away from artificial light. Darting eyes swept the room. The Agent remained silent.

"Good, good, glad you could make it." A brusque greeting which took care not to address the man by name and was far removed from the P.M.'s usually warm approach. "Any progress on the tube train bombers? I really need results, by next Wednesday's House of Commons questions, if possible. Not that politics come into this outrage," he hastened to add as an afterthought.

"Negative," came the reply. The man spoke without moving from the far end of the room,

"Ah, I see," the P.M. moved uncomfortably, rubbing his hands together, the meeting with Goldberg still much in his mind, "Let me be specific on another point. Have you found that youngish scientist fellow you were given instruction to trace and more importantly the brief case which we know he carried? I want it and its contents to be found." His voice became harsh, the mouth twisted. "Also the man was extremely insolent to me and that always spells trouble."

The Agent stepped forward and stood close to the P.M., his eyes veiled by drooping eyelids, his gross features threatening in their very composure. Moments drained away before he spoke. "We have him on footage leaving hospital. The taxi number was obscured by a following vehicle. He was not carrying the briefcase described to us."

"In other words, you've lost him," the P.M moved back, his voice rising to a higher pitch. "This is not good enough. I want man and the material found. You understand?"

"We will find him," the voice was low and even, the eyes measuring and controlling.

"Be sure you do," the P.M. rapped out and in a shrill tone, "How you deal with the man is your own affair, but the brief case, unless recovered, could develop into a leaked document involving National Security in areas of nuclear safety and perhaps other matters, so pay attention."

Without reply The Agent stood motionless, his eyes swung to the operations wall maps, and then with a deliberate slowness, back to the P.M. Minutes ticked by. Neither spoke. Unhurriedly, The Agent turned and walked to the steel door. Looking back he pointed to the button on the desk.

A shaking finger pressed it. The door slid open, soundless. The man in the dark suit stood in the doorway staring. A white face, expressionless.

The P.M. sat heavily and wiped his sweating hands.

CHAPTER ELEVEN

As the Good Sun ripens the Barley

Vague with exhaustion, I wondered *were we sailing*? A tremor of wind, the slap, slap of water on planking, I swayed with the movement aware only of holding onto a mast. A sail came down, the gentle crunch of a keel of sand. Strong arms helped me over the gunnel. The first stars above the dark bulk of a jetty, steps of cut stone, narrow and slippery, a hand rope against the wall. Few words, "Take it easy, boy." The breeze which must have sailed us whispered in the dunes. A rutted track and my fumbling steps took us onto open fields. I felt an arm support me.

Venus lit our path, brilliant and close on the south west horizon. In the far distance across a sheen of water an island floated. A silhouette against the planet's light it rested on the luminance of the sea. Greatly affected I stopped. In the velvet blue of gathered night it appeared as a forgotten place, remote and forlorn, simplicity abandoned to shadows of the past. The man's voice stirred me, "Come away, the island will be there tomorrow." Dew on a rooftop sparkled. Quiet words were spoken at the door. I caught the door post to steady myself. The porch light shone on yellow oilskins and boots that smelt of cattle. Taking my elbow the old man helped me through a kitchen, past the scent of milk and fresh butter, into a warm room.

My eyes opened without grasp of where, when or how I came to be in bed. A beam of evening sunlight crossed a room. Alarmed for a second, the hospital ward returned. Motes of dust swirled in radiant heat, tiny particles in the sun's power.

What equation could predict their antics? My wretched mind thrown back to ten years of screen bound calculations began to visualize the complex mathematics, so much part of that existence. Jostling specks pranced before my eyes, their movements seemingly random. The sun's rays prevented them becoming a layer on the floor. What clever calculation could predict their course, or their relationship one to another?

Dust to dust? For all I knew, I was an infinitesimal speck, a nano second's arrangement of the particles of existence dancing between a life- giving sun and the mystery of its gravity. Could anything in this universe be random, without cause? How far did the past dictate the future? If it did, then all our tomorrows existed in the potential of yesterday. Therefore, all past and futures are here in the present. Perhaps within the matrix of universes there exists only the flow of infinite possibilities? Maybe the particles of our current being are endlessly transmuted on a sea of time, only to reform again. My eyes opened fully and I struggled to throw off the despair of another fit of introverted thinking.

An iron bar propped open the small attic window, cool air wafted over my face bringing the smell of the sea and the rhythmic beat of a gentle swell. Quietly at first, as if from beyond distant hills, came another sound. Closer, closer, a vibrant song, bubbling and clear, I heard, 'cur-lew, cur-lew, cur-lew' rising in tempo. I threw back the sheets and caught hold of the window ledge. A large bird high above the fields, I listened in fascination. On trembling wings it called to un-trodden haunts, wild and treeless. The liquid outpouring faded to lisping notes, the melancholy of places lost. The bird alighted and raised beautifully pointed wings above a dark mottled back. Amongst the rashes it went out of sight.

From the window I looked about the small bedroom. A trance, another bout of hallucination, the sequence of the past days a preordained trick of fate, denying the assumption of free will? That I easily dismissed but not these inexplicable mental pictures, happenings long past, surges of thought plucked from tomorrow; could my reality be parallel phases running out of sync? All future exists split seconds before it becomes reality to our perception. That the sun will rise tomorrow is merely a concept rooted in probability; real time, a flawed abstraction. The future becomes the past faster than our brains function. The past is behind us in an instant. Perhaps it is never erased. Maybe it remains a flux of particles and reality the plausible victim of increasing entropy?

Stop, stop, I clasped my forehead, insanity loomed unless my thoughts would settle. I looked out from the skylight again. The unhurried steps of the old man approached from a field lined with rows of hay. Somewhere in the house I could just make out a woman singing. Quietly, step at a time, I went downstairs.

Supper waited on a scrubtop kitchen table. The three of us ate together without any awkwardness and no questions as to who I might be. They merely accepted my unexpected arrival for what is was, unexpected. My only embarrassment was the repeated coughing. That evening, through in a room across the hallway, we sat at a peat fire. It imparted homeliness to the cushioned wooden chairs and worn rugs. The pink glass of lamp sitting on a polished gate-leg table threw its rosy light on the mellowed wood of tongue and grooved walls. A black piano of some vintage judging by the candle brackets and perched on its lid, glinting in the firelight, a fiddle.

A collie dog pushed at my leg. I dropped a hand and felt a hesitant lick. The old chap's wife joined us, "You'll be the better of this," she smiled putting a glass in my hand. I sipped. My throat burnt. "A powerful charge there, boy," the old man said as I coughed and coughed, rasping and losing breath. The woman stood beside the chair, a shadow of concern on her face.

The coughing eventually subsided, "This cough will kill me yet," I tried to laugh away acute embarrassment. It hadn't occurred to mention my name, nor did they enquire.

My feet prodded the dog. It sprawled across the rug, paws to the fire. The painted mantle shelf swirled a little. Across the hearth, the man sat in a tall ladder back chair. His hair seemed the whiter for ruddy cheeks and a salt- air tan. I saw his look focused on the fire, perhaps weighing my remark. Eventually, raising his head and looking at me intently, he remarked, "Not at all, not at all, you're here now boy. A cough? Hoch, hoch, the good air is near the ground. The old folk knew it, they took the dulse weed from the shore to put strength in the broth and they slept with the breath of the sea on their face." Young eyes smiled from an old face, and he raised his glass, "And as the good sun ripens the barley, so the barley becomes his spirit." Reaching across, he shook my hand with the grip of a man who worked land and sea, "Slainte mhath."

"And to you," I smiled back, remembering clearly how the previous night I'd held the eyes of the old man. Moments, penetrating and thoughtful, passed into the vagueness of recognition and an odd feel of belonging. By and by, my glass was refilled.

Embers in the grate glowed red. We sat. A tiny rustle broke the silence, peat fell against peat. A voice floated on the stillness, strangely familiar, deep and resonant, hollow as a disembodied echo will bridge time and distance. Was the voice in the room or just a welling of memory in my head? "Still the blood is strong. The heart is Highland yet." A flame flickered in the grate. "Stone upon stone, blood upon blood, mind into mind, you will come to know, it is the ultimate power we possess." Words, words, they filled the tiny space of an island room, charged words, driving me forward; foreshadowing obscure happenings?

I sat in the glow of a peat fire, my glass shone golden, its spirit adding to the perplexing euphoria of the past days. I fell to grappling with the fantasy of ideas, drifting in their spell.

"Nothing is as it seems, our attempt to measure accurately the mass, the polarity, or the position of any given particle, at any one moment, is futile. Only an extremely fine approximation exists, the act of measuring is too slow. There is no finite measurement, only indefinable rates of change. Even estimating the degree of probability of any event happening is dependent on the accuracy of the analysis upon which that calculation relies. There always remains the possibility that the basis for the computation is a mistake. Given that nothing can be calculated accurately, certainty has no measure, it does not exist."

Silence. Thoughts passed between us. A presence entered the room. "If fate exists, then we are the tool of its destiny," the old man spoke with the mind of Norse mythology. "So without certainty, there can be no fate." His eyes smiled, "Which is the more probable?"

I was at the mercy of a powerful mind, my arrogant pontificating reduced to scrambling for a verbal escape, a fool in need of bringing down to earth. I continued blatantly on with the same theme, "For us, certainty is an illusion. Given our present form of organic existence, any ultimate reality is unknowable, assuming it too exists. The hybridising of human intelligence and quantum calculating will form another rung on evolution's ladder. Concepts expand, so reality for their calculator exists on the highway of particle transfer. Could only we break that cursed barrier the speed of light and find a wavelength." I raised my glass, "Mind into mind, the journey of imagination." I drank more, coughing fits forgotten in my voluble outburst.

The man listened with his head to one side, behind his intent eyes lurked a smile, far from unkind. "That old sun has made hay for me these past seventy years; good years, bad years, and tomorrow, it will probably do the same again." He looked up at a large photo which hung above the mantle shelf, before turning back to me. "In my life, I've had plenty time and space to think; it's only intuition that tells me the sun will rise tomorrow. My belief that it will is a faith with no more foundation than any religion or your exotic equations. Yesterday's half made hay is not an ultimate proof, only the probability on which I've depended all these years. If the universe is a system of unending change we have no means of converting probability into certainty."

I was thrilled he followed my exaggerated talk and maybe in his quiet way agreed. Our minds were attuned, I could talk to him. Away from the eyes of the old man, my excitement was drawn to the same mahogany framed photo, heavy and old, edges stained with age. As I stared, my focus morphed face into face.

A face looked down, gaunt to the point of death. Eyes glowed out of the ember dimness, socket deep and dreadful. I saw the strength of a gale on breaking seas, the flow of eternity that lies beneath wave and soil. Knuckles were slipping from a gunnel. White hair, in trailing strands. Arms waving, clawing the water, pleading, imploring, as though there remained to be saved something infinitely more precious than an old, worn life.

Gasping, choking, the old man reached out from the stench of antiseptic. Garish light shone over me. Green masks, green, forever green. The horror of a white haired man drowning. Down, down, until only green light. And gradually I looked at a face in a coffin, read the name, heard the thump of sand on a lid.

The old man bent, stirred the last of the embers. They burst into a tiny flame. In their glow his head loomed, a shadow on the wall. I gazed, one to another. Two faces were as one. Their eyes intent and knowing, looking into me, beyond me. "That man you're seeing was my grandfather, Hector MacKenzie of Sandray. Out from the Sound that day, the sea took him," and after a silence the solace of reflection, "over a hundred years ago."

The room shrank to a voice. My eyes filled with the tears for my father. I shook violently,
    "The past is ever at your shoulder. Look back, it's the door of tomorrow's understanding."

I looked down at white knuckles. The arms of a wooden chair were the gunnel of a boat. Its sides were closing in, growing narrow and tall. Coughing and groaning I struggled to look out.

Light faded. Frightened, I touched wood; it was the smooth sides of a coffin.

CHAPTER TWELVE

The Road to Promotion

That's the first fucking sea-gull I've noticed since I don't know when. For brief moments the thought distracted the mind of a pallid faced individual who stood at an office window overlooking the Thames. More than a five' o'clock shadow darkened his cheeks. Rings of sleeplessness pulled down the sagging flesh below his eyes. Impatient fingers drummed lightly together. The Agent paused, clasped his hands before thick pouting lips and breathed out.

Pressure, pressure, always bloody pressure, I've enough to do getting a bloody handle on these damn bombers; it was shaping up O.K., they're still in U.K., that's pretty sure. His mind darted back to last night, did that bitch of a wife know anything? But find a bloody brief case, for the sake of a P.M.'s wounded vanity--- and where the hell had this cheeky bastard vanished to? MacKenzie, he turned the name in his mind. Another bloody Scotsman, his teeth clenched, how he hated their false superiority, that bloody sing-song accent, always stuffing their damn Scotchness down your throat.

"Aaarrr," he growled, drawing back his lips, "Fuck 'em all, I'll get this one alright, briefcase or no briefcase. He'll get something to sing about." He reflected, I'll make this job a personal one, please the brainless politicians, take the easy road to promotion, stuff pleasing that bastard of a Chief, it's the road to nowhere. The Agent glance at his watch, "God, is it that time?" He lit a fag, took a deep drag, and sighed. "What the hell's keeping him?"

A heavily laden barge made slow progress up river against the falling tide, "Stupid bugger," he spoke aloud to an empty room. The dullness of the water mirrored an overcast sky. Black smoke poured from the stern of the barge and coiled over the rippling surface. The gull flapped a few wing beats and sat bobbing in the oily wake. He watched the bird idly, bloody water, better it getting a wet arse than me. Memories returned of pulling a decomposed body out of the mud below Tower Bridge before realising it was weighted. An arm came off as he heaved; not a nice one.

The hubbub of continuous traffic penetrated the double glazing. Across the river, on the far embankment, blue lights were flashing around an ambulance. Not far from the spot they'd lifted his mother off the pavement, he reflected. He never saw her again. The Salvation Army and Dr. Banardo's helped him. That was before a Reform School took charge. Youth's bitterness had turned to resentment these past twenty years. It simmered just below the surface. The Agent hid it behind an unsmiling professional face. Only a handful of people were aware that he hadn't the faintest idea who was his father.

Out of the gutter he'd climbed to a top rank. It'd had taken sheer guts plus all the devious cunning required of his profession. Too well he knew, without the right background of a 'good' school, and the accent it produced, he was never quite accepted by the society to which his position gave access. On many occasions when their upper class politeness cut him out it stung to the core.

A bully at heart, the exercise of power gave him a tingle of elation. To have a cringing victim weeping and pissing themselves, pleading for freedom, yes, even for their life had become the highlight of his job, all in a day's work so to speak. That he was a perverted sadist didn't occur to him; he happily suffered from its addiction, as strongly as any drug. Nothing could be further from The Agent's mind than the example of his mother's heroin craving. His youthful crimes of petty thieving and the resultant 'handlings' he received when in custody had left him with an ingrained hatred of authority, an attitude he was careful to mask. Unaware that trust is reciprocal, The Agent trusted nobody in this 'cesspit of a world' as he described it, totally oblivious to the fact that not a soul trusted him.

Caught off guard, The Agent spun on his heel, lurching forward. Such was his preoccupation at the window that a junior colleague had slipped the room without his hearing. Fuck, he swore under his breath and glared at the man knowing he would gloat to his cronies downstairs. They discussed details of the bombing case, scanning two possible suspects. Progress on one bloke seemed promising. The footage showed the suspect apparently checking the out the street. "OK, lie well back from that one, he's your lead, give him all the rope he needs till you get to the team, then pull it tight, and fucking fast. OK? You know where to take the bastard and don't be soft making him musical." Looking sharply at the man, The Agent lowered his voice, "Remember rules, keep marks to a minimum. If that happens to go wrong, clever boy" he sneered, "erasing them is your problem." Dismissing the man with a nod he selected a button on the desk.

His secretary entered, giving only a fleeting glance in The Agent's direction. The fragrance of this woman excited him. It floated into the room. Brown hair with a natural wave fell loosely about her shoulders. A skirt of Parisian cut clung to the lines of a supple form. No pantie marks; he moved to put a hand under pert contours. A tinge of colour showed upon her cheeks as she quickly sat down at the opposite side of his desk. Without speaking, she kept her eyes focused on the laptop.

Last night floated through his thoughts as mentally he undressed her again. Conscious of a slight tension between them, he wondered, had that bloody hotel porter really recognised her? I won't make that fucking mistake next time. He cleared his throat, dropping his voice an octave,

"Darling, don't be upset, don't spoil last night, never mind that cun.., that porter bloke, he can't know your dear hubby, now can he? Anyway in ten days time, there's a job on hand which justifies Switzerland. It'll be totally private- three days," adding with a snigger, "I'm not out to break any records, know what I mean but a lot can happen in three days."

For the first time her eyes rose to his and she blushed. He walked quietly to her side of the desk. "It's in Geneva. Book two singles, somewhere up the lakeside." Leering down at the top of her head he stroked her hair. She stiffened slightly. "Hotel Du Lac in Vevey has a touch of class about it. Better be two singles, make sure they've got balconies, the view is something else, and," he added with a hint of excitement, "there'll be the Montreux Jazz Festival on about the same time. BA flights, up the front, know what I mean." Nuzzling into her hair, he murmured, "And I'll be your big boy. Know what I mean?"

The instructions had been noted down before the woman began to demur, "I don't, er, I'm not too sure I can make…" The Agent reached round and place a hand over her mouth, "Nonsense darling, this is an order, if you want to keep your job." The woman breathed in sharply, "Sorry, sorry, darling," The Agent soothed, "only joking, know what I mean, just my little joke, naughty me." Then sounding official, "I need you as a cover, we're a sightseeing couple. I need to get into this damn fool particle accelerator they've built in Geneva so nothing too official."

Without taking his hand away from her mouth, he pushed the other under the back of her loose blouse. Swiftly his hand came round, squeezing the nipple of a firm breast.

The exquisitely cut chandelier of a thousand prisms winking with opulence shone its gleaming facets on the immaculate polish of a massive Georgian refectory table. The boardroom of Nuen House, Park Avenue, New York, was nothing if not sumptuous in its furnishings. To appeal to the predilections of wealth and influence, no refinements of taste had been overlooked. It implied a consolidation of assest whose foundations harked to the era of Carnegie and Rockefeller.

Fragrant leather and embroidered draperies embellished the room; whilst most impressive were the ornately gilt framed Victorian oils, all be it most of them excellent copies. Such masters of genre painting as Landseer and Millais, held pride of place against the lustrous mahogany panelling. This was not to be considered the offices of a jazzy, get rich quick, IT outfit, but one of unshakable dominance in the field of both nuclear energy production and the international weapons industry.

Equally polished as the table at which they sat, two rows of Florida tans, looked up as their Chairman entered. Slimmed by regular exercise rather than hard work, he strode purposefully to the head of the table. Jaunty and lightly perfumed, an open necked shirt and golfing flannels emphasised his position amidst the ranks of ties and city suits. To the affectation of paper shuffling and chair scraping, the Board Members rose. Andrew Anderson, Nuen's Chairman sat down.

"Please, be seated Gentlemen." He ran his eye up and down their lines. Good, a full turnout.

For a nation whose accents have yet to solidify into the strata of social class, none the less, that of their Chairman marked him out as a product of Harvard, rather than Coney Island. "Now gentleman, before we get down to work I'd like you to welcome our addition to the Board. Having just retired from a highly distinguished career as Chief Scientific Advisor to the UK Government, Sir Joshua Goldberg has agreed to join us.

We look forward to enjoying the benefits of his expertise on the matters which this company intend to progress and furthermore, his connections outside the scientific field are widespread. Gentlemen, please welcome Sir Joshua."

Discreet applause followed. Goldberg inclined his head in response.

Chairman Anderson continued with the formal business of a board meeting. Comment from round the table was given on matters relating to the minutes of their previous meeting. Agreed as correct, they were proposed, seconded and duly signed with a flourish. Before turning to the agenda's main item, Andrew looked carefully round the table. His eye rested on a leading Wall Street shareholder. Words were not required. After some moments he deliberately shifted his gaze towards a board member with influence in the White House and the ear of the Pentagon. "Gentlemen, I know I can depend on your utmost discretion," the Chairman's tone left the members in no doubt, "you will be aware of the unfortunate slowdown in new building for the nuclear industry and its impact on Company profits. Well I'm able to tell you that Nuen has secured a contract, through one of our subsidiaries, for supplying depleted uranium shells to the war effort in Iraq and gentlemen I'm happy to tell you, it is proving a most lucrative arrangement."

Nods and smiles of approval from round the table pleased Anderson as he continued,
        "Gentleman, given Nuen's considerable involvement in the nuclear industry, as you know we are leaders in both new commissions, the running of plant and waste disposal, I now wish to call on Sir Joshuha to address us on this fast moving field with its widest international implications."

For effect, Sir Joshua Goldberg stood slightly away from the group and spoke without notes. Chairs were pushed back and all their faces turned attentively. "Thank you, Mr. Chairman, I appreciate your welcoming remarks," Goldberg nodded with a calculated deference. "Gentlemen, I have to tell you that the next decade is crucial to the furtherance of the nuclear industry and by obvious consequence, the success of Nuen. Nuclear power capacity may well double worldwide over the next twenty years. Much is happening internationally, the main focus of development currently centres on the Middle East."

He spoke emphatically, adapting his tone to one of authority, "Apart from Iran, nine other countries in the region plan a least a dozen new power plants. For example, both Turkey and Egypt are extremely active. Naturally there is major concern on the part of those nations already well established in the field, over this expected proliferation in uranium enrichment and reprocessing capability. An escalation in the availability of fissile material is the obvious result."

Goldberg paused for effect, "Spent fuel, gentlemen, enough plutonium, gentlemen, for a couple of thousand nuclear warheads. On top of those weapons already existing in the area, we risk turning the Middle East into a nuclear arsenal."

A capable public speaker, Goldberg had looked over the heads of the listeners, but before proceeding he engaged each face in turn. Under heavy lids, his eyes burned intently. "The role of this company in world nuclear energy production could become central. Here lies an oyster of opportunity, a golden chance for us to benefit and of course" he added carefully, "this access to cheaper power would provide the increased living standards and disposable income which developing nations so badly require in the furtherance of trade."

Hurrying to the salient points, he went on, "Two areas are vital. Firstly, there are moves afoot to place the existing enrichment plants under international control and most importantly for Nuen, certain nations are pushing for the construction of new super safe enrichment facilities. In effect, they wish to establish an internationally controlled and operated nuclear fuel bank. Operators, world wide, would draw their fuel supplies from a single source. As I speak the EU has allocated the sum of twenty five million ecu's to the creation of a nuclear fuel stock pile. I suggest to you, gentlemen, the building and management of such a facility would be of great interest to this company."

The impressive speaker again paused. Board members glanced one to another. "Secondly and equally important to Nuen is the question of the disposal of waste by-product," (the words radio-active material he considered to run counter to the interests of Nuen) "This operation could develop in tandem with those of the proposed international nuclear fuel supply. Clearly the leader in one field would engage the respect of governments and the International Atomic Energy Authority. The challenge for Nuen is enormous. Let us not, as board members of such a pre-eminent leader in the nuclear world, shrink from our duty to see the welfare of our fellowmen and women improve and prosper, in safety."

To a man the members rose to their feet and applauded. A beaming Chairman joined in with equal enthusiasm. In spite of the air conditioning, beads of sweat trickled down Sir Joshua's brow.

After their meeting, the Chairman took Goldberg by the elbow, "A word in my office."

The pair retired to easy chairs. Andrew's taste in paintings veered towards modern art. Was that a Jackson Pollock, Goldberg wondered? Impressive. Ah, the trappings of true wealth.

"What a first rate address, Joshua, well done, thank you," the chairman motioned towards a beautiful swan necked decanter. Goldberg shook his head. Anderson poured himself a Bourbon.

"Now it's political agenda as much as practical concern and of course financial for sure. You may have influence in the latter, Joshua?"

The new board member studied the gorgeous Persian carpet upon which his Italian leather shoes rested. "I think that's not a problem, Andrew."

Noting the direction of Goldberg's glance, the Chairman nodded, "Yes, we can depend on friends in that part of the world. However, as I'm sure you will agree, politics are the tricky bit."

"I have a certain friend. He may be leaving high office soon, his feet are under the right tables, a little additional income interests most people. Shall I invite him across?"

Lapsing into the vernacular, "Yeah, Josh, bring him on. I'll fix him a suite at the Waldorf."

CHAPTER THIRTEEN

The Soil of Home

Treeless and empty, hill and headland curved from land into sea with elegance. Not the sharp, abrupt angles I knew of Alpine scenery, its mountains crammed together, neck craning and inaccessible, their forest slopes all pervasive and oppressive. To a child, woodlands were a trap, eerie and frightening. Danger lurked. Branches were claws, black and waving. Trunks hid furtive shapes, stalking and terrifying. The chill, the stillness, my sense of direction lost, I would run. Perhaps an echo of early man's sea-shore existence at rock pool and shallows inflicted my dread of forest gloom and its sunless obscurity.

Thoughts of childhood trauma returned as I stood at the end of the house revelling in the openness of it all. Fields, green and level, a glimpse of the sea through dunes and away beyond the croftland, huge unmoving clouds lay over the mainland, brilliant white statues, their under bellies grey with showers. Away to the north, sapphire hills turned slender lines to distant haze. Westwards, the Atlantic glistened. Morning sun and the safety of space, it erupted before me in a great release. I liked it.

Only one coughing fit overtook me. The collie hadn't barked when I stepped outside, instead his tail thumped the porch floor. "Come in, come in, Hector, you'll be needing your breakfast." The quiet voice startled me, I turned to see the old man's wife standing at the corner of the house. Even more startling, she had used my name. Had I told them last night? I couldn't be certain.

"I was thinking of walking down to the hay field, if that's OK."
I didn't add, to collect my thoughts and speak to the man
who'd brought me here.

"Never heed Eachan," she said, as though reading my
thoughts. "Anyway, he'll be up for a srupach in a little," and
seeing my puzzled look, she laughed, "for a mouthful of tea."

I followed the old man's wife into the kitchen. A glass of milk
sat on the scrubtop table,
    "You'll not be drinking the semi-skimmed from the village
shop," she commented, noticing my look as she handed me the
glass, "There's still a milk cow for the house here; she's about
the last on Halasay. Old like ourselves and I'm getting too stiff
in the knees to be milking her anymore."

Perhaps I seemed uncertain. "Drink up, you'll be the better of
it after your night's blethers with Eachan," and turning to the
stove, "there's porridge on the go, if you take it?"

"Thank you very much. Yes please, I do." This puzzle of my
arrival must be explained, yet still I put off breaking into the
issue in a straightforward way. The abrupt question or blunt
approach in dealing with people didn't seem apt in this
situation. They hadn't asked me one question. Why was being
here so easy? The atmosphere of this home reminded me of the
pleasant, affable manners of my parents. Their approach
towards me came across relaxed and natural, and as if their
style was infectious, the stresses which had twisted my thinking
these past weeks lifted. With a glorious lightness I felt the
stirrings of happiness.

The milk's richness surprised me. Full of cream, its sweetness
reminded me of the scent of wild flowers. I drank heartily,
"This will do more than colour the tea," I laughed over to her.
From the porch came the clump of boots. In walked the old

boy, Eachan, as I now knew him to be. Strands of hay on his shirt carried the scent of cut grass into the kitchen.

I stood up, a shade awkward again after a short burst of coughing, "Good morning, -er, er," I'd nearly said Mister. No formal mould fitted this man. No affectation. He carried a dignity needing no collar, tie, nor title to mark his breeding.

"Yes boy and a good morning it is. Sit down, sit down," he said smiling. A chair scraped on the flag floor. Thanking his wife as she put a bowl of porridge at his elbow, he went on, "If the hay gets another day's sun, it'll do. I'll gather it together and let the coilacks settle."

"Would I be any use? I'd like to give a hand." A large plate of porridge steamed beside me, smelling of fresh oatmeal. "Many thanks, Mrs. MacKenzie," I smiled up. "Don't be calling me that, you'll make me feel old," and behind Eachan's back she winked, "we'll leave that to himself."

"Don't you believe it woman," and turning to me in mock seriousness, "There's plenty young ones down at the pier give me a smile yet." He broke into a grin. "Yes, see and come down to the hay, it's the day for it. I'll get you a pair of boots."

Under a working sun which dried any hint of morning dampness, down to the hay field we went, myself with a spare pitch fork on my shoulder. No jackets, Eachan, shirt sleeves rolled to his elbow, arms burnt almost black. I doubted if they had ever been covered in his lifetime. Walking beside such health and vigour I saw myself, a pale sapling.

The little heaps of hay, tanned like himself and their scent as we began to move them more delicate than I imagined; not the plummy richness of tobacco, rather the sweetness of herbs left to dry on a window ledge. I caught up handfuls and breathed its fragrance. Such was the attraction I took several stalks and chewed them. Now I knew the secret of the sweet milk.

"We'll put three or four coilacks together, make them into a wee stack, like this," and he drove his hay fork into the first one and without apparent effort lifted it onto fresh ground. "The bottom of each coilack draws the damp; we'll put it to the top of the stack, it does as a bonnet." I followed, best as I could, the fork twisted in my hands. There was more knack than I thought.

Without haste we worked away all morning, the sun on our heads, the vast expanse of scenery open as the day. I revelled in it. From time to time we leant on our forks. The leisurely pace, not set by any demand of time or place, I feasted on its freedom, my hunger that of an animal released from a trap. The life about the place seemed equally unhurried, each group doing what best suited the day and its heat. A skylark which sang as we started work fell silent. The sheep grazed their way up to an exposed knoll. I watched the cattle saunter off through the dunes, single file, "They're off to cool their feet," laughed Eachan, noticing my attention. "We'll have a wee seat to ourselves," and he plumped down on a coilack.

All that morning, as we forked the hay into neat lines of round heaps, my eye couldn't leave the island. A Sound ran between us, not wide but silky blue as the day's cloudless sky. Although no ocean swell put a creaming edge to the shores, for there was barely a breeze, still here and there on its glassy waters faint white streaks of foam hinted at the strength of a running tide. Silhouette of Venus on the night of arrival now comely in grassy sun bright pastures rising step by step to a peak of weathered crags. It expressed the challenge of self-reliance, hill land, shore line and where the ground sloped down to greens of abandoned fields, the soil of a home and a living. Perhaps a bay sheltered behind the headland which in times of storm would break Atlantic's power and tipping the skyline, the gable of a house.

Presently, as we stretched our legs and lay back, Eachan must have noticed my total absorption and sitting up he spoke slowly, "Yes, Hector boy, it's an island made of peace." That was the first time he'd used my name. "They called it Sandray," and slowly, "yes, the Viking called it, Sandray." He remained silent. I looked across. His eyes went far beyond the island.

"You should know that." After a long pause, he began again, speaking with difficulty, "I saw you studying the old photo last night, that one above the mantleplace." Slowly he turned to me, "Well now, who better than you should know: That man in the photo was my grandfather, drowned, as I told you and to you, Hector MacKenzie, that man was your great grandfather."

I sat on a croft, amongst hay, having arrived as an alien. The island swam out of focus, from the curtain of moist eyes, into the vision which had become part of my being.

"I knew when I came on you sitting at the jetty who you were. I knew the tilt of head, the sharp face, same as old MacKenzie, the last to live on that island you're studying. You had the cut of his jib, as they say." He motioned towards the island, "There was no hiding the breeding that's in you," and turning to me, "and that, a'bhalaich is where our people began."

How long we sat didn't matter, the hay would make, the tide would ebb and flow, the world could turn. I knew who I was, where I belonged. No longer a life of vague discontent with cities, half formed pictures of what I wanted out of living. The old man's words left me in a great emotional sweep of feeling.

The whole inexplicable process of being drawn here became clear. Attempting a reason was for another day.

What the hell- I grinned stupidly to hide a bursting heart. Without caring of time, I listened to the cry of birds down on the shore. Nothing else broke the silence.

The hay smelt fresh and wholesome and the sun shone.

Nothing mattered, across the Sound lay the soil of home.

CHAPTER FOURTEEN

The Eye of Wisdom

Each day the breeze of settled weather followed round to the west and died away with the evening sun. We built our coilacks of cured hay into little watertight stacks with no more hurry than the cattle who by afternoon wandered up from the beach to graze the machair. I marvelled at their contentment. Cows would stand licking the tail of calves suckling away beside mother's flank. The boldest creatures ventured over to the fence, faces still milky white with froth and round eyes full of unblinking curiosity. Eachan laughed at them. I heard the affection in his laughter and the cows lifted their heads at his voice.

After supper one evening I sat out at the west gable as the sun put its crimson on the sea. Eachan, beside me on the bench, shading his eyes against the glare, began to speak quietly, "You know a' bhalaich, the old grandfather I'm after telling you about could recall what his great granny told him, how her people, Viking plunderers no better than that, came to Sandray. You see it was handed down to her, word of mouth in the days when folk had time to listen. Yes boy, it's an extraordinary story, about a raven, and I tell you, they're nesting there to this day. He was a gifted bodach, he put the story to verse in the way she told it, something in the style of a Norse saga. Think you're hardy, these were hardy, the folk. If you like you can get a read of it."

Eachan rose and in a few moments came out with the manuscript. Though happily tired I took it eagerly. He leant on the wall beside me, "You know this, old Hector told me the way the writing came to him. It was a strange thing. You see, he was very fond of the cailleach." He saw me frown, "the old woman, I mean his great granny. Anyway, on the third night after her death she spoke to him in a dream, told him her story over again. Well, that day, it was clear with the spring air and he went away to a cnoc, a hillock, overlooking the sea and wrote these words. He told me they poured out of his mind as if he were at sea with the Viking rovers through their storm and their coming to that island you've been watching every day. The gift was in him, sure enough as the blood they spilled and the women they took."

Such was the flow of simple writing I seemed a part of it. The sacrifice made by an old woman to help a new born grandson and her people survive through the winter. Her last memories of love and children before the frost had stilled any thoughts How when the baby reached manhood a scarcity of land forced them to set sail. I quickened to the boat builders' belief that the spirit of the tree they'd felled remained in the timbers of the boat it shaped.

Superstitions didn't influence my scientific mind, or so I thought but in reading the tale of the Vikings' faith in the sagacity of a raven which brought them to Sandray, I became increasingly uneasy; a sensation which turned to dread as I read the clarity of the old man's impression of the horror of the drowning that was to be his own fate. Again came this recurrent vision, the streaming white hair, the twisted knuckles that went from gripping a gunnel to the sides of a coffin.

As I read in the falling light of sunset, my hand shook.

They were the words of a Viking saga

Limbs stiff and bent had once entwined, and moss
beneath an ancient larch
knew love's passions flow,
Morbid strands the old crone's hair where tousled
mass was golden spread
in the glow of evening light,
Gums drawn back, teeth stump black, eyes now shadow dark,
that nightly shone for him,
Eyes, once blue as summer long, had watched the empty bay,
were faded dim to a sea washed grey.

Nine had cried, sucked nipples full and red,
her last child saw no bed,
they laid it out upon the hill,
A twisted neck, too frail to feed, she kissed its brow,
the frost cut off his cry.

That night an open door, a birth bed cry,
another hungry maw,
the empty kist their belly store..
She touched blood's new strand of life and knew its pang,
as memories shed their veil.
She heard a cry, her last one died that distant
year upon the hill,
She made a vow,
'This night's child must live, by my sacrifice.'

Softly as the winding sheet that binds, stealthy as the shroud
which covers death's infallibility,
she crept into the night.

Haloed thrice, the moon's white cloak turned the sea to ice,
bound their haven to the shore.
Snapping branches, low swept by winter's weight,
made clawing
arms of patterned light,

And crone of crones, her stumbled path tore
knot worn hands,
and cut each barefoot step.

Against the trunk she sat, twined fingers on an empty lap,
her head to lolling sleep,
Yet through her pain grew summer's bloom and he came
striding,
blue of eye, boat and shore,
Her man she held once more and lips their touch,
till shy young limbs
entwined beneath the crescent moon,
And sunshine bright each calling spring their
barefoot children ran,
and longboats put to sea.

Tangled branches piled a crag above her tree and year on year,
the raven reared its early brood.
Two gawking chicks pressed tight that night, their
head hung low,
no flesh had filled their gut,
Till scent on cringing air, death's presence took
its fingered grip,
and gliding wing, a single croak.

Strike of dawn, bones iron to the ground, icicles her shroud,
they stared upon a smile,
Her sparkled hair, crystal white, two sockets gaping red,
no eyes, the chicks had got their fill.

New babe at breast, a grandchild boy, lusty, sucking bold,
above the pyre of leaping flame,
Her rising soul joined the black of spiral wing.

Rope and cage, the cliff was scaled, one chick must
have her wisdom eye,

must join our family.
A raucous caw, the raven's wing, pinions beat,
a curved bill stooped
close to rip his flesh.
A nestling crouched, black Satan eyes shone
from twig lined bowl,
he grabbed, a vicious bite sank home.

That night, a willow cage hung beside the crib,
dark watching eyes
and newborn child were swinging, side by side.

Blue eyed manhood, bearded blonde, shoulders
wide, and arms
to power a steer-board oar,
Though hands had still to take their gnarl, his face
its hook to carve
by ocean's cutting spume.

His father told, 'Our plough has scraped bare
rock today, worn horses
shoulders raw, no land is here to spare.'

Twenty seasons the larch had shed, needle orange, at its foot.
Axes rang, the crone's tree sang,
'No gale has felled my sway, the north wind sets a Viking free,
my strength goes with your ship.'
Cut and trim, she floated slim, by winter peat
and oil lamp fantasy,
a dragon tongue was carved to lick the sea.

May's the month of siren call, ages past an inner
song to gnaw the heart,
cast eyes to landfalls far.

Mutton barrel, rye bread store, hogs of ale and thirsty sword,
he loaded thirty able men aboard,
Wives and sweethearts, skirts to thigh, carried men
folk down the shore,
shoulder high, one kiss, goodbye.

Crack of rope, the sail unfurled, wing tip wide the
raven soared to terrify,
make carrion of a foe.
Slanted tight she flew, south by west a dipping bow,
her rearing stern
buried homeland's snow clad sky.
Proud larch tossed the dragon prow, and high aloft
in thrumming stay
swung childhood's chick, wisdom's raven now.

Last evening light, the nor-east gale quenched a flaming sun,
dashed crimson crests to the steerman's face,

Feet braced bare, a pitching helm, 'The Raven' skimmed
man and boat, bold mastery.

Moon torrent night is sea nymph's tress, its spray,
beguiling flesh,
a sailor's dream, yet haunt of treachery.

Spindrift coiled in shrieking moan, a gale of devil's glee,
the cage swung violently.

A sudden caw.

He knew the cry.

Swing the helm, full broadside wallow, sail crashed
o'er the dipping deep,
a pitiless wave trough hollow,

Crack, crack, it split the mast, lee rail down, a sail
lay bellied on the sea,
dragging stays, the cage awash.

'Hack the mast, save the sail, to oar, to oar, head
the swell, row boys row,
or it's the gates of hell.'

Rope to waist, deep and green death's choking
cave he caught the cage,
held aloft the raven bird.

Amidst a tower of sea, an emerald plume, a burst
of spray, a hidden rock,
the tip of Orkney.

Angled hard against the crests, bending oar,
with young arm power,
a dragon reared to fight the sea.

Flashing waves, a headland drenched in spray,
seas that drove them close,
'pull my boys, for mighty Odin's sake.'

Shoulders wide, one broken oar? A splintered wreck ashore,
tormented gale, a booming cliff.

Backwash surge, he threw the helm, born seaman's
touch put stern to sea,
and down the shores of wild old Orkney.

Cape Wrath abeam, the turning point, wide Minch ahead,
an island chain, plunder, loot and gain.

Behind the Cape, Sandvarten bay, in they slid beached safe,
beside four stravaiging galleys lay.

*Night time fire weaved spark and star, ale- faced red
told their raven's wisdom call,
he's fit for Odin's shoulder in Valhalla's hall.*

*Drinking horns, five would sail, the bird to be
their guide, sword or strife,
its eye would find a home.*

*A roving wind brought terror down the Western Isles,
slashing axe, blood stained sand,
the raven, silent in his cage.*

*Last headland, soft mist draped island hill, caped
by morning cloud,
'Hecla, Hecla, Hill of Shroud,' the lusty steersman cried.*

Caw, cawing, from the cage.

*'Loose its door,' the raven flew, a circle thrice,
it vanished in the sun cast cloud.*

*Green fields beside the village smoke, a turquoise
bay, beach sand sloped,
and open to the sky.*

An island home,

A Viking home,

By the old crone's eye.

The manuscript slipped out of my hand. The sun had dipped into the faintest pink horizon without my noticing. A challenge stared out of these pages. No rational consideration needed. No practical thoughts or doubts. Shadows of ill health vanished. A new life, heart pounding I came alive, could breathe, stretch body and mind. Abandon civilization, make the island my home. No hesitation, no question, the birth right of my people, make it home.

From the open front door the notes of fiddle music firmed my resolve. The music blended with the glory of approaching summer dim. Tunes soaked in the fabric of island life. Lively, then wistful, a shade melancholy, the old fingers of MacKenzie carried each mood at their tips. I went inside to watch the stroke of his bow. It touched the strings with the delicacy of a painter of sound. In his eyes, the music of his mind.

The lilt took me inside, "Go through," Ella nodded to the sitting room door, "he often takes a tune to himself in an evening; it's a good excuse." I guessed what she meant. Eachan didn't notice me until the down stroke of his bow drew the final notes of a beautiful plaintive air, "Come in, come in, sit over." He must have noticed the sadness in my face. "That last tune was written by a woman who saw her husband and two sons drowned in a freak gale off Halasay Head. You see, the music was in her and her people before her. That tragedy brought it out, gave her comfort, and today that gives thoughts to many who hear it."

Dram and bottle sat on the dresser, "Never mind the sad ones, have a wee toot yourself. I'll give you something livelier." He poured me a 'fair' dram. "Can you play anything yourself?"

I went over to the piano. Ella placed my glass on the lid and off Eachan set with a full down stroke. I guessed the cord. Into vamping, Key of G, did we not make it swing. Ella's foot was tapping, she started clapping to the tempo, birling round the room. "You two'll be playing in the Castleton next. I'll get a dance, we're needing out for a night." We played on. Tunes I'd never heard, but they came to me as naturally as Eachan played them.

Eventually he put down the fiddle, "Well, Hector, you had the old piano bouncing off its casters. Great stuff boy. Slainte mhath!" Our glass raised to the drug of music. Though the evening remained warm, Ella had a peat fire in the grate and as we sat, I commented, "There's quite a stack of peats at the end of the buildings. Where do you get the peat?"

"Oh, there's peat banks out on the hill, not many folks bother with them now." He pointed to the fire. "Those were cut last year and next year's supply Ella and I cut last May. It's a hefty job,"

After a lengthy pause, he took a sip at the glass, "When I was a boy the locals would ceilidh at this house. On nights when the moon was bright, the door would open, no knock, in they came. Sometimes they took a peat but always something that warmed you a little. It warmed a story just as well, a good one could last as long as folk would listen," and laughing, "drams in between and the yarn would improve. Did you enjoy your great grandfather's story? He had the gift with telling a story and could put it to the pen as well. That one would be true, it came down to him as I told you and that's not the end of it."

I could see Eachan differed little from those he'd just described. In the way of his old Highland stock, given a dram, there would be always a story waiting in the wings. I guessed he was as eager to tell more of Sandray's history, just as I was anxious to hear it.

He savoured his dram, "No, that wasn't the end of it. You see, in the days of that story, the folks on Sandray would be at the peat banks in May, same as ourselves. On the day I'm telling you about, a father and son were out at cutting the peat on the north side of the hill. The wind was in the northeast, that always gives a clear day and puts the mainland hills like a pencil line on the horizon, blue and sharp."

His voice was low. I could tell as the story unfolded, it filled his mind's eye. "The father was at the digging and the boy spreading them on the top of the bank, young and sharp-eyed for sure. Anyway, the boy looked up, 'There's five sails rounding Halasay head, slanted hard, drawing full!' he called down. His father jumped out of the bank, startled, 'Death's on the wing,' he groaned, 'the raven soars,' and shouting, 'On you go, run, boy, run!' Well, the loon was fleet of foot, down to the village by the bay. Some of its stones are still about. Anyway, when the boy caught his breath, he ran about the houses shouting his warning, 'The heathens are on us, hurry for your lives, make for the Dun!'

Eachan warming to his story, caught up the glass at his elbow, "Now on the southwest side of Sandray and I'm talking long, long ago, there's the stone walls of a prehistoric fort or a Dun, as we call it. The cliffs there are five hundred feet, sheer, and this Dun sits on a small stack of land, a patch of grass and nesting birds. The sea's been eating away at its connection to Sandray since the Ice Age; there's only a narrow neck of land left, no wider than this room," he spread his arms, "and worse, its sides are straight into the ocean. Well now, the womenfolk gathered their children and the men took what tools or arms they had about them and hurried over to the Dun, single file, a dangerous, slippery path if ever there was."

Fascinated by his face and actions, I raised my glass automatically.

"Wait till I tell you though, living amongst the island folk was a priest, a Holy man, perhaps from Ireland or Iona and he called after the fleeing families, 'God speed you, save you, I alone will stay,' and he stood before his tiny church watching the beach. Raven banners flying, the galleys drove hard onto the sand. Viking leapt over the side, waist deep, horned helmets, blonde hair flying, I tell you, Hector boy, the lust for killing was on them, flaring in their nostrils. Axe and swords were polished, just gleaming. This giant of man, a tall brute, broad as an ox, straight up the beach he came, running. The Holy man knelt at the door of his little shrine, making a prayer to the Virgin Mary, what else?

The big fellow reached him, stood over him. The priest, a poor creature, thin as a lath, held a wooden cross aloft with bony, skinny hands. Their eyes met. Norse blue and Celtic brown. They stood a moment, eyes locked. The priest spoke, not pleading, but gentle, 'In the name of Jesus, the Saviour of all mankind, I forgive you.' Up raised a massive arm, the axe crashed down, split the Holy man down the centre of his crown. There he lay, blood seeping into sand, puny hands gripping a fallen cross, all slippery, red and twitching."

Dumbfounded at the strength of the tale and its telling, I sat rock still, the sickening crunch of blade on bone in my hearing.

Eachan stared up at the photo of his grandfather. "The Norseman, a split head, bleeding at his feet, slowly turned and looked down to the bay. Turquoise waters, sunlight over white sand. What had he destroyed? He stared a long time. I believe he saw beyond the sea, looked into an immeasurable abyss of his own making. The tide turned. In the immensity of the day, would it flow again? Would this clefted head step before him on the pathway of life?"

Stillness deepened into total abstraction. A Viking chief stood by the tide, blue eyes of horror stared into mine. Eventually Eachan spoke again, "The Atlantic boomed away below them, the women in the Dun gathered children about their skirts, wide eyed and frightened. The island men faced sword and axe. That neck of land was their only means of life. The surf, creaming on the rocks. The birds screaming. Either side, a five hundred foot chasm. Climbing, running, up the Sea Rovers came, berserk, howling, swords gleaming.

The Sandray men faced them. In moments, axes were crunching bone, swords slashing flesh. The narrow path was a track of blood. Alive or dying, the echo of falling screams took their bodies to smash on the black rocks below. No man was spared. The ocean was left to sting their wounds and bury the dead."

Was he hearing and seeing the carnage? His voice was low and strong, "That evening as the first star rose in the southwest, the virgin star they called it, a weeping trail of women wound down to the empty village, empty except for their dead Holy man. The villagers gathered about him. A trickle of blood ran from the cloven head. An old woman of the village came forward and knelt by him and slowly she bent to suck its last drop. 'All the sand that ever blew on this island is not fit to drink one drop of blood born to our Saviour Christ.' You see, that humble act was a bridge. It was the union of their Celtic creed and the Cross of Calvary.'

Eachan looked out of the window. I followed his gaze. In the window frame shone the planet I had seen on the night I arrived. We both drank and turned back to the fire. "The evening chill settled in and soon the Viking had fires blazing. They slung their leather hogsheads of ale ashore from the galleys and filled their drinking horns. The ale washed away the blood and they eyed the bonnie women. That night in fear of their lives, they lay below the raven's wing. Dark hills were on the sleeping sea and the great silver moon sailed on the bay. Sobbing women prayed in the words of their Holy man and strangely enough the drunken Viking listened.

Next morning on the flood tide four longboat sailed. One man turned. A huge blonde man, and he stood beside the open grave, bowed his head as they buried the clefted head. And far out on the hill the raven circled, free of its cage."

I moved uneasily, the reality of a bygone horror invaded the room. I clung to the chair. The air chilled. Nothing moved, yet someone was in the room. Breathing? Afraid almost, I looked up to the face in the brown stained photo. Its eyes watched me. My hair rose. The story became a soft voice. His eyes didn't leave me.

"That man's longboat stayed beached. In fullness of the months his child was born. And he took the long-ship's steer-board oar, the same larch he'd cut from his grandmother's tree of death, and fashioned it into a cross. And he gave the island its Norse name, Sandray."

The peats died away, "And that next spring, the raven reared its brood on a cliff at the back of the hill. The hill you've looked at since you came. The one he christened, Hecla, from the helm of his ship. Hecla, he cried, which means, Hill of the Shroud."

Eachan picked up his fiddle.

A tune poured from its strings, from the depth of his story.

CHAPTER FIFTEEN

The Milk of Hills Untouched

"It'll be slack water in the Sound about now. There's quite a run with the flood at half tide. It's better crossing to Sandray just before the tide's on the turn. You could take the boat yourself, if you wanted to. Ach, maybe best not, the old stone slip on the north side of the bay is easy seen, but there's a reef off the headland. I'd better show you, seeing it's your first time across."

Eachan poured another cup of tea for us both. Ella had gone down the field, milk pail and stool on one arm, a bucket of cattle cake on the other. Sitting at the table, I could see her from the kitchen window. The cow stood quietly, her head in the bucket as Ella knelt with her head on the animal's flank and milked away. Their other cattle peered over the fence. After a little I heard her in the dairy at the back of the house, rattling utensils. She'd be sieving the milk through a muslin cloth.

I admired the woman's hardiness and perhaps more than anything, her kindliness. Placid and unruffled, in the fortnight I'd now been in their house, her voice was never raised. Moreover, though Gaelic was their customary tongue, they rarely used it if I were in their presence.

Days had slipped by; I marvelled at the lack of stress. My cough had declined to the odd bout. My limbs had hardened. Blisters on my hands bore evidence of the process. We'd finished the hay, I'd been to the village store on the back of Eachan's tractor and bought suitable clothing. We'd pulled into the 'Castleton "just a quick one," he winked. It extended longer than his description. From counter conversations I learnt that the theme for the locals revolved round the activities which made crofting tick. Surprisingly they drew me in as though I were part of the system.

Sheep, cattle, the quality of the hay crop, 'the early 'tatties' lifted well this year', a whole ability in dealing with fundamentals which passed beneath the concerns of a desk bound public sector juggling figures or the city whizz-kids alternately cheering or cursing their financial data. During these past weeks, I'd come to recognise the yawning gulf which exists between the artificial cleverness of a society that lacks the intelligence to spot its approaching buffers and the landbound skills of those few upon whom these sophisticated lemmings depend.

Crossing the Sound, sailing to Sandray, this could be the complete break. My departure from one intensely complex time and results controlled function to placing myself in a situation which would challenge my woefully inadequate abilities. An isolated island, forebears or no forebears, was I merely wallowing in nostalgia? I hadn't mentioned my plans to Eachan.

"I'll start the outboard if you like. There'll be enough breeze to put us across once we're out of the bay. How about trying the oars?" Eachan moved to the stern. I pulled away. The 'Hilda' moved easily after the first half dozen strokes. Already I had a fondness for her.

"Here's the breeze, boy." I shipped oars and watched Eachan hoist sail. The 'Hilda' sprang to life. He tightened the mainsheet. We headed out. Heeling slightly, the tap, tap on her planking began. Wavelets met us. She threw them aside in small flurries. Swooping over tops, dipping through the hollows she sailed with the ease of a tiny wave skimming stormy petrel. I revelled in the motion. Swaying forests were in her timbers, the tale of the old crone's death and the larch tree's spirit were in the boat they'd built. I vowed no freedom matched the open sea.

In the shallow waters of the bay, slim fork-tailed birds were touching the ripples and fluttering aloft. Their thin twittering cries reached us. Eachan noticed me watching them, "That's the Arctic tern fishing for sprat. They nest on the beaches of Sandray, away from bird watchers and tourists. That's changing fast, Hector boy. There's a fancy new speed boat running out of Castleton. This Londoner built a huge house out from the village, just a couple of years ago, no word about the landscape, only planners needing more rates to pay their salaries would let it through. Anyhow, no doubt with a grant, he bought this craft, not a sea boat but twin forty horse power outboards. She's roomy, does a twenty knot trip round the islands, a wake like a tidal wave to frighten the seals off the beach and you get a cup of tea in the cabin and can see your photos on a laptop."

It was the first time I'd heard a note of bitterness in Eachan's voice. Not truly one of their island fraternity and on many occasions a tourist myself, I said nothing. Cormorants sat silent, their wings outstretched to dry in the warm sun as we rounded the point and out of the bay. Gulls squabbled over a crab which one of them had dropped onto the rocks.

Suddenly, without warning, the ear shattering roar of a fighter jet hit us. I ducked instinctively. Its shadow flashed across the sea. The plane climbed steeply, pouring black exhaust. I'd barely looked up. A second deafening roar, another jet on its tail, in from the Atlantic. They skimmed over the hills of Halasay and banking steeply, headed north. The terns rose screeching and flew wildly in circles. Speechless, my ears ringing, I looked to Eachan.

He shook his head at the departing planes. "They're away to blast rockets into a small island off Cape Wrath. It'll be one of their sales pitches for flogging our latest weaponry round the world. Practise shoots for Afghanistan. Pakistan, maybe Libya or whoever's the next in line for the installation of a puppet government in the guise of democracy."

Quietness returned and the lap, lap at our bow. In sardonic tone his thoughts rumbled on, "Mind you those flying missionaries are already out of date; it's far safer to blast the Taliban by sending in a drone controlled from a bunker under the Pentagon. But just you look at the faces of these Afghan hill men. Whatever their beliefs, right or wrong, these are real men. Compare them to the objects which pass for men and run our degenerate western society. The world is controlled by a collusion of egoistic politicians who've never ducked a bullet, military fools in the grip of a highly profitable arms industry and financiers with the greed of that cormorant over there with its gut crammed with fish."

A dip in the swell exposed a line of rocks off the point. As the Atlantic swell curled over them, they vanished. Just below the surface; dark, vicious and dangerous. Keeping an eye on them, the old man broke into a grin. It better suited his usual easy style. "That's the reef I told you about. It doesn't show after the tide starts to rise. You don't want to find it with the keel. Good spot for a lobster creel though, when you know were they are."

His face grew serious again, "What's an island off the tip of Scotland? Back of beyond, handy for training pilots, kill a few birds, neither here nor there. Eggs or chicks, lost when the parents panic. But it all adds up, Hector boy."

I'd got used to this form of address, it certainly didn't refer to my age. I took it more as a term of familiarity. He hauled the lugsail sheet and we rounded the headland, giving the reef a good offing. The fighter jets had clearly upset him.

"Pilots, trained by bombing an island. In the cross sights, press a button- it could be a school full of children. That's happened. A mistake of course. Apologies; what the hell are apologies for a murder? Try replacing your dead child. What goes through a pilot's tiny mind? Conditioned to kill, trained to protect a fallacy, attempting to continue the folly of believing we can maintain this form of civilisation. My father's brother went over the top at the Somme, a bullet through his brain. That was kind compared to some poor devils. And still we haven't learned, only getting more efficient at the job of killing our fellow man. No, Hector, I've seen the good times, producing food out here. My own boss"

The breeze shifted. I admired Eachan's deft response. For a moment the tiller took care of itself. He hauled over the sail until it filled on the port side and we were heading our way across the Sound. "I'll tell you this, boy," For the first time I heard true anger in his tone. "My old brain has studied all that goes on around me, whether it's the climate, or the croft, or what's left of the bird life, or for that matter the effects I've noticed on the sea, even the beaches of Halasay. New types of seaweed are creeping in, taking over, the birds don't get peace in the nest. Halasay's turned into a playground. It used to produce food, wholesome food. Now it's new houses are the main crop, and big ones too; wait you until they're putting sandbags at the front door when the tide's in."

Obviously he handled the tiller instinctively for the outburst continued, "Climate change, they call it. Well, the oceans hold the trump card. The more carbon dioxide they dissolve from the atmospheric increases we're busy making, the more acid they become and the less their ability to absorb this greenhouse gas. And once you warm the oceans a degree or two, they don't cool down fast like the land does. There's probably enough heat brewing in the sea right now to keep global warming on track supposing you dumped every damned car tomorrow."

The foresight of his comments impressed me and from the look on his face the theme had still a bit to run. The flow of Eachan's derisive observations I took as a mark of despair for the future of all he had known and not least for the desecration of the planet by human folly. "Make no mistake boy, the environment is shifting below our feet faster than many species can keep pace. The more spokes you knock out of a bicycle wheel, the greater the wobble. We're racing down hill on a fixed wheel without brakes and they don't realise just how fast. Talking jargon at a meeting, flown round the world to a conference in an air-conditioned hotel. Scientists," he snorted, "they'd hear more common sense in an hour at the counter of the Castleton bar."

It wasn't the conversation I'd expected. Spanned by islands, the whole width of the Atlantic at my back, the vigour of salt air on my cheek, his words struck a hammer blow. Far from being incongruous, they twisted at my guts. How could we be such criminal perpetrators, helping to destroy the beauty about us, careless of the myriads of species involved; the utter ignorance. Through the passion of Eachan's outburst, I recognised the love of a man for his natural world.

"You see those vapour trails?" Eachan indicated with a nod. I squinted against the light. The flight paths of two trans-Atlantic jets criss-crossed, tiny dots pouring fleecy streams onto a sky burnished by radiant sunlight. "One's just crossed the North Pole, heading for Heathrow no doubt. Who knows where the other's going?" And, looking to the horizon, "I'll tell you boy, neither of them knows where they're heading."

The rumble of their engines floated down to us as he continued unabated, "And the rate of change we're helping to creating is beyond many species' ability to adapt, maybe ours too. Organic life, in some form, has knocked about this planet two or three billion years. It's nearly run out of steam on half a dozen occasions, mass extinctions, cosmic tricks, volcanoes or whatever. Our few thousand years from cave painting to space shuttle, in the time span of this planet's arrival in the solar system's existence," his voice fell away, "it's just a flick of fag ash," He glanced up. "No more than one puff of those jet fumes."

Above us, vapour trails melted into the brilliance of the stratosphere. Down at sea level its same brilliance reflected on wavelets whose glitter vanished under Sandray's headland cliff and into the gloom of storm burrowed caves. Rock falls, cut and carved into statues, were scattered at random. Some smooth, worn fangs, others with jagged, freshly broken edges had their strata exposed, as the purple veins of an old body. In a jet- roaring twenty-first century, the earth felt very ancient. I looked about for reassurance. The terns had gone.

'Hilda' rippled along to the bubbling sounds of a wake which made tiny eddies on the slack waters that come before the turn of the tide. A happy boat, in tune with her element, she restored Eachan's good humour. He held a course for the west side of Sandray, balancing sail and tiller to the least shift of the breeze.

Admiring his skill, I realised that a deep bond existed between the man and his boat. In Eachan's hands she became animate. I saw he treated his boat with the same affection and trust as one of the family. Man and boat complimented each other, the one varnished and trim, the other, bronzed faced and steady, a blending of will powers and both at home on the sea.

The cliff of Sandray's north west headland fell shear to the sea. Eachan ran in close, a couple of boat lengths clear. It loomed over our masthead, a mighty promontory breasting the Atlantic's fury in the tussle between the bastion of the land and the greed of an ocean. Dark gashes drove deep into its bare rock face, the wave riven throat of a storm. Spindly pillars reared, ledge after ledge, climbing into salt green turf. The ocean's tranquility swilled over their boulder strewn feet with barely a murmur.

From ledges streaked by a season's nesting, fulmar peered down, squawking and complaining. Others rode the air on motionless wings. Cormorant flapped off the lowest shelf, swimming, diving, up and over. They popped up ahead of us like corks and took off, beating the surface with hefty splashes. A tight formation of puffins shot from behind the headland, red feet trailing, stubby wings burring like a windup toy.

The intimacy of this self-contained domain, locked in the basics of survival, astonished me. Easy to understand, they had not the means by which to offset the mass intrusion of that exploitive species, the human being. Several smallish birds, black plumaged and dainty, swam a little way off from us. One surfaced with tiny silver fish hanging either side in its sharp pointed bill. I pointed as it flew past us. "That's the guillemot, hardy wee birds. They nest further round the headland. Always lay two eggs. The island folk used to take one and leave one, good for baking scones they said. It's sand eels that one's carrying. It'll be feeding a chick. Guillemots are scarce now and the razorbill too- it's a similar bird."

So far I hadn't heard Eachan even suggest he might be old. "In my young days, this point would be alive with them but these many years the fishing boats have been clearing the waters of their feed stock. Sand eels hoovered up by the thousand tons, ground into protein for these damned salmon farms. One species valueless to us puts smoked salmon on your party menu and in between their fish cages and your dining fork, not a word about the coastal pollution and who in a fancy restaurant cares a damn about that bird's supper?" Contempt rang in Eachan's voice.

I'd made no reply, for in spite of the day's brilliance, studying the cliff tower above our masthead provoked a somber feeling.

It hung on the air, infecting the atmosphere with a chilling dankness. Although each rock platform was home to so many young chicks, the place had a gloomy bleakness, a profound sense of dejection. Was it the cries of the bird life? The piteous note of their incessant wailing that rose above the hiss of a swell which rolled slowly over the dark slab of rock at its foot and just as deliberately fell away into the sunless shadow? Grey pillars rose above the ledge, I saw them as melancholy portals to some abiding tragedy. A feeling of grief surrounded me and I turned to Eachan, "There's something inconsolably sad about this place."

He turned sharply. His blue eyes searching my face before nodding, the old man turned to look steadily at the forbidding crevices, "Don't be surprised," he said quietly. "Our daughter, Hilda, fell from that cliff," adding, "It's a long time ago, but it could be yesterday. She was nine."

Shades of indescribable sadness coloured his voice. Time retreated. The cry of birds drifted from my hearing. Only the gurgle of the swell, far away in cavernous hollows, reached us. Perhaps he too heard it as a voice. "I carried her off that bottom ledge," he gazed at it, black, sloping and gale worn, "before the tide would take her."

Utterly shaken by my prescient feelings giving rise to such a grievous revelation, I ran my hand along the boat's gunnel and the headland slipped past.

Tucked behind the promontory in shelter from the northwest, the bay opened. Shimmering turquoise, clean and fresh, it rolled onto the white sand with the same laziness of the settled weather which had cured the hay on Halasay. The breeze dropped and 'Hilda' drifted slowly towards a stone jetty. I looked into water with the clearness of glass. At a loss to know what I might say that could support the immutability of his image, I asked pathetically, "What's the depth here, Eachan?"

"We're at the bottom of the tide; it's about four fathom, a bit over twenty feet." It might have been inches, such its purity, such the sadness amidst simple grandeur.

Eachan seemed in no hurry. The sail hung limp and 'Hilda' rocked gently on an imperceptible swell. The warmth soaked into my back, salt air and sun healing my lungs. Gulls sat about the curving tide line, oiling and preening their feathers. Hauled out on the south side of the bay the dark bodies of Atlantic seals lay sprawled, basking and scratching. Arctic terns were back fishing, their high pitched twittering cries bright and childlike. An unsullied landscape and its wildlife, untrammelled by man.

The sheen on the water dazzled my eyes, facets of light darted off each ripple. I looked on Sandray; simple lines lacking the grandeur of soaring mountains or endless beach, but a hill and shore touchable and intimate in the homeliness it evoked. "This island is the haven of yesterday." "Just that," Eachan said simply. "The old folk knew it. They called that house, 'Tigh na Cala', House of the Haven."

My life was changing, irrevocably changing.

At little distance from the beach, warm in the sunlight, were the grey stones of the house. A long building of low frontage and rounded gables, it appeared similar from a distance to the upturned boat in which the Viking would have spent a winter. Grown from the soil, a lone house amongst fields of once cared for greenness. Eachan noticed me staring, "That was the home of your great grandfather and his people before him." It was all he said, then slowly, "and my grandfather." Doomsday skyscrapers, spider traffic, city greed and ostentation, the delusions of society. I turned to the Atlantic with open eyes.

"I'll have to handle the sail," his quiet voice stirred me. "Yes, I'll take the oars." "That's fine. Make for the inside of the old jetty and lay her alongside.There'll be no swell at all in there."

He handed up my pack as we lay beside the worn stones. "I'll look back in the late afternoon, I'm away down to Castleton, seeing the day's so good," he winked, "just for the sail."

This, the island of my visions. I stood and watched him row out a little and hoist the Hilda's tanned sail. It filled with tranquility. Somehow I'd seen it before. In the distance, a tiny white -haired figure at the helm. The headland hid an old man and his boat, the headland which had known his daughter's death. How could the evocation of such grief come to me? I'd never asked nor was I told, yet the imprint of the girl's final moment must exist in some transmittable form to which I was receptive. As I turned to walk towards my great grandfather's house its sadness swept over me.

I was alone, the island empty. No other living person. I stood on the flagstone at the door of the old house. The sun round in the south, warm on the stones, the bay spread below, Atlantic's breadth beyond the enclosing headlands. Sadness gradually evaporated. Magnificence engulfed me. The centuries were with me. There was no loneliness, the connection was complete and my heart, happy as the sunshine of spring. All I needed was here, under my feet. Land lived and worked by my people. Their birth and death on this island. The generations were at my side, stretching time, back and back.

Land is all that counts. To be part of it, peace or storm and the sea, the profound, unchanging sea, I wanted it all. The tiny fields, their tumbled dykes, the hill pasture that climbed out to the crags of Hecla. Land circled by sea and sky. I wanted its space with me night and day. And above the green fields a skylark sang.

A large smooth stone lay beside the house's only door. I sat on it leaning against the front wall, touching the rough stones in a manner of greeting. They were warm and friendly. I shared a seat with the past, its vantage over the bay. Our arrival hadn't bothered the seals. Now the tide crept towards them. They shuffled down the sand, barking and grunting. Splash after splash and the bay had dark heads bobbing; the seal folk were away to fish. Who could be lonely?

After a little while I studied the house. Green painted sheets of corrugated iron cleverly fitted its rounded gables and a stubby lum Tiny windows had glass and surprisingly, drawn curtains. In two halves after the style of a stable door, the joining hasp had no lock, only a wooden peg. Tentatively I tried the latch. Should I enter?

Half opening the door, a small porch led into the kitchen. Wooden table and chairs, dresser scrubbed and tidy, "Hello!" I laughed at myself for speaking and stepped over the threshold, all the excitement of a home coming, familiar surroundings after along absence.

A door at the other side of the porch entrance was slightly ajar. I peeped in. The curtains were drawn, making the room a little dim. A large iron bedstead appeared to take up most of the space. Pushing open the door, in I walked.

The sunlit porch threw my shadow onto the farthest wall. Without a sound, the door swung behind me. Heaviness entered the absolute silence. Was I alone? I stood at the foot of the bed, swaying with fear, straining to hear breathing.

Hair on the nape of my neck bristled. I'd been in this room before. The bed faded. A coffin sat on trestles, a dead man stared out, white hair, crooked hands, imploring eyes, the face, the photo. Gradually my focus returned. I unclenched trembling hands from the bed rail, wet with sweat. How long had I stood?

The sun's journey found a chink in the curtains. A slit of light pierced the room. Across the bed onto a small table it fell, in a burning circle of light.

It shone on my briefcase.

I reeled back, stumbling outside.

The Sun erupted. Again the ear bursting pressure.

Screeching steel, choking fumes, screaming terror, blood, drip, drip; through the utter horror of stench and chaos, blue eyes looked into me.

Bursting out of the house, I ran along a track beyond dunes of winnowing grass towards the headland. Lack of breath stopped me on its exposed top. Cliffs were to either side and to my surprise the remains of an enclosure. Stones here and there, some half buried. One leaning stone. I stood looking down at the initials, H.McK. Sand thudded on a wooden lid. The pound of waves?

The stones appeared to be arranged in the shape of a boat, pointed ends, a large boulder, the bow, a flat stone, the stern? I sat leaning against the largest stone. The pimpernels were in bloom at my feet. The ocean sang. Sea birds arose, crying. Afternoon sunshine fell on the stones. Did I sleep? It seemed I looked from a great distance, but still I was present.

Norsemen were farming the land beside the sea, west facing and a kindly soil. A long-house up from the beach saw the panoply of their lives and heard the wail of death. Out on a headland under a pagan sky where a north wing rode the spindrift, they gathered stones. His lifetime boat took shape and they buried their patriach, the last of those who had brought them.

The sea unrolled on the rocks, a soughing melody and over green fields of fledglings safely reared, the skylark sang. The air made eddies of warmth curing hay for the people, filling their barns with the fragrance of meadow grass,

On the evening's stillness were the voices of the girls, calling, calling and the cattle came from the slopes of fescues wild, slowly on their chosen path. Brown arms bent, golden hair tumbled against a mossy flank and the milk tasted of hills untouched. And laughing eyes, blue as the sea, turned their gaze.

Time lingered as the note that waits poised on the fingers of some plaintive air which guides the pain of beauty into trance. The birdlife wheeled. Their cries mingled with the sigh of unfolding ripples. A raven croaked but once. I saw the canvas fill above a making tide and a dragon bow nodded to the swell, to a sun alone upon the hills.

Northwards trailed the islands, their skyline pointed home, took living eyes to a land they saw in sleep, beyond a sea he'd sailed by day to a sea he hoped to cross, in tomorrow's trance of death.

The note book I brought had fallen from my hand, lay open. I'd written those few words without realizing it. The sun had crossed quite a bit of horizon. I made tracks for the house at once. Eachan sat on the boulder beside the door, leaning against the wall, "Well, well, boy, you've made the best of the day and a topper of a day too." At that he disappeared into the house.

Reappearing, he produced glasses and a bottle of malt whisky, "You never know, there could be an emergency over here at any time, I always keep a bottle of first aid kit in the old home. It's the surest paramedic you'll get in these parts." Two stiff ones were poured,

"Hector MacKenzie, here's to your first visit to your great grandfather's island. Man, the sun fairly puts a sparkle on the barley water. Slainte mhath."

"Eachan, to yourself, thank you for taking in me here. I can tell you, it won't be my last visit." We drank heartily.

Grinning at him I put my hand on the wall, "Yes, it's a day to be here. I went along to the headland and sat awhile, indeed I'm sure I snoozed. What's the layout of stones over there?"

"Funny you ask," he gave me a long look. "The raven was croaking away a little ago as I came ashore, not often I hear it. Old grandfather maintained it's the same line of raven that came with the Viking. Those stones you were at, though they've never been excavated, are supposed to be the site of a Norseman's grave. They're laid out in the shape of his galley. The old boy believed that a Norse chief was buried there, the first Viking to come to Sandray he maintained."

Eachan looked thoughtful and before deciding to continue, laid his hand on the stone seat, "You see, how can I put it? Well, old Hector, your great grandfather had 'the sight'. It's been in the family, since generations."

"The sight? I had an idea of his meaning. A tremor passed down my spine.

Having begun, he became keen to explain. "They call it 'the Second Sight'," and nodding to the house, "he had it.

Sometimes he would be sitting on this stone when it came on him. What prompted it I don't know; he could see happenings, long, long past. That poem he wrote, the one I showed you of the Viking coming here, was written out on the hill where the raven nest. Mind you, not only things in the past, deaths and tragedies and such like, he also saw into the future. He'd have premonitions, make predictions. I'll tell you about that sometime. Yes, Hector, boy," he patted the wall, "these stones were put here by the Viking." His voice flattened a little. "Whoever will handle them next?"

We walked down to the boat. "You sail her back, Hector, it'll be good practice for you."

The 'Hilda' sailed so easily, the lightest touch on the tiller brought a response. Sitting in her stern, little more than a couple of feet of freeboard and the sea at my elbow, I was at one with both.

Making a sudden decision, I handed over my note book. "I wrote this, out at the headland. The words came to me without any knowledge of what you told me back there at the house."

Sitting on the centre thwart he read without comment as we sailed. I noticed his attention move to the Atlantic horizon. His stare took on an intense look of dismay. The note book slipped un-noticed from his hands. The tan drained from his face. He became a white- haired old man.

I eased the sail across for the breeze to take us into the bay on Halasay. The handling of the boat was left to me. I helped him ashore and made the 'Hilda' secure. Another small boat lay at the jetty but I made no comment for his mood worried me greatly. I followed him towards the croft. What had passed through his mind, perhaps before his eyes?

Was it Eachan's behaviour which affected me? What dread had come over him? Walking at his heel a strange presentiment grew. Bodies squeezed against me, hurry and sweat, clank, clank. I was back on the tube train, gazing over heads. God save me from this trauma. I struggled.

Out on the croft, a slim figure was hunched beside the house milk cow. I walked over. At my approach a blonde head turned and looked up.

I looked down into smiling eyes,

blue as sunshine makes the sea.

CHAPTER SIXTEEN

Colliding particles

'South Rampart Street Parade,' romped into, 'I can't give you anything but love, Baby.' A full blown Dixieland jamboree stomped the night away. Engine thumping, paddles flailing, its skipper gyrating round the bridge, the good ship Clare de Lune, steering a slightly erratic course, cleaved a mighty bow wave down Lake Geneva.

Cheeks like bellows, a black trumpeter leant back, blowing notes at the stars ten to the bar. The pianist beat out the rhythm one handed, wiping sweat with the other, a drummer kept the bass drum going, swigging his fourth pint. Clarinets circled the jiving crowd. The saloon rocked, the boat swayed, churning paddle wheels kept a glistening tempo. Midnight, moonlight, ships lights zig-zagging across dark waters and the great Alps sparkling like diamond tiaras spread a backdrop only Hollywood could rival. Love was in the air and in several cases, against the ships rail.

And the music, baby, baby--- it roared across the lake, swept from ordered vineyard slopes into tippling wine glasses, rosy red, rosy lips, 'That's a -plenty,' the tempo hot, bodies in a frenzy, top notes on that screeching trumpet hitting the pleasure button. Oh boy, could her hips move, eyes flashing with lust. It'll be an instant, knee bend stand up romance if I don't watch her, the bitch. The Agent's eyes followed his prancing secretary, burning with a mix of hate and jealousy. That fucking young Yank who'd got her up to dance, third time now, swinging her between his legs, nearly had her fucking dress over her head and she's laughing. The cow, I don't think she's got any knickers on. One step too far and and I'll.... I'll...' His fists clenched.

The Agent glowered. Another large whisky made no difference. The day had gone badly, really bloody badly. It kept revolving through his thoughts. Ten in the morning she was still in bed, in the next room, wouldn't let him in for the night, the ungrateful cow and me in the head office of this damned stupid Hadron Collider contraption. Total waste of cash. 'Would I care to see over the installation?' He took another gulp, God--- that burnt his throat. Fuck fast colliding particles, I should've had more sense, through tunnels, along gantries, tubes and pipes everywhere, stupid bastard droning on, bored the arse off me.

Rage was smouldering. His normally white face flushed bright red. He felt the pressure mounting at his temples. A totally wasted day, I'll have to cover this job some how and now this carry on. He glared at the couple. The Yank was right up against her, a smoothie dance. Let him put one hand near her arse. The Agent's jaw tightened. Oh hell, I don't need this, the bitch, she'll pay.

The day wouldn't get out of his edgy mind. Had he overplayed his role as a director of a London Insurance Group? The card had got him in, the bloke, pleasant enough but another of these bloody white coated drones, introduced himself as leader of the main team of physicists. In spite of the racket beating his ears, The Agent's thoughts dwelt on the bits of their conversation that mattered, "We're here for a short break, a spot of jazz, thought I'd look up one of my London pals. I know he's a jazz fanatic, Is he about? Hector MacKenzie, I think he works here." The leader bloke had crossed his knees. The bugger's uneasy, had I sounded genuine? "Isn't he a key member of your project?" No response- maybe I didn't make it casual enough?

The Agent remembered asking, "Where does he fit in, what does he actually do? The chaps down the club often pull his leg about it, bit of a boffin, you know the sort of thing."

A real faux pas, the boffin blinked, straightened his 'specs', "Yes, yes, his work is quite a vital part of this whole project. Indeed it's central to the success and er..er.. the safety of our work." Here he paused, glancing to the door. The Agent noted the guy fiddled with a pencil. The bastard's going to lie to me. "I'm afraid he's, he's not available at the moment, actually went out just before you arrived." Lying wanker. "Pity. I had a spot of news to give him. Does he live in Scotland by any chance? It's a Scottish enough name." The white coated arsehole appeared just a mite flustered, "Yes, I suppose it is."

"Fuck it!" The Agent cursed himself out loud, I went too far. Did I cover my tracks well enough? He remembered leaving with the words, "Not to worry, give him my best regards." "Of course, of course," and the scientific wanker had enquired, "What's the name again?" Fuck it, oh fuck it, The Agent's memory of the meeting had him cursing again, "Fuck me, oh fuck it!" All this bloody, buggering woman trouble, that's why I forgot the name on the card I'd produced. The Agent smarted mentally at the thought of his parting remark to the bloke, "Just keep him guessing, I've a big surprise waiting for him." Fucking right there is, when I catch up with him.

'Sweet Georgia Brown', drove these disturbing thoughts out of his head. The Yank had her up against the bar. The Agent downed his half glass of whisky in a oner. Striding to the bar, he pushed between the couple, catching the Yank roughly by the elbow. The man staggered back. Letting his hands hang loose, The Agent snarled softly, "Hit me now, you poxy bastard." Three steps backwards lost the man in the crowd. Crushing his secretary's hand in a fierce grip, without looking at her face, he dragged her to the gangway. The steamer berthed alongside a jetty, "You and me's going home honey." He stopped a taxi. The Agent's voice, quiet and insinuating, frightened the woman. No more words passed between them, nor did the Agent look at her.

Though the chandeliered reception hall, the heavy carpets muffled their footsteps up the broad curving stairway. Since dragging her from the boat, his grip had not slackened. Now it tightened even more. They stood in the dimly lit corridor outside her bedroom door. "Just leave me, let me go, please just go, please," she pleaded, half weeping. "Open that fucking door," he rasped, screwing her arm up behind her back. She'd left the key hanging in the lock. She fumbled. "Make it snappy, darling," he whispered and with a soft mocking sneer, "just in case your friendly Yank has followed us."

The panelled door swung open. She made a lunge to get in. He spun her round. Quick as lightening her knee shot at his crutch. Twenty years of training, The Agent took it on the thigh. "Baby, I like the way you're feeling," he hissed.

In a jerking Half Nelson, he threw her on the bed. Petrified beyond screaming, she lay. He ripped at her clothes. "No pants eh? That's nice, you filthy cow," he snarled holding her down. Short sharp punches to her stomach. Winded, she gurgled for breath. A hand gripped her throat. He forced his way. Brute force.

Flinging bed sheets over a naked, quaking body, The Agent panted softly, "One word of this little bit of fun gets out and believe me darling, you won't be seeing your baby girl again."

The Agent left her sobbing....

and believing him.

The lithe, bronzed body of Company Chairman, Andrew Anderson relaxed on an inflatable li-lo. Another morning's unbroken Caribbean sunshine required his dark diving goggles to cut out the glare as he turned over to view, not without a measure of pride and affection, the majestic, twin masted, auxiliary schooner. She lay motionless at anchor in a secluded cove of vivid turquoise. Her sweep of white curvaceous lines, from a slender bowsprit to a long counter stern, fully justified her name, 'Sea Nymph'. Beguiling as the Sirens of old who lured sailors into the watery abyss of Charybdis, so his yacht drew Nuen's Chairman towards the whirlpools of financial turbulence.

His Caribbean crew, smart in their white tee-shirts and navy flannels, coiled and recoiled ropes, no splice without a whipping nor clove-hitch left un-tightened. Painting, holystoning of decks, her fresh white canvases lashed immaculately to varnished boom and spar, every touch of seamanlike attention matched the lustre of her extensive brass fittings. Much care and considerable company expense had been lavished upon this aristocrat of the ocean's paths and byways. To emphasis the flowing lines of her femininity the golden hair of a gloriously full breasted mermaid entwined with the elaborate scrolling of her carved name plates. She epitomised the grace of an era when sail was paramount and the men who heard the winds throb, who knew the thrill of a canvas full and drawing, loved their ships above all else.

The sun seemed slow to reach its zenith. That morning the Sea Nymph's anchor chain hung without a ripple. The scent of coconut palms added heaviness to the languorous stillness of a cove upon which the tallness of his yacht's varnished masts stretched with an unbroken image. Indeed the perfection of sunlight and tranquility mirrored the eons of an existence before the decadence of wealth and hurry brought screaming power boats and security men flaunting armpit holsters.

The islands canopy, dense and green, fringed an idyllic beach whose pure mica sand would already burn any bare feet which might venture upon it. Not that this was likely; the small isle was strictly private. Detracting somewhat from the cove's serenity, a large sign in bold red letters read, 'Strictly No Landing. Unauthorised Visitors will be Prosecuted.' On a bluff, above verdant plumes of natural forest, the wide veranda of a spacious wooden bungalow enjoyed whatever cooling breeze might be drawn from the breadth of a shimmering ocean.

From a swivel chair on the bridge, the skipper ordered his crew to holystone the teak -laid foredeck, "Don't go aft," he warned them, aware that the Chairman's wife would be sunbathing topless, or more likely nude. He'd gone astern on one occasion to find the lady stretching on a sun lounger. She'd looked up and smiled. The crew was certainly not to be indulged. His gold braided peak cap lay on the navigating table as he watched the li-lo for any signs of the returning owner.

Splashing a little water over himself, the Chairman turned onto his back and glanced at his Rolex; important visitors due in half an hour. Blast, I've stayed out here too long. Coffee, working lunch, bungalow for dinner, maybe a powerboat zoom to a night club on the main island. On reflection, maybe not. Anyway, business, business--- this nuclear programme is beginning to drag. Action on cash flow, must get action out of this meeting. Pressure built, he knew the problems of febrile thinking. It mustn't show; cool, confident and casual does the trick. Turning over abruptly he sculled rapidly towards the yacht.

One of the crew stood waited on the boarding platform with a towel and robe. Scrambling off the li-lo, Anderson grabbed the towel and took the steps two at a time, calling over his shoulder, "Stay here until a launch arrives, then bring the guests to my Stateroom." At the stern of the yacht, as he hurried to the

Master cabin, his wife lay naked, tummy up, tanned and glistening.

"Darling, I need oil," she reached over, pulling at his trunks as he knelt beside her, "and darling," her voice dropped, "and a big bit of you." He bent and nuzzled her, before jumping to his feet, "Muffty darling, these chaps will be here any minute." With equal alacrity, she sprang to her feet, "You bastard, you horrible bastard," and covering herself with a towel flounced along the deck. "Oh God," he groaned, hurrying to dress, "three days of sulks and silence."

Twin outboards at full throttle and a huge curve of thirty knot foam screamed into the cove. A powerboat roared alongside the yacht's boarding stage, stopping dead. The stage rocked violently, a following wake raked up the beach. A crewman steadying the craft helped onboard the green faced Sir Joshua Goldberg. His companion, affecting boldness with a fixed grin, ignored the crewman's proffered hand and stumbling at the foot of the ladder, clung to the rope.

"Welcome aboard, Josh," Andrew Anderson at the Sea Nymph's rail raised a smart salute. Goldberg, ignoring the welcome, nodded, "Do you mind if I use your toilet?" "Of course, of course not." A steadying hand on the polished brass banister guided the ungainly bulk of Sir Joshua down the vessels wide companionway into the yacht's luxurious teak panelled Stateroom. Its cream coloured carpet rose and fell alarmingly. Goldberg groaned. "Here you are, Joshua." Opening a side door, the Chairman helped the company's scientific advisor inside, not a moment too soon.

Sun tanned and boyish in spite of thinning hair, the ex-incumbent of Westminster's highest office, whistling a Bill Hailey number, wandered round to the aft deck, inadvertently disturbing its sun worshiper. "Oh, oh no, goodness me, I'm so,

I, I do, didn't mean…" Removing his sunglasses he loitered over a fawning apology. Apart from strategically placing her reading material, she ignored him. Recovering his composure he sauntered down the companionway, entering the State Saloon in casual style.

A black Caribbean cabin attendant, smart in white ducks, shirt and blue Company tie, stood awaiting an order. "Grind fresh coffee, Marley." A curt nod from Anderson sent the man away. Goldberg emerged at that point, his sagging face restored to its normal pallor. "Andy, so glad to see you." They clasped shoulders in a light embrace before Sir Joshua turned, "Andy, this is my friend, Anthony," and looking hard at his Chairman, "I may have mentioned him to you before? Anyway," he risked a smirk, "as luck would have it, he happens to be staying down the islands with a pop star friend and I persuaded him to fly up here for the day." Pleasant a visual experience as his deck encounter may have been, Anthony could but assume her to be the Chairman's wife. This conclusion, a shade disconcerting, tempered his manner to a degree. He said nothing.

"Anthony, it's good to meet yah. Your sterling reputation goes before you," the Chairman's reference to currency as an indicator of merit, bordered on a faux pas. The hand grip lingered, a show of bonhomie covered two men attempting to assess each other from behind dark glasses. Choosing to ignore the gaff, Anthony responded with a wide smile, "You too. I know, Chairman you operate a highly progressive energy consortium, I'm sure we'll have common ground."

"Call me, Andy, please. Anyhow, how'd yah like this lil'ol' sailing packet, man?" Anderson's arm swept round the cabin as he mocked the native twang. Waving his visitors towards the push-button leather easy chairs, Nuen's Chairman and principle shareholder tapped one side of his nose, "Handy office for keeping an eye on the offshore perks." The trio laughed and any slight tension passed as they bandied pleasantries. Balancing an array of elaborate silver utensils on one hand, the crewman set down and poured the gentlemen's morning coffee. A "thank you, Marley," abruptly dismissed him.

Carefully steering the conversation, Andrew turned to the ex-politician, "You see a good deal of the Middle East these days, Anthony, the Gaza problem, I don't suppose it'll be solved until Hamas is neutralised and even then what do you do with these people?"

"Please, spare me the Anthony, friends call me, Tone, don't know why." Too wily to be drawn easily, he picked up his cup, "Yes, I'm out there quite a bit, on a peace mission. It's my strong suit," and draining the last of his coffee, "Naturally your country's continued support for Israel is a vital factor in that issue and for the wider area too, given Israel's present nuclear capability and the potential development of weapons elsewhere in the region. Don't forget, the Pakistan/India situation is an equal worry but that's not my remit," adding, "for the moment.".

"Tone, I'm glad you mention the nuclear situations we all face," the Chairman didn't miss his opening. "Josh may have told you, Nuen is a major player on this front, worldwide in fact--- Turkey, the Saudi's, and the rest, apart from Iran, that is." Tone nodded. Andrew concentrated his remarks, "Unfortunately we aren't making development progress in the U.K. as fast as we would like to do. Your renewable energy lobby is gaining ground and I'm told especially so in Scotland. Damn Scottish Nationalists are saying no to nuclear power, they even want to close our joint nuclear submarine base. Think of the jobs that would lose."

"That won't happen, Andrew," the politician was adamant. "The Scots have just lost their two biggest banks in taxpayer bailouts. Don't forget the Westminster treasury holds the Scottish purse," and with a schoolboy grin, "or should I say, their sporran. No seriously, their independence is holed below the waterline. This nuclear game is safe with London and I'm sure your good ship Nuen won't go down either." The trio laughed heartily as the ex-politician leant forward confidentially. "More importantly gentlemen, there are well advanced plans for the next generation of nuclear facilities in Britain. Sure planning impediments have to be eased back a little, but tendering isn't too far away," and looking intently at the pair, "you may well be interested?"

Anderson and Goldberg exchanged a swift glance, "Well, Tone, as you're well aware the capital market is a mite difficult at the moment." Sir Joshua entered the conversation, "I fly into Saudi next week. The pile of petro-dollars isn't as deep as it was at $150 a barrel and believe me there's quite a queue but swapping oil for uranium has its appeal, make no mistake, gentlemen we've got to move smartly before these solar farm projects begin to corner too much cash. Spain, Australia, central Africa, they're waking up to its potential. Climate change and an about turn in policy at the White House are both on their side."

Goldberg glanced again at his Chairman, "Let's not forget, on the plus side, printing money is taking off. Governments have no option; they're just bankers with a heavy millstone they don't know how to manage and with half the national workforce in the bureaucracy, they're running out of tricks. There's never been a sounder time to gather up as much borrowing as possible, interest's down at a saver's suicide rate. Printing money, supply and demand, too many readies sloshing around," Sir Joshua's eyes gleamed. "Just wait for inflation to take off and it will. That cuts through your debts like a knife through cheese. If Nuen were to hold some useful energy and nuclear weapon contracts," he looked from one to another, the inference of his unfinished sentence more potent than words and better suited to a political mindset.

His listeners sat in reflective silence, until broken by 'Tone'. "I fly into Jerusalem next week, Josh, but I can easily come home via Bahrain, or Ryadh, if it's any help." Goldberg looked pleased, "I'm sure we have mutual friends out there." His voice took on a slightly aggressive edge, "By the way, Tone, I've warned you before, this U.K. problem with radioactive waste disposal, remember meeting the Swiss scientist, that report we saw? If we're not careful and its details blow to the Greens it could stymie the whole job. I take it the man and his report are still out there somewhere?"

The ex-politician moved uneasily, "Truth is I'm not too sure on that point, but don't worry. I'll follow that up the moment I'm back in London."

With an appraising glance at his Chairman, Goldberg pressed on in a surprisingly sharp manner, "Look here, Tone, Nuen's going for underground waste storage with potential for handling international shipments. The development site we require demands three main criteria, a stable rock formation, minimum population density, suitably remote and thirdly," his normally evasive eyes fastened on the politician, "an area already under government ownership, so if needs be we can move fast with the least involvement of meddling planners or public enquires and such like delaying tactics which these bloody environmentalist trot out. National security is always a useful screen, wards off this blasted Freedom of Information nonsense."

Seldom was the scientist so outspoken; it created a moment's void. Andrew responded, hoping to cover any embarrassment, "Gentlemen, fresh coffee? Marley!" he shouted. The crewman materialised in seconds. He's too damn close, could be eavesdropping. Showing his displeasure the Chairman snapped, "Tell the chef we'll take lunch under the awning in twenty minutes and get about your duties." The Caribbean face remained impassive, "Yes sir."

Enough business for the moment, guessed Anderson. As the trio responded to the crewman's quiet words, "Lunch is served, sir," and moved to the companionway, he put an arm on the ex-politician's shoulder, "How would a seat on Nuen's board appeal to you, Tone?"

"That's a most interesting thought, "replied the ex-politician, smiling.

CHAPTER SEVENTEEN

Crossing the Divide

The woman stood up and lifting a pail of frothing milk, she put an arm across the cow's back. Dancing eyes smiled, deep set penetrating eyes, full of the rays of an evening sun that bounced off the sea. Her mass of golden hair caught its light and fell glowing on her shoulders in natural waves. Wild as the passions I'd known these months, her steady gaze was the contact of those fleeting seconds, that first charged meeting when our eyes saw into each other came cascading, overflowing with the emotions of that moment. How often she'd been with me, had remained a fantasy helping me through the shadows, those depressing weeks when emptiness devoured my thoughts like the wasting corpse I saw myself to be. I'd longed to glimpse her eyes again, know the woman who lay behind that secret moment.

I remained motionless, staring into the eyes which had been my source of strength. In daydreams I'd stroked her hair, held this woman to me, told all, confessed her eyes had kept me living. Fulfilling wish or inexplicable turn of fate, I cared nothing of that; the beauty of her eyes had brought me to this meeting. They were the heart of my dreams.

Smiling eyes, her cheeks pink and bright, she patted the cow, "This is Morag." No expansive hello, no mighty expression of surprise or astonishment, simple. We stood staring at each other, savouring the meeting, the immediate joining of a presence between us, tangible and lovely. After a long pause she held out her hand and very quietly, "and I'm Eilidh."

Without leaving her eyes, I stepped forward, searching for the words which had so often come to me in fantasy embraces. Instead I took her hand in silence and held it, shy and nervous.

"May I carry the pail?" How pathetic, childish. Rich yellow milk frothed over its rim. The woman's arms bare to her elbow, smooth and brown, just a plain blouse, open at the neck, a turquoise shade, it set off her golden hair truly as the green sea enhances the beaches of sunshine.

We walked towards the house. "How did you enjoy your visit to Sandray?" her voice, soft and musical, matching those I'd met in Castleton as I come off the ferry.

"One of life's more unusual days; as revealing as it's been rewarding," I hated what I'd said the second it left my lips. I didn't mean to sound formal, or evasive, I only wanted to pour out the whole inconceivable happenings. Framing adequate words became impossible. What had been for all these months an imaginary, unreachable woman on a tube train, was walking with me, on an island, on an evening slowly, so slowly, melting the Atlantic into purple.

Only little by little did I overcome shyness and glance openly at her face. A high forehead, neat aquiline nose, a slim jaw line, firm lips and shining skin, tanned and fresh. The strength of character shining through the arresting impact of her eyes failed to hide a girlish femininity. She carried her finely shaped head with the upward tilt I remembered so clearly. The attraction of the woman was riveting, instant and alluring, an arousal beyond any undemanding fascination.

Ella met us at the door, "You haven't lost the knack of milking a cow, Eilidh," and taking the pail from me, "Go you through, Eachan, you're needing a wee toot, he's through there. You'll get supper in a little." It was the first time she'd used the Gaelic of my name and warmth was in its saying. Dazed by the succession of events, I moved to the door, not wanting to leave Eilidh's presence. She began helping Ella by sieving the milk into a bowl on the draining board beside the sink. "Away you go, you're the best excuse he's got tonight," and her smiling eyes followed me.

"Come in boy." Glasses were already on the dresser. Eachan poured with the hand of man not inclined to hain the bottle. Quite often in speaking to me they both mixed in words which they expected me to understand. I'd picked out the word 'hain'. "It's not Gaelic," Ella had told me, "it means, to spare, to save something. I'm sure it came to us from the Norse folk. All about here have a touch of the Viking in their blood."

"Here's to a remarkable day, Eachan," Raising the much needed dram and laughing quietly, "It wouldn't surprise me if you told me Eilidh arrived by longboat this afternoon."

"Look here a'bhalaich you're not too far out, her father's folk are related to Ella, she's a far out cousin of Ella's. Anyway, if my memory's correct, quite a few grandfathers back, Eilidh's forebear, a Harris man, a Norman MacLeod to name, escaped the slaughter after the Battle of Culloden and got a lift over the Minch on a Wester Ross fishing boat. A risky one for them both, the MacLeod fellow and the fisherman."

The old man had the gift of bringing alive the atmosphere of bygone times. I listened engrossed, for as his story unfolded, voices from childhood echoed down a long corridor. "You see, an English Naval vessel was scouring the waters of the Hebrides putting the Redcoats, mostly English soldiers, ashore on each island. Many they suspected of being out for the Jacobite Cause, rightly or wrongly, they were shot without a trial. Others were transported on a one way ticket to a prison hulk anchored in the Thames. No way was it safe for him to return to Harris, so he,

aye the MacLeod man, came ashore on Halasay and as luck
would have it, the Navy ship had sailed north. Well, he wasn't
long ashore when he got his eye on a local girl and you know the
way it is, so it's on Halasay he settled. For sure, the MacLeods
knew how to handle a longboat and that's why Eilidh's got the
sea in her blood," he winked at me. "So there you are, that's
Eilidh's pedigree, but you're safe enough boy, she only came
round from Castleton with her dingy."

I shook my head in wonderment. Memories, I sat on a stool
beside an old woman, rocking back and forth as she spoke. My
grandmother, my mother's mother had told me Eachan's story.
Was this MacLeod the same ancestor she'd spoken about? The
man who'd escaped from Culloden and the slaughtering by
Butcher Cumberland? Were Eilidh and I forty-second cousins,
twice removed as they say?

"Supper's on the table," Eilidh put her head round the door.
Plain, unadorned mutton and potatoes on a scrubtopped
wooden table, rich gravy, carrots from the garden, no
outlandish fare. Simple, wholesome, home produce, it'd helped
my strength return these past weeks. It had kept the old couple
healthy for a lifetime. Red wine appeared, I guessed from
London.

We ate quietly. Conversation flowed between the two women.
Eilidh's London/Glasgow flight the day previous, who she'd
met on the ferry, they spoke away. The old boy teased her,
"You're a long time bringing your man to see us." "Be patient
Eachan, I don't want to frighten him off by meeting you." Her
lighthearted rejoinder caught me off guard. Aware of a profuse
blush I remained silent. Arching her eyebrows and glancing
sideways Eilidh smiled.

Eventually I joined the conversation, strictly without mention
of London or tube trains. Neither Eilidh nor I gave any hint of

our momentary encounter. Certainly on my part and I dared to hope, for her also, it formed a secret communication, an experience too private, too special for sharing, a moment that existed only in two minds; as a current will flash across a divide in the fusion of mutual attraction, so that second's contact had lived with me, an image of desire, feeding my imagination, sustaining a belief in the impossible, somehow, somewhere.

Now, the closeness of her, the incredible blueness of her eyes came again, shining out through the last evening light. The compelling attraction I'd striven to hide overcame me. An inner churning, I couldn't avoid its turmoil, its intense elation amidst the pain, nor did I try. We said little of consequence, the language of the eyes glowed between us, its unspoken vocabulary of emotion unheeding of any other presence. We were two people sharing the elation of an unfathomable attraction; a headlong desire, care free and unstoppable, lightsome as a feather on the river of fate.

Time never served to interrupt conviviality in an island household and the evening was well advanced when Eilidh went over to the window. "The tide will be slack in the Sound. I'll just head away over, it's a clear night and there'll be a moon in a little." "Surely you're not needing to go out to Sandray tonight," Ella stood up, protesting. "Now woman," Eachan spoke a little sharply, "She'll be fine, the sea's down." He went to the door and stood listening. "Yes, the sea's good, and the moon's nearly full, you'll have all the light you need, better than any damn torch. The wind's away to nothing and I filled the outboard this morning, so take the Hilda boat."

Eilidh gathered up a rucksack and thanking the old couple, "Don't worry, Ella, I'll be back across when I've sorted out the old house." Completely taken by surprise, I stammered, "Please, allow me, I'll carry that." Totally unsure of what was expected of me, I followed her out of the front door.

Late summer, its midnight air cool and exhilarating, hinting that a dew would sparkle the dawn. Cleansed by the ocean, the air that night breathed with ethereal purity. We walked in its stillness, together, in silence. Close beside me, her presence felt touchable, breathable. My senses filled the void. Voices whispered of another existence. At the crunch of our steps on starlit sand, oystercatchers flew, crying to a waiting tide. The land seemed transformed, spirited beyond fields and sounds.

Against the radiant dim of a crimson sunset, the dunes were shadows of a remoteness that turned the outline of an island into mystery, an enigma which set wandering the phantoms that haunt an empty shoreline; the ghost of freedom beckoned from beyond the rim of tomorrow's ocean. Never had the incessant voice of escape called so strongly. Cast out yesterday, grasp a life of vision, live today with the sureness of an eternity in the unending beauty of space.

The watching shore, the patient sea, an island empty of people, a waiting boat, I wanted Eilidh in an existence isolated from the grasping, polluted life, the profit motive and shallow happiness in a crumbling world. Take her away to the completeness of the simple and primitive, know her womanliness, find riches on the beaches of entwining thoughts and be together.

Beyond anything, in the fullness of that tremulous night, I wanted Eilidh- mine, completely. How could it be? Her breath, the closeness of her form? We walked quietly. Gently and unsure, dreading, yet willed by unbearable yearning, I took her hand. All the hours and nights she had been with me, eyes alone, we were touching. Our fingers twined, tips touching, stroking, I felt her quivering. The pulse of longing, beating as surely as the heart of all being, joined two people.

We stood on the old stone jetty, hands clasped, looking down at the 'Hilda'. Her dark timbers moved, ever so slightly her mast circled an arc on a moonstone sky. How long had we stood? I would stand to the world's end, stand until the dark island before us would crumble into a waiting sea.

Surely as Eachan told us, the great the mistress of the tide lay golden at our feet.

Ever so softly, it rose, shone lustrous in her hair. Our eyes entwined. For as long as it takes galaxies to turn and stars to burn, all the blueness of an ocean was mine.

She lifted her head, came into the circle of my arms, willingly, passionately. Trembling we clung together, the glory of moonlight on her face.Together in the aura of its blessing, we kissed. In a passion which hungers creation we kissed. Beneath the light of universe upon universe, we kissed.

Slowly our lips relaxed, brushing softly, blissful in the contentment of touching.

There could be no parting. I steered for the ancient headland, stark of rock, mortal in tragedy. The Sound made coils of tide, here in tiny black holes, there in whirls of moon tipped silver. It carried us on a journey, across a divide, to an island and into the pain of love.

In the home of my ancestors, I slept beside her bed and in the balm of a summer's night, I held her hand.

CHAPTER EIGHTEEN

Games of High Finance

"The cow, the fucking cow!" The Agent flung down the letter and throwing his head back on the cushions of his sunlounger, he cursed the sky, the heavens, and his wife in particular. "How the bloody hell did she find out, the bitch, the bitch, she'll ruin me. Divorce! She's taking a chance- by God she'll get as little out of me as, as...."

He looked round at their imposing home. Mature beech trees in full leaf hid the neighbouring property, giving the house an exclusive privacy hard to find in the Thames valley. Virginia creeper covered mellow red brick walls, French windows lay open wide, bunches of grapes hung in a spacious conservatory, the lines of a carefully mowed lawn reached to the bank of the river. The achievement of twenty five gut- slogging, years.

Words twisted out of his mouth, "Operations for those stuffed shirts in the Foreign Office, undercover jobs, eliminating dangerous men, blackmail and corruption, sure a bit could be made, fuck me, I could've been looking up at the grass and they didn't give a wank." He fumed on aloud,
"I've worked my arse off to get this lot. See those greedy, dishonest, shit faced politicians, I've watched them at the dispatch box and I've kept my mouth shut when I could have trailed a leak that reached the top."

Impervious to his own origins, he directed the rant towards his wife, "East End back street; I made that woman, out of the slums, couldn't keep her bloody knickers on." Heaving his bulk off the sunlounger, he glared round an immaculate garden, "Solicitors, I've shit them."

He hadn't seen his wife for at least ten days, not that it worried him, she had a habit of taking off and staying out of contact for weeks at a time. They lived their separate lives. Given the covert nature of The Agent's work and the type of characters involved, 'readies' were never a problem. Number one, he was not in the business of bringing himself to the attention of any policeman. She could go to hell. It crossed his mind, not unpleasantly, maybe that could be arranged.

He strode into the house, poured a triple whisky and returning, lowered his form onto the sunlounger. Contemplation set in. The afternoon's heat drew a tiny breeze from the coolness of the river, the letter, fluttering across the lawn, impaled on the trellis of a climbing rose.

Only a mouthful remained in the decanter. Trees spread dappled evening shadows across rich green lawns. Half shut eyes watched a mistlethrush struggle to pull a worm from the turf. The Agent sneered. This reverence for bird life annoyed him, in particular their green wellied friends. Birds, especially their bloody racket at five in the morning, "I'll bet that's the bastard that wakens me." He tottered through to the study and returned with a cocked twelve bore.

Both barrels rent the tranquillity, turf flew, blue smoke filled his nostrils. Feathers drifted down. He felt better. Leaning the shotgun against the Welsh dresser, The Agent moved the lounger into the last of the sunlight, and stretched out again. Putting hands behind his head and smirking away, he spoke to himself, "That'll teach you, birdie, no more dawn chorus for you. My Christ, I'm still a fucking smart shot. The good God above knows it, guns are a great religion. I love 'em."

Pinpoints of sunset shone through the heavy foliage, creating rainbows in the spray which fell, night and day upon a nude who knelt beside the pond. Her pert breasts reminded him for a moment of the woman he'd once loved. Now he cursed her, repeatedly, obsessively, with a deepening hatred.

Staggering morosely to his feet he put the crystal decanter to his mouth and poured its last drops down his throat. Steadying himself at the French window, he shouted a stream of hysterical obscenities. One mighty hurl. Cut glass smashed against the statue in glittering pieces.

The Agent sank to the floor, sprawling and sobbing, "She won't enjoy the pay off for this," he muttered through a deranged stupor.

Drawing deeply on another cigarette, The Agent screwed his eyes in thought, allowing the smoke to curl from his nostrils. It drifted towards the ceiling. He stubbed out another butt viciously. The ashtray filled with twisted cigarette ends. Thick black coffee stained the lip of a cup. He poured another. It struck him he should open the office window. The Super might just come in unannounced. Of course, he realised the window didn't open. Instead, he vacantly switched on the air conditioning and remained standing.

Pulsing temples and vague thoughts lacking any coherence, he scowled down at the river. Sea mist clawed in from the Isle of Dogs. The Thames, grey and turgid, flowed towards some imperceptible horizon.

Divorce, O.K. big deal, yeah so what the hell? But lose the house over it? Thoughts rolled about his splitting head. Two months had passed since the Geneva trip with that secretary bitch. It still rankled. She's off sick, maybe chucked her job. So what, she only did the bookings, didn't know anything about the operational work. I'll let that one lie. It doesn't take much to figure out who'd put the boot in, set up the wife to call time on this marriage cock up. Secretary, honey you need the special treatment.

Money, I need some 'readies'. An accident isn't hard to arrange, might take a couple of months, a bit of surveillance. Stolen car, hit and run, there's plenty of the right guys owe me a turn, they don't come cheap, not the professionals. Money- cash, but no bank business. God save me, I've enough 'heavy leans' to pull in the ponies.

Bitterness filled The Agent's sullen mind. "I should be bloody millionaire, I've enough inside info. to bring down the whole fucking government. That pre Iraq stuff I did, weapons of mass destruction, my arse, bloody risky though. Never mind, it helped towards the house. Mean sods, I only got half what the job deserved."

His words rambled over the injustice he'd suffered. "As for what I did for them on special rendition. Me, out there in Morocco, the bloody heat in that 'safe house' and the flies, they didn't like 'em buzzing round their balls when their wrists were chained."

He warmed to the memory, speaking absently to himself, "Can't beat a bit of screaming for getting results, you don't need to tell me. Jesus, that water boarding, great sport to watch, beats football any day and the sputtering bastards getting another sploosh and pissing themselves, no shit left in 'em," and laughing aloud, "That bloke hanging from his wrists, dancing on tip toes, blubbering and screaming for his mother, stupid bugger. Oh boy, if the punters only knew the half."

His thoughts steadied, "Hypocritical bastards up at the top, pleading innocence, turning a blind eye and that dressing down for using the word 'torture'. All I said, if you want results Sir, then all you need is a little gentle torture, oh God, didn't he look frightened, rabbit in a snare. 'Don't ever use that word again, you understand?' the prat, Christ Almighty, my cover work on that one would fuck 'em all. See Prime Ministers, I could have them all on trial at The Hague, Court of Justice." His flow of bile subsided, "No, no, that's not the way, I'd be top on their expendable list."

Fog, in great clotted rolls, blotted out the river, yellow and damp. High above the City, jet streams criss-crossed, rosy puffs in a morning sunrise. The Agent turned away and sat heavily. Half a dozen code numbered assignments awaited his attention. Delegating each case to the right man, given the arcane nature of the information and possible duplicity involved, called for much convoluted thinking on the part of The Agent.

Several presently ongoing involved checking on colleagues working in the arms trade. Posing as foreign buyers, they were expected to inform on illegal U.K. arms sales, but no way could you trust the buggers. The whole labyrinth of deceit required a ruthless disregard for trusting anyone and where necessary a complete disregard for any colleague caught making a mistake.

The Agent flicked through codes. Only his memorised key opened each file. Which case could yield a little profit? Most were too dangerous for a nice little pay off, too many other colleagues involved. The whole Geneva episode came into his mind as the initials M.H. came up.

A minor operation, he'd only taken it as an excuse to get that bloody woman away for a free trip and please a politician. M.H., umm, the name back to front. MacKenzie, Hector, nuclear research papers. Briefcase must be neutralised. Man incidental.

He considered the case more careful. A better prospect than it first appeared. Behind all the political dressing up, there'll be big funds pushing this nuclear job, U.S. for sure. Waving his clenched fists in the air, that's it, I've got it. Why hadn't he bothered before? Too much attention paid to that damn woman. If this bloke's research work hit the headlines, might stymie any quick progress on their nuclear energy game, certainly in the U.K. Let the anti-Trident submarine lobby get a whiff of it. The contents of this briefcase could be a real show stopper.

Brilliant thinking. He felt pleased with myself. Just what I need, a neat private exercise. His mind's eye already saw himself flying into New York, a meeting in the Waldorf or somewhere like it with the nuke fanatics; plenty folk about the place, for safety. Name my price, I'll do some work on that one, might be half a million!

Verify an electronic transfer to my Cayman account, before parting with the briefcase. Play it real safe, make sure they know I have a copy, ready to hand it over to their man as I step on the home flight. Simple to cover the job with the Chief back here at HQ. I'd just be across in the US checking our under cover in the Pentagon. Never liked that creep anyway, I'd love to nail him.

The Agent warming to the stratagem talked it through his mind. Swap my Cayman account the moment their money's safe in it, maybe into my Swiss holding. I'll think about that detail. Main thing, don't get separated, stay in the hotel and keep a wall at your back. Above all, don't trust them. The bastards could blackmail me, try and get their bloody cash back. Worse, I could end in the Hudson River. "Not on your life, not me," he gloated aloud, "This briefcase could be loaded and I don't mean stuffed stupid with science."

His mind began to tick. Where would a man with a bloody Scotch name make for? Picking up the internal phone, a backroom boffin answered immediately, "Yes, Sir?" "Get me any address, bank reference, occupation, size of collar, know what I mean, everything the cross computers can pick up; everything we have on anyone with movements on a U.K. passport in the past twelve months with the name, Hector MacKenzie. There won't be many with that amount of Scotch mist for a handle. Eliminate those under thirty, over fifty-five, get a line on them all, pronto. Have the info. on my screen by midday, without fail."

"Yes, Sir."

Action invigorated The Agent. Swinging out of his office, he hurried down back stairs to a secluded exit and into a side street. A few hundred yards of smart walking put him discreetly away from the building. Confidence mounting, he looked carefully about the street and hailed a taxi.

Now to deal with arrangements for that secretary bitch. The wife could wait. Two arrangements close together would not be wise.

"Gentlemen, we face serious issues so I make no apology for calling a meeting at such short notice. Some of you I know will have had to fly in from holiday and I fully realise the inconvenience this may have involved. I myself have flown up from the British Virgin Islands this morning, nevertheless, let me assure you gentlemen, I am not wasting your time. The international energy business and other related matters are moving more rapidly then we anticipated."

Nuen Chairman, Andrew Anderson rapped on the table. "May I have your attention?"

Chaffing conversations faltered. Smiles faded. Anderson kept the meeting awaiting his next words, a tactic he used to great effect in enhancing his position. Around the boardroom table, tropical island suntans turned gravely toward a Chairman who chose his words with precision.

"Our first item, gentlemen. The initials, S.S.P. may mean nothing to you for the moment but I guarantee they will do so before too long. Their impact on Nuen's future prospects and far beyond could be considerable."

Practised at handling a board of directors, the Chairman's deliberate phrasing imparted the level of gravitas with which he sought to impress its members. Chosen in relation to their shareholding and influence within a particular business sphere they were certainly important by their own estimations and required careful handling for best results.

Anderson played the aloof card, "The Companies scientific advisor and our new U.K. board member, whom I introduced to you at our previous meeting, are now in a position to report to us on their several joint visits and meetings with heads of State in Bahrain and elsewhere in that region. The rapid fall off in world trade coupled with the bailing out of national banking systems which over egged their assets and to some extent concealed their liabilities, has seen a great deal of wealth, shall we say, on the move."

Grey heads being in the majority, a more youthful Anderson, albeit his hair was dyed, realized that lecturing from the chair would be counter productive, not least given some of his Board were now a great deal wealthier by neatly anticipating the monetary cash which they themselves had no small hand in creating. "Sir Joshua, would you care to elaborate on the current financial position?"

"Thank you, Chairman." Sir Joshua Goldberg rose laboriously to his feet. Sweat marks were already staining his shirt. "Excuse me, do you mind if I turn up the air conditioning?"

Anderson waved a hand. Their scientific advisor stepped over to the door, adjusted the control and puffing slightly, returned to stand at the back of his chair. Goldberg also an expert in holding a meeting's attention knew the value of suspense.

Privately during these past months Sir Joshua had set his mind on controlling Nuen. Not gifted with modesty, he believed that a judicious manipulation of his contacts in the rarefied stratas of high finance, coupled with his adroit understanding of how to apply the latest scientific advances would yield him, not only the Chairmanship but given a little time, also a significant shareholding.

His first step in the game, gain an insight into Nuen's overall position. He had befriended the Finance Director. "Sir Joshua, stagnation is fatal. We look to you, in some degree, to deliver the extra capital required to ensure the expansion needed to alleviate our present downturn." The Directors words rang like the chimes of a cash register. Negotiate the company's latest monetary requirements, keep it on hold. Engineer a cash crisis, call for an extraordinary board meeting, propose a vote of no confidence. Announce his negotiated financial deal. Bingo, Anderson deposed. Who would the members elect? They'd vote for me, or see their inflated director's fees, plus any shareholdings, sailing down the Hudson.

Tailoring his delivery carefully, "Gentlemen," he began, his intense dark eyes deep within black circles of jet lag and rich living, "Gentlemen, our Chairman is perfectly correct in warning that the situation which Nuen faces is serious," nothing beats the oil of sycophancy before a going for the kill, "and for several reasons." Faces round the table looked equally serious.

"The developed world's finances, in terms of government's debts, are a rising percentage of their various GDP's. Falling company profits equal a lower taxation take. Rising unemployment equals higher benefits and so forth. An angry and frightened consumer society turning on the instruments of control needs careful handling." Nothing like suggesting a hint of social unrest.

"However banking systems, now subject to inappropriate levels of political meddling, are set to retrench for their own survival. No matter where one turns, the world of finance is not only tight, but very finely balanced, as some of you at this table are only too well aware." He inclined his head to the coterie of bankers who sat at the far end of the table avoiding his gaze. "None the less, my Middle Eastern trip, if not as yet delivering the funding I sought for the extending of our nuclear programmes, did yield some extremely important information."

At this point Sir Joshua asked that the company secretary should, 'lift his pen', as he put it. The Chairman nodded and minute taking was suspended. Goldberg reached for his glass of water.

"I was favoured, not least in view of my scientific credentials," a comment Sir Joshua inserted with a complacent smile. "I was favoured by two strictly private meetings with the heads of a certain oil cartel, in fact the largest grouping in that region. Our discussions were far reaching."

Adopting a statesman like pose, "Naturally the cartel is concerned over falling oil revenues, obviously due to world recession. Slashing interest rates is one thing but of considerably more concern is the extent of the fiscal stimulus taken by the U.S. and U.K. governments. The term used is 'quantative easing', which you bankers recognise as simply politicians printing money. Both these measures, designed to counter what may yet turn into a mammoth global depression, have our oil rich friends, to put it mildly, rather alarmed."

Not a paper shuffled, two lines of faces watched Goldberg intently. "Falling sales are compounded by the weakness of the petro-dollar. Privately and under pressure from the relatively buoyant Chinese economy, the major oil producers are toying with the concept of ditching the pricing of their output in dollars and turning to a more favourable currency. Dare I say the petro-yen?" This bold suggestion registered in a shock wave round the room. "Meantime gentlemen the cartels main concern, down the line, is dollar inflation. They know sure as geese lay golden eggs, inflation will kill the goose."

Heads nodded. Sir Joshua drew himself up, not without sound reason, to deliver the main thrust of his speech. "The power of oil as an energy source will decline over the next decade, a fact which our Middle East friends find uncomfortable. Depressions come and go, global energy consumption, by comparison, is a steady linear curve upwards. Having enjoyed the crown of oil worship, they don't intend to vacate its lordly throne."

Goldberg primed himself for the dagger blow. "Make no mistake, gentlemen, they are looking to transfer the sovereignty of oil into the next source of wealth creation. Whilst there remain funds which are still interested in nuclear, the initials, S.S.P. stand for," he paused for dramatic effect, "Sahara Solar Power."

A look of surprise registered round the table, board members glanced at one another. Gratified at the impact on his listeners, Sir Joshua allowed the name to sink in. "Gentlemen, a consortium of oil producers is putting an initial three billion dollars into this project. The challenge of accelerating climate change requires joined up planning. Already here in the U.S. I must say, trusting I give no offence, at last we have some intelligent leadership from the White House."

Several heads nodded, the bankers, Republican to a man, remained stony faced. Making a mental note of the various reactions to his comment, he continued, "The intention to develop a national grid network of super cooled electricity cables to carry Californian sunshine to the Eastern States of America, using high voltage direct current, is attracting much interest in the Middle East. Transmission of high voltage DC is vastly more efficient than lines carrying the Alternating Current. Obviously the installation of a series of transformer stations is required at strategic points of uptake to convert the current into household and general usage."

He allowed his supercilious manner to dominate the table, "Sahara Solar Power envisages the export of North African sunshine right across Europe using similar generating technology and employing a comparable network of power lines. They intend also to integrate wind and wave generation within the system so as to level out variations in generating flow. Sub-sea cables would link remote areas into a mega pan-European grid. Indeed, such is the scale of this proposed system it could well make coal and gas generation obsolete in fifty years time."

Sir Joshua had the board where he wanted them, dependent on his scientific understanding. Now to deal his next hand, finance. "Gentlemen, this is major thinking, its costs will run into trillions of dollars. More importantly for Nuen, not only is it diversion of funds away from our needs, it could prove a colossal threat to the future nuclear generation. Naturally we are not without allies, in particular the Pentagon over here and in UK the Ministry of Defense."

Important shareholders in the room studied his words. Any undercurrent of meaning might translate into share movement. Aware his last comment might sound too down beat, their scientific guru hastened to add more reassuring words, "All is not lost, far from it. The recent bailing out of numerous banks resulting their semi- nationalisation by a number of governments, gives us a great opportunity to find useful funding."

This touched a raw nerve with already nervous banking members on the board. "UK is a case in point. Two Scottish banks, now virtually taxpayer owned, happen to have a number offshore subsidiaries to help with their clients' profits at both company and individual level which are not subject to record in Britain. Guernsey, Gibraltar, Cayman, etc. all maintain offshore registrations which do not fall under UK taxation schedules. It's rather uncomfortable for holders of funds in these tax havens to find the eyes of Her Majesties Collector of Taxes now able to pry into their accounts."

An uneasy shuffle went around the boardroom. "Indeed, as a result of this possible exposure, billions of pounds have already moved very smartly to new homes, Hong Kong, Panama, Singapore, and of special interest to me, into Dubai. I shall say no more except to add, it is in the latter United Emirates that I have considerable influence and some of the funds to which I just have referred can, I'm sure, be made available to Nuen. Thank you for your attention gentlemen."

Sir Joshua resumed his seat. Smiles, nods, and gushing words of thanks came from the Chairman. It went exactly as he planned. What he didn't disclose, two a billion dollars, just a phone call away, were available from an oil sheikh wishing to diversify into nuclear Let the board sweat a little, thought their scientific advisor, timing will be of my choosing.

Coffee, biscuits and general chatter, Chairman Anderson signalled Goldberg to his side. They moved away from the table and displaying an obvious concern he spoke quietly, "Well done Josh, but look, do you think I should inform the directors of the thwarted cyber-attack on the control system of our Sea Island reactor last week? After all, the virus was deflected without having an emergency shut down, or God help us, worse. If that bit of news leaked out, Nuen's equity will fall like a stone."

Anderson was an anxious man. Another implication alarmed him to an even greater extent. A precipitous jail sentence would result from an oversight of this magnitude. He'd lain awake for the past few nights, wondering, worrying. Who could he depend on who was completely discreet, shrewd enough to offer sound advice? Who to trust? It had to be Goldberg.

"By the way, Josh I haven't told the UK Atomic Energy Authority either. I've kept it in house. Only your good self and that chap on the monitor knows, so far as I'm aware. I'm ninety-nine percent certain that's the case. Anyway, a useful bonus should keep him on our side. I am bit worried about the data records, they might show up on the next inspection. It's kept me awake for a week. What do you think?"

Far better that Anderson be solely to blame should this gross oversight come to light. Privately delighted at his Chairman's invidious position, Goldberg, looking deliberately over the man's head, allowed several minutes go by before bending confidentially and speaking in a low voice, "Don't trust any of your Board Members, especially not the bankers. Say nothing and don't think bonuses, it's a bad principle. Just give that employee a few shares and maybe he'll not want to damage the Company," Inwardly amused at the thought of creating more sleepless night for the Chairman he added in his silkiest voice, "unless of course some ferreting media outlet offers him mega bucks."

A look of alarm registered in Anderson's eyes but conscious of showing weakness he snapped, "Sir Joshua, one other matter, I want action on that UK nuclear waste facility and pronto; a hell of a lot rides on it."

Furious at the Chairman's superior manner Goldberg abruptly turned his back and left the meeting without replying. Descending the wide marble stairway he paused to view a full length portrait in oils of the first Andrew Anderson, founder of Nuen. It hung at a turn in the stairs and clever lighting ensured the painting dominated the Company's spacious hallway. Under his breath Goldberg sneered, another aloof bloody Scot. They always imagine they've an ancient pedigree somewhere in the cupboard. I hate the lot of them.

A sardonic smile reached the corners of Sir Joshua's flabby mouth,

"That portrait deserves a fresh coat of paint."

CHAPTER NINETEEN

Long Climbing days

Eilidh lay asleep. I stood watching her quiet breathing. I'd lain on the wooden floor beside her bed all night and in the closeness of reaching up to hold her hand sleep had been immeasurably happy. She lay with an arm still outstretched, more attractive than I had possibly imagined in all my months of seeing her in my thoughts. No need of makeup, health shone from a clear skin tinged with the vigour of fresh air and sunshine, her face elegant and refined, slender jaw, thin shapely nose, her lips slightly parted in the tranquility of untroubled sleep. A beautiful woman, natural and feminine. How could a single glance on a train bring us together, forge the strength of my emotions? Her golden hair, thick and wavy spread loose across the pillow. I reached to stroke it but drew back, afraid to waken her.

An empty island awaited sunrise. Early light reflecting off the bay flittered through the tiny window onto my night's crumpled covering. Silently folding the rough woollen blankets, I put them to one side and in the half light my hand touched something which felt like leather.

Gingerly my hand traced to a cut handle. My cursed briefcase. Any memory of the wretched item being in the house had been forgotten, completely erased by the mystery of yesterday. Its half bent shape leant repulsively against the wall. Dimly on its flap I could make out the black initials, H.M. Without any reason it produced a grotesque feeling of menace. Its God-forsaken contents, my reports on the dangers of radio- active material, imbued a simple briefcase with a presentiment of catastrophe, awful and sickening. Did it stand between me and escape? I glanced to the bed- stand between us and our future?

Did it move? I recoiled. Impossible and yet its shrunken blood stained leather became a hideous malformed object shrivelling before me. In dread, I backed to the door and stepped outside.

Out into a crispness, the herald of sunrise and the freshness of atmosphere innocent of malice. Revulsion towards the briefcase vanished as quickly as I'd been affected. The harmony of my surroundings lifted any unease. I set my face to climb the hill. Away from the back of the house ran ground that once supported family after family. A thousand years, three thousand, who would know what history rested below this soil? And my people, the last to turn a furrow. Affection for its uncared acres grew at each upward step, urging possession, demanding what by dint of a thousand years was mine.

Reaching the crest of the hill and unprepared for what lay below, I sat on an outcrop of rock to gaze down upon a vast open bay. Gently shelving sand followed a perfect curve. Without cliffs, its enclosing headlands tapered into an expanse of sea, cast in a deep mauve. Far, far distant, ranging away to the northeast, jagged mainland peaks tipped the horizon, indigo and mystical. I waited, absorbed by the immensity of an unfolding landscape. Revolving, unknowable, indifferent to the despoiling of what it had spawned, as it had breasted earth's peaks and ridges longer than life had existed, so the sun burst across the sea, glorious and golden and I longed for Eilidh.

I sat, and sat, alone with the sun in the silence of its rising. Alone? From the crags of the Hill of the Shroud there came a raucous call. I looked up. Fingered black wings spiralled high above me. A raven greeted the first warmth. Its single call, harsh and arresting.

The Viking saga, written by my great, grandfather, ranged through my head. The eye of wisdom pecked from the dead crone by a raven and fed to its nestling chick. In that acute awareness which defeats the passage of time nothing separated me from the generation which brought it here. The raven circled, cawed again. A greeting, a warning? In its wisdom, what did the raven foresee? Destruction, death?

Amidst the rising sun the story lived, banners unfurled, longboats crunched the sand. Bearded giants leapt gunnels, shrieking fiends, swords spilling guts, axes slashing limbs. I saw the clefted head bleeding on the sand, watched the kneeling, sobbing, women. From the encompassing elements of sea and fiord the longboat men had found a new home. Amidst the beauty of this island, they had bred my forebears. Intimate as the great orange orb of the sun will be to a man alone, I heard the laughter of children.

Down by the tiny fields of tumbled dyke I ran breathless, to the door of the old home, "Eilidh, Eilidh!" I called excitedly. Her bed was made. The room empty. A stab of concern ran through me. Back outside, I looked about urgently. There, in a bay of our own, a head bobbed out of the water. Not dark as the seal would be, but golden in the first rays of sunrise breaking free of the hill. And seeing me, she waved.

Waving both arms eagerly, happy at her in sudden appearance, I turned to the stone beside the door. Seat of many thoughts by Eachan's telling. Maybe of the trance that relives yesterday. Perhaps of the gift of 'sight' that opens tomorrow. Naturally, as to a chair of long habit, I sat. The people were on the fields, bent to the cutting of their harvest, gathering it in hand bound sheaves. I could see them; scaling the bird cliffs, fishing the mackerel sea, pendant nets dripping the moonlight jewels of a cresent night. And the laughing children from the playground of a hill, long climbing days, collecting honey from the wild bees' nests, how bright the bird song hill of summer flowers.

The peat hearth of winter, childbirth pain and firelight suckle. The driving rain on huddled thatch and the drum of a thunder sea that fed young hearts, glistening- eyed at granny's knee, stout manhood tales of longboat morn, of crashing seas sunrise torn and Raven banners born.

I rose still bemused by the weirdness. Had the stimulation arisen from the force of my hilltop vision, the longboat, children's laughter, or the raven's croak? By what freak of inspiration could they summon up themes related to the island of a thousand years ago or insert themselves in to a train of thought? The speed of writing those few verses had imperative command of dictation. The thought came strongly to me; by some means I was a pawn of supernatural elements which lingered amongst the island's feel of the natural and un-spoilt ways.

I watched Eilidh swimming amidst the colours which were transforming the day. The last sparkle of dew still on the green sward, white sand against the blackness of rock, a turquoise bay pouring itself into the ultra marine of the Atlantic and presently there was a woman running towards me, golden and beautiful.

Eilidh stood before me barefoot, a towel about her, laughing as she shook her hair. Shyness overcame me, embarrassment and excitement together. I blushed deeply, looking only into her merry eyes. "Eilidh," was all I could muster. She laughed, "Hector, I presume?" and pretending to be serious, "one egg or two?" My tongue loosened, "two, please, if I may, one only, if they're not from Ella's hens."

She skipped into the house. I could hear singing and laughing through in the bedroom. Before long the rattle of dishes sounded in the kitchen. Time I became useful. Putting my head in the door, "Anything I can do to help?" Eyes smiled from under arching eyebrows and handing me a galvanized pail, "Would you like to get more water, please?

Swinging the bucket, I made for the burn. Tucked a little from its bank I came upon the well, a neat circle of built stone. Water straight off the hill, filtered by the soil. I scooped a cupped handful. Cool and sweet, without any taint, fresh as the breezes on its source. I walked back to the house, my first steps towards remoteness living.

Putting the pail down in the kitchen and shaking with excitement I caught the woman around the waist. "Eilidh, I'm going to live here." I whispered into her hair. She twisted to face me. Her arms went to my shoulders, "Oh, Hector" she breathed my name softly. Her arms circled my neck. I bent, our eyes joined. The depth of attraction reached my inner self as no emotion before. Our eyes closed and in the security of shared passion we kissed, the eager kiss of longing.

An outgoing tide left bare the stonework of the jetty, a tribute to hands that could cut and craft. Red and purple sea urchin inched their way across its rocks. Stranded starfish, orange bright on white sand awaited the sea's return. Seals, dark and idle, hauled out on the sloping rock of the farthest headland and slept away the lull. Only the gulls busied themselves, strutting and probing the limpid pools which remained. From time to time a cloud would block the sun. A shadow would flit across the bay before sunlight returned and sand and sea glistened once more.

The boat lay heeled and safe and we sat on her gunnel, barefoot on the warmth of the sand. Content and relaxed, I watched the receding waters, conscious our bare arms were touching.

The peace of the bay brought us close, nobody in the entire world to listen or intrude, the wildlife about us neither upset nor caring. We were accepted, a kindred life, part of their wide domain, its sun and cloud, the faint rumble of the uncurling Atlantic. Seclusion, absolute, and the slowness of time, servant only of a turning tide.

Gently, I put my arm round her waist, "You brought me here, Eilidh. I think my life is owed to you," and very quietly, as I turned to look to the hill, "and I hope, my future."

She rested her head on my shoulder, her deep, thick, golden hair against my face. "It wasn't my usual train, I happened to be early but standing in the crush of that rush hour carriage seemed quite strange, almost like being in a trance. I didn't will it to happen, but gradually the tube train didn't exist. I was here on Sanday, seeing it all. I've known the island since childhood, walked the cliffs, watching the sea for a boat."

She lifted her head, gazed away to the horizon and in a very distant voice, "A presence walked with me, along the cliffs, powerful, totally compelling... was walking with me on Sandray. There in London, amidst the City's unending clatter, in that noisy, smelly train."

I waited, stunned and silent. Her description mirrored the image which had come so emotively to me in the few seconds I'd gazed at her blonde hair across that fatal carriage.

Slowly her head rested back on my shoulder. That first sight of her returned as she spoke. I'd replayed its memory time and again these many months, remembered the thrill of its instant attraction, the vividness of the wild associations it aroused. Now at its recall, beyond reliving the passion of those dreaming moments there came a yearning

Silent with emotion, I pressed my lips to her head. My fingers tips caressed the golden hair, warm and downy. Words would be empty tokens, what need of uttered bond? For simple as nature abounding, happy as the sun is young, joy flowed between us.

She stirred a little, "I felt eyes were looking at me, I knew an intense presence was close," and lifting her wondrous eyes to me, "the sensation forced me to turn. When I did, and we looked at each other, though we'd never met, I knew who you were and," she whispered, burying her head in my arms, "I knew we would meet again," and ever so quietly, "meet again, like this."

Tears closed her eyes. She was crying. Gently lifting her chin, I brushed her wet cheeks and each in turn, I kissed her tears.

Tiny rolls of foam uncurled about our feet, spread their bubbling fans of clear water across the shelving sand. A delicate shade of turquoise returned to the bay. Summer was waning, the tang of autumn's approach on the air but still the midday sun reflected a warmth from the settled water. Those in a world without time are in the land where all that has gone before and all which may be of tomorrow, rest in one moment.

The boat stirred slightly. She lay in the shelter of the jetty, tucked behind its sturdy masonry. How imperceptible the quietness of her coming awake. Without our noticing the water stole below her keel. Suddenly jumping up from our seat on the boats gunnel and splashing out of the shallows before I could catch her, Eilidh was away, running, calling, "Come on, Hector, I'll race you to the house." Up the dunes, bare feet, sand flying, she arrived at the door yards ahead of me. I hung onto the door frame, panting, amazed both at her speed and the recovery of my lungs.

She put an arm round my waist, "Poor Hector, that wasn't kind, I'm sorry," and giving me a squeeze, she whispered, "but I'm so happy." We went inside. "Eilidh, with any luck I'll catch you yet." She laughed from the other side of the table as I dived round and lifted her off her feet. "That was just a test run, anyway I'm cured, no sign of a cough. Sea air and sunshine, it beats all the patent cough drops put together."

Perhaps it was the mention of that wretched cough which had plagued me months past. Eilidh began to prepare some of the food we'd taken over the previous night, her face solemn and the tone cautious, "I'm afraid when I saw the rescue team cut that briefcase from your wrist to get you clear of the carnage, although you were still alive, I thought it was touch and go,"

She put some of Ella's home baking on the table. We sat gazing at each other, two minds locked again in a horror transcending present time and place. Behind her head, through a window, the bay, the boat, our morning, were they all far in the future? Were they a fabrication of an imagination which, able to span the centuries gone by, could just as easily project the act of consciousness into the yet to be? How could one's mind encompass this unending gallery of experiences, comprehend the dovetailing of sensations which were the living, dreaming, pulsating act of being? Through the open bedroom door, against the wall, lay the crumpled briefcase.

A catch came to Eilidh's voice. I reached across and took her shaking hand in mine, "People fell against me, I got a bit of bruising that's all; the blast had gone the other way. I struggled clear and made towards you. It's funny now, the stretcher boys were commenting on your size, but they did a tremendous job, these men are some of life's true heroes. In all the confusion I picked up the briefcase." Its mention brought back the flashing explosion.

"The ambulance crew couldn't have been more considerate. As they were loading you into the back, I said to one of them, 'May I go with him'? Eilidh bent her head and dropping her eyes to the table, she gripped my hand quite tightly. There came a long pause. I saw her blush deepen, setting her face in a beautiful glow and I pressed her hand in reassurance.

"They were closing the door and he hesitated, so I just said to him," I waited. Eilidh lifted her head and in a small voice, she went on, "I said to him, 'It's my husband.' The man couldn't have been more sympathetic, 'Yes, of course you can,' and he helped me aboard. I remember him saying, 'He'll be OK missus, he's a big strong lad.' I just held your hand until they wheeled you into the emergency. I stayed until a surgeon came out, hours later, to tell me he thought you'd pull through. I called to see you quite a few times but you always seemed to be sleeping. Finally I had to go away but I left your case and some things. Hector, I never opened the briefcase."

I went to her. We clung together, shaking with distress. I stroked her lovely hair, "Eilidh, I'm here. I won't leave you, if it's what you want." She nodded, and buried her head in my chest.

Afternoon's warmth brought a breeze off an Atlantic whose vastness stretched away, blue upon blue. How many suns had painted it so, given life to the tiny scrolls of brightness which exist only moments on a day such as this. We walked the cliffs on a crest of happiness and the sea sparkled and amongst the Viking stones where the scarlet pimpernel bloomed, we sat. Shyness left me and with it all reluctance to speak and tell. I told of the drowning vision, an old white haired man in the coffin, his hands, his warning look, the funeral, my name on the coffin lid.

Eilidh spoke. And in the remoteness of her words it seemed she saw my image staring out of the swell which echoed in the caverns below our feet. "Since I was a child coming to the house of Ach na Mara, I've looked at that picture above the fireplace, the old man whose eyes follow you about the room. When I turned and saw you on the train, I knew who you were. Hector, it's in our people, your people, you can live the past, you can see into the future. Poor Eachan, like his grandfather, he has the gift, or curse. He foresaw the death of Hilda, his daughter. It haunted him, he knew she was condemned. Had he destined her death?"

Eilidh's eyes lost their brightness, "The scar is on his mind. Nor will it heal." And she turned fully to me, "These are the cliffs of our past visions, today our happiness and," her voice, a whisper, "they are the cliffs of sadness."

We sat on, amidst the stones of past hope, amidst the frailty of tiny flowers. Quietly, I read her the poems I'd written. She listened. As though in a trance, she looked away to the faint trail of islands which vanished to an incalculable distance.

"Oh Hector, Hector," was all she said.

From the little kitchen window I watched the land growing into shadows, only the sea preserved the radiance of the day. Fragments of cloud, slender skiffs of purple far beyond the horizon, marked the sun's last rays with their crimson edges. Without stars, the transparency of the sky had only distance, the opening to some endless unknown, a void unfettered by dimension. Was there a crossing, a boat to sail the waves of imagination?

Darkening headlands, unpretentious outlines of rock, cut and tossed, ground and broken into the soil of our existence. Simple and unadorned works of art, neither bleak nor austere, did they point towards some great indefinable force? Perhaps a solitary

Anchorite in his stone cell journeyed as far as is possible? I saw the people of old watching that same setting sun. Its rays governed their survival, from its tranquility came their peace.

I dreamed and Eilidh, quiet and thoughtful, lit the candles. Summer had passed its zenith, and nights without darkness were becoming the evenings of the long gloaming. The whistling calls of birdlife feeding along the shoreline, faint but clear enough, emphasized the quietness of the room. I turned from the window, out of sunset thoughts and into the flicker of candlelight.

The serenity of the place, the nearness of the woman, no tension, no stress, the harmony of being alone together, in a place of natures making, "Eilidh, this is home. I want to make it home."

She came to me, wide arms and bright eyes. "Hector, you of all people have the right to this island, a thousand years of right. Whatever you were born, whatever your life before now, this place is in you, deep in you as the Atlantic sunset."

Her words, slow and foreshadowing, "My people knew the north wind that brought you here. Like the tunes of yesterday, the feelings are buried beneath their notes. This island is a hidden melody. Take it, hold it. It won't deceive you, nor leave you."

Her arms were about me, "Eilidh," I spoke into her hair, "I hear the music. Perhaps it's a lament for what has been. Perhaps I'm searching within its notes for the secret of its expression, the mystery of a beauty that haunts me. It's in everything about us. It's in what I write, in all I want that melody to be."

Our arms entwined. It was difficult to speak, "Eilidh, there is no melody, without you."

The candles wavered, burnt low. Eilidh moved away slightly and spoke in a tiny voice. I could barely hear her, "Hector, I have to go down to London. Tomorrow." And after a little, "The tide is early."

I rolled in the old blankets on the floor, beside her bed. I stared out of the tiny window. The island, the world, dropped into an empty pit of despair. And tipping the topmost window pane appeared a moon without sleep, full and alone.

A hand reached down, stroked my cheek. "Hector. My Hector, don't fret. Wait for me. I'll come back. When the tide is high and moon is full again, I'll come back to you."

Dawn was without a breath. In half light a fog hung on the sea, a narrow band of mist that lay on the Sound at the meeting of the waters, twixt ebb and flood. Out of its cloying white vapour floated the headland, a black embodiment of some archaic upheaval without solid foundation. We rounded it close in. The bird life was silent. Fingers of mist clawed up deep crevices. It needed little to conjure the grinding eons which deify our illusion of constancy.

Eilidh had taken the helm, confident and capable, her eye on a compass box at the foot of the mast. "A bearing of twenty five degrees avoids the reef and puts us to the landing at Eachan's croft." Droplets of mist settled on her hair. With a laugh she shook them off. Glum as I felt,
    "Look here woman," in mock annoyance I brushed them off my jacket and we laughed together.

Ella had breakfast on the stove. Its welcome reached us on the lifting fog. Out at the sheep fank, Eachan loaded lambs into a trailer. I went over to him. "Well boy, you're back. How's the old grandfather's house?" he winked, "Needing a nail or two?"

"Wind and water tight, it'll do fine," I smiled, no longer surprised at his quickness of insight, nor his ability to express thoughts by inference. Unlike the directness of the culture I'd left, the Highland style of leaving the listener to read between the words suited me fine.

His trailer load of lambs was headed for a mainland sheep sale. Halasay's winding single track road skirted the furthest fields of Ach na Mara and with Eachan at the controls of a wheezing Land Rover, Eilidh and I squeezed alongside him until we reached the pier in Castleton. The ship lay stern in, roll-on-roll-off fashion. A trickle of exhaust at her red funnel, the radar scanner turning above her bridge, it all seemed modern, strangely out of touch.

A sheep float awaited, ramp down and ready. Eachan backed the trailer into position with skill. I gave a hand, grabbing lambs which attempted to escape. Much bleating and scrabbling feet forced lambs onto a mainland float and the lorry rolled aboard the ferry. It was not the parting I'd expected. Sheep and business kept emotion at bay.

Eilidh stood at the gangplank in conversation with the youngish chap who'd spoken the evening of my arrival. I walked up, not very clean. He smiled at me, "You're still here." I thought I heard pride in Eilidh's voice. "Neil, this is Hector." We shook hands and he grinned, "You've caught the island infection," and with, "See you up by," he went off to attend the ship's ropes.

"That's a cousin, far out, so I suppose he's related to you somehow, even further out," her eyes glowed with merriment, "if you're not careful you'll get him 'up by' after the ferry's away." I guessed that 'up by', meant the Castleton bar.

How could I be down cast? All the activity, practical hands on work, satisfying and with a purpose. Yet looking at Eilidh, beautiful to more eyes than mine, I knew emptiness would come, a constant missing, wondering; a longing fraught with uncertainty and the pangs of jealousy.

She stared at me, the eyes of our first contact. I felt their meaning and she leant and kissed me lightly on the cheek, "Don't fret, Hector, I'll come back. Our minds are together. When you're thinking of me, I'll know. I won't sleep until you speak." She ran up the gangway and turned with a wave.

I stood and the ship's propellers churned. The missing of Eilidh had begun.

CHAPTER TWENTY

Hard work and a Good Woman

Eachan came to my elbow, "Come away boy, we'll go up for a 'wee toot'. I don't go over to the mainland with the lambs any more." The bar was crowded and possibly because I smelt of sheep and my hands were dirty, nobody seemed curious. I didn't feel out of place and the barman was already giving two glasses a double press below the optics as we came through the swing door. They were set on the counter before us as he and Eachan greeted each other in Gaelic. I made to pay the round but the man held up his hand, "It's on the house, MacKenzie. Welcome to Halasay, and don't worry," he laughed, nodding at Eachan, "you're in good company." I got his drift.

Another round appeared from down the counter. Neil from the pier raised a glass. Several rounds later I ventured to say quietly to Eachan, "Who's the barman?" "Oh, he's the chap who owns the place, Angus MacLeod," and looking at his glass, "I think I'm right, he's related to Ella," and looking at me, "generations back." Shaking my head, I emptied my glass, nothing by way of relations surprised me now but curious, I asked, "How did he know I'm a MacKenzie?" Eachan laughed, not unkindly, "See that old photo that hangs over the fireplace, well a' bhalaich, take a look in the mirror."

Conviviality gathered pace around us, locals congregated, elbow to elbow, crofters, fishermen, blue boiler suits, yellow oilskins and much wisecrack. Not all of it registered. Eilidh didn't leave my thoughts. I realised neither she nor I had asked how we each earned our living. It hadn't mattered then, nor now; nothing could take away from the happiness of touching minds.

Perhaps Eachan noted my dullness. In a moments lull, he remarked casually, "Eilidh will be on the mainland shortly. I wonder she goes away, she's so fond of the place but there's nothing for her here on Halasay; the crofting life is finished," adding, with a long look at me, "for most folk these days, unless they're dropouts from the south."

I paid attention, "She said London to me." Wondering momentarily if she went to join a friend down there, possibly a relationship, again neither of us had asked nor given any indication that we might have a partner. Our feelings towards each other had been so immediate and sacrosanct that with a touch of shame I pushed it out of my thoughts.

Eachan's powers of deduction didn't fail him. By his next comment I felt he'd read me. "Yes, she's got some fancy job down there. She's a scientist of course, graduated in Cambridge some years ago but I think she's not long back from doing research work in Siberia. Anyway, part of her work involves informing the government on some aspect of climate change. I'ts important work but I heard her say she's dealing with fools. They're not her type of folk and Hector boy it's a long way from the crofting style over here. Who knows, maybe there'll be a connection to bring her back." Over his glass he winked. My colour rose; by now I knew Eachan's quiet way of letting his meaning lie between the words. I smiled, "Who knows?"

He went on, "You see, she was born and reared on a croft on the north end of Halasay. The crofting life is in her but her folks are dead, quite a while back. Her brother has the croft. That's him over by the piano. Iain to name and a good hand at the cattle, a hardy chap I tell you."

Later, quite a little later, Eilidh's brother lifted down an accordion which sat, perhaps for reasons of safety, on the lid of a beer circled upright piano. Despite fingers which looked anything but those of the delicate handed musician, he put a lift in his playing I found irresistible, "O.K. if I try out the piano?" "Aye, give it the works," and with a straight look, "You'll be Eilidh's friend," his grip doubled my fingers together. "Good to meet you." I was taken aback at the speed of the island's information network but more than pleased to admit the friendship.

Iain struck an A chord; we were off, into a pipe tune. I hammered out harmony with the syncopation of a jazz band. We zipped through marches, jigs, stately Gaelic waltzes, music runs like a river in spate through Highland blood; following his playing was no problem. Old tunes, fast ones, slow ones, feet tapped, fingers drummed tables, "Give us, Donald MacLean's Farewell to Oban," or someone would call, "What about Headlands, or Crossing the Minch?" It appeared Iain could play to order. Drams arrived, bouncing on the piano lid. It seemed the barman could pour to order just as smartly. The crowd gathered round us. A little more encouragement from the bar; an impromptu ceilidh was building.

"Give us a song Eachan." The bar fell silent. I stopped playing. Somebody spoke to him in the Gaelic. I saw him nod, emptying his glass before standing. Quietly, with muted notes Iain accompanied him. The subtlety of its minor notes, the inflection in the old man's voice, I listened quite stunned, a truly beautiful tune. The last verse and Iain played through the tune slowly, bringing out all its exquisite charm. As clapping died away, I asked for the tune's name. At once Iain said its Gaelic name, 'Nighean Donn a'Chuainein Riomhaich.' "What does it mean?" He thought a moment and breaking into a smile which brought the look of his sister Eilidh into his eyes, he replied, "In the English it means, *the lassie with golden hair*." I looked down at the piano keys and thought of the woman I missed.

We played on. Musicians at full toot are hard to stop. Eventually Iain put down the accordion, "There you go Hector, we'll make a band yet. Take a look over sometime, Eachan knows the way alright." "You're on, Iain." We shook goodnight. The feeling of affinity, instinctive and reassuring, we shared the same race and back many generations, came of the same stock.

Leaving his stance behind the bar Angus MacLeod came to the door with us, detaining me with a nod. Eachan walked out of earshot and the hotelier spoke privately, "Hector, there was a man on the phone the other day, asking for you, I'm sure it would be yourself. You know I could be wrong but he said to me, 'Has a Hector MacKenzie arrived on your island recently?'

MacLeod laughed gently, "Now, I didn't just go with his tone, so I said, oh there's several here already. This is a busy place you know, they come and go. Which one will you be wanting? "

Having cut away completely from any previous life, I wanted no connections. Cursing inwardly at the message, I thanked him, "Don't be afraid to keep it vague, that's the way I like it" Shaking my hand as we parted, he assured me, "Vagueness, you're talking to an expert and I'll tell you what, the old piano hasn't sweated like it in years. Come in anytime."

"You've made it," Ella put bowls of soup on the table along with thick slices of home baking. It needed no enquiry as to the whereabouts of our venue, "Was The Castleton busy?" "Busy enough to please your cousin," replied Eachan, hoping that would halt the subject.

Ignoring that comment and addressing me, Ella countered with, "Eilidh phoned a little ago to say she was across in Oban, the ferry made good time. She wondered if you two had made as quick a journey back from The Castleton? What could I say?"

Eachan took on a vague manner. A mix of innocence, evasion and excuse which passed for an apology, "You see, Ella, we got a little involved. Your brother, Iain started playing the accordion, you know what the man's like, there's no stopping him, one tune leads to another,"

Eachan neatly deflected the blame and kept my name in the clear.

Ella put on a mock scold, "Each MacKenzie, I know too well who's the last to stop." Eachan let that pass. I concentrated on the soup, "And, Hector," she continued, "that man of mine would have you off the straight and narrow quicker than a blind horse would have you in the ditch."

I looked up, "Did Eilidh say she would phone back?" "No, she's away to her bed." The pleasure of the hours spent in The Castleton turned sour. Bitterness, sharp and painful. I should have realised she would phone. I had let her down and it hurt, badly. As women will, Ella noticed, "I told her I was sending you to Sandray," and nodding at Eachan, "to be out of harm's way. She said tell him to use my boat. I think she sounded a wee bit upset, tell him to take care whatever."

Eachan and I sat long after Ella bid us 'Goodnight'. After missing the phone call, it seemed a night to talk. We settled down with mugs of tea. I wanted to work round to asking about the practicalities of living on Sandray. I knew from Ella their daughters had all left Halasay; two were married in Australia, another nursing in New Zealand and the youngest married to a business man in Vancouver; grandchildren but no son, no pair of hands to take over the land. Eachan seemed in reflective mood. I hesitated to break into his thoughts but after a while I asked,

"What went wrong for crofting life? I've heard you say a few times it's finished." He gave no immediate reply. Somewhere, down on the shore, migrating redshank were whistling. Syllables, wild and sharp, until each call became fainter and fainter and just the sea remained.

"After they cut the Panama Canal, the ship loads of guano arrived. Centuries of sea bird droppings, solid stuff, they cut it off the cliffs of Chile and shipped it into Glasgow. That was the beginning of the nitrogen era, natural stuff the guano, but next came the Sulphate of Ammonia, a powder, but powerful, would grow grass, high as your knee, then after the war, they got to producing oil based nitrogen fertilizer. The clever lads in the Agricultural Colleges praised its use to high heaven and farmers couldn't see the advisors were really on the side of the public. Blinkered by the myth of increasing efficiency, farmers sent their sons to college; they came home stuffed with ideas that raped the land. They'd lost their love of the soil; it was the beginning of the end for a belief in natural fertility."

Our tea grew cold. That didn't matter, Eachan's ability to reduce an issue to its salient point was minimalist art in words. Frequently uncompromising, gleaned by age and observation, often spiced with a taste of an underlying philosophy, I could only describe it as a holistic view of life.

"Farmers grabbed the new systems of producing food. Hunted for higher profits, egged on by the degree brigade and commercial interests. Bigger farms, fewer people on the land, extractive chemical methods, intensive mono-cultural units; the old cycle of soil fertility, clover, livestock and dung was laughed out. Pesticides dealt with the soil bacteria and the wildlife and adulterated the food the public ate; no word of today's cancer epidemic Except in terms of the cost of environmental damage, which was discounted, food became cheap. No longer the item which swallowed the workers wages packet and it put the skids under the economics of crofting."

Though he spoke quietly, the force of words and cogency of argument was dramatic,

"The advent of this artificially cheap food allowed an expanding population to engage in superfluous activity; a world of consumer delights, build fancy houses, bigger and faster cars, time to play at tourism, fly to the beach. The gap between a natural world and what passes for civilisation widened to the degree that food has become a byproduct of the citizens' global playground with the wildlife driven into a corner."

There was no stopping him, "So the old systems were priced out, crofting included. But wait you, Hector boy, unbridle a horse and he'll canter about the field till the barbed wire cuts him. Hedonism comes at a price and that price is the killing of the environment upon which we depend. I took my pleasure from a turning furrow and the gulls at my heel but that's old hat. The new pleasures are on an escalator, a joy ride, so far without bound but the barbed wire's in sight. Shed off the responsibility of producing food, abandon any caring for all the other companions in life which share this planet with us, I tell you boy, it will end in the tears of destruction. Capitalism will kill the planet."

His face became old as the photo above the fireplace. He crossed to the dresser, "One for you and me, Hector," and handing me a glass, he said quite simply, "I heard the redshank calling out there tonight. It's a pity. The innocents will go down with the guilty."

Fired by the strength of Eachan's words, I spoke bluntly, "Do you think it's possible to live on Sandray, make it a home?"

He studied his glass, as I had seen him do before, "Yes, it's a kindly place, the water's pure, its fields lie to the sun and," his voice fell away to a sigh, perhaps a yearning for something lost in the sadness of knowing, "the old home has peace and freedom."

He drained his glass and brightened, "Forget the planners, damn regulations. Throw your mobile phone in the Sound. Yes, Hector boy, hard work and a good woman will make it a home."

Eilidh- I reached out to her, bridging the distance between us in thought.

CHAPTER TWENTY-ONE

Pay Off

The spacious dinning room of Glasgow's most expensive west end hotel was busy. Kilted gentlemen, portly and white kneed, sported a wide variety of tartans. Every clan, shade and hue seemed present from the heather dye of the Hunting MacSporran to the latest tartan off the drawing board, the mustard and purple Dress Walkers Shortbread. Subdued lighting picked out the silver buttons of Bonnie Prince Charlie jackets, bottle green and tight. Immaculate shirts, cuffs an inch below the sleeve and extra chins snuggled under lacy silk ruffs. Equally formal were the ladies. Long skirts clung expensive and shape revealing, tartan sashes sought to constrain the contents of tastefully matching blouses. No less than the great and the good, in some cases the not so good, were assembled for Scotland's premier Highland Ball. From the Lord Provost to the pick of the Nation's legal profession, not to mention baillies, bankers and just a sprinkling of lesser quality, every person of standing in the City was present.

Elaborately coiffured for such an occasion, the ladies when aided by the guile of soft lights, revealed hitherto unsuspected depths of glamour. The City's sun beds had been booked solid for weeks, not a cleavage but it hinted of topless abandon in the Seychelles. An attractive prospect for the taller men and in some cases a surprise to hubbies. All in all, a colourful spectacle awaiting the skirl of the pipes to march them, couple by couple, behind the Provost and his Lady from dining table to dance floor. One sharp squeeze of his bag and the piper roused the concourse with, 'A Man's a Man for a' That'. No fair hand to be seen without the sparkle of diamonds held high in genteel style as the handsome couples circled the dance floor in the Grand Parade, the termination of which tended to be the bar.

On a small dais a Scottish Dance Band twiddled with microphones, spaced out drum kit and speakers. Last minute pints were stashed discretely behind chairs. The fiddler asked for an A, the drummer rattled a drum or two, the leader tapped his mike, "Testing, one two, one two." All systems were live, "Lord Provost, ladies and gentlemen, take your partners please for the first waltz of the evening." The lead accordionist nodded round the musicians and struck C major. They launched into the placid notes of 'Annie Laurie'.

Dancers sallied onto the floor, a night of formal Highland reeling became a kaleidoscope of colour. Swirling kilts and elaborate steps circled the ballroom, elegant and decorous. The display inflicted upon proud tartans by the revolving balls of chequered light which shone down on the gracious couples was equally wondrous. Bold kilts oscillated between bright red and muddy brown, yellow tartans changed in rapid sequence from pea green to an outrageous purple. Even bald heads could be seen alternating red, blue and a ghastly grey. Many guests were affronted.

But the band had seen it all before, they'd played The Dashing White Sergeant when he was just a corporal. They knew full well by eleven, thanks to certain of the guests, best described as the coarser end of Glasgow society, dancers would be hollering for a rock-an-roll. Men of standing would have taken to lying down, jackets off; the ladies, their costly hair styles sadly bedraggled would be spotted hitching up long skirts and to appease the shouting the musicians would be forced to break into, 'Come on let's twist again'. It was nothing new to the band, nor did they doubt by mid-night and six deep at the bar, many bottoms would have been surreptitiously felt and twenty pound notes still showering the till like confetti at a toff's wedding.

"Will Sir take coffee in the lounge?" The Agent didn't lift an eye from his copy of The Sun newspaper. Several other papers also sprawled open across the table. The waiter, standing respectfully a little to his left, awaited a reply.

Oblivious to the Highland Ball, The Agent's eye rested on a newsprint headline,

'Hit and Run, Toddler Dies in Mother's Arms.'

Dishes long since cleared after each course, the cheese board alone remained to accompany a third carafe of vintage red which The Agent had demanded. At least the meal came up to standard. Indeed so satisfying that without noticing he belched loudly. The news, anything but satisfactory. Gulping more wine and scowling at the item, without speaking or looking up, he pointed at the dining table. Completely engrossed, he read and re-read the story.

"As you wish, Sir," and picking up the crumpled napkin from the carpet, the waiter hurrying to the kitchen, returned with a coffee tray. The last remaining diner, The Agent grunted and waved the waiter away. "The stupid bugger, botched the bloody job," he muttered aloud, absently pouring another wine, insensible to any music or dancing. 'The Sun' gave the most graphic account,

'BADLY INJURED MOTHER CRADLES DYING DAUGHTER.' A hit and run driver veered onto the pavement outside an East London kindergarten fatally injuring a four year old toddler and severely injuring his mother. The infant died as the pair lay on the pavement. The mother who herself suffered multiple injuries struggled to support her dying child until the ambulance arrived. The incident occurred as the mother and child were walking home from their local play group. The driver, who has not so far been identified, drove off at speed. A stolen car, thought to be the vehicle involved, was found abandoned three streets away. The mother is in intensive care but not thought to be critical. It is understood the woman works as a secretary in Government security and the police are at her bedside.'

"God, what next?" Only half a fucking job. If that cow squeals to the police?" He swilled his wine, "That bastard music's getting on my tit. For Christ's sake, I told him get the bloody woman first. A fifty-fifty job's no use, worse, when it's only the brat of a kid." He raved away to himself. "He needn't think he'll get paid. Two thousand down, he'll bloody well not see the other half, not a chance."

A half empty carafe, the coffee long cold, what to do? Tomorrow a ferry trip, out to some damned wilderness island. Those computer thick heads back at base had better have it right. He scanned the coded message again. Its gist, a person called Hector MacKenzie fitting the given description travelled to the island of Halasay on June 20th and has not so far left the island by any known form of transport. This man's whereabouts on that island are not known. As per instructions local police have not been informed. He folded the message, this needed thought.

Opening his wallet The Agent scanned the reservation, "The Castleton Hotel, Isle of Halasay. What the fuck place will that be? Wonder should I cancel this trip? Maybe better to be back at base in case this botched job needs handling at top level. Easy to say I discovered she knew too bloody much, the boss'll understand, it'll be a simple fix. He wouldn't believe her cock and bull story anyway." In spite of himself he laughed at the analogue. His smile quickly passed, that bastard music really began to annoy him

Coloured light beams still illuminated a dance floor now full of whirling kilts flying at thigh level. Tired of the constraints of long skirts, ladies bottoms gyrated and the dance band, rid of fancy reels and Petronellas, was letting rip. Their interval behind the bar was taking hold.

Leaving his newspapers littering the table, The Agent considered options. Hit the town? No bugger that, it'll be full of these insufferable bloody Scotch layabouts with their singsong voices. Nightcap? O.K. He swayed to his feet knocking over the half empty carafe. It spilled across the table and dripped onto the carpet. He laughed at it. So like blood. Good, he felt better.

Ignoring the mess The Agent made for the bar. Crossing the dance floor, he pushed between a leg flinging couple doing something approximating to The Charleston. A voice panted, "I say, do you mind?" "Yeah fucking matey I do and I'm not a wanker poncing about in a skirt."

A sweating barman eyed The Agent, "A large malt and ice, on room eighty-two." "I'm sorry Sir, don't you think you've had enough to drink?"

At that point a hand gripped The Agents elbow, "I think you owe the lady an apology." A large flush faced man swam into his sights.

"Don't you touch me Jocky boy." Two carafes of wine impaired his aim. The punched flew harmlessly past the dancer's ear. Two hefty guys materialised.

Sunshine and a splitting head awakened The Agent in room eighty-two.

Sir Joshua Goldberg, dressed only in an embroidered purple bath robe, reclined on a chaise longue, propping his back with oriental silk cushions. Erotic Indian carvings ran along the sofas mahogany sides to curl at the headrest into plump cherubic figures. Lion claw feet supported the significant bulk of a Knight of the Realm.

A spacious room, its discreet uplighting shone from behind palm tree greenery to illuminate massive tapestry drapes which covered the walls and the arched entrance to his bedchamber. Desert scenes of camel trains and turbaned nomads crossing trackless dunes towards lofty turrets and sun baked fortresses, the asceticism depicted somewhat in contrast to rich Turkish carpets providing luxury for Sir Joshua's bare feet as he padded about the apartment. Intricate patterns indicated the rugs were of unique design. Adding an erotic element to the sumptuous furnishings, from votary urns of glazed clay in each corner there wafted the heady scents of Arabia. Twenty-five stories up in a Manhattan penthouse no disquieting sounds from the unending traffic below, nor indeed the stench of diesel fumes were allowed to penetrate the exotically scented atmosphere. The ambiance of the apartment rivalling the opulence of a desert sheikdom lacked only date palms and a Palomino stallion.

The Scientific Advisor to Nuen reached for a grape from the Venetian bowl at his elbow. The bath robe fell open revealing Sir Joshua's thin legs and hairy paunch. He tapped a number into his mobile, "Nicky, so pleased to get you, sorry it's so late," he paused to listen, a smile crossing his face, "Yes, perhaps, why not taxi across for a night cap," and smiling wider as he listened again, "Well, if you're in that frame of mind, you never know. Yes Nicky, see you in ten minutes."

The advisor scratched his stomach, ate another grape and feeling for the remote control turned down the lighting to a flattering softness. This needed careful handling, on several fronts. He pulled his bath robe together as the intercom bleeped.

Nicky's voice sounded, "Come on up Nicky." Sir Joshua crossed to the door. His visitor came gushing into the apartment, slacks and open shirt obviously thrown on in a hurry. Towering over the rotund Goldberg, he bent and they embraced affectionately, "Josh, it's always a thrill to see you, and dressed so appropriately," he ran his hand down the scientist back

"Nicky, Nicky, behave," Sir Joshua disentangled himself, "there's a good chap, we must talk a little business," and patting the couch, "sit here and be good."

Nicky Fellows sat as he was told, casually draping an arm over his friend's raised knees. Tall and baby faced, dyed blonde hair, carefully crimped, a loose mouth weak and effeminate, his otherwise small and even features were marred by a slight boss-eye. One of the more influential board members at Nuen, he also directed the billion dollar funds of an international investment company with offices in London and New York. The pair had been friendly, on and off, for years.

Handing his companion a bunch of grapes, after a few pleasantries, Goldberg began cautiously, "I see Nuen shares have dropped nearly forty percent over the past three months. Chairman Andy is a very worried chap. It's rather a spectacular fall don't you think?"

Nicky smiled with feigned innocence. They might be close friends and fond of Josh as he was, the nature of his business intervened. Disclose nothing, trust nobody, "Yes, surprising isn't it."

"How far down d'you reckon they go, Nicky?" Goldberg drew up his knees a shade further allowing his robe to fall open a little. An excited Fellows moved closer, "Oh, maybe another twenty percent, I suppose they might drop to three dollars over the next week or so, once things start, who would know," he stroked Josh's leg.

Goldberg smacked the hand away and spoke harshly, "Look Nicky, when they hit a three dollar low I'll promptly call for an extra-ordinary meeting of the Board. I want a vote of no confidence in the Chairman organized and passed, without fail, before there's any chance of an outside rally," he leaned forward and caught Nicky's plump cheeks, "and, no fooling about, leave the buy back to me," and with a final tweak "rest assured it'll be your own interests."

Nicky pouted, "Joshy, don't worry," and coyly he slipped his hand under the bath robe, "you know Josh I'm always your big friend."

They sat silently for several minutes until with edginess Nicky drew away his hand. "But don't be greedy Josh, think of me." At that he became serious, "It's very, very high risk, took a heap of borrowing to get the price down, even to today's level. It's an art, Josh. Sell shares too fast, and all the noses are sniffing the wind. Might take another sale, then a small buy back to steady the price, before the big off load. You sure of your backing, if you get my nod?" and realizing he'd said more than was wise he stood up, glaring down on Goldberg, "This conversation hasn't happened, don't speak to me again about it."

Sir Joshua swallowed hard and nodded. Looking viciously at his host now squirming uncomfortably on the couch, Fellows added, "Make no mistake, Josh, I need a lot of fun out of this little run." There could be no doubting the menace. "Make one mistake my dear friend and you'll know where to find your paddle," Goldberg shuddered and straightened his legs

Fellows measured his words, "And I mean a lot for this little game, if not it's curtains for more than Anderson."

And catching Goldberg gently by the hand his guest turned to a wheedling manner, "Come on Joshy, cheer up, that's business over for tonight, now be a sport and we can be friends again."

Squeezing the Scientific Advisor's clammy hand, he drew him towards the bedchamber.

CHAPTER TWENTY-TWO

The Briefcase

At breakfast on the morning after my musical engagement with Eilidh's brother in The Castleton I'd disclosed my full ambitions to Eachan, "Maybe you'll think the idea's not practical but I fancy living on Sandray, I'd like to see the old house a home again." Approval was instant. "On you go, boy, you're the man for Sandray and good luck. I'll help you all I can," he'd said, unable to hide the enthusiasm of someone half his age. The prospect of Sandray being home once more to a MacKenzie after nearly a century fired Eachan's thoughts. No mention of Eilidh of course but as Ella sat porridge down before us I thought I spotted a hint of womanly knowing in her smile.

Whilst we ate I learnt that Eachan owned the old Sandray house and its byre. In Norse style his forebears and their cattle had lived in a longhouse for more generations than he knew and as the old man had told me with bitterness in his words, "My great grandfather was to lucky escape the Highland Clearances, Sandray was too remote for the landlord to bother about." The harsh treatment metered out to Highland families in the eighteen hundreds left an indelible mark.

English nouveau riche land owners and sometimes Clan Chiefs with the support of Church Ministers fearing loss of their stipends, had ordered Highland estates cleared of people. Border sheep farmers, able to pay higher rents than the indigenous population, moved their stock onto grazing left fertile by the cattle economy of droving days. People out, sheep in. Many families physically evicted from ancestral homes had thatched roofs burnt over their heads and cattle taken to pay arrears of rent. Listening to Eachan I realized that the minds of both those who escaped dispossession and those who filled the emigrant ships remained deeply scarred. The New World and the Antipodes got a blood transfusion and the Highlands got the destructive mono-culture of sheep.

All was not lost. In recognition of the parlous position of those remaining on the land Parliamentary legislation granted them the security of tenure for their crofts in perpetuity. Furthermore in many areas of the Highlands the Government took ownership of the land. Halasay, along with the whole of Sandray came under Government ownership and thanks to the guaranteed tenure, Eachan inherited from his father both the croft of Ach na Mara and Sandray. Significantly the tenancy of the island could pass to his successor. Little then did I appreciate this gem of information.

The old boy sat before a half finished plate of porridge. I knew the signs, his eyes focused on an inner scene and keen as always to share the view, he began, "The old house is in fair condition, plenty fit to live in. Tigh na Cala, that was the name my grandfather and his people before him had on it, House of the Haven. Tigh na Cala," he repeated it fondly, going on slowly, "If you follow those marks heading south across the fields, it's the track to what was once a clachan, you'll find plenty of foundations, aye and maybe still the odd gables standing. I haven't been over to that side of the island since we gathered the sheep for the last time and ferried them over here and that's how many years ago now Ella?"

His wife spread her hands on the table, "If you start a story now, Eachan, the rest of your porridge will be stone cold before you're half finished." Pretending annoyance, he put an old and worn hand over hers, "Quiet woman, I'm only telling the boy what he needs to hear. There's a burying ground on a cnoc up from the village, that's where your great grandfather's buried, him that was drowned out in the Sound. The clachan's almost buried as well. A southerly gale, takes the top off the dunes. My grandfather carted away the best of the stone, put gables to the Tigh na Cala, raised the walls, put on a new roof and so forth. What a pair of hands was on the bodach." Maybe hands follow families. As he spoke I looked from Eachan's to mine; certainly my own had some way to go before they would look as useful.

"That clachan, a dozen or more houses, there'd been people living in it I'm sure since thousands of years, probably since the Iron Age, there's standing stones out on a flat to the west. You see their land lay to the south, fine for the crops but the landing is exposed." The length of Eachan's stories being unpredictable, Ella poured a cup of tea and sat.

"Anyway it was the Viking that took it over. I dare say they thinned out the folks, but that south beach wouldn't have suited their longboats, the east side of the island has more shelter and its to there they went to farm. The outline of a Viking longhouse is there yet, easily seen by the overgrown mounds. Far bigger house than the Celts ever built. But the finest shelter on the island, yes and as good as anywhere in the Hebrides, is in the bay below the house where you're planning to live. You see, Tigh na Cala and the ground they farmed about it was a Viking homestead and according to the old grandfather, the original house was the hall of a chief."

He allowed that bit of folk lore to sink in, "You know and it could be in ourselves. The Norse weren't great for living in communities, they liked to have plenty land round about them and keep a mile or two between themselves and their neighbours," he winked at me, "except when there was a party on the go." I laughed and rose from the table.

No hesitation, that morning I started. Eachan responded immediately, "You'll need to take the tractor to Castleton." I plundered my bank card. All manner of tools, spade, pick and shovel, coils of piping to take water to the house, a surprise for Eilidh's return; food supplies, porridge oats high on the list; corned beef, packet soup, candles, outboard fuel, dozens of items, plus a pail of salt herring from Ella; all stowed under a bulging tarpaulin aboard Eilidh's sturdy sixteen foot dingy. She lacked the length of the 'Hilda' but could carry enough to keep me fed and busy for a month.

No telephone, mobile or modern means of contact. Slack water, middle-day, Eachan's final words were simple, "Watch the tides, put a white sheet out on the headland if there's any problem. That's the way they signalled across in my young days." He stood a moment, lifted a hand and turned away, his step heavy with thoughts. I sailed the Sound, into a new life.

Anticipation turned to excitement, any tiny doubts swallowed by enthusiasm. Up from Sandray jetty I lugged tools, supplies and the piping. By late afternoon the rolled out coils of pipe stretched along the track to a pool in the burn. My private water system would need a small dam, stone and concrete, maybe a settling tank. I poured water in the end of the pipe and ran down to the house. A dribble wet the ground at the gable. Gravitation worked! Two hundred yards of digging would put the pipe out of sight. Thirty yards a day? I laughed "Surely, Mackenzie, you're fit for that," and set to work.

Stripped to the waist, evening sun on a back already browned at Eachan's hay making and a breeze off the sea to keep me cool, I made a start. When the house stood dark against an ocean sunset, twelve yards of pipe had vanished into a trench. I straightened up and put my shirt over a now lean body. Working muscles relaxed. Disappearing fast were the ladylike hands of modern man, hard, rough lined hands would take their place, curl easily round a spade shaft with a grip to match. Add the pleasure of gaining strength and fitness, a stimulation to feed the mind and I was highly pleased. Four more days of digging and I laid aside pick and spade, fitted a rose on the pipe, soaped down and at the gable of the house danced naked with shock under a fountain of cold water.

I'd thought as I dug. Make a sustainable home with some modern comforts involved utilising sun and wind power effectively. The sun didn't always shine but when it didn't, generally the wind blew. Neither clocked up a meter. South facing roof, perfect, re-roofing, yes, some glass, extra light, solar panels, maybe photo voltaic tiles. In my wildest theory, I'd concentrate sunlight through lenses, make steam, drive a generator. Enthusiasm galloped away with me, it would be a sunshine home, sunshine, we only use one percent of it. What falls on three percent of the world's deserts would power the planet, a fraction of world expenditure on armaments could do the trick.

Next day- better still, build a small turbine system further up the burn at a point where its waters fell vertically over a ledge. A fall of twenty odd feet meant power, especially given winter rainfall. Electricity at the flick of a switch, controlling the voltage, no problem in today's technology. Fridge and washing machine, maybe there'd be a T,V. signal; on reflection no television but for certain there'd be light and heating. 'Unlimited clean power', the phrase resounded in my head. I had heard it before, in a meeting in London.

One evening I climbed excitedly to the spot which might just suit a mini-hydro electric project. Clear from the hill, falling and twisting, stones and boulders, over a rock shelf the burn poured into a chasm so narrow I guessed only a sun nearing the end of day would intrude. Lank grass hung over steep rock walls which enclosed its sides, thick cushions of moss, bright and green grew thick on ledges where churning water kept it moist. I stood at the edge of a deep pool. My grand scheme would require a small building to house the turbine and a three inch pipe from a dam at the top of the waterfall to feed this mini-power station. Controlling its output, not difficult, wiring my new home whilst avoiding damage to its wooden tongue and grove lining, more tricky.

The constant hiss of falling spray; I listened, it sang of the wildness of hill places. The last rays from a sunlit horizon glistened on wet rock. Dankness brightened. Rich mosses were the furnishing of a grotto hidden in a little green world of the wee folk. A sudden updraft from off the sea blew tumbling waters into the air. The rhythmic splash, splash ceased. Rocks and water and a streak of sunshine turned the falls to a cascade of yellow droplets. In the seclusion of this tiny piece of the earth's crust the elements which gave us the power of creative thought had built beauty. How easy for me to contemplate harnessing the innocence of a waterfall, destroy its simplicity. The wind dropped as suddenly as it arrived and the spray of water fell again into a dark pool and with it my plans vanished into fresh understanding. Progress cuts a wide swath. How did the old folk manage, ten children and no washing machine? I stripped off and stood under the falls. Racing back to the house, drying in the breeze, electricity couldn't match an inner radiance.

A food supply and how best to tackle the land, bring it back into production. My forebears possessed the knack. Relearning it by trial and error might take seasons of success and failure. Eachan would know. Marks on the field I'd trenched across to bury the water pipe followed a series of corrugations, distinct humps, maybe two yards wide. Horse plough or hand work? Digging through the humps turned up soil, black and rich, the sweat of caring generations. A foot down I came into sand and broken shell, the work of wind and tide. Good soil and sunlight could put warmth and energy into food via a poly-tunnel. Sheltering any structure from winter gales would be a challenge. It would grow our basic needs. Already I thought as 'we'.

Would it really be possible to exist on Sandray without the latest props of modern living? Millions in the west were changing from iPods to iPhones, calculators to computers, building interaction with high tec. chips, wrapping their lives around face book, blogging and twittering, talking by text, sharing their existence with the growing dictatorship of an overarching network of manipulative communications and gadgets which replaced self reliance; a fast growing network of social influence increasingly subject to political interference and subterfuge. The more I experienced the interplay of observation, common sense and the ability to improvise, the more I respected the resourceful intelligence of previous generations. No pressing buttons for help or information, they had relied on sharp wits.

Falling into the new pattern of living couldn't have come more easily to me. Apart from the drone of an occasional plane heading for Heathrow, no artificial noise, no need of time keeping. I'd put my watch on a kitchen shelf, didn't need it. My stomach and a glance at the sky told me a midday snack was due. Keeping tally of the days presented more of a challenge. I started a note book. Jottings soon filled pages. The birdlife which caught my attention, sketches of flowers strange to me, the activity of the seals, cloud formations and their relevance to the next day's weather. After an evening meal I wrote and drew, adding the thoughts which had occurred as I worked. Two candles on the table gave surprising warmth and turned the kitchens bareness to friendly shadows.

A week of heavy work passed without any outside contact. Alone, the island to myself and not a shred of loneliness,

I learnt the meaning of peace. It seeped into me, altering my state of mind. There were no tensions left, only an infusion of supreme contentment. And strange as it may sound, I knew a companionship with the island. The weather changing its mood from happiness to discontent, affected me. Elation, when streaks of sun lifted the morning mist, dullness on a day of raw drizzle. Distant thoughts came as dark cloud shadows flitted across the face of the Hill of the Shroud, or became black forms racing over the sea before the emerald sun returned. The life of the elements became intimate, comforting as a heartbeat.

And each night I blew out the kitchen candles and went to my tent. Sleeping in Eilidh's bed seemed presumptuous, nor had I ventured into her bedroom. The door stood open, there was nothing to prevent me and yet, strangely to do so suggested an infringement of her privacy, the taking for granted of an inviolable trust. Our being together, in spite of its brevity, seemed to me an unshakeable bond; still we were independent, uncommitted individuals and that I respected.

My brief case remained a stained leather object against the gable wall, its cut straps dangling. Feelings conflicted, would I destroy it, burn it, along with its cursed contents? Several times I'd hesitated, about to go in and take it, yet a reluctance to break some sort of connection prevented any action. In the recent convoluted events, this brief case had proved the key to my meeting Eilidh, central to the enigma of our finding each other. Obviously Eilidh had brought it here, to this house and to that I attached respect but surely no strategy on her part could have placed the case back within my grasp. Foresight maybe, intuition possibly, how could she believe I'd phone that number or take the ferry? The brief case's return to me had to be outwith any form of deliberate plan on her part. Yet Eilidh's words on the tube train, 'We shall meet again' rang with certainty beyond a simple hunch. In the quiet of nights alone, remote from any contact save the sound of the elements I began to believe there might be powers of another world of communication.

One shelf of the dresser carried an unusual collection of books. Somebody of catholic taste mixed Walter Scott, Conrad, and O.Henry's short stories, with Bertrand Russell's, History of Western Philosophy and Kauffman's, At Home in the Universe. Alone, I read by candlelight. The wind rustling at the door, fluttered yellow light across the pages. Words quivered with fresh meaning. The ideas, theories and passions generated by the writer's thoughts, fed my own imagination like a stream of energy. Within the interwoven strands of force which mediate all known connections, did one strand rove the extrasensory? Each night, I looked through the open door at Eilidh's blankets, neatly folded, at the end of an iron bedstead and I talked to her.

In a kitchen cupboard I'd found a tent and sleeping bag. Beside the west gable of the old house where the short cropped grass smelt of earth, I'd pitched camp. My clothes made a pillow and through an open tent flap before sleep, I could watch and listen to the life of the bay. Sometimes the querulous bickering of oystercatchers as they poked amongst the seaweed, and as darkness closed, often the whistling of birds passing unseen, perhaps migrants heading south by the compass of the stars, maybe the same earth's magnetism which brought them to this island. Breathing the scent of the sea my eyes would close, I'd drift into sleep feeling an affinity with others' lives whose activities were equally as important to them, as was mine, to the conscious perspective of survival.

One night I wakened to the clamour of geese and clear on the thin air, the flapping of many wings. I arose to watch. The tip of the moon dipped into the Atlantic and gliding out of its dying glow many dark bodies emerged, bird after bird. Momentarily they hung with beating wings before dropping to earth. Voyagers from the Arctic, they came to rest out on the headland. At first light a restless chorus told me they were leaving. Squadrons formed high above me, long necks pointing south and the morning sun, still below my horizon, gleamed on their white under parts.

No light dimmed the October stars, nor when the night was fine, tarnished the image of our own galaxy, for it stretched in a great sway of brilliance across the still Atlantic. I lay imagining its magnificent shape from another point in space. I looked down on the curls of a giant spiral galaxy. A hundred billion stars, a hundred thousand light years across, an immensity beyond our grasp; and yet in its vastness no bigger a part of the colossus of all the created heavens than a coiling ammonite shell on the prehistoric beaches of this tiny, tiny speck we call earth.

Watching the patchwork of countless galaxies emerge from the darkening abyss of outer space brought an unusual feeling of intimacy. Within the source of their flickering light hid a mysterious world of quasi-particles, an infinitesimally small electro-magnetic domain of particle collisions. The creation of particles whose lifespan, as a parcel of energy, decayed and transformed on timescales equally minute as the timescale of cosmic change is immense. And still by some means a vast integrated system of interchange between matter and energy existed in unending realms of birth and annihilation. What and where its pulse?

On clear nights, I slept under the open sky, beneath another electro-magnetic realm; gigantic beyond calculation, equally full of collision, monstrous cataclysms ripping apart stars and their galaxies, warping time and space. I came to see the micro and macro were the same system, bonded in fantastically varying degrees of density, of energy and movement, time and distance. Not before had I realised it so clearly or simply. Be it the space and attraction between an electron circling a mother atom or the sun nursing its planets; be it our own Milky Way holding onto satellite galaxies, or the immeasurable galaxies swirling above me, one about the other in an expanding universe, was attraction and repulsion the ultimate synergy? The pulse which drove all universes? If so, what and where its heart?

Each evening I took an unhurried stroll down to the jetty to check Eilidh's boat lay snug. That night, for the tide was full, she floated clear of the stone work and I pulled her alongside to bail out an afternoon's heavy showers. With their clearance, came a crispness. The autumn air held its breath and utter stillness engulfed a bay whose placid surface remained as luminous as the afterglow of some great stratospheric happening.

I sat in her stern, unwilling to disturb a mirror of the surrounding island, afraid to break an image created by the elements to which my consciousness owed its being. The closeness of the stars, all about me, the air I breathed, its purity, the calmness of the night, its beauty born from the furnace of the stars, perhaps some gigantic supernova in the ever changing universe. A shiver passed over me, as though I were to be privy to the unfolding of secrets not given to mortal understanding. No movement, no bird cried into the deepening night. Alone, my breathing only, I waited. And from the shoulder of the Hill of the Shroud the light grew, until golden tipped, the moon cast its shapely peak across the water, a momentous shadow, unstoppable as the play of light on a fragile mirror.

No tendril mist to hide a far-off shore, an island peak reached out, its dimensions crept towards me. Where lay the haven of its power, the phantom of its consciousness? I watched the stars live a second on the still, black bay, a reflection of their span in the scale of cosmic birth and death.

Photons falling, incandescent from a dark vellum, Electrons, atoms, planets, suns and spiral galaxies, matter a fragile skeleton for their energy. If universe circles universe, born to crash and die, what place have we?

I reached into an abyss, greater, deeper, more penetrating than earth's paltry night, a blackness elemental and absolute. The Universe became a spiral, spinning tighter, faster, tighter, faster, ever tighter, until a density beyond the laws of science law crunched mass to energy, heat and energy to the n'th degree, the forge of creation.

And yet is there a war of oscillating universes? Dark energy versus gravity, matter against antimatter, attraction or repulsion, expansion everlasting or contraction to oblivion, is there a dualism eternal where victory is annihilation? No, in domains of quantum gravity density curves time and space, grinds time to an instant that is the limit of all dimension. The speed of spin defies the crush of gravity and time and space burst free.

Burst free from a singularity, rupture the rotating orifice, through which all has passed and all will pass as the bundled twists of space which are the base of energy, infinitus. Understanding is the anvil on which imbalance heats the singularity, entwining knowledge is the energy, the powerhouse of the heavens. Of all the universes that have been and all that are to be, imagination is the pulse which drives their beating heart. And at their heart is still the mystery of infinity.

The Hill of Shroud looked down, a lonely hunched dark form and at the dead of night it wore a silver crown.

A redshank whistled from across the bay and I waited at the edge of understanding.

CHAPTER TWENTY-THREE

"There's no depth to them."

The Agent sprawled across three seats in the ships lounge, groaning. The motion felt bad enough, add in that sing song jabbering in a foreign language and these bloody islands! The whole scenario was getting to him. This ferry crossing was hideous. A group of English tourists at his back waxed loud and profound about the consummate attraction of the Hebrides. The Agent raised his head, "You lot must be off your trolley. Who the hell would stay out here for a second even if they had to sleep on a bench on the Thames Embankment?"

The shock of his comment sank in, "We've been coming here for years; its lovely, we just love these Scotch people and their scenery... well, it's out of this world." "It bloody well should be, and the damned Scotch as well," The Agent snarled, his hatred of all things Scottish deepened, grinding his already queasy guts. He rose, barely making the ship's toilets. A steward helped The Agent back to his seat, "Don't worry Sir, I'll clean up." "Yeah, can't your fool of a captain keep the boat still?"

Green faced and in the foulest humour, The Agent came gingerly down the gang plank. "Get me to the Castleton Hotel," he barked at the young man handling the ships ropes, "Are there no taxis here?" "No I'm sorry, he's away just, the man that has it."

The Agent's face twisted, "Where is this hotel?" The young chap seemed in no hurry to reply. "I said, where is this place?" Looking into The Agent's eye without a waver, the reply came equally deliberately, "That's no problem, it's only a step or two, at the top of the street." Glaring at the young man, The Agent snapped, "I'm not used to insolence, you'll hear more of this, what's your name and company number?" A slight grin appeared before the pier hand replied, "Ach we don't worry much with numbers, everybody about here knows me," and he flicked the ships rope off a bollard. Walking stiffly up the brae, The Agent spoke aloud, "Cheeky young bastard."

Signing himself into the Castleton Hotel involved little thought. He scribbled, David Williams, Lymetree Gardens, Swansea. A wry smile crossed his face, it happened to be an alias he found amusing. Years back Mr. Williams owed him money, refused to pay up and strangely enough was killed in a hit and run accident. The hotelier's wife showed him up to a bedroom overlooking the bay. He glanced out. The wake of fishing boats in from the Minch spread silver ripples, shore to shore, in the late evening sun. With a flourish he drew the curtains and snapped, "What time's dinner?" "Just when it suits you, Mr. Williams, there's no hurry."

The green bile of seasickness left The Agent weak. He dumped himself on the bed, not before noticing dust on the bedside table. He wakened after nine, got to his feet, opened the only other door in the room, "For God's sake, a bloody cupboard, no ensuite." Chain chairs, jug and wash hand basin on the dresser, "What a dump." He strode down creaking stairs to find the dining room empty.

Pushing through various doors, he landed in an echoing passage, lino on the floor and beer kegs stacked against the wall, "Fuck me, not more of that bloody Scotch music." The strains of an accordion reached him. He opened the end door to find himself behind the bar.

Faces lined the counter, glowing from salt air and elbow exercise, "Hello, Mr. Williams, you missed your way but you came aground in the right place. What can I get you.?" Hotelier MacLeod seemed not the least surprised. The Agent's manner changed abruptly. He needed co-operation.

"No, no, let me and give these chaps a round on me," he insisted. "They've had a hard day I'm sure. I watched boats coming in from the bedroom, a fascinating sight." He smiled down the line of local faces. In due course glasses were raised to him. "Put it on my room. Something for yourself, Mr. um, Mr.?" "No I'm fine just now thanks," Macleod didn't supply the name but added, "Where would you like your supper, er, dinner?" It flashed through The Agent's mind, one more note from that bloody instrument and I'll, I'll, but no.... with an ingratiating smile he replied, "I'd be happy amongst the crowd, local colour you know, perhaps a table towards the back?"

A steak arrived inch thick and pouring with gravy, worth the racket all round him. A large dram appeared, one of those fishing types he guessed, raising it to the crowd at the bar. His ear caught an English voice at the next table and nodding across The Agent queried affably, "Over here on holiday?" "Oh no, I live here now, quite a native, ten years you know. You on holiday?" and without waiting for an answer, "I'm Trevor by the way, like myself you're from London, I can tell. It's the accent you know, can't hide it old chap."

Thinking fast, "Well I'm actually here on work and pleasure. I'm an archaeologist," The Agent laughed, "for my sins." "Oh really, how awfully interesting," the new native pulled across his chair, "don't mind if I join you? By the way, didn't catch the name."

The Agent made space, "David," he replied grudgingly after a second's thought whilst filling his mouth with steak. Blast that accordion spoiling the meal. It'll give me indigestion and now this prat beside me. A youngish girl began to sing, the bar fell silent, "What language is that?" enquired The Agent in as mild a voice as he could muster. "Oh that's Gaelic, I'm trying to learn it. All oks, ochs, I should say, very difficult to get the right sounds you know, Davie." "I can believe that," The Agent commented dryly as her song ended to enthusiastic applause.

They chattered about London. Getting busier, not what it used to be, too many foreigners, illegal types, through the Channel Tunnel and all that carry on. Barely drawing breath, The Agent's companion spoke with a penetrating voice, "Wing a few, that's what I'd do, stop 'em in their tracks, you know. Johnnie foreigner, a lot of scroungers, no sooner in good old Blighty than they're getting more benefits than you and I'll ever sniff. And this stupid Human Rights that they shelter behind. Human Rights, don't get me started. Wing 'em when they come out of the tunnel, that's what I say."

He rambled on, obviously pleased to have the company of a fellow Londoner and someone who appeared to listen, "Used to do a bit of shooting when I was down there, sadly not illegal immigrants, ha,ha. No, pheasant mostly, the odd partridge, getting scarce of course, not really much up here in the sporting line. Mostly I go to the mainland, friends've got an estate in the Highlands, he used to be a newspaper editor, I drop the odd stag, you know, it's quite fun. No, I have to content myself, I just wander along the beach below my house when the mood takes me. I have to say migrating curlew make the best sport."

Between you and me," The Agent's new confidante leant closer, spoke a little more quietly, "I pulled off a nice one in The City and here I am. Bought a rundown croft, let the local chappie have a few sheep on it," and laughing loudly, "saves me cutting the grass, you know." The Agent struggled to appear interested but on reflection it occurred to him this conceited fool might be the very man to give him information he'd never prise out of these damned evasive locals.

"Strictly between ourselves, I've a nice little income, David, stacked up a good pension, indexed of course, saw the stock market crash coming, cashed the chips and bingo! Living's cheap, here, locals are helpful, if you buy them the odd dram. Mind you I have to say, that's beginning to change, they're not so friendly as they were, incomers arriving all the time you see, rather a pity I have to say," and lowering his voice, "I'm not racist, absolutely not, David, never have been but last week a Pakistani couple came off the ferry, I tell you," holding up his hands the man from Bow Bells emitted a hollow laugh.

The Agent signalled the bar with a snap of his fingers. It took several attempts before the barman stood at his elbow, "You took your time. Bring two large malts, put them on my room," and picking up their conversation, "Funny you should mention incomers, I heard of a chap who came up here from London just a month or two back- scientist bloke, I wonder"

His voluble new friend cut in, "Oh yes, I heard about him," he put a finger to the side of his nose, "the good old grapevine never fails in these parts you know, they're a nosy lot really. Yes, he's over on that island south of here, Sandray they call it, desolate place, full of Viking ruins, graves and such like, of course the locals don't care about them as you'd expect, too busy counting sheep droppings, but you'd find it absolutly fascinating." Their glasses emptied rapidly.

The London crofter put his hand on The Agent's arm, "I must tell you, I happen to have a speed boat, just a little fun thing, do a spot of fishing you know, don't catch much, but it's amusing you know. I'd be happy to run you over anytime, tomorrow if you like, here's my mobile number. Don't ring before ten, ha,ha. I say would you care for another snifter?" He waved to the bar, held up his glass and pointed to it. They waited. Had the barman noticed? "This happens quite a lot you know, especially when I'm here with my friends. I often think that fellow's blind, the service here can be gharstly and he owns the place, always talking to those fishermen at the counter. It's so rude." Trevor stood up and waved. MacLeod nodded and after an interval another round arrived.

"I'm so glad we met, David you said, didn't you? I have to tell you, Strictly entre nous of course, I get a mite tired of these locals, always talking sheep and cattle, that's all right in its place, but there's absoluty no depth to them, know what I mean?" the ex-pat rattled on. "Their music's worse, no tune, so repetitive, once you've heard one you've heard the lot. Sometimes a bloke comes in with bagpipes. Well, I must say when that squealing starts I have to leave, how's that for business. Used to play the piano myself, just for friends of course," and pointing to the piano at the other side of the bar, "that old instrumen'ts well past its sell by date, wouldn't dream of touching it with a barge pole. Do you play anything David?" and without waiting for a reply, "I'm a bit of an opera buff myself, never missed a new production at Covent Garden. You've been there of course."

The Agent groaned inwardly, he'd dealt with this type before. If they're going to be any use, you have to string them along and this buffoon could certainly be put to use.

From behind the bar Angus MacLeod watched them thoughtfully. He was a shrewd judge of his fellow man. All sorts of characters, shades and persuasions passed through the swing doors. It clicked, Williams was the man with a London voice enquiring on the phone for Hector MacKenzie.

Two o' clock, closing time, "Drink up please." MacLeod took a few more orders and the bar slowly emptied.

The Londoners shook hands and parted firm friends, "Davie, old pal, phone me in the morning," and slapping The Agent on the back, "not before ten, absolutely not, ha,ha."

"Be delighted, Trev."

The steadying hand of the hotelier guided The Agent to his bedroom.

David Williams is not quite what he claims to be thought MacLeod, closing the door.

CHAPTER TWENTY-FOUR

Morning coffee

After a midday snack of oat cake and cheese I sat on the stone by the door writing out my scribbled words of the previous evening. Sounds carry far over calm water and my attention drifted from the note pad to the high pitched whine of a powerful outboard engine. Occasionally a fishing boat steamed past the island homeward bound from the Atlantic. Riding low in the water with a heavy catch on board, they'd be pushing a hefty bow wave and if the day was still I'd even feel the throb of their engines.

This was different. I looked up and listened. Seconds later a twin engine speed boat banked in from behind the headland and planed across the bay with a curve of flying spray. It stopped suddenly just yards of the jetty. A mound of wake rolled onto the beach, panicking the seals and sending gulls squawking to the hill. A peaked cap bobbed over the Perspex shield and taxied the craft alongside the jetty. After some heaving a man managed to get himself onto the landing.

Shouting voices reached me. "I'll be a least couple of hours, Trev, I've got your mobile punched in. If it's O.K. I'll bell you when I'm finished." The reply from a man at the throttle floated across, "Alright by me, David, absolutely no problem. I'll maybe throw out the odd hook, smack the water for a shark, you know." I heard laughs. "Won't come over till you bell. It'll only take minutes to nip across for you."

Outboards screamed to full throttle. Reverberations echoed round the bay. A couple of revs and with a flourish which left a wide arc of curling water, the nose of the craft lifted and it planed round the headland with blue smoke pouring from the stern. Before a succession of waves swept onto the beach, operator and speed boat had vanished. The man who'd come ashore stood looking carefully at Eilidh's boat before walking the length of the jetty, deliberately studying all around him.

A vicious feeling of possession overcame me. Furious at the intrusion and especially the manner of arrival, it took much restraint to stop my walking smartly down to challenge this uninvited visitor. A fortnight here and already the island was mine. I hadn't missed a telephone, definitely not the T,V, surely I wasn't becoming a recluse? The rearrangement of my priorities had been startling; the change in a sense of values, dramatic. It took a moment or two before I steadied enough to realise that this sense of ownership, compelling as it felt, had no basis except in emotion. Deciding the man couldn't have spotted me, I stepped into the house, closed the door and sat down to calm myself. From the window I could see him staring down at the dingy. His behaviour struck me as odd. What was he weighing up? Inner rage gradually turned to a palpable unease.

The Agent watched the speed boat roaring away, "A bloody fool, but useful," he muttered, "seemed to think this is where this MacKenzie bastard is holed up." He stood some time looking down at the wooden dingy moored carefully to the jetty; umm, if this is the man I'm after.... his mind already hunting possibilities for dealing with him. Hope to hell he's alone. It's quiet enough, but what a God damn awful place, fucking ghastly, bloody seals and birds and miles of bugger all. No sane creature would come here unless they'd a hell of a lot to hide. That means this bastard could be dangerous." Checking under his left armpit and still grumbling, he walked deliberately up the track from the jetty to the house.

A sharp rap on the door. I didn't hurry. It came again, more heavily. I opened the door to a man who stood well to one side. Medium height, thinning hair; a heavy, ill- featured face and indoor pallor. Out of puffy black circles, small hooded eyes, attentive and penetrating, flicked over me. Collar, tie, jacket and slacks, city clothes, casual but expensive, a raincoat over his arm. An official? Instantly he meant London, tube trains, politicians, their duplicity and implied threats.

Having rapped smartly on the door, The Agent stepped deftly out of direct line. Nothing. He knocked again. After several minutes, a tall man opened the door. An obvious look of displeasure, if not arrogance on a bronzed faced. Immediately, before uttering a word The Agent sized him up, young, athletic, this bugger could be quick and strong. Play it easy, "Good morning. Hope you don't mind me calling. Not intruding, am I?" and with a sweep of his arm, "It's such a beautiful island, lucky you." He followed with a gracious smile, "D'you live here?"

The 'toffish' accent at once struck me as false, however I relaxed a little, "Good morning, yes, it's a bonnie place on a good day." Ignoring his question, I awaited his next comment.

The Agent considered carefully.... I need to get into the house... and reaching out his hand. "My name's David Williams, do hope this isn't being a bother to you, but perhaps you might be able to help me? I'm an archaeologist, for my sins. You local by any chance? I've got a map here," and looking pointedly into the house, "I wondered perhaps if you might give me some directions?"

Out of good manners I shook hands to find he had a remarkable grip. Archaeologist? I wondered. He didn't strike me as a man involved in digging. The chap began struggling to open a map he'd taken from his raincoat pocket. Perhaps out of curiosity, I invited him into the kitchen. "I'm just about to have a coffee, would you care for a cup?"

"Why not, don't mind if I do. O.K. if I use your table for the map." No point in waiting for an answer from this surly bugger and spreading his map on the table, The Agent sat himself down. "What a fine little place you've got here, nice and quiet. Sorry, I didn't catch your name, not another MacKenzie by any chance?"

I busied myself at the Calor gas stove, fending off his direct question with a laugh, "Oh, well, Mr. Williams there's as many MacKenzies in these islands as I'm sure there's Williams in Wales," and washing the cups with my back to the visitor, "Sorry I've only powdered milk."

Bastard isn't going to tell me his name, same as that evasive clown I spoke to on the phone. The Agent's eyes swivelled round the room. What a shitty little hell hole. Bare boards and an old stone sink. Galvanised pails, wooden shelves, who the hell? Only a wanted murderer would shack up here. He stared through the open bedroom door. God save the Prince of Wales. His heart bounded. A briefcase against the wall, cut straps and battered looking, dark stains.

That's it, that's it! Oh you beauty, this is the man, that's the briefcase. By Christ there's something special in it when it landed in this crazy joint. No wonder that bloody politician seemed so keen. 'Get the case,' he told me, 'the man is your own affair.' Torture or elimination, I never knew one of these top political sidewinders that ever took the risk or the rap, always just a nod, do what's needed. The creeping louse will pay for this little trip. This is going to be the real thing.

I turned to put the coffee cups on the table, "I'm afraid there's only oatcake." I stopped in mid sentence. The man's eyes sparkled, tiny dots, glittering out of the flush of bright scarlet which covered his face. Intense and cunning, I thought of a stalking fox. The look lasted only seconds before he glanced down to the map, pointing with a thick finger, "Forgive me, I've just made a brilliant discovery. You see this headland? It's possible, according to my information, that this may well be the site of a Viking ship grave. By the way here's my card."

The Agent fumbled through the numerous cards in his wallet. I must get the bugger out of the house. Finding the card, thank Christ for that, he smiled and handed it across the table. Sipping the coffee, "Thanks for the unexpected 'elevenses,' saved the day. No, I won't have an oatcake, but thanks. Got to watch the old weight you know." This is the foulest piss I've ever had to drink.

I read the card, 'Professor David Williams, B.Sc. (Archaeology). Advisor to The Commission for Ancient Monuments. Maybe. I'd seen plenty of professional cards. This one struck me as bogus. Looking up, I became aware that whilst studying the map he was actually watching me closely. The unease which I'd first felt when seeing him land, grew to a tautness.

Outside, the day lost its early brightness, the dullness of a pending change. Flurries of a wind from the east rattled the bedroom window. Getting up from the table I closed the door. The man's eyes flickered, his face hardened.

Instinct warned me, this visit is not what it seems. Weather's worsening. I must get him off the island, pronto. The horrifying thought of his being stuck here, perhaps days. No, no. Should I offer to run him back to Halasay? Force the issue? "It's slack water about midday, after that I'm afraid the weather will soon make for a dangerous crossing, especially as winds away round to the east. Is your boatman due back shortly? If not, I would run you over the Sound, really, I mean as soon as possible."

The Agent jumped to his feet. Action, exhilaration, this job will need to be an out-door one, "Yes, yes, I see what you mean. I say, would it be too much trouble if you could possibly show me out to this Viking site. I must report something back to base you know," he gave a little laugh, "just a quickie, would tell me if it's significant enough to recommend an exploratory dig."

Exploratory dig! Rage swept me. If this were true, the sanctity of a thousand years would be uprooted, desecrated by a gang of dilettantes who'd put their 'finds' in some museum remote in feelings and location. No matter how remote in time, these graves were my people and my kinship with them a profoundly spiritual matter. Utter distaste, even fury, must have shown on my face.

Getting this man out of here was paramount, "Yes, of course I'll come down with you to the headland and then, if your man isn't showing up we can make straight for my boat." To leave the man in no doubt I added, "Before it gets too stormy." "Of course, of course," the man agreed. A peculiar glow shone from his eyes. The atavistic glint of intense hunger? Or premeditation?

A tingling came over The Agent, prickling the nape of his neck. He shivered as if an electric charge passed into his body, lifting his hair. The sensation thrilled him. He ground his teeth, felt a primitive desire to pounce. His palms sweated a little; a tightness in his head. He moistened his lips. I'll have this arrogant bastard beg for mercy. Just watching his face, that'll be lovely, seen it before, better than sex anytime. I'll make this one last, have him on his knees, crying like a baby.

I walked quickly, very quickly. Ruffled by the wind, small white wave tops crossed the bay. I veered towards the headland, increased my pace. The man didn't leave my heel. I heard his raincoat flapping but didn't turn. My back felt desperately unprotected.

This fucker thinks he can tire me out. No way. By God, he'll find who goes first. What a place, better than I could have arranged. The wind, the wildness, the prospect of fun, it all fuelled The Agent's intense excitement. He trembled.

Already clouds were becoming leaden streaks, their edges tattered and sailing. Cold gusts winnowed through the brown grass of autumn. Moss on the stones, now grey. Barrenness flowed over headland. "This is all there is to show you," I stood beside the man amongst the Viking burial stones. My nerves stretched taut. Evil surrounded me, in the wind, the very taste of the air. I became acutely alert, "I think we should hurry, before the tide turns."

"Don't worry my friend," the man's voice, high pitched and rasping, "you won't need to hurry where you're going."

It pressed into my spine. Hard and boring, twisting, forcing. I knew immediately. "Walk, you clever bastard." Ten paces. I balanced on the edge of the cliff. The gun moved up my spine. It stopped. Pressed into my neck. "Now isn't that a bonnie sight, just what a bloody Scotch twat like you would call it, Mr. Hector, cocky, MacKenzie."

Surging waves frothed onto the ledges two hundred feet below me, dark, licking, awaiting. In a hissing voice the man spoke, "What a pleasure this is for me to be able to offer you a choice. Very decent of me." His laugh more of a screech, "Which do you prefer, a jump without a parachute or the bullet first? Wait, wait, I'll be kind to you, I'll give a brave Scotch bastard like you a chance."

Now," he screamed, "down on your fucking knees."

Pressure. Click.

An uncoiling spring, I swung, hit him, the back of my wrist across his neck. Crack, a violent burning on the side of my head.

The man swayed, moments passed. Attempted to grab me. Missed.

I stumbled, clawed at grass. It gave. Came away in my hands. I slithered over the edge, stared into space, the chasm of imminent death.

In slow motion, I began to fall. Time slowed. Eilidh came to me. I saw her again, her eyes in mine, talking to me.

The man pitched forward, his eyes bulging with the terror of death. He hurtled past me, arms flailing, floating almost, his raincoat spread by the wind.

Screaming, falling headlong, down, down. I heard the thud. The crunch of bone.

I slipped down the rock, my whole body pressed against it. Torn fingers searched for hand holds, feeling over a cold wet surface, gripping the tiniest roughness. Slowly, five feet, ten feet.

Suddenly my hands lost their hold. Faster, faster. In the terror of death the sweetness of life came to me with an overwhelming sadness. My boots caught something. I fought to hang on.

Legs buckling with fear, wind buffeting the narrow ledge. This, the end of a glorious saga? Hopes, ideals, all tomorrow's promise brought to a futile end below a Viking grave?

I saw Eilidh weeping, I touched her hair. She looked up and I kissed her. A longboat put to sea, a fair wind billowed its raven sail. I journeyed back through time, no longer afraid of dying.

Calmer now, I found hand holds, my legs steadied and turning my head, I glanced down.

Face up, on a shelf of bare rock he lay, beside the Sound, grey and flecked. Broken- backed, fully conscious but immobile.

A wave backed off, came frothing in again and lapped around him. Blood trickled from his mouth. The next wave surged to his face. He spluttered, arms waving franticly.

Unable to move, each wave came and went, indifferently. The tide rose slowly.

Balancing precariously on the narrow ledge, I looked down. He saw me. Fresh screams carried up the cliff, crying, pleading, "Save me, climb down, for Christ's sake, please, please."

Waves began to lift The Agent's body, gradually at first, wrapping a raincoat about his useless legs.

Still he clung, snatching at the rock between surges, the dripping shelf his only haven.

Another wave covered his face, retreated, drew back into the gurgling depths, gathered momentum and white tongued, it came licking towards him again.

Vomiting water and gasping, I could see the man's eyes bulging in abject fear. He waited each wave, gulping air between each measured space, powerless in the agony of breathing death.

They came. Slow, hissing waves, deliberately unfolding, washing him up the shelf and then, with rattling detachment, unhurriedly sucking him down.

Little by little, without compassion, they dragged my visitor towards a sinuous grave.

Without remorse, I watched his drowning.

Gradually his threshing body below a floating raincoat ceased to move; a mere dot, no more than a piece of flotsam rising and falling with the swell, he drifted into the Sound.

And the uncaring sea covered his bloated face in a veil of waves.

CHAPTER TWENTY-FIVE

Shorted and Shafted

Nuen spared nothing, least of all expense, in moving from its New York, Park Avenue offices to a prestigious site overlooking a bend of the Hudson River. Fifty million dollars down and forty floors up, on the rooftop of the flamboyant Nuen Building, Chairman Anderson paced back and forth the full length of his lavish sunshine garden. This dream child, which the Chairman had conceived after several viewings of 'Jurassic Park', involved him in the expending of many creative hours and it might be said, a prodigal amount of the company's petty cash.

Rock piled upon rock climbed to a summit pool from which, by virtue of the cleverly arranged sound recording, there tinkled an icy waterfall. Splashing ledge by ledge with a sparkle enhanced by hidden lighting, it descended as a delightfully musical cascade until it vanished into the enveloping steam of a heated lagoon. Realistically moulded dinosaurs perched on outcrops overlooking the swimmers, pterodactyls flew past on invisible wires and to boost the effect, a growling Tyrannosaurus Rex belched flame at the flick of a switch. Every rocky crevice bloomed with fragrant plant life, miniature jacaranda trees blossomed in the background, date palms leaned over the lagoon's blue effect water and to perfect the vision, on a sandy bank facing the sun sat a Tahitian beach hut complete with cocktail bar. Perhaps the only discordant feature of the garden's pretentiousness was its helipad. Given a succession of celebrities dropping in by private chopper to the Chairman's 'novel' all night swimming parties the downdrafts tended not only to defoliate the vegetation but in some cases to ravage the more flimsy outfits of his female guests.

Andrew Anderson's great grandfather ploughed his last furrow on the family farm, turned his back on a Shetland homestead and around the 1840s joined the peak years of migration from Scotland. His people, fishermen, crofters and fiercely independent in true Norse character had a parcel of land beside a west facing voe on the wind swept treeless island of Unst. To the youngest son it held no more prospect than rye bread and cockle soup. For a restless young man born by the sea, seeking adventure and fortune, it meant following the westering sun. Six hundred miles and a pack on his back, sail and steerage out of Liverpool, three Scots pounds and his father's blessing, eight weeks later he landed on Staten Island at the mouth of the Hudson river.

Following the sun, he headed northwest, fur trapping his way through forest and mountain. Down the wide MacKenzie River and up to the Yukon he travelled, to the gold nugget days of the 'Forty-niners'. Fellow Scots all the way, batwing doors, hard drink, hard fists, wine, women and song, and not too much of the song. On the Atlantic passage he'd met a Scots girl, in her teens and from the Hebrides. Tina MacAulay, she, with her parents, heading for Pittsburg. In spite of his raking, on nights rolled in a blanket when the frost at twenty degrees put the stars on the pine tops, her face came to him and pay dirt in his pouch, he worked his way towards a sun which rose in more ways than one over the steel smelters of Mr. Carnegie.

Future father-in-law, MacAulay, by then foreman at a Carnegie foundry, willingly provided a job for any man with a good Scots tongue in his head. Anderson had such credentials and smartly progressed from pouring pig iron to pressing for Tina's hand in marriage. Pioneers to the very flapjack, young Anderson, plus bride,was soon honeymooning west by covered wagon; this time the prodigal son building bridges with Carnegie steel, as railroad companies conquered the Rockies.

Mix a harsh upbringing with the genes for hardiness and enterprise, you're liable to breed success and sure enough the Scots couple's boy, born in the back of a covered wagon, founded a company involved in the early days of electricity generation. Father to son, each brood added to the company's expansion, until under the forceful drive of Andrew Anderson senior, diversification led directly to the creation of Nuen and its extensive operations in nuclear energy production. Top secret U.S. government contracts followed, immensely lucrative arrangements involving the supply of weapons grade plutonium for the latest military developments.

Of particular interest to Anderson junior were the nuclear warheads and fueling requirements of U.S. navy submarines. Indeed he'd paid a visit to Scotland's nuclear submarine base on the Clyde when a new project was mooted. Visiting Shetland crossed his mind but his American wife who'd accompanied him took a pathological hatred of Scotland, any homecoming to seek his roots she firmly vetoed. It piqued Anderson a mite but more to the point his trip had led to fresh contracts. Naturally such agreements between Nuen and the U.S. administration were strictly off the books and most definitely well away from any prying public attention. All of which meant that Chairman Anderson was no stranger to the Pentagon, by the back door.

How his family had built their wealth had been preached to him as a child and when business pressures mounted the Chairman would chill out from his office, two floors down and leaning on the balustrade of his rooftop play garden he'd watch the busy shipping ply the Hudson River. Staten Island ferries scooting back and forth, top heavy container ships, liners, inward bound from Le Havre, Oslo, Liverpool; shipping of the world towed by tugs below the Statue of Liberty, docking, pouring people ashore, sometimes it awakened his father's preaching, 'My grandfather left the poverty of a Shetland farm, sail and steerage, a canvas cover at the stern of a square rigger but I can tell you this, his longing for the island never left him. He always wanted to go back, return to its basic ways but he was trapped on a treadmill of serving the fortune he'd made.'

Anderson looked round at what he'd inherited and the opulence it had created. That night there happened to be an invite to another party, one of an interminable round which circled the city and well beyond. Beneath a frivolous surface they amounted to highly competitive affairs, pretentious occasions for networking and being networked. A system for doing business, meeting important people, politicians heavily loaded with hangers on, and spare me, the dreadful women, half an inch of makeup, three inches of cleavage and voices that would drown a chain saw. Was this social roundabout just a gross expression of self indulgent values, he sometimes wondered? Greed at its most sophisticated, unmitigated self interest crawling round in empty vessels? Perhaps it might be his current mood; he spun on his heel and shouted, "A thousand acquaintances, and not a friend to trust amongst the lot of them!"

Beyond the mercantile panorama which the Chairman's rooftop retreat enjoyed, it also looked to a forest of New York skyscrapers, each vying for air space and a larger slice of the world's finances. Though not averse to using their money, Anderson privately considered bankers and their minions to be sneaky manipulators of other people's hard work, only trustworthy so long as self interest wasn't threatened. And when not covering their backs at the customer's expense, still taking a fee and passing the package of risk down the line. Fat, bonus inflated operations little better than a loathsome form of extortion. He raged inwardly, with good reason. It was money matters which had him striding the roof amongst the exotic foliage and cursing banks and bankers in general.

For six months now, a straight line drawn through the graph of Nuen share price headed down at a forty-five degree angle. Small rallies there had been, especially when he, as Chairman, albeit obliged to borrow heavily against his other assets, had bought up shares in the hope of steadying their fall. Why, why this collapse in Nuen's equity value? Slow progress in the expansion of fresh nuclear plants? The threat from 'renewables', especially this damn Sahara Solar Power? Worse, maybe the company was being 'shorted'? Acutely aware of the latter possibility, somebody borrowing shares and offloading them to get the price down but who would do it?

Only a week ago, Anderson's main personal banker had asked for an interview. Not the normal sherry and chat, no, an unpleasant demand for more collateral to support the volume of shares being chalked up to the Chairman. Every morning as Wall Street trading opened, Nuen's shares flashed red. Nothing seemed to halt the slide. O.K. stock markets round the world might be tottering, great finance houses rotten to their foundations but from a high of over twenty dollars, Nuen's fall steepened, twelve dollars, five dollars, the breaking point approached.

Newspaper headlines, shares were rated 'loss/sell' by leading brokers, Abrahams. More selling, Anderson phoned Sir Joshua Goldberg, "Josh, the accountants are having difficulty in tracing who's doing all this selling. D'you think somebody with access to holdings is 'shorting' our shares?" Goldberg's voice, calm and reassuring, "No, Andy, impossible, it's just the market's volatility, don't worry, Nuen isn't toxic debt. If I'd only the means, Andy, at five dollars they're a steal."

Anderson threw in another ten million dollars. A blue flash on the Wall Street screen, Nuen shares rose fifty cents. Was this the turnaround? Next day the shares dropped to four dollars and a demand from his Board of Directors for an immediate special meeting arrived on his desk. The morning before the meeting, their price hit two dollars. Nuen faced insolvency. Anderson stared at personal bankruptcy.

"Don't forget it's the Oppenhiemer's party tonight, darling. My hairdresser's coming here at six, taxis at nine." His wife sat up, ruffled her tousled hair and putting her feet over the edge of their carved mahogany four poster, she stood up. Letting a diaphanous silk negligee slip to the floor, she walked over to the full length tilting mirror. Pressing in her stomach and lifting her bosom, she announced, "Can't wear that black Dior off the shoulder creation, I've worn it once already, that hellishly boring Soras party and it was too tight." Viewing her tanned body, she carefully examined her breasts, pushing them together, "Darling, would you turn on the sun bed?" and noticing his clothes, "Going out again Andrew, you're never here to help me."

Anderson, shaved and city suited, hesitated before bending to kiss the back of her neck, "It's a vital meeting today, honey." He patted her bottom. Knocking away his hand, she threw a look over her shoulder and crossed to the bedside telephone, "Meetings, always damned meetings. This is no life. Andrew, you're so bloody selfish." As he gently closed the bedroom door his wife's voice, shouting down the phone, followed him round the first bend of their magnificent Georgian stairway, "I want you here at eleven, bring that backless cross fronted dress you designed for me the other month, we'll check it for fit." Pause. "Yes, today, of course it's important. You'll have to cancel your other arrange----." He hurried down the last flight and out of earshot.

A full length oil of Anderson, the Shetland immigrant, filled one wall of their spacious hallway. From habit he glanced up. Its imperious pose and ice blue eyes had haunted his childhood days. A black servant handing the portrait's great grandson his coat, held open the front door.

The chauffeur in maroon livery touched his cap. The Chairman nodded. His Company Rolls Royce, making barely more sound than its tyres on the gravel, coasted down a driveway whose canopy of leafless branches glistened white with the crystals of November's first frost.

Not even the bright light of the cut crystal chandelier hanging above the board table could enliven the grey faces, deliberately studying their papers as the Chairman entered, "Morning gentlemen, welcome to this special meeting which you quite rightly have requested," Anderson began briskly. Standing before them and surveying bowed heads, a coldness entered his voice, "I'm glad you could all arrange to be present. As you know we have much to deal with, gloomy as that may seem. As my father would say, nothing beats a challenge," he forced a laugh.

Not a head looked up.

"I fully realise this a matter of us all having trust in our company. You will be aware of the recent fall in our equity value." That bought the first response, nods around the table. Anderson continued at length, claiming a lack of liquidity in the world's banking sector, the impact of a down turn in world wide GDP, the volatility of international stock markets; indeed he touched on anything which could have a bearing upon the fortunes of Nuen.

Winding up his explanations their Chairman appealed to his directors in a far from humble manner. "You too will have much to contribute. Difficult times are ahead. We must all pull together in trust, confidence and mutual support. Gentlemen, I welcome your comment and advice." Hard faced and challenging, he demanded allegiance from a Board which his inner senses told him was fast descending into the pit of self interest. His stance mirrored the family portrait. Anderson's fierce blue eyes held a look of contempt, if not scorn.

No face lifted nor, it seemed, dared look towards him. Twelve men sat. Some looked sideways. Others gazed across at the paintings which graced the walls. November coughs, ritual nose blowing, fingers twiddled pencils, then silence. Forty floors up and into rooms from the freeway below, the wail of a police siren came and went.

Nicky Fellows glanced towards Sir Joshua who sat impassively at the bottom of the table. Goldberg gave the merest shift of his hollow eyes. Fellows stood, his hands grasping the lapels of his stripped suit to steady their tremble, "Mr. Anderson, I feel nothing but dismay at what I have to say but given the parlous state of the company's financial position I feel I have no option but to table a motion of no confidence in you, sir, our Chairman."

His eyes flicked back to Sir Joshua as he sank into his chair. Not a move, not a paper rustled. The Company secretary fixed his gaze on the wall clock at the far end of the room. Its minute arm counted time in jerks. He waited for its next jerk and its next. The passage of time had become spasmodic. Late November sun stabbed obliquely through the window.

Andrew Anderson appeared not to have heard. He looked over the heads of men who confirmed his deeply held private opinion. Though many of his Board had positions of high office in their respective professions, politics, banking, or whatever, suddenly a veil lifted. He saw them for what they were, blood sucking parasites whose skillful machinations provided a hearty meal of self-interest from the public at large. Corporate greed which ignored the social consequences. His jaw tightened. The soft facial curves of city living gave way to their underlying hardness. It became the face of a man of decision. Squaring himself, he cleared his throat and spoke with dignity,

"Gentlemen, there is a motion of no confidence in this Chair on the table before you. May I have the motion seconded? Eyes reverted to the table. Eventually a palm lifted. Nuen's banker, blushing deeply and barely audible, "I second the motion." A sharp indrawing of breath circled the room. Well used to sizing up their clients, be they failing businessman, or a congressman trading on his influence, a table of shrewd operators attempted to gauge the banker's motives.

"Thank you, sir," Anderson showed no emotion. "Now gentlemen, may I have a show of hands. Those in favour of the motion?" Fellows lifted a shaky hand, followed by the banker. Eleven hands, one after another, rose shoulder level. Only Sir Joshua remained head down, hands on the table. Anderson visibly shook and hesitating slightly, "If you please, those against the motion of no confidence in my Chairmanship?" Hands slipped out of sight except for that of a smiling Sir Joshua. Carefully avoiding eye contact with the Chairman, the Scientific Advisor lifted his hand and looked round the table from face to face.

"Gentlemen the motion is carried," Anderson bowed his head, inwardly aghast; his lone supporter, Sir Josuha Goldberg. Hardly credible, the move so well co-ordinated. Had there been a plot to oust him? Who would do it? The question now immaterial, he needed to find out urgently. His personal position would require considerable help, perhaps his friend Goldberg might know?

Anderson stood silently, letting his eye fall on each member in turn, haughtily, disdainfully; they would not forget. He saw them clearly, despicable, cringing objects, slyness dressed in a city suits. "In relinquishing the chair of a company which my grandfather father founded, I thank you for the support given to me and our organisation over many years and I wish success to an incoming Chairman. The meeting is the hands of your Vice Chairman. Good afternoon gentlemen."

The ex-Chairman, ignoring his papers, walked quietly to his private office without a sideways look and closed the door. Elbows on the arms of his swivel, he pursed his fingers before his mouth and thought.

A stunned Vice Chairman stood behind the newly vacated seat, "Board members, I, er, I feel, I believe, indeed I'm sure, we must act promptly. Any delay, any, er any hint of, I shall be blunt, the news of this change at the top of Nuen and headline news it will be, must be of a smooth transition of leadership, progressive bolstering of the company's position, otherwise gentlemen, well, today's share price affects us all, a further panic dumping of our shares on Wall Street, I mean..." his voice trailed off.

Pulling himself together he conferred in whispers with the company secretary. Member leaned towards member. Much subdued murmuring, some already standing aside, speaking urgently into mobile phones. Were they buying or selling? A rap on the table and the Vice Chairman brought members to their seats. "It falls to me to call for nominations to the Chairmanship of Nuen." A stir of anticipation...

Nick Fellows, adjusting his half spectacles, read from a note, "It gives me the greatest honour to put forward the name of Sir Joshua Goldberg. New to us though he is, his scientific background is of paramount importance in our present difficulties, his connections, rather I should say, his understanding of the financial world, make him our obvious choice."

Many, "Here, here's" and no further nominations sealed the take over. Sir Joshua padded round to the top seat,

squeezing his friend Nicky fondly on the shoulder as he
walked past.

The faint glow from a safety light illuminated the ex-
Chairman's face, family portraits and historic shots of the
Carnegie smelter hung side by side with those of Nuen's
nuclear plants. Rags to riches, at least an Anderson had made
it to the fourth generation. Rags again? Only one person
came in to see him after their meeting ended, his personal
banker. "You know Andrew your drawings in the past two
years have been exceptional and if you don't mind my saying
so, especially those of Mrs. Anderson. I have to be plain,
Andrew, unless you provide more security against these
borrowings, well, shall I say the bank will be forced to take
a final view. I'm sure you understand what I mean."
Anderson dismissed the banker with a nod and sat on in the
gathering gloom.

A photo of his wife smiled up at him from the desk top. For a
long time he looked at her. Intimate memories crowded in.
Twenty-two years, but no children; she didn't want a family but
the home building, the holidays, just together, and then
increasingly, the social whirl. His thoughts of her gradually
soured, emotions dug into feelings which hurt. Slowly, he
turned the photo face down. Without switching on the light he
crossed to the door. It shut behind him with a click.

The steam which lies on a November river, hung in a gritty rime
about the front portico of the Nuen Building. Normally his
limousine and chauffeur waited, no matter the hour. The door
porter stepped forward with a smart salute but said nothing.
"Where's my car, tonight, Jones?" "It went away about three
hours ago, Sir." "Went away?" The man coughed awkwardly.
"Yes, sir." "Well?" "Yes, sir, Sir Joshua Goldberg got in and
I think, Mr. Fellows." Now he knew.

The gravelled carriageway to their mansion wound between oak and beech. A blaze of house lights flickered through bare branches. Anderson stepped out of a taxi. Another taxi sat ticking over. Spotlights on the lawn played over the white façade of their spacious mock colonial home. Through the open door he could see his wife, even from a distance, in a blaze of jewels. He leant a shoulder against a marble pillar and waited. Violent shouting reached him from the top step, "I've been ready for twenty minutes." She looked down, eyes aflame, her voice snarling, "You're so Goddamn selfish, Andrew. This is another of your mean, pinch penny tricks and look at you, scruffy, filthy. It'll be another twenty minutes before you're changed. You horrid, uncaring wretch; you knew, you knew it. I've looked forward to this party for weeks."

Moving closer to her, out of earshot of the taxi driver, he cut her short, "Honey, I ain't going to no party tonight. And two things for your information, sweetheart, I've just been voted out of the Nuen Chair and the bank are threatening to pull the plug. Bankruptcy, yeah, bankrupt. That might change your little story. So see me baby, I ain't in no party mood right now."

She took a step back. Red dots of fury appeared on white cheeks, "Not in party mood! Not going," she dropped her voice to a sneer. "Don't come crying to me with your miserable problems. You're pathetic, I don't need this shit," and bursting into a crescendo of sobbing and screaming, "You can't do this to me. Beast, you beast! I hate you, hate you! I'm going, you hear me, I'm going now and you can please your lousy self."

Taxi lights flickered along the lines of black sentinel trunks, lit their gaunt leafless arms. For a moment its back window framed her head. He stood listening. The engine roared out onto the freeway and he went inside, to the phone,

"You've reached Pan Am, Sir. How can I help you?"

CHAPTER TWENTY-SIX

Waves of Thought

We are but what the heavens made us,
And in the arc of curving space,
Every particle therein,
Is our kith and kin.

No more now than a piece of flesh, awaiting decay, tossing wave to wave on the Sound. A would be murderer's body, a corpse slowly bloating by the salt water of its drowning, caught and twirled by the current; gulp after gulp, I'd watched his repeated sputtering and vomiting until the sea filled his lungs. I'd heard the screaming, the pleading of a man with faith in nothing. I'd seen the bulging eyes, the abject terror of a man afraid to die.

Waves sluiced over the ledge of his drowning, the worn rock shelf now almost out of sight. Wind over the rising tide sent white tops scurrying across the narrow waters. A nor-east wind, whetted to sharpness by the grey November sea. I looked down on the shelf. Two lives had found it their deathbed, known the enormity of approaching death, a sudden death and yet still there would be space in those seconds of falling to compress life into final thoughts. The shelf of death, young adventurous Hilda and a man with a revolver. Would it claim a third?

Twenty feet, above me, I glimpsed the turf edge of the cliff. The ledge which had saved me appeared to widen as it turned out of my view. There were no hand holds. A rock fall would have sheered them off. I began to quiver, jaw trembling. Fright and cold. I clenched my teeth. Get out of this cutting wind. Torn fingers, still bleeding slightly, were numbing. Soon they would be useless, render any climbing impossible. I looked down, nearly two hundred feet. Dive out? Hope to miss the shelf. Hit it. Death! Miss it, and drown?

Slippery, oozing bird droppings but no option, I had to move. Move and fall? I spoke inwardly, trying to gain control. Don't hug the rock, your feet will shoot out. I balanced backwards, a little off the face. One foot, steady, next foot, hold, examine every tiny scratch, it might give a finger hold. The ledge kept turning, widening; I worked round, just inches at a move. Wind not so harsh now, instead the acrid stench of bird droppings. More shelter, my knees were juddering. I rested.

The sea beneath, boiling off the shelf, poured in a black curve hitting jagged fangs of rock, bursting into white salvos, falling back to seething froth. I edged another few yards. The rock face began to lean out towards me, an overhang. I stopped. Ahead I could hear the wind gusting, sometimes a whistle, eerie, calling a human tone, whining above the boom of each surge below.

A last yard- the ledge ended. I looked into a great crevice, splitting the cliff top to bottom. A rock chimney, an organ pipe to wind and sea, a great mound of boulders at its base, daylight at its top. The overhang, too great, it leant out above my ledge. No way to pass round it and try to climb the chimney. Shaking with despair after the risk of moving along the ledge was I beaten?

Legs getting weak, I had to try and sit. I moved back a few yards until at least out of the wind. Gingerly, slithering my hands down the rock, I sat. Feet over the edge, truly dangerous. I knew that much. Now I faced the sea. Faint pale light crossed rolling wave backs. The November sun deep in a hollow of hodden clouds sank green and sickly. A trail of gulls, flying close to the surface, followed deepening wave troughs. Their wailing carried to me, not the raucous screams of anger but in long single notes of desolation, the cries of worsening weather.

The wind in the chimney rose and fell with an incessant chant. Without option, I listened. Its moaning dirge would swell to a rush of exhaling breath, and fade again to a soughing whisper. Dire thoughts forced themselves upon me. I fought to banish them with thoughts of Eilidh, a longing for what might have been. Alone on the island, she had become an inseparable part of my life. Now hanging on to that very life, my passion for her became unbearable. I saw her eyes, spoke her name aloud, over and over again, choking with ineffable sadness in its saying, "Oh, Eilidh,"

Even with my back against a cliff, out of anguish a poem wrote itself in my mind. I encompassed the universe in a poem. The fear of death faded, there is no death, only loss of a loved one and a reunion in the strength of shared hope. I spoke to Eilidh, "We shall meet again."

The cold, the wind, the isolation. I looked fixedly down at the sea. Swaying far below, its hypnotic motion was becoming compelling, begging a choice.

By my own hand, or move and just one slip?

I was being drawn inexorably to a final decision.

"Is that you, Eilidh? Hang on a moment," Ella brushed flour off her hands and picked up the phone again, "Yes, Eilidh I'm hearing you. Are you alright?" Without answering the question, "Ella, is Eachan there?" and before Ella could reply, "Ella, something has happened to Hector, something terrible,

I don't know what it is. He needs help, help at once. Is he still on Sandray?"

A shocked Ella, "Yes he's on the island. Eachan's in the village," Eilidh broke in, "Ella, Ella, I know it's bad. Can you get Eachan?" "Yes, Eilidh, I can phone down and get him home." "Oh thanks, thanks Ella, I'm in London, I'll phone you back in five minutes."

The tractor rattled into the yard. Eachan strode in without smile. "Is there a problem?" Somehow he knew before Ella replied, "Eilidh's been on the phone, really, really upset. She's certain something has happened to Hector but she's in London." Eachan, saying nothing, went to the porch door and walked a few steps down the croft. Out on Sandray, the dense white sheets of cloud were trailed by the wind across The Hill of the Shroud. He listened for the sea. Its faint rumble told him the set of waves. A rising tide would mean wind over current, it could be rough.

"Tide's on the turn, I'll head across before it gets dark. Look for a torch at five'o'clock." Ella knew by the brusqueness of his tone to say nothing. Instead she filled a thermos of coffee, packed bread, a bottle of whisky and watched him, waterproof jacket and leggings, head down to the jetty.

That Eilidh's concern would prove correct was without doubt. Too often he'd known the passing of emotions between people far apart, their warnings, the prior knowledge of happenings, no matter the distance. He was too much a Highlander to scoff at Eilidh's premonition.

The Hilda boat lay ready. Eachan slipped her ropes, jumped aboard and about to cast off, he stopped. Was it memories? An inner prompting came to him too strong to be ignored.

Back to his shed, a little searching and he found the safety harness a yachtsman had left on the jetty many years back.

Adding a couple of pulleys and a heavy coil of rope, the old man lugged it aboard. Loosing all but one of the sail ties, he made the sheets ready for a quick hoist and started the outboard engine.

Pausing only to glance at a cloud tearing cloudscape, Eachan swung the stern of his boat before a rising sea.

My last thoughts were with Eilidh, somehow I knew they reached her, telling her all I felt. Music ran through my head, melodies of unsurpassed beauty. I listened entranced, as I had as a child, to the sublime Mozart, the swelling choruses of his great Mass, a legacy to mankind outshining all forms of human conception; its message beyond our arrogant invention of a divinity. Simple, an encapsulation of beauty, direct to our sense of the ultimate indestructible eternity.

It prepared me. I was ready to jump. Leap out as far as possible. Take my chance with the sea. Pulling my legs under me, I got onto hands and knees. Stiffly, cautiously, I stood up. Unafraid now, breathing deeply, I started a count, ten, nine, eight, seven...... I stopped.

Against the fading outline of Halasay, a shower of spray rose from the bow of a plunging boat. Instantly life returned, the beating of hope, care my only thought, no false moves now.

The Hilda, I knew, it had to be. She was running a beam sea. I watched her helmsman bring her nose into the wave peaks, a burst of spray. Through them she rode, into the trough, running the trough, over the next peak. Oh boy, it had to be Eachan, handling his boat, fearless, dancing with the sea, a master. Would he see me, dark against the rock? He had to round the cliff to make it into the bay. Dare he chance coming in close?

Hilda riding it, great little sea boat, yes, he was running the headland close, what a heave on the sea, what a risk, lose control, matchwood on the shelf? Man and boat close in. Eachan seemed to be looking at me. Had he spotted me? Would I jump? Would I jump? Eachan lifted his hand. He'd seen me, must have read my mind. He stood up, swaying with his boat's rolls, waved both hands, sideways, negative. He veered off and making for the bay, out of my sight. I fought to stop the shuddering. On wings of happiness in an unbelievable uplift of euphoria, I shouted to Eilidh.

Half an hour's light left, maybe. Time stretched. Waiting, waiting. How long till he'd reach me? I was shaking quite violently, dangerously so, my back against the cliff, totally numb.

Eachan's voice came first, calling, trying to locate me. I shouted. Turning to look upwards could easily unbalance me. Head to the side, I squinted up, his face looked down, unperturbed and steady. Relief gushed through me. "Here's a harness, put it over----," the updraft of wind took his voice. Two minutes and the safety harness dangled beside me on the end of a rope. Putting it on, could be the most dangerous move. Holding the rope in one hand, I wriggled an arm through the straps. The other arm.... clips came together round my chest.

A pulley block came down, clanking against the rock, "Hook it onto the har----", words blown away. I was swaying now, managed to hook it on the ring, chanced to look up, he was watching. "Loose off the first rope." It vanished up the cliff. Eachan was out of sight. He reappeared, "I'll lower you down to that bottom shelf, the tide's rising. When I have the strain let yourself..." I guessed the rest.

The rope tightened, almost lifting me. I held it, stepped off the ledge, feet against the rock, out into space, waves pounding below. I pushed myself to an angle with the cliff face. Faith in Eachan and the rope harness chokingly tight.

I descended, foot by foot, the sea closer, frothing over the shelf, my feet slithering off the rock. I hung, fighting for breath, harness cutting into my chest. Down again, able to contact rock, lean back, push with my feet. I glanced behind me. Black-backed waves licked across the shelf, booming into spray against the rock face. A moment's ominous lull before they poured back down in white streaks, to wait the next onrush.

Two more drops. I touched the shelf, water swirling to my waist. The rope went slack. A surge lifted me, sweeping me off the ledge into the sea. Frantically I clung onto the rope. It came. The wave sucked off the shelf, taking me with it. Gulping and spluttering, I fought drowning.

The rope tightened, I dangled over the sheer under water face of the shelf. On three yards of slack rope, I hung in the sea, up to my chest. Was I to be pounded senseless against the rock? To a shivering body, the water seemed strangely warm. The next wave rose below me. It lifted, I clawed up the rope. Back on the shelf, holding loops of rope, I hung on.

Buffeting seas dragged me off my feet, washing me to the end of the rope until the swamping passed and my feet found rock again. Cut hands burnt with salt, eyes stinging, side of my head painful. I fought each swirl. Twice, they completely submerged me. Green light closed above. I surfaced, choking and coughing water.

Weakness was taking over. My arms ached. A fast rising tide. Another immersion? I counted the surges, the next big one? Drowning was close.

Sound of an outboard. Round the headland, The Hilda, heaving and bursting spray.

Eachan brought her nose near to the shelf. He stood in her stern, calm and unflustered. For a moment he left the helm. A coil of rope snaked out. I floundered, grabbing at it, mouth full of water. Got it! "Tie it round your waist," I thought him almost laughing. "Tie a bowline."

I fumbled with the knot, "Let off the pulley. Hector." The Hilda surged in, he backed off, a wave passed under her. Eachan came ahead again, two yards off, a yard,

"Now boy!" I launched myself at the bow, half aboard, a hand grabbed my collar, hauled me the rest. He stepped swiftly back to the stern. Her bow dipped, a wave was taking her stern. Lying on the bottom boards, I waited for the splintering crash. It would tell the drowning of two men.

The engine revved, she hung, stern in the air. I heard the propeller spinning clear of the water. Forward she went, the prop dug. Slowly she pulled astern. I clung to the gunnels, looked to Eachan. He watched the next curling top, swung her off into the trough. Boat and judgment.

The headland of Sandray, close and perilous, reared above us. I looked fearfully from its merciless grandeur to Eachan. His face spoke his thoughts. Hilda, his lost daughter… it was on his face, the vision, her broken body lying, the self same shelf, the same forsaken place…. it was in his eyes. Such the sadness in his expression, were we to be lost, swept and drowned from a splintered boat which bore her name, so be it.

It could claim us yet. Jagged rocks ahead, breaking, black teeth fallen from the chimney shaft. We clawed off, running the troughs. Eachan nursed his boat, daren't force her. Waves climbed the headland, burst and fell back into jostling white foam. Slowly we pulled clear.

I lurched down to the centre thwart. Stern seas, the worst, swept us to the point. He ran out, swung beam to the swell, before taking it head on to make the rounding. Spray lashed us until gradually, the wind off the land, we were into the shelter of the bay. Eachan grinned at me, "Hoch, hoch, boy, you've had a close one."

Ten minutes brought us alongside the Sandray jetty. True to Highland good manners, no comment, no questions, his only observation, "Well, Hector boy, you'll be needing a dram."

I sank down on the stones. A thermos cup was put in my hand, warm coffee and whisky. Sip at a time, before the pain of returning warmth. I staggered up to the house. Eachan busied about, the kitchen, tea, another dram. "It'll be about five o'clock, I said I would wave a torch at five o'clock, Ella will be watching and she'll know we're fine." He took the torch and went out.

Warmth from the calor stove, an inner glow from Eachan's bottle of cure all and I wakened to find my head down on the table and the room in darkness. Regaining a vague awareness and believing Eilidh through in her bedroom, I spoke quietly, "Eilidh, are you alright?" No reply, and more urgently, "Eilidh." For a second in the darkness she stood over me. I reached out to her hand, the vision faded. Only then I realised she wasn't physically in the house, yet the feeling she was beside me remained.

Gradually the recent events reshaped themselves and for the first time I ran fingers warily over the side of my head, now smarting unpleasantly. A warm oozing smeared my hand. Blood. The realisation, neither a shock nor relief, just more disorientated thinking. The crack of a pistol shot, real enough, a bullet through the brain, instead, alive by a fraction of an inch. The unexplained appearance of Eachan, impossible he'd have come across on chance, not on such a day.

Never more strongly did I feel a pawn in some torturously predetermined sequence of events. In truth I could offer no rationale for my chosen direction. Why these uncanny circumstances, these apparitions, this harking back to Viking days, ancestral graves, drownings, were they real? The explosion ---was it real? It had to be. I remembered Eilidh's eyes, the flash, the screams.

Perhaps I was no more than a vegetable in a wheelchair viewing some incredible phantasm being played inside my brain, a conscious mind existing only at the mercy of its imagination; a brain oblivious to physical incapacity, being fed a holographic image by some external force? I dreaded slipping back into spasms of mental anguish, struggling to separate the threads of sanity and insanity. Sensory perceptions objectively presented, their cause physical or psychological, a game play of virtual reality beyond my control?

A stirring across the table, I could make out Eachan coming awake from the opposite chair, "Madainn mhath," he yawned and stretching, "Ah Dia, I've slept on softer chairs." Immediately alert, I got up and lit the camping light. An empty bottle stood on the table. Half dry clothes, my back needing a dry shirt, our stomachs, solid food. It must be the early hours. The impact of the ordeal still so numbing I couldn't speak, instead I went to the cooker and got busy.

Porridge with honey on it, two plates steamed under the hanging lamp. Eachan made no comment about my departure from his customary salt. Looking over the last spoonful, "I heard you calling to Eilidh when I wakened," and in a serious tone, "you were calling to the right person. If she hadn't phoned yesterday morning with a message you were in some sort of trouble, I wouldn't be eating sweet porridge," adding a great deal more seriously, "and neither would you."

"Eilidh phoned?" "Yes she did and she was in some state of upset." "She phoned?" I stammered, staring at her bedroom door, incredulous, "From London?" "Yes and I came across straight away." "How could she know?" my words trailed off. On the cliff, never before had I thought of her so passionately. I faced falling to my death and she filled every corner of my mind. "What time did she phone?" "It was quite sharp, I was down the village, maybe half ten, eleven o'clock time."

Middle morning, the man at the door, my first unease and Eilidh phoned. The theme of the poem that wrote itself in my mind, I must catch it, write it down. Bit by bit I gave Eachan my story. I described the speedboat, "Aye, that's a character who arrived in Halasay a year or two back, you hear him before you see him, that's the way his kind tend to be."

Listening to my account of the happenings he showed no surprise, only a thoughtful face, angular and shrewd. "Are you coming back to Halasay with me?" Obviously he'd the police station in his mind, though reporting the matter wasn't mentioned. "No, I don't think so. I'll stay here, if that's OK with you. The evidence is in the Atlantic. I'll come over, maybe on the slack water late this afternoon." Understanding as always, "Aye, whatever you think, no problem, it'll be time enough."

A hint of light showed through the little glass panes of the kitchen window. Dawn cut into our conversation. We went outside and stood at the end of the house. Across the Sound the peaks of Halasay, dark and lonesome were emerging on an eastern sky washed to rosy pink. Below us, the mauve waters of a November bay. The wind had lost its chill, and yesterday's storm was barely a memory on the surface of the sea.

"That's the weather passing east before the sun. Now it's on the mend I'll head over, it's about the bottom of the tide," and pulling on his oilskins, "Take care if you come across later. Don't worry if you aren't wanting to go back to the cliff, just now, but if you get a chance, I left that long rope and pulleys."

Whatever he thought of the whole episode remained unsaid. I saw him off at the jetty and climbing to a point behind the house, watched the tiny dot of the 'Hilda' until it vanished into the bay which lay below the croft of Ach na Mara. There would be another time to thank Eachan, "Please phone Eilidh," had been my last words to him.

The isles of the ocean have ways of making amends, the morning breeze came round to the south, mild and relaxing. The sun, no longer bleak and green, warmed the stones. At middle day, after much perplexing thought, I walked slowly towards the headland. The grass, lank and ungrazed these many, many years lay matted, russet and wasted, the soil upon which it grew might be superfluous to present man's requirements, yet not to that of the little yellow tormentil. Oncoming winter had still to deter its miniature bloom. Independent plant, it grew, not in clumps, but singly, here and there. Open to the sun, amidst the dying sedges, their tiny petals dotted my path, the last of summer's profusion.

I stopped to look down on a single plant, unprotected and vulnerable, one tiny bloom in a vast landscape and still bright and eager, keen to live. That few moments pause answered all the morning's reflections. The who, the why, the nausea of contemplating death, it all left me. The island soil was as important to that tiny flower's survival as it was to me. I walked on, my spirit regained, as a folk singer might strum, with the sun on my shoulder. Out onto the headland and the Viking grave, its stones in place a thousand years, cleaned by salt and gale.

A large stone symbolised the longboat's prow. Narrow but uncarved, it leant forward, and firmly round its base Eachan had wound a strop of rope, an anchor for the pulley block. The long rope stretched out, disappeared over the edge of the cliff. Hand over hand, I hauled, hearing the clank, clank of the lower pulley hitting rock. Up it came, yard by yard. The coil at my feet grew. It stuck, I pulled. Pulled harder. Still stuck.

Had I courage to go the edge and look over? It took force of will. Crawling to the edge, I squinted down. Twenty feet, and more, the ledge, narrow, spattered with bird droppings. Air wafted up to me, acid and putrid. Away below, the shelf, wave washed, devoid of life and utterly mournful.

Giddy with vertigo, the cliff seemed to be tilting. In terror of slipping, I gripped the sparse tufts of grass. My head swam. My depth of thought for Eilidh returned. The passion that dwarfed my contemplation of falling, came again, replaced all fear. The poem and its baffling relevance to Eilidh's phone call spoke through my head. Words and theme presented themselves, still fresh. Are there paths by which some great emotion may communicate? I lay on the turf edge staring down at a pattern of ripples on the waves. They seemed as ripples in space and my grip relaxed.

Steady now, keep focused. I flicked the rope to one side, crawled back from the cliff and stood up. Flicking the rope again and hauling, with a jerk, it came. The last few yards dragged the pulley over the edge to my feet. Carefully I coiled the rope, as thought it were a mooring line.

With marked respect I unwound the rope belay from around the grave ship's prow stone. Perhaps early settlers gathered it from the taking in of the land. The grave pointed north. Symbol of a Viking's returning voyage. Island headland, oceans wide, no pilot marks, into space unknown, beyond the speckled heavens; from death into life, as it had held me.

November sun made shadows of the stones, my back was to the prow stone. The people of the graves were at my side, I saw them at fireside homes bound in winter snows and evening tales. And with them, I gloried in the daring voyage of imagination

The lichen stones were without a sun, it crept into northern night and a flake filled gale caked the leaning birch. Aurora's torch shone red and green on drifted snow and I heard frost bound steps crunched to neighbour's tread. In the dancing blue the firelight flames spun tales of daring late into each wide eyed night. Song and verse, a winter passed until sunshine spring brought blackbird song to a catkined river edge and plovers called and whimbrel probed worm casts on the shore. Then was the time and shoulders heaved, stout lines were rove and milk-blue melt from snow capped hills put longboats back to sea.

Tapestry days of shape and colour, when perspectives long in a mid-night loom were latitudes play on light and hue. Images came, the hollow wave a cave of green, in the curling storm they saw a sailor's grave, wind twisted branches, the waving arms that plucked knowledge from the stars. Ideas alive, fresh as the gleam of new turned soil, clear as the air that set their voyage, wide as minds that journeyed the realms of fantasy, roved the seas of uncertainty and sailed beyond this universe, plunderers of imagination's seam.

The massless photon, energy's fastest source, outpaces speed of thought but are there paths on which insight and great emotions may exist, may communicate on wavelength within dimensions which defy the speed of light, perhaps become a force within the bubble of this universe? Does imagination's boundaries grow,or is consciousness a hollow tunnel? Does the universe exist to pander to our thoughts? What may still emerge, evolve beyond this brain, or atomic functions grow

without a carbon base? Amalgams yet may blossom just as the
stars are born to spin the Hole of Death, the fruits of quasi-
particles which swirl its stellar tomb.

Atoms perhaps are not as real, float only in a mystery of
possibilities without end, where potential and uncertainty
alone exist, in dimensions beyond the myth of science. Are all
things possible on uncertainty's endless path? Within the
framework of our brain, we struggle to break the synapse' trap,
It's a snail like pace of sodium ions, the neuron's organic grasp.

Unleash electro-magnet's bending force, accelerate ideas
beyond the photon's cosmic hold, forget the Gods which
we conceive, become the ghost of energy's vast turmoil. Join
the particles of space and be at one, in the mystery of
'Entanglement.'

We are but what the heavens made us and in the arc of curving
space, every particle therein is our kith and kin.

Completely unaware of my surroundings, I'd strained excitedly
to catch the fresh ideas which hovered within my grasp before
they flitted into some unknown vacuum. Finding a set of words
to define elusive concepts imposed total absorption. When my
spate of thoughts finally settled the weather had cleared from
the west. Sauntering back to the house, I came round by the bay
to find the south wind had died to nothing and left behind a
pocket of warmth.

The air had all saltiness of the tangle of the isles, the scent of
dream and song. I laughed, for where the rocks on the far side
of the bay formed a wee cove of their own, the sea had heaped
tons of fertiliser and tomorrow, romantic scent or no, I would
gather my seaweed harvest clear of the tide. Ocean's bounty for
the 'lazy beds' I'd dig next spring. Gulls circled the beach,
returned from a day's searching. Perhaps they'd followed a

fishing boat, ranging their world of chance. I blessed the game of chance and stood beside the jetty watching them until they, like my ideas, became floating concepts, vague shapes in the last rays of a sunset which bounced off the dying Atlantic swell. Gone November's rawness, the terrors of yesterday; in their place the peacefulness of the island gathered about me, tangible and livable. The old house indeed a haven.

The camping light on the table threw a small circle of warmth. Pushing aside my dishes, I made a fair copy of the poem. After its title I wrote, 'Headlands' and sat thinking. Ella would have phoned Eilidh, for certain. How much of the drama had she been told? None I hoped. Tomorrow, I must phone, maybe head for London. Nothing except meeting her again could ever drag me back to London. First it had to be the police station. I fingered the furrow of dried blood on my skull.

How to make anybody believe such a wild story? Police questioning, "What were you doing staying alone these past weeks on an uninhabited island? Explain that one, Mr.MacKenzie. Were you perhaps, hiding?" From most people's stand point, it looked suspicious, or at the very kindest analysis, the behaviour of an eccentric. Maybe the body had floated ashore, been identified by the speedboat guy. He'd have been expecting a return trip to pick up this supposed archaeologist, or as chance would have it, a failed murderer. Certainly I'd acted in self defense. I'm not guilty of murder, surely not even manslaughter. Or was I? Would I face arrest? Who was this madman anyway, and why his fascination with my damned briefcase? Long since I'd forgotten the vague threat I sensed during that London interview. An assassination attempt, surely not?

Strangely, during these weeks alone I hadn't bothered the bottle, it remained a yellow glint up on the shelf. I poured a 'night cap'. Before it could even wet my lips, out of the evenings stillness there arose a sound, a strange wailing, a chorus of high pitched notes. Putting down the glass, I went to the door. The cries of some hideous plight quivered on the thinness of the November air, some creatures or some persons? Where, down at the bay?

A waxing moon newly risen, crater pocked and ice white, cast long shadows as I walked slowly towards the shore. It seemed there were many voices, a beseeching, primal sound, beyond any human grief. My breath rose, tiny coils in the sharp light, the hair on the nape of my neck, stiff and tingling. I stepped towards the shore, tense and alert. Stones rattled with staccato clicks.

Breasting the last of the dunes the bay spread below me in a great sheet of reflected light. The moon floated, a disc of brightness on the water. No human voices could create such piteous music, know such melancholy. A lone voice rose above the rest, psalm- like in private grief. I stood, an intruder on sorrow, the calling of unearthly spirits. Out on the distant ledges silhouetted against a moon green sea, dark bodies swayed, slender heads raised vibrant throats. The seal folk sang before their goddess of the tide.

I walked quietly round to the jetty and sat listening. Little by little their voices died to a soft keening. Deep from the pores of night the People of the Sea unlocked sepulchral caves, offered a last coronach to those who'd perished by the ocean's call. In the sadness of their departing notes remained the lost souls of those who dwelt within the chrysalis of their sealskin tombs. Did they cry to me, who cheated the hungry sea?

A faintest breeze came off the wide Atlantic bringing with it a balm from the warmth which remains in a winter sea. I stirred myself, unwilling to leave, for the mystery of the supernatural still clung to the silence. At last, rising to leave for home, I stopped in utter disbelief, in quick dismay. Outlined on the glitter of moonlit water, mast and sail set, a boat appeared from behind the black mass of the headland. The 'Hilda', I knew her lines. Eachan, it had to be, only he would sail her at night.

Did he come to warn me of a missing person's search? More likely they'd found the body. Only a special reason would have Eachan sailing the Sound at night. Alone? No, the local Policeman would be with him, Halasay's single arm of the law. Sure, he'd ask me to come quietly.

The truth, who would believe it? Evade capture? I rejected the thought immediately, yet the threat of being taken off the island dismayed me, I braced for the shattering of a foolish idyll.

Silent, effortless, an apparition gliding in the moonlight, the Hilda sailed the horizon as if by phantom hand.

Her sail came across to the faintest breeze.

Ghostly as the dying voices of the seals,

she laid her course for the jetty.

I waited.

CHAPTER TWENTY-SEVEN

The elation of free fall

Sitting in the executive class of a five hour flight down to the Caribbean gave Andrew Anderson much needed thinking time. His wife had failed to come home from the Oppenhiemer party, so what? He hadn't slept, eaten or spoken to the servants. A small attaché case carried a few details of consequence for his home office, he didn't leave his wife a note and now aboard an early plane, lack of sleep and the shock of being voted out of Nuen's Chairmanship was written in black lines below his eyes.

It mattered little that the peaks of the distant Appalachian Mountains sailed on a frieze of pink mist; sun rise came at a heavy price. He stared out moodily, America's Eastern seaboard thirty thousand below, he could just make it out, the long indented coastline, that white edge would be surf on Florida beaches, for a moment it created a hankering, and he felt a flicker of relief. From what? Financial and social disgrace, pretty certainly a divorce, he balanced on the precipice of ruin. Should he step back from the edge and fight? Jump and savour the elation of free fall? That child- haunting portrait of his austere grandfather, had he seen it for the last time?

Bouts of inner rage seethed though him, clenching his fists; Goldberg; I should have figured him at the start, too smooth by far and that plummy English accent, he swore aloud, "The sneaking bastard, just let him wait." The Air Hostess looked at him sharply. Recovering his composure he sat and glowered. Please fasten your seat belts. The plane banked above Roadtown, about to touch down in the Virgin Islands, land of the lotus eater's diet of palm beaches, rum and music. More importantly the location of a strictly private bank account, unknown to that creep of a banker in New York and every bit as critical, unknown to his ruinously extravagant wife. And there, anchored in the village bay amongst a plethora of millionaire sail and luxury cruiser, Anderson made out the tall masts of his yacht, the graceful Sea Nymph. Good, the crew had got his message.

Have breakfast, shave and then a smart visit to the bank. Ex-chairman Anderson stepped across the shimmering tarmac into a coconut rich aroma. His spirit soared. Dazzling sunlight, the fragrance of exotic blooms filling the warmth of the trade wind; the stupor of the past twenty-four hours was clearing. Ideas were forming. His taxi followed the coastline, colours separated into primary splendour under the brilliant light. Unending lines of surf, green and vibrant, rolled in from Africa bursting on vast white sands which painted their fringe of palm trunks black and slender. Back from the beach, amidst cool dark foliage, houses of colonial grandeur, sprawling patios and gardener trimmed lawns, had their windows to the sea. Beneath palm tree shade were the shanty huts of corrugated iron, kitchen gardens of hoe and plenty. Roaming hens fled squawking before the taxi, Caribbean kids on bikes dodged them both. Local women sat watching the passing world from front veranda, their gay dresses matching garlands of flowers which hung, reds, purples, and sunflower yellows. Smiling islands of music and laughter, the illusion of happiness?

None of the scene was new to a thoughtful Anderson, he'd spent many holidays out here between his yacht and hilltop villa. On this occasion for the first time, he saw it differently. Why face the stress of business, being driven by this disease of making money? Goldberg returned to his mind, he saw him now as a skillful manipulator suffering from the psychosis of unmitigated greed, living in a manner on the way to killing him.

Let him shoulder the worries of Nuen, dealing with sly bankers, the endless lobbying of shifty politicians, top level intrigues, glamorous stuff until you realized what perfidious creatures inhabit the upper echelons of power. Watching the rolling breakers seemed to be cleansing his mind. Find a way out they said, feed the hunger of the wind, be a man again.

A cruise liner towering above the quay disgorged a procession of camera wielding tourists as the cab dropped him at a hotel on the waterfront. A tidied up ex-Chairman ate breakfast at a palm shaded table. Across ultramarine waters he could appraise the liveliness of a tropical playground. The bay churned with boats, island ferries, tourist laden, flashy millionaire gin palaces and their swimming platforms, local fishing boats piled with nets and dotted about, the odd dinghy being rowed lazily ashore. An old style gaff- rigged schooner hoisted her spread of canvas, sails clawing up the mast until drawing before the Trades they'd heel her over and drive foam from her bow. Maybe she'd be leaving for a distant landfall, a thrill tempered by anticipation. Others arriving dropped sail and anchored. Single-handed sailor would know the satisfaction of making a good passage and feel the strength of self reliance.

He watched the Sea Nymph rocking to the swell of an outgoing liner. Sleek and beautiful, she needed a crew of five and always her skipper making the decisions, how much canvas to set, when to tack, where to anchor. The appeal of adventure was stirring. The sea was talking to him.

Puffs of a hot breeze lifted tiny swirls of dust from the sidewalks. He walked past prestigious company offices that double as counting houses for the manna which fell on a luxurious tax haven.Banks, multi-national institutions, each was dedicated to ensuring that wealth, however obtained, remained in the accounts of those who'd discovered tax loopholes larger than the eye of a needle; in a perplexing mix of the grasping, the insouciant and the carefree, an old lady sat at her shop door, absentmindedly fanning herself. Hens at the gutter fluffed their feathers in a dust bath. It neared noon and the town took time out to rest. Anderson crossed a quiet street and caught the automatic doors of Scotland's largest bank before it closed for a much extended lunch hour. Fans whirled above his head, scenting deliciously cool air. Being well known to the staff he was admitted without any security formality and shown politely into the head banker's office.

A bald head just in sight over the top of a sumptuous Spanish leather couch might indicate the banker was anticipating his lunch time siesta and hadn't heard the discreet knock. Getting to his feet on realizing somebody important must have been ushered in, he stepped across the spacious room, "Andrew, it's always great to see you," a Scots accent and the name, Fraser gave away his origins and by way of an excuse for not being behind a massively carved Indian desk, he added, "I was just sitting thinking." They shook hands cordially, "Sherry, or something better?" the banker enquired already halfway to a cocktail locker. "Something better, if you please, Simon."

Two large malts were poured. They'd always struck a note of accord, the banker feeling an affinity towards a man he regarded as a Scot even after a couple of generations in America. By the same token, Anderson was in many ways more at ease with Fraser than with his fellow countrymen. They chatted, touching gently on the recent banking crash and the disgrace of Scottish Banks.

"You know, Andrew when a top executive's ego outstrips his business acumen and a bonus culture feeds down the ranks, then one day he finds his bank's lending forty times its deposits and the system he controls has becomes a pack of dominoes. Pull out the bottom one, in this case the housing market and because you're such a big player in the finance game, it's hello Mr. Taxpayer." The banker's eye wandered to a window which looked out on a bay full of yachts. "But make no mistake, only the tax paying punters at the bottom are caught out. The cunning lads creep from behind the skirting boards, crawl over the pickings and the cycle starts again."

The frankness of Fraser's comments surprised Anderson, he warmed to the man. Looking round at the room's trappings of wealth, from past bankers' portraits down to an ornate crystal inkstand, it mirrored the ostentation of his own social class, objects symbolic of status, no better than a PR exercise to impress the like minded. The feeble minded, who could tot up the price of your furnishings, trade share markets up and down, but didn't know the value of trust.

"Simon, I'm finished with Nuen," his face became as hard as the decision, his voice brittle with emotion, "sell the yacht and the villa at your earliest opportunity, remit what's generated to my bank in New York," and speaking rapidly, "Transfer fifty thousand dollars from my private account with you to that small account I run in Switzerland." Downing his dram, he finished emphatically, "I'll call in for some ready cash tomorrow and we shall see what's next."

Fraser showed no surprise. Saying nothing, he crossed to the cocktail locker and came back with the decanter. Pouring another two fingers each he stood silently at the window. They sipped their whisky, neither quite ready to break private thoughts. Eventually Anderson throwing back the last of his glass spoke with difficulty, "My great grandfather left Shetland with the few Scots pounds he'd been given by his father, only the clothes on his back. Across there in the bay is a symbol of what grew from the soil of those islands, their harshness made him fit for a challenge. Look at my hands, soft living thins the blood. Maybe mine needs revitalizing."

Putting his back to the window, the banker stood squarely before his client, "Disposing of your assets is not a problem, money flows into this hole like water down a drain. Nobody sees the effects of wealth better than a banker and a barman. I see what it does to many out here, they flounder in it, some sink, a few put it to good works, charity, if you like, mostly it saps them of any challenge, baring the next round." The man's steady gaze seemed tinged with hidden regret, "Andrew, I grew out of a Glasgow tenement, my father was a dock worker on the Clyde. My folks had nothing, nothing except the value of honesty and now I wallow in all the wealth that fills an empty barrel." Fraser reached out his hand, "Young man, I admire your decision. Good luck."

Anderson took the hand without a word. Its grip was that of a man's man. It sealed a momentous decision, a turning point; the handshake of a deal with fate.

A short distance beyond the harbour, a yachting marina filled a sheltered cove. He could see a forest of masts and walked towards it. Nobody about, the town quiet, no tooting cars, screeching parrots or warbling pigeons, the island snoozed away in a heat which burnt the soles of his feet. At the locked gate of the compound he stopped and waited. Sunning itself on a heap of stones too hot to touch, a lizard sat motionless, only the slow inflation of its sack like gizzard suggested other than a mock up. A loud snoring emanated from under an awning. Several rattles at the gate roused a tall smiling Caribbean who gave him access and promptly vanished beneath his sunshade.

Anderson sauntered about the boat yard. Yachts were of every size and type, some moored at pontoons, others ashore and propped on legs, some he wouldn't even chance sailing across the bay. Wandering amongst the craft brought an inexplicable feeling of anticipation. Dodging round the stern of a flat bottomed motor cruiser he came upon a yacht which stopped him in his stride. Her bow lifted with a sheer fit to cleave any foaming top, her full length keel and wide beam would give stability, her canoe shaped stern would rise to any following sea. Perhaps thirty-six feet on the waterline and a simple Bermudan rig, she was an ocean going princess. A yacht for single handed sailing and hanging on her taffrail a sign, 'For Sale'.

An old white haired seadog slept on a deckchair in the shade of her hull surrounded by paint tins and brushes steeping in turpentine. Mahogany face and lank brown arms, Anderson stood looking down on him. A sixth sense which goes with the sea awakened the man. "Sorry to disturb you, but I noticed your sign on the stern." "Yes," the old man reached out and patted her keel, "she's followed the Trade Winds, knows every island in the Pacific, round the Horn and back again." He searched the distance shore before looking up, "never a truer friend."

Anderson walked to the bow of the yacht and read her name, 'Valkyrie.'

The fourth floor windows of a luxury suite in one of London's exclusive hotels overlooked Hyde Park. A naked and yawning Sir Joshua Goldberg drew back the heavy velvet curtains and stood looking out on a drizzle which settled lightly on November trees. The shades of autumn had still to lay their carpet of colour, the deep auburn of chestnut trees and the dying leaves of the oaks, yellow and brown. Early walkers shielded themselves with umbrellas and there clattering along the tarmac, a mounted troop of The Queen's Life Guards on morning exercise. This was a London loved by the freshly installed Nuen Chairman, style and affluence, Royal traditions, knighthoods, a civility which gave quality its place, "Nicky, Nicky, come and see this, a troop of the Household Cavalry are out in the park." Nicky Fellows, merchant banker and friend rolled out of their canopied bed and stood sleepily at the window.

"Wait till you see them on ceremonial duty, what a lovely sight, beautiful uniforms, lovely boys," Sir Joshua enthused. The American blinked at a jingling cavalcade of head tossing horses and soldiers bobbing along in their saddles. His contact lenses were still on the dressing table. "Josh this is marvellous, what a good boy you are persuading me to visit London," and he patted the Chairman's bare bottom affectionately. Goldberg, forcing a smile, squeezed his friend's hand, "Not at all, Nicky, you were the good boy, helping me to oust Anderson." "Sure thing, Josh we sent him running like a cottontail."

Turning from the window they sat side by side on the bed, the sagging white flesh of a Knight of the Realm with its creases of layered fat in contrast to the bony naked torso of Nick Fellows, tanned and scrawny. Nicky allowed their elbows to touch, ever so gently.

Sir Joshua's thoughts centered on the business ahead rather than the attentions of his friend. He looked down on a floppy girth which hid his private parts. This affair was becoming tiresome. Fellows, yes a splendid chap, as far as most bankers went; not intelligent types, their noses too near the trough, clever but not intelligent. Nicky had certainly facilitated the run on Nuen's stock, couldn't grudge him that and now the shares were climbing nicely again, but today's meeting had to be of the highest secrecy. Financiers couldn't be trusted; once Nuen became indispensable to the interests of both the Pentagon and Westminster, this relationship would have served its purpose and could be broken off; anyway Fellows was painfully demanding.

Hoping to distract his friend, Goldberg attempted a serious note, "You know Nicky, deposing Anderson is one thing, protecting Nuen's nuclear interests is another. Solar energy's our real danger. I noticed the other day the US Energy Department is funding work on photovoltaic panels which can be embedded into roads and car parks. Its sounds outlandish but paving the US road network with solar panels would supply the nation's entire energy needs. As for this damned Sahara Solar set up," Sir Joshua mused on, "and just wait until China and India along with Brazil and the Middle East block stop trading oil in dollars, that'll stuff the US economy big style, no wonder gold's taken off, a real shift power is round the corner."

Fellows stroked Goldberg's flaccid thigh. Before the hand could stray further, Sir Joshua got up, "Now, now, Nicky don't be naughty, I think I told you I'm meeting an old member of staff for coffee, a bit boring for you, I'll drop you off at the National Gallery, you must see the Turners. Now then shower and breakfast, what d' you say?"

Nicky sounded petulant, "Whatever you say, Josh, but let me soap you down," and pulling his friend off the bed they went into the shower together

----

An obscure café in China Town served the purpose of two men dressed casually in sports jackets and flannels; neither would be recognized or even noticed by the mix of clientele who sipped green tea or took their morning coffee. The pair met on the street outside and sauntered to a table away from the window. Dragon lanterns did little to alleviate the general dimness; instead they cast a yellowish light on richly embroidered silken drapes. Mustiness pervaded the thick atmosphere, a cloak- like incense of spice and exotic fruit in which secrecy might hide. Cane tables and rattan chairs were not the style of furnishing which Nuen's Chairman favoured, nor did oriental beverages have any appeal.

The click, click of a bead curtain and a Chinese waiter stood awaiting their order, polite and deadpan. "Two black coffees," Goldberg spoke without looking up. As silently as he appeared, the waiter withdrew into some dark recess behind the curtain. Perhaps the unreadable mood of the place, maybe the nature of their business, glancing at each other both men became aware care must be taken. They sat chatting, drinking coffee, to all appearances an innocuous meeting of two old colleagues.

Neither papers nor briefcases, no names used, the two men knew each other from Goldberg's days as UK's top Scientific Advisor. Nothing to be recorded or spelt out, both men's minds perfectly able to convey their respective position and requirements without any openness. In spite of their affable conversation Sir Joshua watched the Permanent Secretary to the UK Government's Minister of Defense with a concentration which turned his dark eyes to glittering avaricious dots.

Taking a casual approach, Goldberg observed, "Of course there's so much common ground between yourselves and my friends in your sister establishment, issues of overall strategy don't present any problem. We work towards mutual goals, it benefits all round." Nodding agreement the Permanent Secretary ran slender fingers through a greying Etonian haircut, thoroughly aware that Goldberg referred to the Pentagon and his own Defense Department.

Sir Joshua spoke airily, "Perhaps I should say that my organisation has the closest ties with the chaps on our side of the pond. In fact we supply the key material for their existing requirements and also to their more advanced programmes."

Brushing a military moustache with his index finger the Secretary had so far said nothing, his clean face remained impassive, only a faint flush came to the morning's aftershave.

This could prove a risky conversation. He glanced round the tables.

Goldberg felt his heart pulsing, a slight pain in his chest, the coffee too strong? "You may well wish to use our services in that direction, re-fuelling if you like to put it that way." The Defense Secretary inclined his head, his eyes staring down a long aquiline nose at nothing in particular. Sir Joshua attempted a laugh, "Naturally if we can help you, perhaps your influence in another area could help us and you know, old chap, my organization is only too willing to help; we supply under brown wraps as well," The Secretary mustered a quizzical grin.

They sipped coffee. The Secretary's face lost its grin, Goldberg was getting to the salient, "Let me be honest, any progress on that other issue of energy production is being hampered by a lack of adequate facility in disposing of some of our more unwanted products and make no mistake this could be of international interest as others have the same problem too."

Although the Defense Secretary easily followed Goldberg's theme, the words international interest puzzled him for a moment. "International?" he raised an eyebrow.

"Absolutly", Sir Joshua lent over the table, "there could well be a worldwide demand for the facility we at Nuen envisage, could pay your bosses handsomely. It would be quite a warren, given the right situation. It goes without saying that our helping you out with your private requirements would tie in quite nicely with the planned expansion of the generating units which are presently still behind closed doors."

Far from being oblivious to Goldberg's hinted proposal, the Private Secretary, who gave the impression of only a vague grasp of this torrent of innuendo, was thinking well ahead. Nuen's paramount position in the nuclear industry was well known to him. To have Nuen quietly supplying weapons grade plutonium to the Ministry of Defense whilst busying themselves sinking their money and UK's present and future nuclear waste into a storage facility would be the kind of deal of great appeal to the Treasury. Shipping in other nations' waste would truly whet their appetite. Mustn't let Goldberg cool off, he smiled graciously, "I quite understand your position, most interesting," and rounding off, he nodded, "food for thought."

Sir Joshua's chest tighten, practiced at deciphering the bureaucratic code, he smelt progress, "We have several locations in mind for this facility and would appreciate it if you chaps could arrange a fly-by for us, rather than us pushing in somewhere to the glare of flashlights."

The Defense Secretary stood abruptly, just a shade flustered, this interview must be terminated before Goldberg became too specific. He'd already decided that under the guise of a small military training exercise Goldberg or his minion should be shown to wherever it might be necessary for a survey. One snag, deaths in Afghanistan and current helicopter availability.

Ignoring Nuen's Chairman, he walked out onto the street. Cursing under his breath Goldberg paid for the coffees, took the change and followed. Chinatown bustled round the pair, intimate and smelling of food, though daylight was not its medium. The cheapness of the venue had pleased neither party but then the Secretary reflected, one must make sacrifices in furthering the National interests. He must bear in mind that nursing Goldberg and Nuen, to a large extent the result of a certain other Company Directors' influence, had the approval of Downing Street.

Looking over Sir Joshua's head, the mandarin spoke in an undertone, "Our transport is busy elsewhere as we speak but within several months I can arrange a helicop..." he cut short. Confound it, stiffly he corrected himself, "I shall arrange suitable transport. Expect a private communication in due course and by the way, your thoughts will be relayed to the highest quarters."

Anxious to bolster hopes of future business but in no ways wishing to compromise himself he lowered his eyes to give Goldberg final a penetrating stare, "Rest assured, Sir Joshua, the UK's nuclear programme remains under active consideration, of course in the Nation's interests certain planning procedures must be reviewed." Goldberg moved to shake the Secretary's hand, too late, afraid he might have said too much, with a curt nod the Permanent Secretary to the Ministry of Defense strode away.

Hidden by the crowd he smiled sourly, "Goldberg's risen to the fly, um... he might be useful." Shoulders back, military bearing; equally at home, be it casting flies on a salmon river, potting grouse on a Scottish moor or networking a Royal Garden Party, he epitomised the vested power behind politics, happy as always to watch his puppets dancing.

CHAPTER TWENTY-EIGHT

Entanglement

Eilidh was in London, that much I knew, no more, no less. Alone on the jetty I fretted for her. The crying of the seals which drew me to the bay had faded away to a profound stillness, the long, long hiss of gently spreading foam upon the sand, the only sound. It was a night for sharing. The vast firmament shone without a trace of cloud, no man made illumination to dim unbounded space, to detract from the purity of a light which enveloped land and ocean in a milk-white glow; a time to be together in the solitude of a place untouched; a haven where the past was a wraith which grieved for the spectre of tomorrow; a night to watch the turning heavens in their timeless configurations and journey to the limit of entwining thought.

Something drew me away from watching the play of light and shade across the bay. Dark forms at the turn of my head had a movement which caught the corner of my eye. Without reason, for several moments, a considerable unease affected me, almost a dread. An impending force seemed poised above the island. I stared into empty space. Its wavering silence seemed the echo of a long past celestial happening, some momentous cataclysm in the annals of the rocks. Its sinister threat vanished as quickly as it had taken hold. Instantly I dismissed the impression as no more than the auto-suggestive impact of dramatic lighting effects and the mournful wailing of the seals.

Although the keening of the seal-folk had died away, there lingered still the phantoms of my imagination, the souls without rest who'd lamented their drowning through the voices of the seal women; the spectral dead who roamed the beach by the fullness of a moon which infused the bay with a radiance of palest turquoise. And upon that eerie glow the Hilda glided, far out, stealthy as a dream, silently as a chimera might float into the mind on seas of fantasy.

Had I succumbed to the strangeness of the night, glimpsed of the tangled wavelengths of other worlds amidst the unending undulations of time? Out of an impenetrable distance, beyond the edge of our puny dot of existence, the arc of outer space grew in luminosity as it soared towards the circled brilliance of a haloed moon. From the vaulted heavens to the floating orb at my feet creation turned on an axis of light.

Familiar shapes were walls of black outline, silver reflection and shadows the animation of rock and shore; together the carved land of a bygone era, the creatures of the tide, the journeying photons which gave their energy to light the sea; I stood in a hallowed amphitheatre and in the secrecy of the night came their holistic enjoining. It seemed as if all the elemental forms were gathered below night's curving dome, weeping with the pathos of the crying of the seals.

Slowly that bizarre impression faded and I thought again of Eilidh in London. And in so doing, to my horror, tube train doors were closing. Over a swaying crowd I saw her golden head. Aware of immediate danger I fought my way desperately towards her.

I struggled to rid the night of its stupid fantasies as the Hilda glided imperceptibly towards the jetty. The strength of the light cast her shadow upon opal waters. She sailed closer. I caught the faint creaking of her timber as a small pocket of the breeze filled her canvas. She was no illusion. Her crew were hidden by the spread of her sail. How many I wondered?

Eachan for sure and doubtless a police officer, maybe two of them; I smiled ruefully, yes, there'd be two of them, make certain I left the island quietly, hopefully without being handcuffed. Had they seen me standing on the jetty? Hiding on Sandray wouldn't be difficult, it again crossed my mind, but then I'd be a fugitive and if suspected of murder, it might only confirm my guilt in the eyes of the law enforcement. I did not relish a heavyweight interrogation. No boy, stand and tell the truth.

Such was the transient beauty of the night, the impending police questioning or arrest seemed of no consequence on the great scale of happenings. An appreciation of the minutiae of any individual on the scale of the universe I'd been gazing upon emptied me of anxiety. Short of planetary disintegration through escalating climate change or playing with massive nuclear devices, nothing that mankind might do to disfigure or destroy the face of this earth could impact on the inexorable march towards this planet's cosmic fate. What would be, would be. Eilidh was with me in thought, the island was part of me; both would travel in my mind and beyond.

I waited; tiny puffs of warm air brushed my cheeks. The Hilda moved with the tide. Three boat lengths off the jetty, the merest breath and the helmsman brought his boat slowly round.

In her turning the moonlight shone on golden hair.

Transfixed, I neither spoke nor moved. The Hilda drew gracefully alongside the jetty. A coil of rope landed at my feet. Mechanically I secured it to a mooring ring and looked down on Eilidh. She looked up, laughing eyes, outshining the night. Neither of us spoke. In the meeting of our eyes was all that was needed, binding us, bringing us together. I reached down, caught her stretching hands and she was in my arms, crying sobs of happiness. Crushing her to me, "Eilidh," was all I managed to say. Astonished at her coming to me, the hardiness of her sailing alone; a night which had filled me with longing and imagination, now found me shaking with inexpressible joy. My longing dissolved into elation, I held the woman I craved.

I stroked her lustrous hair, holding flowing strands to the light; moonlight ran through my fingers. I buried my face in silky thickness of golden hair and breathed her fragrance. The soft growl of loving came to my throat. Caressing her shapely head, soothing and caring, gradually the sobbing eased as though a great stress were passing. Her face stayed hidden against me. Her body trembled. Gently I lifted her chin and bent my head; lips and tears were mingled.

We kissed the unbroken kiss that knows no time, nor bounds of thought- knows just the bliss of touching, the touch which sweeps two people into the harmony of being in each other's arms. Under the heavens, in the unbroken peace of an island, two people were in love.

I struggled to comprehend how it could be she was here, by the bay, in my arms, that we were holding each other. How, it mattered not, I was overwhelmed by happiness, this woman had come to me. Out of the hideous trauma of these past days, staring death in the face, the woman that I'd called to, of whom I'd thought of beyond all else in those desperate hours, had come to me.

Only the steadfast moon and the gently making tide counted time, for to us, it held no meaning. The world could turn until its complexity became the simplicity of beauty in a realm where only the waves of entanglement exist. I looked over Eilidh's head to the silver water and the stark outlines of the headland of death and knew that when minds were one, there would be no parting.

With an unexpected laugh Eilidh sprang out of my arms and ran helter-skelter to the edge of the tide. A shade bewildered,

I watched. In moments her clothes were a discarded pile on the sand. White as the moonlight she skipped into the sea, splashing and calling. "Come on Hector, it's warm."

In moments her head shone golden on the moon pale water. Down the shore I ran in wild excitement, peeling off garments on the beach, leaping in strides through the shallow water, flinging up showers of glistening droplets. One mighty dive, I swam out to her. Under a silver moon in the glowing ripples of a phosphorescent sea, our bodies clung together.

Our every move created a trail of gleaming specks, minute forms of ocean life they clung to our limbs, glowing for a second, shedding their tiny store of photons. I turned Eilidh's lithe body and held her on my chest as I floated. Our heads were together. Moonbeams surrounded us. We swam in a circle of light. I whispered, "Eilidh, just the three of us." "Yes, three of us" and she gave a little laugh.

The rustle of our swimming alone broke the silence. Suddenly crashing sounds carried over the bay. Startled for a moment we trod water. Amidst much grunting and splashing the seals plunged off their roosting ledges. Churning waters shone out of the shadows. In moments curious heads bobbed around us. Big dark eyes gazed, unblinking. Eye level contact, before, with a snort, each black dome slid out of sight. We followed their every twist and turn by the trails of a million sparkling golden dots. Lowly life? Only human hubris believes in the pyramid of life.

"Race you to the house." Eilidh set off with a flurry of strokes. Laughing, I caught her foot. We were in the shallows, hugging and kissing. Breaking free, grabbing her bundle of clothes, she was off, running through the dunes until bare feet were in the softness of meadow grass. She turned at the house, panting and laughing at the same time and held out her arms to me.

Without a word, lifting her off her feet I carried her round to the gable. Still holding her I turned the tap of my makeshift shower. Cold fresh water straight off the hill, her squeaks carried to the Hill of the Shroud. In a minute I was back, soap and towel. We washed off salt water. Exhilaration, every artery pounded as the warmth grew. I dried Eilidh with tenderness, she was beauteous woman. I hugged her again with the towel about us.

It was then I realised how few words had been spoken. There was no need, the ecstasy of enfolding arms, the glory of the night, what need of speech? Taking her hand I led her into the house. There was no light inside, only the sinking moon through a window pane. Two bodies together and in the shaft of white light, one brown, one a ghostly white.

I began to say, "goodnight,"... tent and sleeping bag waited. I crossed to the door. Reading my thoughts Eilidh quietly took my hand. Putting her arms around my neck she whispered, "My Hector."

We lay in the bed I'd at looked at each day. And the woman I'd wanted to be with, to be mine in its purest meaning since our eyes first met on a tube train, in a teeming city, was beside me now, giving herself to me, warm and loving.

The moon laid her tip on the edge of the Atlantic, the last of her light a silver path across the bay; it shone at our window in the old House of the Haven. Slowly it faded, a reflection of all things past.

Tenderly my kiss closed her eyes and together in that passion which knows no tomorrow, we reached into the endless galaxies, entangled, body and mind.

CHAPTER TWENTY-NINE

"A serious matter."

They'd known each other since prep school days and indeed in later years for a couple of terms at Eton, in fact, young Tim Winthrop-Bagley, now Sir Timothy Winthrop-Bagley, to much leg pulling, had fagged for Jeffrey Norton-Winters. Both received adequate instruction in the handholds that allowed them to climb the slippery pole, or more correctly, ascend the backstairs of political power. Naturally a knighthood for Winthrop-Bagley, or 'Windy Bags' as he was called by his familiars, reflected his rise to the post of Senior Permanent Secretary to Her Majesty's Treasury, whereas his erstwhile 'senior boy', the 'Shivering Jeff' Winters, had to make do with the cloth cap position of Permanent Secretary to the Department of Trade and Energy.

Each week they lunched together at their favourite French restaurant, just off Mayfair, discreet and it must be said, thanks to its exotic menu, rather exclusive, not that the bill concerned either gentlemen, the tab went to the taxpayer. After all, important policy issues concerning their respective roles in the running of the country could be discussed, minus the ear or note taking of assistant secretaries, in short the justification of a working lunch with the benefit of a frank exchange of views. At best, when joined casually as it were by the captains of finance and industry, they kept their fingers on the pulse of the Nation.

Norton-Winters swilled round the drop of Reserve red, tasted it, nodded a grudging approval to the waiter, allowed him to pour and waved him away, "Saw you'd made it down to the old Nail and Garter last night Bagley. Must say 'Bags' old sport you looked a bit miffed about something,"

"By God 'Shivers' old chap you couldn't be more right, had one hell of a day with that numbskull of a Chancellor, talking about flogging orf the family silver. Has to be, I'm afraid," Sir Winthrop tried his wine, "let any tuppenny banker orf the leash, nose for a bonus, better than my best Pointer when he's onto a Woodcock, as for these expense happy politicians buying votes with their soft cushion economy, then blaming the Yanky-doodles," a flush tinged his heavy jowls,

"I tell you Jeff, they couldn't have blarsted a bigger hole in the vaults if I'd supplied them with a charge of TNT. No Jeff, it's over to Mr.Taxpayer to fill the crater, raise the standard rate, that's what it'll be. Selling the silver, won't make a blind bit of difference, even flogging the Channel Tunnel. Mind you," he paused, an idea occurred, "umm, remember old 'Floppy Prick' Hankey, he's done rather well for himself considering the rumpus over that takeover job. Not a bad shot for the chap who won Wanker of the Year Award, I say what." They laughed together. Norton-Winters steered away from the topic.

"By the way, 'Bags' before 'Goldilocks' turns up, he's always late, you might have heard, courtesy of this damn fool Freedom of Information Act and that's something which should be tightened up, it'll be the undoing of our democratic system," Sir Winthrop nodded emphatically, "Absolutly, couldn't agree more, worse than any leak, far harder to control, no saying how deep this exposure of Westminster expenses could go. A leak, you can turn it orf at source, simple, bring the press hounds to heel, they know what's good for them."

"Quite so, but I should mention 'Bags, you may have got a snippet, anyway the nuclear boys up in Scotland, I think somewhere on their God forsaken north coast, have been caught pants down holding hundreds of tons of radio active waste, came from all over Europe. Damn'reptiles' have splashed the story; ideal Green fodder and helps the wretched Scotch Nats' anti-nuclear lobby no end. Don't understand what actually happens, I think they stuff it into barrels, anyway to put a good head on it they've poured in a dollop which seemingly arrived from 'Down Under'."

"Really," Sir Winthrop-Bagley looked mildly shocked, "Australia of all places, my son's out there, just pulled orf a job in Canberra, Private Secretary to Her Majesty's Governor, he's young of course, something better's bound to turn up. You know 'Shivers', the flight's so awfully boring, still we may go out for the Christmas break, I have to say Anthea so feels the benefit of their wonderfully dry weather, her arthritis....."

Norton-Winters interrupted, "Point is about this nuclear stuff, 'Bags', we agreed to return it to the countries of origin, but storage is such a nice little earner, keeps everybody happy and can't think of a better dustbin than Scotland; and now that's blown. There's got be a way round this little problem. Talking of selling silver, never mind the Met Office, we must get 'Goldilocks' and his company to offer for the new range of nuclear facilities that's on the drawing board. Naturally the French are keen, but Josh is such a bloodhound when there's a whiff of lucre in the wind; either way offloading our nuclear worries should put a bob or two in your begging bowl."

"Good thinking Jeff, totally with you." Looking out from their secluded alcove, Winthrop-Bagley spotted the polished dome of their school chum. As a waiter helped Sir Joshua Goldberg off with his winter coat, 'Bags' whispered hoarsely, "Look here, 'Shivers', don't mention this bally climate change issue to 'Goldilocks', he's such a bore, caught me at the Club last week, seems to think it's quite a serious matter. I suspect rather importantly from his point of view, it has the infinitely more serious prospect of being a cash dispenser. He went on and on, this nuclear thing, our only solution to keeping temperatures down, such a bore, I told him its varstly more pleasant in the garden these days, nectarines've never done better, even Anthea's hip has improved, Finally fell asleep, wakened up, he was still bloody well talking."

They both rose to greet Sir Joshua, "Josh, how awfully good to see you and so nice you can spend a little time on this side of the pond and looking so spruce. Capital, so glad you made it, do sit down." The waiter tucked a chair beneath the Nuen's chairman's ample posterior spread a linen napkin across his knees and to a nod from Bagley vanished silently to reappear with a fresh bottle of Reserve.

"How jolly splendid to see you both," Goldberg responded to their greeting just a shade less effusively never having quite forgotten his 'three of the best' administered in the Prefects' Room by senior boy, Winthrop-Bagley. The flat of a cricket bat on bare buttocks amongst a group of smirking cronies left him smarting for days and inflected an indelible mark on his mind.

Pleasantries and platitudes and not a little gossip passed concerning the foibles and fornications amongst bureaucracies ruling orders, until 'Shivers Norton' found an opening to comment darkly, "You realise our dependency on this wretched Russian gas pipe could have a ghastly effect on UK energy prices. I know old 'Barmy Blakensop' at the Foreign Office is working hard with MI6 to find some way to blunt the Sickle before the Hammer crushes our goollies."

Goldilocks rose to the fly, "Now, that's exactly where I can help you chaps. This climate change lark, all the rage at the moment, international conferences! Enough hot air to put a degree on the graph," he warmed to the theme, unaware behind his back

'Windy Bags' Winthrop's eyes reached for the ceiling, "we at Nuen have the complete answer." To gain effect, Goldberg allowed his eyelids to fall.

"Really, how interesting," exclaimed the wide eyed Permanent Secretary to the Department of Energy playing innocent curiosity, privately delighted that Goldberg appeared hooked.

Sir Joshua looked carefully behind him "Give us the green light, ha, ha, perhaps I should say the go-ahead, a dash of fiscal simulation on your part, we'll build your next generation of power plants, pollution free, give you all the energy the country can utilise. We'll halt the spread of these revolving blots on the landscape; bally windmills, disastrous for the grouse and tidal turbines are sure to mangle the salmon, either way they're a complete waste of resources."

Winthrop-Bagley's eyes were drooping. He sat up with a start at a carefully aimed under the table kick, "Did I catch you saying fiscal support? Dangerous words these days." Winters-Norton, not wishing Sir Winthrop to dilute the wine with a splash of Treasury cold water, tightened the line, ready to land Goldilocks, "I dare say some accommodation could be made, I can't speak for 'Bags' but we at Energy have a useful budget." 'Windy-Bags' frowned but remained silent.

"Look here chaps, I can't be more honest," Goldberg unaware of the hook he'd swallowed attacked full frontal, "Off the top of my head, for a round figure," as he rolled his eyes in a rapid calculations they both glanced from Sir Joshua's bald plate to the straining buttons of his striped shirt, "could be the order of six billion per facility. Give us the three new plants, by tender of course and any current decommissioning work at costs plus. You come up front with six, we'll capitalise the remaining twelve billion, thirty years against you at say," he tapped his forehead, "say, nine percent quarterly over Bank of England base and any extraneous problems by negotiation."

The pair sat back aware of the potential for a deal. By tender of course, highest standards of verisimilitude must be observed at all times. The waiter, long experienced in being privy to Governmental affairs, recognised a critical juncture. He approached with a ready uncorked bottle of the Special Reserve.

Driving home his point, Goldberg breathed in sonorously, "And if it's any interest to you both, I'm being flown quietly up to Scotland by the Minis---," he checked himself deliberately, "when the weather improves that is. I'll do a survey, couple of sites in mind for handing this small matter of waste disposal. I know I can count on your help in that area particularly. We want to construct storage that's adequate for dealing with material from nuclear facilities far beyond the UK," in fact he said airily, "for example there's no reason why we couldn't oblige Japan."

Count on our help, the suggestion of a wider international trade in nuclear material came as music to the overly large ears of 'Shivers Norton'. He'd suffered ridicule since childhood, indeed night and day for years his mother insisted he wear a hat with flaps tied below his chin in a futile attempt to curb their protuberant nature. When finally exposed to the general amusement of his school chums they steeled a young mind with the determination to outwit his fellow beings. It could be said his ears had been the making of the man. Now glowing bright red, they gave away the combination of Special Reserve and a degree of attention which he strove to hide from his fellow diners.

"How very interesting Josh, why don't we get together, talk things through. Care to come down to Windy Nook for a weekend? Pre-Christmas shoot, always a jolly affair, plenty of room at the manor you know, say a week Thursday? Gladys and I are having an informal party, few friends, think the Chancellor will look in, one or two more. Pheasant are breaking cover high this year. I'll lend you a 12 bore if yours happens to be in Yankie Doodle land. By the way who did you say was providing your transport up to Scotland? May we help?

Sir Joshua an accomplished hand at playing one Government Department against another left Winters-Norton wondering might it just be the MOD providing his transport and if so why? Noting the bushy eyebrows of the Treasury Secretary were drawn together with more than a hint of displeasure, he realised care would be needed, "Wouldn't dream of troubling you Jeff old chap, nothing arranged yet, but I'd be delighted to come over to the Nookie, got to nip back to the Big Apple for a couple of days beforehand, that's nothing, yes I'll be down, mind if I bring a friend?"

"Please do," gushed 'Shivers', privately thrilled he'd outflanked 'Windy Bags' whom he'd taken care not to include on the guest list, just in case the P.M. might turn up. Nor had he forgotten Bagley nobbled a knighthood, as his dear wife frequently reminded him. The trio turned to debating the luncheon menu. The best part of some time elapsed before they parted, ostensibly genial friends.

One moment a fresh crescendo of screeching, next the moaning of a demented soul, the cravings of a gale are fed only by death. It tore at streaming hair, sucked air from the lungs of a crouching man and at his ear, beneath each lusting shriek boomed the mighty rollers pitching headlong into a pit of watery blackness. No blessings of the halcyon days but the embodiment of an evil that whispered through the lightness in his head, lone sailor, know the portals of your tomb are wide, you will be our sacrifice.

There is no fury on this earth beyond the wrath of an Atlantic gale, no sound the more terrifying than an ocean's requiem for its countless solitary drownings, no greater release of the ascending human spirit than to be taken by the glory of wild abandoned beauty. So the sailor prepared to be a part of that which man strives to subdue. He watched in awe the beasts of untamed passion, felt his soul about to share the grandeur of their freedom. Elation conquered fear.

Across the wastelands of an ocean the great combers reared unbridled; rank upon rank, they fused the writhing strips of cloud and dashing tops; set golden light dancing tip to tip. Cloud, waves and sunset were one, there was no horizon, nothing save the flickering colours of violent motion to stay a fast falling night. Each succeeding onslaught ripped arching peaks and flung them, white sheets of unleashed spume into a purple sky. Darkest ultramarine surged to deepest green, huge collapsing crests turned the slanted sunlight into orange fragments of bursting spray and on the bellies of twisting clouds blazed the crimson fires of nightfall.

Andrew Anderson clung to the cockpit of his yacht, hands without feeling, one to the winch, one on the tiller, salt water lashing his neck, blinding his eyes, a strop of rope to a ring bolt held him; the faith of a man in his boat against a thousand miles of sea which held no mercy; human frailty, a plaything to be tossed before demonic whim.

Ten days sailing and eight hundred miles astern lay the Caribbean islands. Luxury living and the Nuen Company office were two thousand miles northwest, a lifetime away in his thoughts. The abandoning of all the froth of sophisticated living had fallen at one stroke, a single decision, final and total.

That sun braced morning in Roadtown, at his bank, on the waterfront, amidst every form of seafaring vessel, in the marina he'd come upon a yacht. No second look or careful appraisal, he knew without recourse to thought or painstaking deliberation, she was the yacht; his sudden instinct told him, the awakening of some innate feeling for the true relationship between sail and sea was enough. She would take the place of all that had gone before, in challenge and affection.

There and then, standing at the yacht's bow, Anderson shook the hand of an old seafaring man, looked into faded eyes, the washed out blue of day after day of glittering sun on the breadth of an ocean, "She will be as faithful to you as you will be to her." Nothing more was said. The old sailor put his hand on the yacht and stroked her shapely hull. His eyes filled with the tears of memory, and he walked quietly away. A witness to that parting of man and boat, Andrew Anderson understood why at the very last a skipper goes down with his ship.

The ferocity which might yet claim him forged that bond. 'Valkyrie' would see him through, or carry him beyond; courage and faith alone his lifeline.

The stern of the 'Valkyrie' reared higher, higher, her bow plunged down and down. The crest of the wave which surged away ahead of them became taller than her masthead, an immense greyback streaked with veins of froth, powering into chaos. The yacht's angle steepened, the tiller twisted in his hand. He fought to keep her square to the rising wave.

It came. Up, up, steeper, steeper, the yacht tipped nose down. Andrew Anderson looked into a hole in the sea, gaping open, devoid of light, a bottomless grave. Growling grew to roaring. He glanced astern. Water towered above him, a perpendicular face of black water. Its great white crest hung poised, curled, about to topple, a second, two, three....

The hollow cave of water began to fall, slow motion, falling, falling. The yacht plunged, deeper, steeper. If the bow buried, she would pitch pole, end for end.

The monstrous comber cut off the gale, for moments only a hiss of cascading water, down it came, a jeering face, a breaking seething torrent.

Rushing, crushing, it fell onto 'Valkyrie'. A thunderous crash of solid water, a mass of swirling foam; tiller torn from his grasp, it washed a helpless Anderson to the end of the strop of rope which secured him to his yacht.

No hold of the boat, gasping, choking, all green and silent.

The rope tugged. Coughing water, his head cleared the surface.

What lies deep will out, "Valkyrie, Valkyrie, for Odin's sake."

He cried to the God of his Viking blood.

CHAPTER THIRTY

Tomorrow's journey

I wakened in the stillness of the old house to the warmth of our bodies together. Eilidh lay with her back to me in the circle of my arms, just the way we had slept throughout the night. I felt her breathing against my chest, soft and easy, her beautiful body in the cup of my hands. Gently I buried my face in the spread of her golden hair. Its fragrance brought her closer. At the slight move of my arm Eilidh awoke. She turned with the sigh of contentment. Her eyes expressed the strength our feelings, all a woman may give, all that any man can return. Slowly we kissed. The long, long kiss that brings bodies and minds together.

The first hint of sunrise drew light to our tiny window. Soon it would lift the chill of a fresh November morning. We nestled, unspeaking, unwilling to return to man made time; sufficient the pace of a world which lived at our doorstep. We were in love, impossibly in love. All that mattered revolved around us, we existed in a capsule bound by the force which entangled our thoughts, united us in that beautiful melody which reaches to the heart of all being.

I lifted the tresses of hair which covered our pillow, caressed the softness of her skin; almost afraid of the question which arose in my thoughts. I whispered, "Eilidh, how did you know to come to me, what was it?"

Pulling my head to her breasts, she whimpered a little. I felt the beat of her heart quicken and after a long, long silence I caught her low murmuring, "It came over me, in middle of another useless meeting, without any warning a sudden pang of agony. It was dreadful, I felt sick and got up and walked out. They thought I was ill."

I looked up, startled by what I was hearing. She smiled at me, stroked my face, "Hector, I'd been happy thinking about you through the day, missing you, dreadfully sometimes but talking to you as I went to sleep each night made me more content," a catch came in her throat, "Hector, in that frightening moment of agony, I thought you'd been killed," she seemed barely able to speak, "I though you were dead."

A violent tremor seized her. At last, in what seemed as a child's voice, she whispered, "and I wanted to die beside you." My arms crushed her to me, "Eilidh, my only Eilidh, I will be with you, as we are now."

It was a long time before I collected my thoughts sufficiently. With Eilidh beside me, the events of cliff top and rescue seemed far in the past. Breathing into her hair I told her gently as I could, "My end was as close as it will ever be," her body went rigid, "our being apart was the only thing which filled my mind, talking to you the one thing that kept me from falling." Bit by bit I unfolded the whole story. We lay comforting each other, no longer was I incredulous at her arrival, the peaks of great emotion have pathways beyond our understanding.

The Hilda boat would need to go back to Halasay, slack water was at mid-day but neither of us wanted to relinquish the delight of simply lying side by side. For once the tide could wait. Whatever the future might involve, I certainly had no intention of it involving our being apart, "Eilidh, I won't be separated from you again, it may mean leaving Sandray, I've set my mind on this island but nothing, nothing is more important to me than being with you." She nodded, and speaking almost shyly, "It's what I want beyond anything."

Eventually sounding more like herself, Eilidh announced, "I'm finished with London, packing in my job, I've had enough of trying to talk common sense into politicians. I've been heavily involved with research on climate change, especially its impact on the release of methane from the blanket tundras of Canada and Siberia. I can't stand anymore of their petty back biting machinations. The poor natives of Sub-Sahara watch their livestock dying of drought knowing their children will be next. They face a four degree temperature rise and twentyfive percent less rain, fine proud people, and whilst they lead their camels to slaughter, I have to talk to the degenerate objects who struggle to get out of their fancy limousines. I tell you, Hector I'm so sick at heart. "

I took her hand realising that her pent up anger needed a listening ear, it certainly had my full sympathy. I wanted her to talk and ease the fretting which had taken hold. After a little she began again, "There's no leadership from the front, nobody in a position to make decisions who's prepared to set an example, no Prime Minister who'd swallow his pride and drive a little eco-friendly car. No, they're busy building more roads, believing a bigger dose of economic development is what's needed, happy letting bailed out banks loose to fund the pollution of oil extraction from the tar sands deposits of central Canada, I've seen the machine ripping gigantic holes in the ground." The outburst astounded me. Her eyes were aflame with an unreserved passion.

"Now they decide that all we need are systems of power production which don't emit CO_2. They can't grasp the fact it's our escalating energy usage which provides us with a playtime planet to wreck. Even tampering with the earth's crust, never mind the shift of weight distribution due to melting poles and rising sea levels, breaking through the rock strata to bury carbon dioxide or other forms of waste is liable to release more problems than it can ever solve, as for meeting CO_2 emission targets, not a hope. The relative stability of our planetary climate during the past twenty thousand years is passing a tipping point of no return; we are heading into multiple uncharted effects, each one re-enforcing the next in a domino collapse." I nodded, not wanting to her to stop, being so much in agreement with views which had the flavour of one of my rants.

"I feel so helpless, Hector. I've seen the starving pot bellied kids, vultures picking over the carcases of their parents' cattle. The impact on the world's poor will be catastrophic. Affluent Westerners will only abandon their consumer conspicuous lifestyles when the waters lap round their ankles, the wealthy will pull up their drawbridges thinking they're safe. It's the blind, unstoppable greed of financial institutions and the myopia of multinational economics versus an environment which in the end holds the cards, the planet will remain in one piece until it's fried by the sun."

Poor Eilidh, her concerns tumbled out. She rounded off, "I've had enough of a world where millions waste their day texting and twittering, we're top heavy with talkers. Politics is a media performance with no more substance than a celebrity act, we're being led by ill- informed fools who wouldn't know what a spade looks like and certainly wouldn't want to know. I was booked to address the Climate Change Conference next month, but honestly, Hector, I couldn't stand more hypocrisy." Shaking a little after her outburst, she snuggled into me again, "anyway, I wanted to be here," and at last she laughed, "to see what you are up to, my boy." In spite of being shocked by her distress and deeply sorry, I laughed with her. "Eilidh," I put a finger on her lips and took her to me.

Although Eilidh had told Ella she would be back by that afternoon, strange to relate we missed the midday tide. Both boats were to go across, Eilidh's which I'd been using and the Hilda. The moon had yet to rise. No light took away the stars, their radiance peopled the treacle blackness of the Sound. Like old Eachan, Eilidh handled the Hilda boat with a confidence in her every action. Ropes came to hand with sureness, the sail's least need trimmed to the faintest of breeze. She sat at the tiller with the lift of a head that welcomed a friend. Legacy of the northlands, the sea was hers.

We turned the Sandray headland, Halasay stood clear against the stars. The tail of The Plough pointed our course. Along the swathing path of the Milky Way we sailed a sleeping Atlantic. Eilidh's form moved with the boat, they waltzed to the motion of the sea, natural as the faraway islands on the edge of a journey. I watched the woman and knew the aching of an immense happiness.

I glanced astern. Sandray had vanished. The breeze died, we drifted into a cotton wool fog. It rolled over the Sound, thick and clinging. A tide on the turn curled under the boat. It would sweep us into the Atlantic, perhaps onto the rocks of Sandray head. Neither of us spoke, I slung the outboard on the stern. Eilidh dropped and stowed the sail. In case the engine refused to start she laid out the oars. A couple of pulls and the engine broke a clammy silence. I knew the bearing which should get us across and could just make out the compass needle. Eilidh perched at the bow, a black form in a white blanket, seemed happy to depend on my navigation.

How far had we sailed, more than half way? I allowed a degree for the set of the current and we motored ahead. My eye didn't leave the compass. A single gull banked over the mast; head to one side, it looked down at me. Had the bird had risen from the beach? Eilidh signalled slow, we crept ahead. Fog, once the sailor's dread, now I knew why. To combined surprise and relief, the dark mass of the jetty appeared just yards off the bow. Born sailor, Eilidh was ashore with a rope, laughing down to me, "Well done, skipper!"

The skylight of the byre at Tigh na Mara, beamed up into the murkiness. We walked towards it and pushing open the byre door there was Ella, back to us, sitting in at the milking of their house cow. It looked round, lifted its head and sniffed. The single bulb from amongst a network of cobwebs shone on big round inquisitive eyes. Animal warmth and the rich milky smell of cattle met us. Eachan emerged from the barn under a pitch fork full of the hay and more, he carried the scent of summer days. Before pitching it into the hay rack above the cow's head, quite matter of fact without mention of fog or danger, he winked at me, "Well now you've made it. I didn't look for you until tomorrow," always a laugh lay behind his words and look, far from unkind; it was his way of comment, polite but with a hint of mischief. I knew it well and blushed.

Ella, lifting milk pail and stool, stood up stiffly, "Now you pair, was there no tide at middle day, unless you missed it?" I knew she laughed inwardly. Eilidh bent and untied the cow's tail from its hind leg. Even by the one bulb I noticed she blushed, "Ach, since this boy's taken to living over there he's lost his sense of time, and don't worry, I'm giving him a hair cut." They laughed together and Eilidh carrying the enamel milk pail, the two of them headed for house and kitchen.

Taking up the spare hay fork I helped the old man fill the racks above his remaining six cows. I noticed the dung from yesterday lay in the 'grip' behind the cows. Straightaway I went for the shovel and wheel barrow. Perhaps it could be the light, I thought he'd failed a good deal in the few days since the stress of my rescue. He made to take the shovel from me, "That's my job, Hector boy," "No, no Eachan it's not a problem to me." He sat on the milking stool as I worked, the years showed their lines on a face suddenly old. After emptying the barrow on the midden I leant on the wall beside him. "What a fine lassie that is, boat or island," he commented slowly looking out of the byre door. I guessed his line of thought but then in an abrupt change of thinking he sat up, "By the way, they got a body on the beach up from Castleton; it came ashore on the morning tide."

The vivid incident of falling seared my mind. Its seconds had stretched horror into slow motion. I realised now that perceptions of time are succeeding frames of experience which can run at different speeds; now the whole sordid business of briefcase and attempted murder seemed surprisingly long ago. I was silent. The sound and smell of the cattle pulling hay from their racks brought back the scent of the hay fields; one arched her back and made water, I watched it trickle down the 'grip'. The old fashioned style offered a security away from the rampant pace of change.

After a while Eachan said slowly, "That important fellow who races about in his speed boat, aye the one who ferried the man over to Sandray, well he was in at the police station stating his case, identifying the body and so forth. MacNeil the bobby in Castleton a Barraman and plenty Gaelic, he's an OK bloke, if you don't go too far over the score with the car. He looked in this afternoon, I told him not to be coming here inspecting the sheep dipping, that regulation finished here years ago, maybe not in Barra, it's very backward you know. He laughed but wouldn't take a dram, Ella gave him tea. Ach we get on fine, he doesn't take things too seriously. 'When your relation comes across from Sandray, ask him to give me a call,' was all he said from the car window. Anyway the remains are off on the Glasgow plane."

Peaks and troughs; my father used to say, 'Happiness is an illusive commodity, you only know it through sorrow.' A chasm opened, I remained silent. Eachan got up from the milking stool, an old man overnight, "Come on, a' bhalaich, you're needing your supper."

A dram somewhat changed the picture and barely were the dishes being cleared to the sink after roast beef and tatties when the front door opened. "Hello, hello," in walked Eilidh's brother Iain, followed by a bonnie dark haired woman whom I took to be his wife. Eachan was on his feet at once, "How in the world did you get here in this fog? We lost our way coming in from the byre."

Iain put a bottle on the table and replied seriously, "We counted the fence posts, and look here, there's two broken at the bottom of the road." Eachan laughed and admiring the bottle, "We didn't need this." Iain made to put it back in his jacket pocket, "If you say so." "You'd better leave it where it's safe on the table, in case you might fall on it," was the old man's response. Their infectious banter lifted my thoughts. My musical friend of our last encounter pretended not to know me, "Is it yourself, Hector?" I brushed back a mop of hair, laughed for the first time that evening.

At once Eilidh turned from washing dishes and took my hand, "This is Hector," she said to the dark haired woman, "wait you till I've given him a hair cut. Hector this is my sister in law, Katrina." Shyly we shook hands. "No ceremonies here, away through." Ella shooed us to the 'room' and the warmth of a peat fire. Getting into his stride, Eachan at the dresser poured three 'bumpers.'

The two men talked cattle prices, trade had risen amazingly at the last Castleton sale. "The croft will pay yet boy. Is that all your calves away?" Only the women folk coming through changed the topic, "Now ladies, what will you be having, gin and tonics or something better?

"How's life on Sandray?" Iain asked me, it was the closest our conversation came to an incident which was gladly drifting out of my thoughts. Eachan called over to the young crofter, "Surely you took the accordion, MacLeod, we'd do with a tune." No second telling, out to the car, Iain was back in moment. Eachan lifted his fiddle off the top of the piano. A wee tuning session before they burst into 'Father John MacMillan's Welcome to Barra' and nodding to me, "Come on pianist." Straight away to the piano, my fingers soon loosened up, I beat out the base notes. Reels and jigs filled the room. Eilidh took a chair to the top end of the piano, could she play! I moved down an octave, the instrument bounced on its casters. "You two'll have that old thing through the floor," Ella shouted over the racket, clapping time to the beat and hoping it might.

Eilidh and I stopped to draw breath. Not Eachan, he slowed the tempo to a Gaelic waltz. The old man had become young again. He and Iain played softly, drawing out the notes. The richness of the melody came through after each minor note. For a moment I thought of my father's words, happiness and sadness. Ella pushed back the ancient sofa, I took Eilidh in my arms and we danced and danced, there could be no hiding our feelings, our eyes must have shown it all, and I was proud to give away our secret.

Still holding Eilidh, "What was that tune, Eachan" I asked as they let the music slowly fade. He thought and putting it into English, 'Mary of the Witching Eyes,' he told me, winking at Iain's wife. Seeing my arms were tightly around Eilidh's waist, the pair took up another waltz. We danced together, close and loving; its beautiful melody flowed with us, 'Lassie of the Golden Hair', and our happiness filled the room.

I could see Eachan was much affected. Ella went over to him and put her hand on his arm He said something to her in Gaelic. "What did he say?" I whispered into Eilidh's ear. She looked up at me, a shadow in her eyes, "Those tunes, Ella, will see me on tomorrow's journey." I knew what the old man meant and knew a moment's true sadness amongst the night's happiness.

282

More drams, the fire was dying, Iain put down the accordion and stood staring at the photo of Eachan's grandfather which hung over the fireplace. "You three are as alike as peas in a pod," shaking his head he dropped his gaze and looked from the photo to Eachan and myself.

The fog had lifted, "Don't let that man drive," Eachan at the front door spoke to Iain's wife. "he'll only go breaking more fence posts." Away they went with Katrina waving an arm out of the car window and calling "Don't worry, Eachan I'll send him back to mend the last two he broke!"

Eilidh and I waited a little on the doorstep before going into the room. Eachan poured a nightcap, the two women went to the kitchen leaving us alone. I heard the rattle of cups and before they would join us, I lifted my glass, "Eachan, if you hadn't lifted me off that ledge I wouldn't be thanking you tonight for saving my life." He looked hard into my eyes, "Not at all, Hector boy, I was only saving there being one hell of a heart-broken woman."

Ella put tea down beside her man. Eilidh took me by the hand, there was no awkwardness; we said our thanks and goodnights and climbed the stairs to the bedroom which I now thought of as being mine. Even in the darkness Eiludh's body seemed to glow as she slipped under the sheets.

I opened the skylight and listened. Up from the shore came the whistling of a redshank, perhaps heralding a change in the weather for beneath its notes the sea was booming.

Fair or storm, happiness or sorrow,

We were in each other's arms.

CHAPTER THIRTY-ONE

Shafted by Sunshine

Sir Joshua Goldberg balanced his generous proportions, all be it a mite precariously, on a shooting stick at the edge of a dignified stand of ancient woodland. Ancient indeed, the antiquity of the forest being of some considerable pride to its owner, Jeffery Norton-Winters, Esq. He was wont to inform his shooting guests, "Doomsday Records prove it to have been personally planted by William the Conqueror." Moreover when in a suitable frame of mind, as their luncheon hamper emptied he was given to declaring, "It pains me to tell you these glades provided a favourite haunt for Robin Hood and his band of Merry Layabouts."… a troupe of ne'er-do-wells whose inclination towards the redistribution of wealth Norton-Winters regarded as the precursor of the wastefulness of today's Welfare State.

"Cock over now sir, high to your left, sir," the cartridge loader, smart in tweed jacket and moleskin breeches, stood respectfully behind his guest issuing directions for the gentleman's first target of the day. Up into the blue rose a squawking pheasant, a whirring russet flash. Up went the barrels of Sir Joshua's 12 bore, a swing to the right, he sighted a trifle high, BANG! Perhaps a shade out of practice the gun's recoil took him by surprise. Up into air shot the portly legs of Nuen's Knight of the Realm. With commendable presence of mind his gun loader skipped neatly aside, not a moment too soon. Such was the Company Chairman's alarm at finding himself so abruptly brought down, he pulled the second trigger, BANG!

Beech leaves fluttered down to settle on the winded form of Sir Joshua in an auburn coverlet, to be followed seconds later by a splatter of descending lead shot. A crowing pheasant settled several fields away. The Chairman's knickerbockered legs stopped beating the air, "I say, it's confoundedly slippery here," he panted as his loader set him back on his feet.

The unseasonably warm afternoon's sunlight created a mosaic on the rustling carpet of autumn, and still the aging oak and beech had leaves to shed. Early December and yet still no frosts to have squirrels snoozing in their tails. Even the pheasant, though plumped for the shoot by the corn in their feed hoppers, were able to feast on a variety of insects as they awaited their turn for dietary shift to lead pellets. During their alfresco luncheon one shooter was moved to comment, "Global warming, bit of a lark I say, can't wait to get the vines into the garden, far healthier."

Quite annoyingly however for the thatched Ann Hathaway hamlet of which Norton-Winters regarded himself as its rightful squire, the trout stream's normal leisurely saunter past the Morris Dancing green and ducking stool had taken on new dimensions; already the village had been swamped three times. The last occasion being so rapid it found their Vicar, after choir practice, stranded in his vestry with the lady organist. As one fireman reported after carrying the pair to safety, "They were both up to their knees in water. It was not a time for an organ recital."

The cavalcade of Range Rovers and assorted three litre 4x4's loaded with an exultant shooting party and heaps of pheasant strung together in pairs, toiled away from the woodland towards Norton-Winter's manor house, in tracks of mud a foot deep. Touching his cap and looking ruefully at the quagmire, the gamekeeper observed, "Aarr, m'Lord, the weather it is a-changing." Hoping his respectful address might be overheard, a beaming Winters nodded, "Oh if I were you Williams, I wouldn't let that worry you, you've given us an excellent day's sport." The squire had yet to be ennobled but then for rather differing reasons the use of a title pleased both parties.

Oak panelling, family portraits and a raftered ceiling, the dining room spoke of an era of doublet and hose. Mellow lighting and a blazing log fire drew the shooting party to the cosiness of an inglenook. To warm the guests before they bathed and changed for dinner, and it has to be said to enhance the Elizabethan impression, a comely wench in no small danger of having her bottom pinched, poured copious draughts of rum punch into large silver goblets recently engraved with the Norton-Winters Coat of Arms. In keeping with the trend towards boasting one's humble origins, Jeffery was wont to assert, "My thirty-fourth grandfather, paternal, was a swineherd in the New Forest on the day William Rufus was shot." An honour reflected in the heraldic device, a boar sitting on an oak leaf. The researches of the genealogist had involved considerable ingenuity and amounted to rather more than he'd hoped to pay,

Faces shining from fresh air and bath salts sat before trenchers groaning under roasts of prime Aberdeen-Angus and wild boar, all the more satisfying when washed down with an exclusive red, the renowned Chateau Noir, 1939. As one devotee of the grape explained to the table whilst standing on his chair, "That was the larst decent summer we enjoyed down in Brighton before we tackled the Hun." Gulping more vintage, "Chamberlain, bit of a wet I'd say, I remember perfectly those appalling sirens, dreadful air raid shelters; naturally Pater would have none of it, shouldered the elephant rifle which saw him through the Boer War and made straight for the Cliffs of Dover." The evening's historian later retired under the table to shelter from the effects of his memory.

Meal finished, a few of the diners tottered to the kitchen to thank to the cook. "Henrietta, how lucky to own such a wonderful chef," purred a dowager unaware the chef was hired for the night. Winter's wife beamed, "Shall we withdraw ladies and leave the men folk to their boring politics?" The ladies adjourned with much swishing of silk dresses to the Drawing Room. The men gathered to their host's end of the antique Jacobean dining piece; the butler, also hired for the occasion, polished the crystal glasses for a third time and soon beneath a blue haze of the finest cut cigars, the brandy bottle circulated the table.

Not every after dinner exchange of opinions enjoyed those of a Chancellor of the Exchequer and a Westminster Under Secretary. Goldberg, not quite by accident, found himself beside the power behind the UK's energy police, his school chum, Norton-Winters. Their conversation deepened; Sir Joshua leaned close, "Look here Jeff, do you realise that the world's biggest energy project so far devised is shortly to be developed in the Sahara, twenty major German Corporations are forming a consortium to build a series of solar thermal generation planets, stuffing sunshine into a steam boiler to drive a turbine, it's the same as canning sunshine, and they aim to supply an initial fifteen per cent of Europe's needs; a peak output of a hundred gigawatts, that's about a hundred of the your dirty coal fired power stations you're dithering over building. "

Winters swirled his brandy glass in an unconcerned manner. Sir Joshua's face twisted in anger, "and this crowd are putting up four hundred billion ecu's of funding, where the hell are they finding that amount, four hundred billion." He breathed heavily at the thought of such a sum, "And what Jeff are you doing to help our nuclear programme get started, just what might I ask?"

Norton-Winters looked coldly at the friend he knew too well from school days, and aware that the Chancellor seemed to be chattering amiably to an American financier whom Goldberg had brought for the weekend, he said quite firmly, "Look here Josh, the Government's cutting through the local planning red tape and next week we shall be designating sites for ten nuclear installations. My clear advice to you, my friend, is to cut the first turf in your nuclear waste plant; believe me many cards will then fall into place. We might even help you by a little, shall we say, by an adjustment of the carbon tax on emissions, but as you will be well aware both here in UK and in America the Nuclear Safety Inspectorates are questioning some of the aspects of the design you're proposing, so you'd better get any design fault rectified, pronto."

He let that sink in before looking directly at Sir Joshua with obvious annoyance, "By the way I do happen to know of your arrangements behind my back for supplying the M.O.D. with weapons' grade plutonium, whilst promising to dump the rotting nuclear submarines which they're scrapping."

Not used to being on the receiving end, Goldberg swallowed hard and choosing to ignore any comment on design problems, forced an ingratiating smile, "Jeff old chap, you know how touchy the M.O.D. can be, especially the way things are out in Helman." Norton-Winters turned to speak to another guest and Sir Joshua was left sullenly watching his friend, Nicky Fellows, the financial manipulator from America, laughing and joking with the Chancellor of the Exchequer.

Always the considerate host, Norton-Winters arose and carefully holding onto the table, announced, "Shall we join the ladies?" No longer able to stand the jollity of the night, Goldberg shot a penetrating look at Nick Fellows and carefully negotiating the stairway with a little help from mahogany balustrade, he stomped up to his bedroom.

The porcelain bedside clock approached three am.before the door opened to admit a grinning Fellows, "Gee man, what a party, and that Chancellor guy, sure we got on just great, just..." "Come in Nicky, I want to talk to you, clear of all that tomfoolery downstairs." "Josh, don't be so nasty to your own little Nicky," and supported by one the pillars of the four-poster bed, Fellows patted the corpulent figure of Sir Joshua, "Joshy, I've had a wonderful conversation with the guy. Man, man, he's going to break up those Scottish banks he got his hands on, break 'em up man." Fellows rolled his eyes, "Josh just think of the pickings out of that lot with sterling on its knees, just begging man, just begging," and falling onto the bed in a roar of guffaws, "Josh, just think of it, stuffing the British taxpayer; I'll fund your miserable little nuclear dump on the strength of it."

Far from being mollified by his friend's three am offer of support, and knowing full well the impact a grey dawn can spread over even the brightest ideas, Goldberg snapped, "Yes, yes Nicky, I appreciate your consideration," and as his friend, slumped beside him on the bed, "unless Nuen can move fast, and by that I mean in the next few months, this confounded Sahara Solar project will catch on and pull in even more funding. Even the stupid UK government might wake up. Do you realise all Europe's electricity could be supplied from an area of only two hundred and fifty square kilometres? Cooling water's the problem obviously, but damn it they're talking desalinisation and supplying water for crop irrigation; it's horrendous."

Fellows merely grunted. "This is serious Nicky," Sir Joshua was talking to himself, "plans are afoot for solar farms in Israel and China. Australia's going solar, the Germans are sticking solar panels on every damn roof and now they're pulling the strings in Africa, California's leading the way in America, I tell you, apart from the M.O.D., that dope of a chap Shivering

Winters and his Ministry of Trade and Energy is our best hope of any future business."

"Nicky my dear chap," he prodded his snoring friend, "Nuen needs the cash for this waste bunker, and fast, otherwise without more political influence in the right quarters our nuclear job, thanks to this bloody Sahara Power project, is going to be shafted by sunshine."

Breaking over with the brittle crash of splintering crystal, the wave crest toppled towards a mammoth hole in the ocean. The screaming gale reached a higher note, foaming white a cascade poured down, the Valkyrie became a smothered hull. She began to roll. Anderson washed into the falling torrent, took a gasp of air. In the seconds with his head above water, he saw her mast coming towards him. She's going over. This will be the end. He was being dragged down, a rushing gurgle pounding his ears; pressure crushing his lungs. He fought against breathing. Water filled his nose, all was going black and deathly silent.

Each Atlantic gale will create the few immense waves which remain a terrifying vision in those who survive their greed. Seeded by falling pressure and a rising wind these mountains of the sea are sucked towards the sky; in a relentless urge they devour their smaller brethren, grow in height and might, and prowl the trackless wastes to seek a victim. Top heavy giants, they crash. The ocean's pit of a sailor's dread is filled, acres of sea are flattened, the remains of a majestic peak are reduced to the foam streaked carcass of a departing greyback; and the laughter of a gale.

The Valkyrie lay on her side, knocked down by the inexorable will of the elements. They hear no prayer, nor care. Only the power of the old Viking Gods, the Hero's of Asgard in their Halls of Valhalla might save one of their own. Strange a modern man in his moment of need should cry to a long dead belief. What power a myth to force itself from the mouth of a drowning man?

Any man who has seen beyond the ultimate eclipse of this life's conscious being, glimpsed in his final vision a glory which shines out, that draws him moth like to the eternal flame, to the indestructible energy of a universe which knows not death, only unending change; such a man is transformed, no longer a helpless victim of mindless faith but the possessor of inner knowledge.

Andrew Anderson's eyes opened to the sky, conscious that he lay across the yacht's boom. He felt it lifting him. Vomiting water, retching and coughing, he clung to the spar, vaguely able to see the Valkyrie's mast slowly rising. The yacht fought to right herself. His feet dangled in a flooded cockpit; seas pouring off her decks she lay, a stricken vessel on a great black shoulder of water. The cascading mass, having flattened the sea, forged into the darkness, streaked with anger. Thwarted? The devil is never defeated. The gale raged into the chasms of nightfall.

Regaining breath Anderson swung off the boom, aware the snagging of his rope on the spar as it lay in the water had saved him, saved him, so far? The Valkyrie, swinging broadside to wave and gale lay ahull, at the mercy of the whole weight of any freshly breaking crest.

Action. The yacht sat heavily, no longer her buoyant self but a flooded hull. He opened the hatch, water sloshing at bunk level. A yacht half full, the next dump of sea would...? He reached for the instrument switches, panel dead, no power, no electric bilge pump, cockpit hand pump too slow, a pail the only way. The yacht rolled alarmingly, dipping her gunnel to coach roof level as each wave drove under her; swilling cabin water added to each roll; to a fatal list?

Pail's in the 'heads'. He unhitched the rope strop, clambered below, waded through the cabin, grabbed the pail, floundered back to the hatch. Balance and bale, bale with each roll of the boat, get the water out before another wave crashes over her, hatch open- another would smother her she'd fill and sink.

Working frantically; save the yacht, no fear for himself, the spirit of Valkyrie spoke to him, her voice was at his shoulder, "Together we live or go down, be with me and we live." The soul of man and boat fused in a bond of kinship known only to those in peril.

Pails of water flung over the stern. The boat rolled hideously, rode the crest of another shattering top. Another truly big one would bury the Valkyrie, make the Atlantic their grave.

Sea anchor and ride the storm? Water level down, out of the cabin he climbed, groping along the deck, not tied on, handholds only to the for'ard hatch. She rolled, he fell, arm broken? Huge waves, always far apart. Wait the next lull. Pain, soaked and frozen, fumbling the catch.

Watching the sea he lugged the anchor from the hatch, a huge canvas cone, heaved it over the bow. Paid out rope, fathom by fathom, secured it to the Samson post.

Would her head come round, face the onslaught? Ride the crests?

He looked northwards. Out of the night, a window of light, a star showed.

Did the God of his forebears look down?

Was faith alone his anchor?

292

CHAPTER THIRTY-TWO

Aurora Night

On the beaches of our consciousness wash
countless grains of time
That change with every tide, with every fresh born galaxy
Whose mineral palette is the swirling photon brush
Which paints the beauty of the cosmos
As love's simplicity.

Eilidh and I spent our first Christmas on Sandray, alone together in Tigh na Cala. The old house and its bothy style of bare essentials had been blitzed. Creaking chairs and enamel basins were out, our supplies no longer sat in wooden fish boxes declaring,' Lochinver Fish Selling Co. No Unauthorised Use'. A number of boat trips transported some practical comfort. Easy chairs were in; under a woman's hand, cushions, curtains and a bedroom carpet appeared. From tablecloth to tapestry wall hangings, Eilidh's flair for bright colours had a distinctive style, the rooms came to life, we had a home, and to prove it Eachan and Ella came over the Sound on Boxing Day. "Ach," said Eachan, "I'd never heard of this Boxing Day stunt until I was twenty and then it was just a practice for Hogmanay," adding with a wink at me, "not that some were ever out of practice." "And who knows that better than yourself, Eachan MacKenzie?" Ella piped up. He pretended not to hear.

Whilst the two women discussed our home's next improvements, Eachan sat quietly. Not a man given to showing emotion, to see the house of his childhood rescued from dereliction affected him greatly. A dram eventually brought out the stories of his youth, how they'd gathered the island sheep, the danger of the sea cliffs to sheep and men, "I once lost a dog, 'Shep' to name, a topper of a dog, he cut out to the far side of sheep that were making to dodge down the cliff, running fast, his eye was on the sheep, over he went, poor beast. I blamed myself." he said slowly. The names of his father's collies came to him, laughingly he went on, "the bodach would work one dog in the Gaelic and the other in English, sometimes he got it mixed, so I dare say the dogs were bi-lingual." Each cnoc and hollow flitted through his mind as he saw the lines of sheep drawing towards the stone built pens, all Gaelic names which told of the lie of the land or the nature of the ground. I wrote it down as he spoke. Were any left of the generations who knew the features of the island with the intimacy of tramping feet? His reminiscences paused as I poured another wee 'toot', "Who else could tell me these names today?" I asked him. "Nobody," was his slow response, and then with a fixed look at me, "but I'm telling you, Hector boy." His meaning was not lost.

We'd taken in the bells in our own home and sailed the Sound in the cold early hours of a star bright night to be the first foot at Ach na Mara. Lights blazed from every croft on Halasay. We made it. Eilidh lifted a peat from the stack beside the house, "This'll do, we'll have ours next year." First to cross the old couple's doorstep and put a peat to their fire, "Happy New Year!"; oh boy the welcome! Eachan swept Eilidh off her feet, "Woman, I wish I was young again," they were so fond of each other. I hugged Ella till she gasped to Eilidh, "I'll bet he's as wicked as his namesake." "I'm beginning to think that." A laughing Eilidh flush-faced from the sail looked beautiful. No shyness at our second kiss of the New Year, and the old couple took our cue.

No knocking and waiting either, the door opened and neighbours carrying clinking supplies appeared in droves. Good cheer came in more than a bottle, this was a community of like people, no pretensions, as natural as the land they crofted. Lively folk brimming with music and not a little refreshment. Soon they were singing, dancing and for those who would listen or could hear over the laughter and Iain's accordion, some were telling stories. Ensuring all glasses were charged, though not for the first time, Eachan called the toast, "To absent friends." It was echoed round a tiny crowded room. I remembered the old Scots song, 'My ain Folk', my father at the piano, mother singing; in words and music an exile's longing, the missing of 'the lang syne days, the old folks ways, and the hills of the heart's romance,' as he used to quote. I asked Eachan and Iain to play it in their memory. My first New Year in the Highlands, 'at hame with my ain folk,' and I'll swear by five in the morning old great grandfather of the photo above the mantle shelf was smiling down.

New Year's night and dancing down in Castleton. The following evening on a circuit of village friends, it occurred to me that months had passed and I'd yet to call at the Police Station. Eachan looked serious, "What's the hurry?" I put it off, wisely so, in the circumstances. Another night around various crofts, I marvelled at the stamina. "Wait you for the Old New Year," Eachan warned. I must have looked puzzled, "the old folks always kept the twelfth of January as their New Year and some of us still keep up the tradition, out of respect you understand, so now we have two celebrations." On the fourth day we retreated to Sandray for a sleep. A Highland New Year was not to be under estimated.

By the first week in January I could tell a difference in the length of day. Settled weather hung over an oily Atlantic, vague mists drifted its flat calm surface, ideal for working the land. I hauled up kelp from the shore, set to digging the lines of 'lazybeds' which would take our first planting of tatties. Eilidh sailed back and forth to Halasay, food supplies, kitchen equipment, piping, wood and fittings, boat loads of 'home improvement' trips. Each evening by the hissing lamp, I fitted sink and draining boards, cupboards. A week and Eilidh could turn on a kitchen tap, cold water admittedly but the solar panels and a boiler were on order. One corner would host a peat burning stove. By May, I'd be at the peat bank cutting for next winter. Hugging each other to sleep each night we talked plans, sheep, maybe cattle, fencing a field for hay, pioneer homemaking, "What about a collie pup," my last words and a tired Eilidh nodded in her sleep.

The winter sun had rolled along the horizon each day to give us weeks of dry invigorating weather. A break coming? I felt it on my skin as late one evening we crossed salt bleached grazings on the gentle rise towards the headland. Deep in the conflicting energies which surround the planet a disturbance was about to strike, a maelstrom of electrons were funnelling into the earth's upper atmosphere, I'd seen its first flickers from the doorstep, "Come on Eilidh," Putting down a cushion she was sewing and joining me she whispered at my elbow, "Yes, Hector we must see this tonight." Pulling on jackets, for the night had the chill of January's end, Eilidh took my hand and off we set.

The night held a curiously anxious feel, as we walked it seemed electrified. The planet faced violence from the sun; a geomagnetic conflict. Hot plasma hurtled towards the earth in a cascade of high energy particles. From the north came a cosmic outburst, flashing onto the sky, filling the horizon. The planet's magnetic shield was fending off a massive onslaught of charged particles, a solar storm. Stars faded and died. Vast curtains of green light appeared, hung in swirling drapes from the firmament. Totally incongruous colours were suspended from a mammoth screen, flickering with intensity, pierced with leaping white flares. It moved by unseen hand.

Gradually the swaying green canopy gave way; orange searchlights shot skywards, a garish mauve covered cliff and sea. Ripples of violent discharge spread far beyond earth's orbit. In turn their brilliance morphed to sheets of a deepest pink reaching outwards and upwards, hanging over us. Immense magnetic fields were thrashing the heavens. The omnipotent power of the solar wind, a hurricane of the sun's ejected electrons rushed past the planet, millions of kilometres an hour, smashing molecules in the upper atmosphere, whipping the earth's girdling magnetosphere into a frenzy of twisting electric fields. Potential havoc to satellites and power lines could be the very least; were our protective shield to fail, the solar wind would slowly strip away earth's atmosphere. Exposed to toxic carcinogenic rays life would shrivel and die. The Sun would triumph.

The grandeur of space weather played out above our heads. One moment the bleached grass at our feet shone green, the weathered stones tinted by its weaving eeriness, and the sea a deep green empire until shafts of white gave way to changing shades; pale green faded and the heavens were immersed in a deep rose pink. The sea before us became dark crimson.

We neared the headland. Against a lurid sky the prow stone of the old Viking grave ship stood out, a huge black figure. Ancient hand- placed stones, their mica glinted as sparks of a fire ignited by the sky. A funeral longboat burnt again. The dancing aurora were bearing away one of their own, carrying his soul to the land which had grown the timbers of his ship, back to the northlands of larch clad fiords, and the raven crags of wisdom.

We sat with our backs to that prow stone. The people of sword and longship sailed the galaxies of belief, plundered the cosmic beaches, put fire to the heavens and feasted by its light. Shadows fell about us, regal in their shades; the myths were alive, an unquenchable mystery buried deep within layer upon layer of generations who'd watched in awe from their arctic vastness.

Slowly the skies were fading, the stars returning. The Gods drew their raiment about them, and left the night to us. Low on the horizon the lights were dimmed below the Halls of Valhalla.

The woman beside me shivered, I drew her close. We were both greatly affected by the weirdness of the night. No man- made light, two people alone beside a wondering ocean, crouching within the stones of a boat grave, the symbol of death's aspirations.

Together we'd witnessed the most powerful forces of nature, had seen threading currents rip through nearby space; remoteness brought closeness and with it came a reverence for that which may lie beyond.

I listened to the rustle of the sea beneath the cliff, conscious of my close encounter with death, "Eildh," I whispered, "Whoever lies buried within this ship lived with a vision, he looked north from this headland, held fast to an unshakeable belief that one day he would sail the cosmic oceans of his mind. Nothing has changed. Since humans first felt the presence of the stars on the road of discovery the myths of man's religion have simply invented fresh gods. I believe there will be no end, only fresh beginnings. The celestial forces bind our destiny to the pathway of infinite knowledge."

She was silent for a long time, looking to the last glimmer of the aurora. Reaching to me she held both my hands, "Hector," her voice, a tremor of excitement, "Hector, we're having a baby."

Dumfounded by joy but unable for a moment to shake off the drama in the skies, my first thought tumbled out, "A child of destiny."

Gently I took her to me.

The night was in our arms, a night for loving,

and only the stars to know.

CHAPTER THIRTY-THREE

"Get me out of here."

The pilot banked steeply. Green Atlantic rollers broke their three thousand miles of freedom in spouting white plumes. The jagged cliffs of a small island were close. Sir Joshua Goldberg clung nervously to the rear seat of a small helicopter. Both the engine noise, and from looking out of the window, an awareness of the proximity of the sea were unsettling Sir Joshua's stomach. Certainly not the Executive Class travel normally associated with his Chairmanship at Nuen or his penchant for the refinements of life. This would not be repeated, only a strong hint from the highest level of a forthcoming building contract plus the insistence of the Permanent Secretary at the M.O.D. had persuaded him to undertake a survey of prospective nuclear waste sites by such primitive means.

Nuen's thrust into the UK's nuclear industry was moving smartly, in spite of Goldberg finding the atmosphere in 10 Downing Street markedly different from that of the previous incumbent, who so happened to be one of his more influential Board members; gone the easy going arm round the shoulder politics, the sofa and coffee decisions taken along with T.V. news bulletins and the guiding hand of Hatchet Face. In place of the nonchalant pop star approach, a grim formality met Sir Joshua as he was shown into the P.M.'s private office. Prompted by Nuen's UK man on the Board, the meeting had been arranged by Sir Timothy Winthrope-Bagley, top man at the Treasury, who sat beside the P.M. with barely concealed arrogance. Two others came discreetly into the room,

Jeff Norton-Winters, whom Goldberg knew well and a face unfamiliar to him. Not a little to Sir Joshua's annoyance greetings were perfunctory.

Without a smile the P.M. shook hands, "Perhaps you know these gentlemen," he motioned towards the trio with a curt gesture. The faces of Bagley and Winters remained impassive, not a sign of recognition to indicate they were all chums at Eton. However the stranger to Goldberg leaned forward and offered a limp hand, "Jerry Switherington, I'm at Health and Safety," adding nervously, "for my sins." Not a smile passed any lips, the P.M.'s eyes narrowed. Given the extent of Westminster expenses scandal the word 'sin' was something of a faux pas. Sir Joshua immediately wrote the man off as a nincompoop. "Please sit down." They sat without a word. Putting the tips of his fingers together and looking at the desk, the P.M. continued, "I shouldn't need to mention it gentlemen, this meeting is strictly private and informal," he raised his head with a meaningful stare. "Would you care to speak, Sir Timothy?"

It seemed to be the last thing Winthrope-Bagley wished to do; he took some moments before saying in a faintly supercilious tone, "Thank you Prime Minister, I think we all understand these new builds are urgently required to met our emission reductions targets by twenty-twenty and beyond. I have to say, Sir Joshua, the details of Nuen's tender are the most interesting," and at a glance from the P.M., "on the face of it that is. As we speak, Sir Joshua, our accountants are in touch with your men in New York," clearly Sir Timothy had no wish to commit himself further. A distinct silence, the Prime Minister looked decidedly preoccupied and studied his fingers.

To Goldberg's surprise Switherington cleared his throat, "Prime Minister, may I put a question to Sir Joshua," he received a brusque nod, "I understand from my engineers they have some major reservations about certain safety aspects of the design Nuen will be building, perhaps you could comment. Secondly sir, are you aware that (the some) highly toxic waste storage being held at one of our main facilities is currently in stainless steel tanks of a limited life span, and thirdly the stability of the rock formation is paramount in terms of earthquake activity? I believe Nuen have undertaken to deal with issues in the terms of their contract."

Sir Joshua's two friends, colouring markedly, fingered their notes on the table. What a fool, their fool of a colleague had alerted Goldberg that they intended to grant Nuen the contract. Puffs of red showed on the P.M.'s pallor, it was he who'd insisted on this Secretary's attendance. The Prime Minister rose abruptly. "Excuse us gentlemen," and glaring at Switherington, "we have another meeting at three, if you don't mind Sir Joshua. I'm sure Sir Timothy and Mr. Norton-Winters can conclude this meeting," and with merely a nod he marched out with the Health and Safety's Chief Secretary at his heel.

His two school friends coolly ushered Goldberg out of Number 10 via the garden. Unknown to those he'd just left, Sir Joshua's next informal meeting was round at the M.O.D. Nuen already delivered nuclear submarine fuel to the Scottish base. Moreover, in a top secret arrangement, totally breaching UK's signature to the International Non-proliferation Treaty, his company were the regular suppliers of vital neutron generators, the key to enabling the firing of a nuclear weapon. What better lever for obtaining these new reactor builds. Maybe too dangerous to pull. Goldberg reflected upon one scientific officer now sadly deceased. It tempered his approach. Those who opened their mouths too wide were apt to find themselves in very unfortunate circumstances.

The Defence Ministry were also pressing Nuen for more weapons grade plutonium, but payment only dribbled out. In an extremely brief, one to one meeting with the official who'd previously refrained from identifying himself, Goldberg was told abruptly, "fulfil our requirements and staged transfers of funds will be forthcoming to the Caribbean subsidiary which you indicated." Sir Joshua cringed inwardly at mention of the Caribbean connection. Did this incognito official guess his little private siphon? How the hell did they find out? It weakened his bargaining power.

That night, as though by chance, 'Shivering Jeff' Winters happened to appear at their club. "Look here Jeff," Goldberg remembered saying, "I've just read a report, two Japanese companies are developing a technique for harvesting solar energy from space using satellites, they'll beam it down to earth by lasers or microwaves, a prototype's going be launched in the next few years. The sooner these new builds are started the better, and that fool Switherington opening his mouth Jeff. D'you think his comments would concern the P.M.?" Realising his anxiety showed, Sir Joshua took a tougher line, "I know the contract just awaits my signature but you can tell 'Windy Bags' he'd better open the Treasury safe. If you all want a deal I need at least fifteen percent up front to cover the design points that ass was making, and don't forget 'Shivers', you'd better let 'Windy Bags' and your busy Mr. Prime Minister know if you don't want Nuen to run your new reactors it just so happens we own the largest uranium mines in Western Australia and like oil, supplies of the stuff won't last another forty years."

Norton-Winters busied himself attracting the waiter's attention and seemed not to have heard him. The last words from 'Shivers' stuck in Goldberg's mind, "Don't worry about the politicians, Josh," Winters confided tapping the side of his remarkably large nose, "just carry on, fix this damned waste dump and you'll have real friends. By the way, if you're interested, a beautiful riverside property on the Thames came up for sale last week; things could be arranged for an old friend." He'd poured more wine, "for old times sake, Josh. You can trust 'Windy' and me."

Trust- the word left Sir Joshua hollow inside. Old school pals? Who the hell could he trust? Bloody bureaucrats and politicians, a fatal mix of slippery characters hiding behind one another's backs, loathing each other in private, always offloading responsibility, the business world required honesty, that is one might say, within reason. At least one should be swindled honestly.

Goldberg groaned, no more looking out of the helicopter window, his bowels wouldn't stand it. The whirring rotors ceased. He opened his eyes, struggled hurriedly out of his seat and from the hatch doorway could see they'd touched down on a broad hilltop. Nuen's Chief Engineer and a leading geologist in the party helped Sir Joshua down the ladder. He staggered over to an outcrop of rock which barely hid his flapping shirt tail. A smile passed round the experts as they turned their backs and began unloading their surveying equipment.

The impact of a primordial scene drew minds to consider a starkness little changed since the great glacial melts scraped rocks to their origins those thousand years past. Moss, in tiny verdant patches, clung to hollows amongst stones flaked and shattered by the keen edge of Atlantic gales. Nothing but the supremely hardy could survive. The late winter barrenness found personification in the harsh croaking of two birds, the only sound to be heard above a biting March wind with ice in its teeth. The Helicopter rocked to each succeeding gust.

A squatting Goldberg shivered, looked about him and began vehemently cursing the place, the land, the sea; its unremitting bleakness frightened him. The thought of being marooned brought fresh spasms. Get these rock borings done and get to hell out of here. This hideous place will do, all it'll ever be fit for, a vacant, useless, wilderness. In needed taming and by God, Nuen would do it.

Perished and shaking, Sir Joshua was at last able to stand and take in the prospects of constructing a viable deep waste repository. Eye and mind swept over the topography. We'll blast the top off this ugly pile of a hill, build a breakwater and harbour with it, right down there, extend that promontory to shelter the bay, depth might be critical, level that green area for accommodation and the rock crushing equipment, that'll deal with the spoil from the underground storage cavern, it's bound to be road building material, sell it south, nice little earner. Electricity, that major wind farm project planned on islands to the north, plus their own generator backup, yes, a high rise pylon spur across that stretch of water should be feasible. No people on the island, no blasted environmental brigade, so there'd be no damn planning regulations which couldn't be handled by the usual method.

Well accustomed to macro-planning, Goldberg covered the site's possibilities in minutes. It freed his thoughts to consider the real questions, the probable billions required by Nuen; tapping the UK Government for more finance once the ink dried on the contract and they'd detonated their first charge; and paramount to his thinking- profit.

Hurrying back to the helicopter Sir Joshua tripped and fell quite heavily. Abandoning survey operations the team ran across to find their leader sprawled across a rock. "I think I've broken my fucking ankle," he screamed at them, "get me out of here!" Nuen's Chairman began to sob, "This wretched, goddamn awful bloody place, I'll... I'll..." he spluttered to a stop. Through the intense pain Goldberg vowed revenge on a remote island with a feeling of hatred beyond anything he'd known.

Above the hill a pair of raven circled.

In the cliff below crouched their early brood

Forty fathoms of stout rope and a sea anchor, the survival of a yacht and the life of Andrew Anderson depended on it. Should the Valkyrie remain lying abeam amidst such mountainous seas, the next crescendo of gale and breaking crest would come bearing down on them, draw the yacht beneath its great curling top into a green cave of oblivion. Away on the horizon reared a monster wave, a freak, it towered over the surrounding chaos. Anderson standing at the bow clung to the jib stay with his undamaged arm. Unless the sea anchor bit the sea and held, nothing could save him, unless the spin of fate. He watched its approach, a leviathan of the deep. It crept up the horizon, gathering steepness and height with the deliberation of a predator about to devour man and boat.

The thunder of seas put words in his mouth, unbidden words. He called on the mighty Thor, man's Viking saviour in times of distress, "God of my people save me now!" It seemed above the gale the sonorous rumbling of the ocean became a voice; the deity of a long banished faith. Over him came a strange lightness, the exaltation of spirit given to those who approach death with out fear.

The anchor rope no longer a dipping curve stretched taut. The sea anchor gripped below the crests. Slowly the bow of his yacht came round. The monster came. The Valkyrie faced a pillar of water bow on. Anderson stood, head back, watching, waiting for the peak to crumble. It did. Solid water roared over the boat, immersing her stem to stern, washing a helpless man down the foredeck. The yacht's nose broke free. Water poured off the decks in torrents. Anderson struggled to his feet, her mast had saved him. The gush of water surging over his body pinned him around the foot of the mast, head one side, legs the other; he was held there by the sheer weight of water.

Behind the collapsing wave came the respite granted by an ocean which has overreached itself. Disentangling himself, he crawled down a deck stripped of stanchion rails and equipment. The cockpit self draining was emptying, cabin doors undamaged. He toppled down the companionway and lay for a little on the cabin floor. No more water down below. The Valkyrie felt buoyant again. Anderson, wet bedraggled and hurt pulled himself onto a bunk. The boat had saved him and now would save herself. And he slept with the voice of the sea in his ear.

A ship's fog horn wakened him. The wind had dropped and a large fishing boat stood off a cable to starboard. Cupped hands shouted down, did he need help? They too had come through the storm, were bound for the Azores and repairs. Anderson shouted up from the cockpit, "No electrics, no engine, my left arm is smashed." Two fishermen came aboard and rigged a towing cable. Thirty-six hours later the Valkyrie lay alongside the jetty in the island harbour of Horta; the sun broke through to salute once again the seaman's code of helping a fellow mariner in distress.

Greatly to Anderson's relief, concern for a brave sailor had kept the Azores customs officials from taking more than a passing glance over Valkyrie. A certain container retrieved from his villa in the Caribbean for the time being acted as ballast, and in due course he had a job for it.

Walking up the quay each day Anderson read the names of visiting yachts which their seamen painted over the years on the walls of the harbour; small, famous or otherwise, all recorded by men proud of their ships. "Valkyrie," he told her, "you're my first true friend."

Three months and a cracked arm healed, a trim yacht waiting, a souwest breeze and northbound terns skimming the sea, the roving fever in a man's blood returned.

Wind in her main, the Valkyrie dipped her bow towards home.

CHAPTER THIRTY-FOUR

A heap of dust

March sunshine and longer days gave us hot water at the kitchen tap and my first shave by solar power. I'd fitted panels on the roof and a tank in the tiny roof space above the sink gurgled quietly the moment the sun rose over the Hill of the Shroud. Before the arrival of the baby, a bathroom and second bedroom on the east gable in a re-roofed byre, build sheep pens, fence and drain; work a plenty with energy to match. Together we prowled the land with a feeling of possession, though in reality we were no more than squatters staking out a home. Roots of a thousand years meaning nothing in modern law, meant everything to the strength of affinity. Centuries of pressure from the south usurped the old Viking Udal Law. It permitted a settler to enclose the unoccupied land he chose to cultivate without regarding any his superior, no feudal forelock tugging, the stamp of Norse independence. Sandray felt ours by right.

Each day's work a part of nature's renewal. Spring air, I'd run to the jetty before breakfast to check the boat, the smell of the tide damp with salt from lines of tangle, bright orange in the keen light. Flocks of waders peopled the shoreline, dunlin or curlew, golden plover, dozens of tiny black legged sanderling running along the tidal froth edge, picking insects. Excited whistling, lisping bird talk, stretching their pinions aloft, a redshank zigzagging away, wing bars white and smart, by mid-morning the tide would covered their feeding, I'd look up from digging to smoke trails on the horizon, their flocks would be hurrying north.

A climbing sun and warmth opened the first daisies, greened a land awaiting skylark song, whatever I put my back too each day there was time to straighten up. Work finished and supper waiting, on the hush of evening a drumming sound would resonate, sheep- like bleat floating from the hill pastures, an eerie wavering at great distance. I'd look up and spot a tiny dot of birdlife diving towards the ground, the snipe were back to their haunts of nest and chick. I'd call to Eilidh and we'd stand at the door listening and happy.

Even with the first signs of her tummy expanding, Eiildh helped me to spread seaweed on the 'lazybeds'. "I need plenty exercise," she insisted, having already decided that the baby should be born on Sandray. Excited by just turning the soil, we worked side by side, luxury days which gathered their freshness from the sea. Eilidh had never appeared so bonnie, her clear skin shone tanned and rosy. Unhurried weeks of achievement, we slept the tiredness of simple, healthy work. Each night as I hugged her goodnight, out of the silence still the whistling birdlife hurried to their nesting lands in the north. Other creatures had home making plans, and we felt a part of their plans.

Already the empty ground which surrounded the house was taking on the feel of a croft. Even the pastures, unploughed in a hundred years began to grow the sweet early grass. It needed lambing ewes. We made the decision to bring sheep across to Sandray. The island would be re-stocked, I'd rebuild the fallen stone sheep pens, and Eilidh on a trip to Halasay would speak to her brother. Alone that day of March I worked hard, enjoying the prospects of becoming a shepherd. March blow warm, blow cold, the wind, round to the east, had a searching chill. Any sounds apart from those natural to the island were exceptional. It took me a second to realise I was hearing the throbbing of a heavy engine.

Looking up sharply from the digging I saw what appeared by its size to be an Army helicopter landing on the high ground above the raven cliffs. The birds were circling, obviously alarmed; I could tell from their rapid wing beats. Our raven, as we considered them to be, were very much part of island life. Some weeks previous, I'd shuffled to the edge of the cliff and spied down on their huge nest of heather stalks and seaweed; the site had been in use for centuries. Two young chicks with spiky feathers lay tight together for warmth; lucky parents, hardy birds.

A helicopter on our island, the intrusion infuriated me. Throwing down the spade in rage I set off climbing the hill. Ten minutes from the summit, I could hear the racket of engine and flailing blades starting up. Damn it, I hurried. Moments later the contraption roared out to sea, heading east. Whoever it was, I'd missed finding out. I reached the flat top. Wheel marks on the thin turf. What in the world could they be up to? Some damn fool army exercise? I walked about, puzzled, until over on a large flag of bare rock, I spotted a heap of dust. Smoothing it exposed a small bore hole, only an inch in diameter but deep. Testing the rock? Possible reasons flashed through my mind. The ravens circled in great agitation, flapping and cawing. I left straight away, very uneasy, indeed very worried.

Sighting Eilidh's boat turning the headland down the slope I ran, arriving breathless to catch the rope as she came skilfully alongside the jetty. Mischievous eyes warned me, another surprise? She reached for a large cardboard box from under the thwart and passed it up. I put the box down to help her ashore, "Open it, open it." Baler twine indicated a croft was involved. I undid the knot and lifted the lid. Two big round puppy's eyes looked out at me. "Eilidh, you rascal girl, now we have to start a flock of sheep," adding, "as well as a family," and I hugged her, not too hard, the baby bump was beginning to show.

"It's a bitch pup, Iain kept it for us, his good breeding bitch had eight, this is the pick of the litter. He said if ever we get married it'll save him a wedding present." The wee black and white thing made a little whine and licked my finger, "What a beauty, has she got a name?" Eilidh had given it thought, "I heard them say the last collie on Sandray belonged to Eachan's father, she was Muille, it's a pet name in the Gaelic." "Muille," I said her name as I lifted her out of the box and put her down on the jetty. She sniffed my boots and wagged a tail no longer than my finger, and Muille she became at once, a wee pet.

The helicopter intrusion remained very much a concern but reluctant to cast a shadow over the arrival of an apprentice sheep dog, I said nothing and we laughed our way up to the house, Eilidh with the puppy in her arms, me carrying boxes of food. Later that evening, Muille, having explored the house slept on Eilidh's lap, I described the incident and gently mentioned my fear. "Drilling the rock, testing its soundness, for what?" I hadn't dared to tempt the fates by mentioning my true concern, but I sensed she herself had the same dread. "I knew something had happened Hector, something to do with the island was troubling you." The colour left her cheeks, a sadness I hadn't seen before filled expressive eyes. I cursed myself for causing her worry, at the same time startled again by the ability of our emotions to behave in empathy.

After supper she began to talk quietly, the helicopter visit clearly behind her thinking. "I sometimes wonder, Hector if we are being selfish in cutting ourselves off from an outside world that's heading for turmoil and may need our help in some way. We're abandoning your expertise in nuclear physics and my work on models of climate change. Somebody else my have read my paper to the International Conference, it's set to fail anyway in getting a legally binding agreement on carbon reductions but I feel guilty letting them down." She stroked the puppy, "I wonder, are we being defeatist by hiding here on Sandray?"

The chill of Eilidh's misgivings struck home. I fought off qualms of uncertainty. No longer the island crofter, she began to speak as the eminent scientist I knew her to be, "Even if the politicians can reach an international agreement which is practical, and more difficult, one which suits the finance markets, then the species is embarking on its most critical experiment so far. By attempting to regulate the amount of atmospheric CO_2, the hope is to stabilise global temperature at an ambient level which suits western society's current behaviour patterns."

The scorn in her voice grew, "Major modifications to western lifestyles are required, will be forced on us before too long, and tomorrow isn't too soon. Less air travel is certainly one aspect, ordinary folk won't be able to afford to jet off to the sun anyway. Sadly we're too stupid to prioritise, we imagine that temperature control alone will enable us to continue with our consumer affluence. That's a myth, our profligate living is oblivious to the finite resource base on which it depends" I enjoyed scope of her views.

How like Eachan she sounded, I watched her bonnie face flush with passion, "In spite of CO_2 level rising steeply, there's plenty of vested interests who whip up sceptics through the media, dismiss the data as scaremongering, scientists fiddling the figures to up their research grants. Of course the temperature rise is due to naturally occurring solar trends but for human activity to be adding to this increase is highly dangerous."

Darkness had fallen as she spoke, "We can't easily destroy the basic fabric of the planet, it will spin on regardless of the excesses of the American Dream, many microbes will survive no matter what we do, but for us humans to survive then depending on diceing with the atmosphere really is a shot in the dark. There are too many variables over which we will never gain control, the crucial role of volcanic activity in affecting the climate is one and the stability of the earth's crust is certainly beyond our control. Already some of our operations in that area are liable to trigger activities which will be hard to plug once they take off.

Her tone became decidedly emphatic, "Make no mistake, this will be a bold attempt at global temperature manipulation, climate control if you like; what's still to dawn on politicians and even on some environmental specialists, is that we are endeavouring to manage our planet's climate, insulate it from the impact of solar emissions, sunspot cycles or the planets long scale elliptical orbit, wrest power from the major phenomena ruling the entire solar system."

I stroked her hair and though she smiled, a tear glistened in the lamplight, "An arbitrary cut in consumer lifestyles applied on a socially fair basis is unlikely to happen. The wealthy will survive the longest, the poor will go to the wall. Only a survival attitude based on altruistic behaviour has any hope of saving us. Greed is gobbling the planet." Her final words were the measure of her true sympathies; they lay with the approaching plight of the poor she'd witnessed struggling to survive on the flood plains of a river delta, those fighting the encroaching deserts, those who will go to the wall, as she'd put it.

For me one futile attempt at influencing myopic politicians had been convincing enough. In planning actions to combat a macro-environmental threat, they were neither free nor capable of making rational judgements. Eilidh was right, their masters, the major international financiers, thinking themselves safe in their counting houses, stay well out of reach of reason. Six billion people and rising to nine. How few people control the planet's destiny. The smaller the number, the greater the menace of megalomania, the greater the danger of destruction. We sat quietly. My admiration of Eilidh's views and values grew to new concepts. Her zeal for the cause of common humanity was infectious. I took her hand and sat thinking.

The puppy wakened, I took her outside for a snuffle and stood awhile watching the changing shape of the clouds. Sometimes a passage opened amidst their beautiful roundness, tunnels into the sanctuary of an outer space which looks back in time. That night they changed imperceptibly, drifting one into another, layered as undulations in radiation merge time into motion. The splendour of their differing shades, cold white cushions hiding the moon slowly became the blue, black masses resting on an incurious sea.

For a moment my belief in a life on Sandray had wavered. I knew the clouds as paramount to our climate's stability, a safeguard against the sun's rapacious energy; now I saw them differently, no longer a vital scientific fact, for as the oceans grow into clouds of seemingly aimless beauty so they restored my faith in simplicity.

Whimpering noises at my feet aroused me. I lifted Muille and went inside. Tip-toeing into the bedroom I slipped her under the blankets.

Tired of waiting for me, Eilidh lay sound asleep,

I too snuggled in beside her warmth.

CHAPTER THIRTY-FIVE

"There is no present."

The message came via Eilidh's visit that Eachan would have five sacks of seed potatoes ready for me to collect. I'd dug close to an acre of ground for our 'Lazybeds'. The soil would be warmed by the decaying seaweed heaped beneath their long lines, planting the 'tatties' would be the next operation on the road to self sufficiency and my hands had calluses any man worth calling himself a man would be proud to own.

A reluctant dawn awaited me on the Sound. To catch slack water I'd left early, the last stars bright enough to give me clear outlines. Once out in the open the morning became darker. A mist through which no sun would penetrate spread high above the Sound. The wind, slight as it was, backed round, I felt it on the nape of my neck and as animals will do, I turned to sniff the weather. It would not be a day to ceilidh too long at the croft of Ach na Mara.

Ella shook my hand at the door, "We're so pleased to hear about the baby," and with a light dancing in her eye, "aren't you the boy, and Eilidh determined to have the birth on the island." Proud but a mite embarrassed, I blushed. "Anyway come away in, you'll be needing your breakfast." Presently Eachan appeared from the byre, together with a fine smell of cattle. He clapped me on the back, "Well, well boy, didn't I say to herself the first day I saw you two together, it won't be...." "Now Eachan," guessing what he might say, Ella cut off further comment. Not to be outflanked, he went on, "I was going to say, I was the last child to be born on Sandray," and turning to me for the first time, he told of the rest of his brothers and sisters. We were just a family of five, not a lot for those days, Hector boy. I'd two sisters, one went to Australia, the other to New Zealand, young women, off they went in the thirties' depression. Never came back, my mother never saw them again. The Australian one lost her man in the second world war."

Not wishing to ask questions, I was pleased when he continued, "My two elder brothers, big strapping boys and only sixteen and seventeen; I might have been two years old, but I can see it as well as telling," and speaking quietly, "you see the recruiting officer came to the door, on Sandray mind you, kilt and all, he didn't question their ages too much, just offered them glory in the ranks and a silver shilling to fight the Germans. Off to Inverness they went, joined the Seaforth Highlanders. Nineteen fourteen, into the front line, the war to end wars they called it," and giving a snort, "It was as much to keep England's social order in place," adding softly. "The trenches of France did for them both before they were twenty, and it finished the cailleach, mentally anyway, ah Dia, how my mother hated the English toffs."

We sat in to the table but I waited until the porridge plates emptied before telling of the helicopter visit and, for it seemed important to me, I went on to mention the raven's distress. At this last, the old man looked startled. Although he turned to look out of the window, his eyes strayed far beyond the peak of Sandray. Their focal point appeared riveted on the image of some approaching terror.

Ella sat silently, watching him closely. In the overcast light of that morning his face aged with a frightening suddenness. Out of its strange aspect materialised his grandfather, hovering in the form of Eachan, dull in the shadows, an apparition, its presence a trick of mind? I recoiled, shrank into my chair.

Eachan rose. Possessed by another he walked round the table, his eyes burning with intensity. A vision gripped him. I knew it, the room closed about us, suddenly old, as from another existence. A shiver lifted the hair on my neck, playing over me, the stealth of a deathly hand; the coldness of a ripple in the unending curve of space-time where all existences are a stream of particles, and those that once have been, are cold; cold in the vacuum of death.

Crossing behind me Eachan stood starring out of the window, his hands raised, his fingers spread, a patriarchal figure, white of hair and noble of feature, he remained motionless as though fending off a grotesque evil force, and then, in a voice not his own, "The raven of our forebears will return to the land of their ancestors, never again will they breed on Sandray." His mental anguish, if it can be described as that, passed off as quickly as it had taken him and he sat back at the table; nevertheless his gaunt features had a greyness. Eating very little, he remained silent.

Ella packed a box and with a hug of goodbye and, "Look after Eilidh," Eachan and I hurried back to the boat without speaking. A tarpaulin covered five bags of seed tatties. He passed them down to me. Not a day for delaying. The wind strengthened from the south. Only then I did I learn his mind as he stood on the pier, rope in his hand, about to cast me off. I glanced up, ready to catch and coil. The man, his eyes unblinking, stared across the Sound to the Hill of the Shroud. I stood, rocking with boat, unwilling to intrude. Lines of gulls circled in from the Atlantic; their metallic screeching carried a warning which roused him.

Still holding the mooring lines, finally he looked down, "Hector a' bhalaich, about the croft, you'll know I'm sure, our family are scattered to the four winds, doing well, the lot of them, Australia, Canada and where ever else, they'll not see crofting, no nor the Highlands, again. I'd like to keep the name Mackenzie on the place, know what I mean. Now then, there's particulars in the house drawn up and agreed by the estate and the Crofters Commission which hands Ach na Mara over to you when I plough my last furrow."

He spoke in a manner surprising by its unaccustomed bluntness, "The house belongs to me and that will go to Ella. Sandray is more difficult, anyway you have just to agree if that's what you have a mind to do. Think about it, Hector." He looked down on me, eyes intent, searching mine as they had the night we first met. No words passed to offer my answer, none was needed. My eyes expressed a pledge beyond words.

Home from a threatening sea the herring gulls sheltered in the lee of the dunes. Gusts of wind plucked at their feathers. One by one, stretching necks to the sky, their utterances carried over the bay in snatches of sorrow. Perhaps it was the mood that was on us, but their cries were of another age, another happening, of an undreamed desolation. Tautness came to Eachan's jaw, his thin lips straightened, his voice had strength, "Remember Hector, when my hand is off the tiller, you'll bury me on Sandray, in the grave out on the headland."

Our eyes met in that understanding which is transmitted by means greater than words. He threw the rope into the bow of the boat, shouting into the rising wind as I pulled away, "There's tide under you now and this south wind'll put up a sea, take the Sandray headland close for the shelter until you have to round it, make out in a trough and cross the crest well off and you can head in along the hollows!" Without more words and judging the sky by a glance, he turned for home. Neither of us had made reference to what passed in the kitchen. I knew no saner man. Was he the unwitting medium of a power beyond this earthly place?

The old boy was far from wrong; once in the Sound wind over tide began to throw up triangular crests. They met with loud clapping sounds, vicious peaks jostling in the conflicting forces, tossing sheets of spray in the air. They stung my eyes. I licked the taste of salt from my lips, it filled my mouth. A big lump of sea sloshed over the gunnel. Tiller below an armpit I bailed smartly, weaving amongst the confused waters. Coming under the Sandray headland, I ran in close. Conditions eased and taking my eye off the seas for a second, I glanced up.

High above me on the cliff edge, Eildh carrying Mullie. her hair blowing in a wild golden mass. She waved down. Past horror sprang at me. Instantly I stood up, signalling- go back from the edge. She vanished. My confidence rose, my woman with me, watching and willing.

Atlantic rollers were passing the point, I ran out along the lee of a hefty one. Clear of land, out of shelter, I sailed the hollow. Ahead its peak began to break. Open boat, a curling top fast unzipping, racing towards me, ready to swamp us. Ride its crest before the curl reaches. I swung the boat, put her shoulder to it, up she climbed, a violent lurch, over its mighty hump we sailed. The crest toppled over behind me. Now, swing in for the bay on its curving back. The boat so small I sat amongst the waves. Man, boat, wind and sea, the glory of a relationship which breeds lasting respect and affection; there is no mastery of the sea, only a joy in being part of its unquenchable spirit.

A glowing Eilidh caught the mooring line. Muille's inquisitive head appeared over the jetty before she scampered back to hide behind Eilidh's legs. I jumped ashore, two minds and four arms entwined; there could be no leaving Sandray. A lovely woman, lucky man and a little dog.

Safe home, that night we lay snug and listening. The tap, tap of slates kept us awake. Out of respect for the old man I hadn't mentioned Eachan's alarming behaviour at the window, yet Eilidh seemed aware I'd been present at a strange manifestation of the Highlander's visionary power. She'd spoken in a hushed voice, "A gift or a curse, who would know? Eachan always had that turn of mind, they said it came from his grandfather, born and died on Sandray, full of poetry," and with a quiet laugh, "Your great grandfather. You know Eachan sometimes seems possessed by the depths of great emotion, past happenings, tragedies or loss; then again he seems to see into a future few would care to contemplate." Only then, hiding my surprise, did I tell her.

I waited for the roaring of the gale to abate a little, "I think Eachan's strength of character has saved him, his state of mind may be a form of awareness, an antenna that can sweep the continuum of events which pass into each other, the long past and the what will come to be," and after a little thought I went on, "he's able to see an over view of the dovetailing of the past and future which defies our belief in an instant of time." Eilidh's head on the pillow nodded, "Yes," she whispered, "there is no present."

A candle stood on the pine dresser. Its yellow light on played on the walls, making dark patterns of our sparse furniture. I watched the wax melting, drip by drip. A drumming on the window pane came and went, loud then softly, twitching at the curtains. Flickering shadows moved on the ceiling, reminding me of Eachan's strangeness, his outstretched fingers. The atmosphere took on a chill, the same uncanny chill which had pervaded their kitchen. I had the claustrophobic sensation of entering a cave without ending.

Our talk had been of Eachan's wish to make over Ach na Mara to me, how much that would change our lives if it were to happen. Once more we returned to his singular behaviour of that morning and why should it happen after I'd mentioned the raven. What ghastly vision beset him, brought about his pronouncement that the birds would abandon Sandray? More worrying was the wish he imparted down at the jetty, "Bury me on the headland." Neither of us cared to put thoughts into words. Was it a premonition?

The door handle rattled, once, and again. Crash, the door flew open. The candle gutted. Blackness. A cold draught blew over our faces. I reached beside the bed for a torch. Wafting gently in its beam, the door stood ajar. Had somebody entered? I swept the beam round the room. Nobody? Before I could rise to close the door, it slammed shut.

An Atlantic gale seeking out the old house, did its spirit wander the darkness? Suddenly I knew, surely as I saw the dying waves of a receding tide stretch into the emptiness of an ocean blue and immensely empty. Surely I knew.

"Eilidh," I held her tenderly, "Eilidh," I said simply, "Eachan is dead."

She lay still, I listened to her breathing, until stirring a little she said, "I know." Her soft words reached into the abyss of sadness and sobbing gently she buried her head beneath my chin. The candle burned low, its shadows no longer unearthly and I heard her murmur, "Eachan would have been born in this room. And now he's back and I'm happy for him."

Rollers pounding the beach sent shock waves through the ground. The House of the Haven trembled. The gale's ferocity, its determination to enter the house, no longer surprised us. An hour passed in the utter desolation of our loss.

Gradually the storm veered into the north, soughing at the gable. Poor Eachan, as fine a man as it had been my privilege to know. An intellect and wisdom which surpassed degrees or narrow cleverness: unassuming, he carried a dignity beyond the squalid interests of money and social station. The sanctity of life in its countless expressions was paramount.

We said little more, the loss too great. Needing the open skies and knowing the tide was on the flood, I whispered, "I'm away down to check on the boat." At once she made to get up, "You keep the bed warm, I won't be long." Pulling on shirt and trousers I was out before she could stop me. It wasn't altogether our boat's safety which prompted me to head for the jetty, something made me uneasy. Danger was afoot.

The midnight sky gave little light, only when shredding clouds opened a window of stars did it shine on the flecks of spume dancing over the fields weightless as bobs of cotton wool. The weight of each falling comber shook the earth, a mighty thump and roaring up the beach. They were ravaging the dunes. Though the wind was dropping, tide and gale had done their work. Dunes were collapsing. A massive swell tore at their bases. Huge slices of sand faces were falling, being sucked down the shore, staining the rippling backwash. Another dune toppled. I watched the devastation. It vanished, no more than a child's sand castle.

How obvious that melting ice caps and rising sea levels would obliterate the dunes of Sandray, ultimately take the croft, strip away the soil by which succeeding generations might live. If Sandray, where else? What of the millions of mouths?

Back tracking from the shore I reached the jetty in safety. Our sole life line to the outside world rode safe and comfortable. I'd moored her so that she lay across the elbow of the pier. I checked the ropes for chafe and by way of habit before making for home, walked to the end of the pier to scan the conditions. As I turned, was that a flash of green, far out, a starboard navigation light?

Never, it had to be a star tipping the horizon. Again it blinked, a starboard light, well out from the bay, a vessel of some kind? The colossal swell would account for the pause. A minute passed. Next appearance, green and red, both lights showed for twenty seconds and vanished. No doubting now, the ship had brought her head round, making for the bay, running a lee shore in a gale, every sailor's nightmare.

Our kit box stood at the top of the pier, I ran up grabbed a torch and began shining its beam slowly from side to side. Don't attempt to enter the bay. Hard judging distance at night, would the skipper spot my signal, put up his helm, swing to port? Had he room to clear the headland, make for the Sound?

On the vessel came; a mast rose against the southern sky; a yacht, in these conditions, my God, are they mad? Shipwrecked on the beach, drowned in the swell? She drew level with the jetty, centre of the bay, just outside the rolling tops. Red and green lights came round to face me. She's swinging, heading out? To my amazement her white aft light shone. Surely not trying to anchor?

Eilidh appeared, breathless, "Hector, are you OK?" I gave her a quick hug, "That yacht's in danger, she's going to anchor, I'll run out and take them off, if it goes wrong." "No, no, Hector don't, you'll be swamped." Loosing the aft rope off, I hauled our boat head in to the jetty and leapt aboard, "Eilidh, I need to help, could you cast off the bow line?" Perhaps my tone of voice- she slipped the rope. Outboard revving, I cleared the jetty's stonework, running broadside to a steep incoming swell. Not breaking, that would be fatal.

The yacht appeared to be drifting astern. In the glow of her green navigation light, I could make out a figure kneeling at the bow. In spite of the tension, I laughed. Dropping an anchor I hoped, not praying. At hailing distance I throttled back, nosing the rollers, "Do you need help?" A gust took the reply. Taking it as yes, I flicked out fenders and ran close in to the yacht's hull, both boats now rolling through forty degrees.

A bearded figure in yellow oil-skins stood above me, arm looped in the shrouds, balancing to a gyrating hull. I flung a line. Wind took it. Re-coil, second throw. Neatly caught, I was hauled tight alongside. Wait for the yacht's gunnel dipping towards me. One step, I was aboard, clinging to the rigging.

A man's voice at my ear, "I'm trying to get out two anchors, one's out. Can you ease away to starboard? Controls in the cockpit, gear lever goes down for ahead, throttle's the small lever. Go easy into gear," and looking at the narrowing gap astern, "don't stall the engine." Using every hand hold he clawed his way along the deck to the bow. I worked my way astern to the rattling of chain being hauled from a locker.

The bucking and rolling getting more erratic, we must still be drifting. Almost thrown overboard I grabbed the winch, dropped into a deep safe cockpit. Close one. Unlash the tiller, it thrashed wildly for a second, I gripped it between my thighs, hung on one handed, reached for the controls. At my right hand, fine, a touch of throttle, very gently into the gear. I steered us carefully to starboard. Violent rolling, it's getting shallow. Should we take to the wee boat, run the swell, leave the yacht before she struck?

A bellow from the bow, "Steady at that!" a rattle of chain, anchor down. I glanced astern. White lines of rollers were smashing into spray on the rocks, the only lightness which showed. Ledges close. Cream breakers ran up the gullies, burst in plumes, fell back sissing. A cable off, if the anchors failed, both boats would splinter on the black seal rocks.

The man fought his way aft and stood in the cockpit beside me.Neither of us spoke, tense and alert, watching. The engine might well tick over, it could never take us out of here.

Would the rolling turn to pitching? Her bow swing to the swell? Tell us the anchors were holding?

I saw Eilidh, high above the breakers. For myself I had no fear, but I felt the anguish of her watching.

The boom and hiss became louder.

Shipwreck closer.

CHAPTER THIRTY-SIX

The nude Sun God

Ten p.m. and Sir Joshua Goldberg sat in his strictly private office pouring over Nuen's actual and projected profits. In the absence of the thrill of handling raw cash the pleasure of studying figures ending with seven noughts ran a close second. He lit a cigar and blew thoughtful rings. Tomorrow his first report to the Nuen's Annual General Meeting as its Chairman would be a catalogue of success. His delivery must leave nothing to chance, must side step any awkward questions from the shareholding punters, vis a vis his predecessor Anderson's abrupt departure. He needed to concentrate, fix the whole performance in his mind, make it look off the cuff.

Previous minutes proposed and seconded, they'd be followed by a series of graphs together with short videos of the Company's latest projects, thence to coffee, that always got the shareholders relaxed. He'd begin by drawing attention to Nuen's escalating capital assets, touch modestly on the eighteen percent improvement in profits, magnanimously announce a quarter of one percent increase in dividends and end dramatically by sketching their future global prospects.

Should he keep this gem to the last? He saw himself speaking with statesmanlike gravitas. Shareholders, it pleases me, slight pause, and your good suportive selves, here there would be laughter, to inform you all of the significant news which is emerging from Canada as I speak. Nine times all the oil we've so far consumed since the invention of internal combustion engine is contained in the tar sands of Alberta. Naturally we have to contend with the environmental lobby; no, no, cut that, they're just a shower of green layabouts, easily discredited, given my media mogul friend's ability to cast them as fanatical extremists bent on killing ecomomic growth and fomenting anarchy. Best to say, you see gentlemen separating oil from sand is energy hungry, extremely energy hungry but not surprisingly, given your Company's eminence, it presents Nuen with a brilliant opportunity. Already I've been approached to construct two nuclear power facilities near the main extraction sites, and rest assured I can confidently predict that many smaller plants will follow.

Sir Joshua imagined he heard the indrawn gasps of surprise and approval. Very privately, his fund management friend' Nicky', during the past few months, had been quietly buying him more Nuen shares, nothing too obvious, just acquiring them for a small holding company registered in the British Virgin Islands. He'd called it Elixir Investments. Without doubt, releasing the news of fresh contracts would massage the one thing which interested all finance punters, the price. How he loathed these petty shareholders, loyal only to profit, but there you are, humoured they must be.

Feed them a snippit. The Mining Act of 1872 gives all US citizens the right to mine on public land and fellow shareholders, we at Nuen, on your behalf, are about to exercise that very right. We shall commence extracting ore from the major uranium deposits above the Grand Canyons National Park. Republicans to a share they'd love it, stuff the environmental Democrats. Go west young man. Covered wagons, Colt 45's, conquer the land, the Gold Rush over again, from a touch pad.

One enthusiastic burst of applause after another, the very anticipation swelled his mind with pleasure. He'd bow his head modestly before holding up a hand to quell the standing ovation he'd asked Nicky to arrange, a nice touch, he congratulated himself, rather clever, just moments before proposing with due humility a small increase in his Chairman's emoluments. More applause, maybe cheering and a voice from the back of the conference hall, Nicky would see to that, "Due reward Sir Joshua for your skill in guiding Nuen's affairs." Nobody would dare to question the amount. The figure involved, about forty percent and the doubling of Director's bonuses to a figure not remote from six million dollars, must await their next monthly board meeting, prudence dear boy, prudence.

Another attack of palpitations and a slight pain gripped his chest. It had plagued him on and off since the morning's disturbing event. He belched loudly, and grabbing a bottle from his desk draw swilled down a handful of pills. Fluent cursing followed. By mistake he'd swallowed the blue tablets kept for 'special occasions'. Now something else would plague him all day!

Much had gone well since the pathetic Andrew Anderson's very necessary replacement. Getting his screeching wife out of the office that morning proved more difficult. 'How the mischief did this diabolical woman get past the doorman?' was Goldberg's first angry thought, but she had. He'd eyed her without speaking. A wall of perfume advanced towards him. As she perched on the edge of his desk and leant over him, he deliberately switched on the extractor fan. Not exactly his penchant; the ample display of expensive Botox treatment left Sir Joshua unmoved.

"Joshie darling I had to see you, I've nobody to help me." Tears glistened, "Andy sure has vanished, just gone, left little me alone, helpless." Mascara dripped from her eyelashes. Between sobs she added, "The cruel, heartless monster." Goldberg gave a nonchalant wave of his hand, "So be it my dear woman and no, I don't know where your husband has gone." Given that almost twelve months had elapsed since Goldberg first heard of Anderson's mysterious departure, it crossed his mind that the discovery of her husband's absence seemed somewhat belated.

His coolness appeared to fan a flame. She flung her arms around his neck. "I'm running out of money," and wailing hysterically, "I might have to sell the house." With considerable difficulty he disentangled her arms shouting, "That, Mrs. Anderson is not my concern!" and praying the stench of perfume wouldn't cling to his suit, he'd attempted to thrust her out of the room.

Bright red finger nails ripped down his left cheek. A leopard skin handbag hit him squarely under the right jaw, the accuracy of the blow suggested practice. He'd staggered back. Equally accurate, she aimed a kick. The pain was excruciating. The door slammed. She'd gone. Holding himself and staggering across the office he locked it, just in the nick of time. A stream of obscenity filtered through the keyhole. Hefty kicking from outwith thumped round the room. He made it to his desk and telephone before being sick.

The kicking stopped. At the hands of his doorman, the screeching departed down the corridor. Sir Joshua sank down, clutching at himself, rocking back and forth in agony. Later the Doctor examined him carefully, "Gee, that sure is some swelling, Sir Josh." An observation Goldberg considered totally unnecessary as he lay exposed across his desk. At the next comment, "Yeah man, she sure did hit the bull's eye," the patient seethed inwardly, the sheer impudence. This Doctor would wait a long time for his money.

So the day had been trying, and still at his desk, late as it was, Chairman Goldberg finally pushed aside his copy of the Company Accounts, lit another cigar and inhaling deeply, lay back in his swivel chair. Smoke trickled from his nostrils. From time to time his hand hovered over the afflicted parts. Damn tablets, they'd double the pain. Stirring himself, he poured another two fingers of brandy. Thoughts of the morning's fiendish attack were soothed away. Sir Joshua took to mulling over issues which certainly didn't lend themselves to disclosure but rather to the pleasure of a little self congratulation.

Strictly off the books, his dealings with the Pentagon and the UK's M.O.D. were bearing fruit; the weight of his little 'piggy bank' as he fondly described his offshore tax haven, nicely proved it. The forthcoming round of this damned International Non-Proliferation Treaty could be tricky. Whether the enriched plutonium which Nuen supplied went into defensive weaponry or otherwise was not his concern and wars had to be fought. Anyway nobody but himself and one Board member, that most helpful ex Westminster P.M., knew of the arrangements. The Company Chief Executive might have a shrewd idea. Given the man's salary, only a complete idiot would open his mouth. Naturally Anderson would know. Any hint of trouble from that quarter and a certain team of 'security experts' would ensure an effect far from beneficial to the health of Nuen's past Chairman.

Blue cigar smoke hung above his desk. Watching it trail gently towards the ceiling, he allowed his thoughts to envisage the conquest of far horizons. A wall map displaying a considerable part of the globe was already bedecked by Nuen symbols. Propping his heavy left jowl in a cupped hand, he looked proudly across to it. Uranium mines, Africa, Australia, Grand Canyon, big deposits there, the price of ore climbing nicely as demand increased, sites for the next range of eleven nuclear plants in America be flagged up, more pins in the map, where next in a world thirsty for cheap energy and luxury? Iran was out of bounds for several reasons, rather a pity. As much as he mistrusted the Iranians, business was business.

Anyway, hurrah at last! UK's top priority, an agreement on the underground nuclear waste repository, was through. The secret test drill, given a slight adjustment to the results, did the trick, solid rock. The Nuclear Safety Authority raised no objections, National security interests had side- stepped tiresome planning consent; work would begin in the autumn. The next generation of nuclear power stations to be built in England were 'privately' in the bag. Sir Joshua gazed fondly at the map.

Nuclear energy to all nations, it will save the planet, the world would worship him yet.

Cigar smoke and a brandy at his elbow, how soothing; he screwed another cigar stub into an ornate silver ash tray which sat on his calf leather inlayed desk. This glittering little object d'art depicted a reclining nude Apollo, the embodiment of masculine pulchritude. He smiled, it'd been a naughty present from Nicky Fellows, his 'funds management friend', bent on becoming a billionaire, poor chap. As Goldberg was wont to reflect, beware of megalomaniacs and religious fanatics, or worse, a combination of both and never, never trust a man who's fond of money. Sir Joshua's half closed eyes focused on the heap of smouldering ash, his last cigar. Slowly it crumbled to nothing.

Its dying wisp of smoke curled around the perfectly formed statuette. This was not the day for such a tantalising exposure to come to his attention. Feeling himself gingerly, Sir Joshua winced.

Pouring a nightcap, he scowled. A faint recollection of classical history lessons at Eton became a painful memory, the mortar board and gown, the swish of a cane.

Bare buttocks and embarrassment, a group of sniggering sixth-formers; he groped towards some obscure fact. His mind drifted from a school day to the figure on an ash tray.

Apollo. Yes, the beautiful Greek Sun God, nude and mocking. Grabbing the ash tray he flung it across the room. Apollo snapped off his base.

"Bloody sunshine, bloody sunshine, the sun's my only enemy."

CHAPTER THIRTY-SEVEN

"We made us a bond."

Tense and watching we stood in the yacht's cockpit braced against its wild rolling. The boom thrashed from side to side above our heads. Grabbing a hank of rope the man lashed it to a cleat. The peak of her mast careered across the sky, an arc so wide and violent I feared we'd be de-masted. Another ten degrees and she must founder. The engine ticked over. Every seventh wave is a giant; it came, a truly frightening beast, the roll buried her stern and exhaust pipe. A few chuffing coughs, the engine died. A red light glowed. Without comment the man bent and switched it off, his manner, calm and impassive. A choked engine; danger mounting, it tightened the sinews.

The closer to shore, the steeper the crests, from the peak of this mighty escalator I counted. Astern three waves powered ashore, their foam streaked backs separated us from the seal rocks. A white curtain of water detonated skywards, fell slowly into a massive hollow. Water streamed down black fangs of rock. We were close. To starboard heavy swell uncoiled into graceful arches of a moment's beauty before thundering onto the sand. A cross wind whipped spray across the beach in horizontal sheets. Seething torrents roared into the fragile dunes. The atmosphere spiralled about us, moist and salty, laden with sound. Loud is the beat which carries the note of doom, slender the umbilical of life. Two men, total strangers, waited; both aware should the anchors fail, the rocks would taste the timbers of a yacht.

No lover of the sea believes he will drown. If the keel were to smash down upon the rocks we'd be flung from the cockpit, washed powerless up ledges green with slime. Somehow I'd stop myself slithering back, dodge the next pounding, claw my way to safety. Eilidh stood high above the land devouring surf weighing our chances, a woman thinking of her baby, born by the shock of seeing its father's drown. An island girl, she knew. The sea has no belief, offers no idle hope, knows only the hovering ordination of fate.

Out of the darkness the flash of exploding plumes marked our drift towards the rocks. If she struck, abandoning the yacht was our only chance.. risk making for the jetty, let the wee boat take the storm beam on, maybe get swept up the beach, leaving the man was no option unless the yacht settled. I spoke at his ear, "There's good holding ground beneath us, the anchors should grip," and in attempting to appear unconcerned after one extremely violent roll put her gunnels under, I ventured, "If you don't mind my asking, where are you bound?"

The bearded face looked straight at me. Deep grooves in thin cheeks were worn by exposure, if nothing else a hard- jawed ocean wanderer. Steel blue eyes carried an aura of calmness, a man unruffled by the clamour of running surf which might shortly grind his boat to smithereens. The reply didn't surprise me. A smile broke from a thick red beard, "Five months of hard thinking and a near drowning, my friend, I just follow the compass of the heart."

The wind veered sharply north, stripping the wave tops and lashing us with spray. "D'you want to come ashore?" at once I regretted the question, intuition knowing the answer. It sounded an insult. His eyes were bright, those of a man relishing danger, "Me and this Valkyrie girl, we made us a bond." He patted her gunnel, "We've put a bridle on the Atlantic seahorses before and if this lot buck us off, we go together." I nodded approval.

The yacht's rolling shifted, she began to plunge and rear. We looked at each other, the anchors were holding. She buried her nose, waves swilled along the deck, poured over the stern. She reared and chain clanked taut on the stem head. Challenge turned to spray. Now embayed on a lee shore? Not the act of an experienced skipper, the mystery of the man about as mythical as the name of his yacht.

Anxious to reach Eilidh, I stepped out of the cockpit. He caught my arm and reaching into the hatch pulled out a lifejacket. "No thanks, I'll be fine," not adding my thoughts,' it just prolongs a drowning'. Holding a stanchion and swaying to each dip the yachtsman held out a hand, "Thanks for coming aboard, you saved me a lot of bother. I'm Andrew Anderson." Instinctively I liked him, liked the ring of his name. An iron grip said the rest.

Reluctant always to offer my name, I'd have parted happily without any such exchange. A shade woodenly, I told him. "That name doesn't surprise me none, I was aiming for an island called Halasay, my radar got blown to hell, reckon I've missed it some, but you kinda look what I expected about these parts."

A swell lifted my boat level with the deck of Valkyrie. I jumped aboard, "You missed the entrance to the Sound," I shouted up to him, "this is Sandray, just south of Halasay, if you've a mind, give us a call when this blows over." Lifting a hand in acknowledgement, seamanlike he tossed a neatly coiled rope into the bow and cast me off.

The ability to handle a small open boat back across the bay in such vicious conditions had to be instinctive, in the blood, every move of the tiller felt the sea. I thrilled to the response of the boat, I wasn't fighting the storm. I revelled in its rawness, the soaring elements, the intoxication of danger.

A waiting Eilidh caught the coil of rope which snaked up to her hand. "Sorry, sorry leaving you alone, poor woman, that was really unkind of me." "No need to be sorry, Hector, you did what a sailor would do," she hugged a shivering man, "You did the right thing."

Laughing with the exhilaration, I spoke before realising it wasn't funny, "I once heard a Prime Minister say that before he sanctioned a hundred thousand innocent deaths."

CHAPTER THIRTY-EIGHT

The Disc

All that morning the sea ran strongly. The Valkyrie rode it out beyond the seal rocks where she'd anchored. Neither boat nor man was in our thoughts. There could be no crossing the Sound to be with Ella, she would understand. Neither of us doubted our premonition. Eachan had died at the height of last night's gale. We spoke more quietly. The old house felt it, not the cheery home of yesterday; not sullen, but respectful. An odd silence dwelt in each room, the essence of his being waited here on the island. An amorphous soul hooded by death awaited release, some token that all was not the end.

No religious contemplations nagged our thoughts, offering comfort as it did too many, his presence sufficed. Quietly I said to Eilidh, "I think Eachan foresaw his death, that prophecy of the raven leaving Sandray, perhaps they were symbolic words, maybe an omen. He seemed always to regard the raven as being the link to his ancestors and whatever was the horror he contemplated who would know, but almost his last words to me were, 'Bury me on the headland."

Eilidh listened with her head down. I spoke of the man she'd known since childhood, "He'd no orthodox religious belief, his mind ranged too wide for that, I remember him saying to me one night, 'religions come and go, they change according to manmade concepts, today's belief is tomorrow's myth, God is just a bit of anthropomorphic imagination." Deep down, perhaps subconsciously, he was highly superstitious, and since coming here I learnt why; the closer you live dependent on the whim of the elements the more credibility you give to the ominous supernatural and the need to guard against its wilful tripwires. Over a noggin one night, Eachan and I came to the conclusion that religion is just superstition in fancy dress."

She looked at me steadily. There was no crying, just a dullness of eye I hadn't seen before. "I believe all he said, there's no logic in religion, only hope, nothing to replace a loss for those left, but I understand why Eachan wanted to be buried on the headland" She said no more than that, and knowing his reverence for his ancestors, I agreed.

The drabness of the sky awaited a clearance from the west to strip away the cloud. Taking spade and punch, that afternoon I walked over to the headland. The storm had died to a cheerless day, lacklustre seas slopped about the cliff. Eilidh had wanted to help. I shook my head. She watched from the door, reading my thoughts. I wanted to work alone. Delving into a monument sacred to the beliefs of another age was a task I approached with some misgiving.

What secret, if any, lay amongst the stones? A boat grave entrusted to the keeping of these silent guardians, a lone cairn set amidst sea, hill and sky, its aura of tomb and standing stone, dare I chance its defilement? I recoiled and stood looking about me. I was being watched, the sensation of crossing a divide from which there would be no return whispered sacrilege. What curse might befall the trespass of this desecration? On a slight mound, amongst the waiting stones, I marked out the shape of a coffin.

Suspecting it would prove difficult in finding depth for a burial I cut the first turf. It lifted with surprising ease. Down my spade went, brown clinging peat, its acrid smell of decay getting stronger at each level. Sticky earth piled above me on the bank. Although warm from digging, I began to shake. This ground had been moved before, maybe a thousand years or more ago, a sacred resting to believers in adventure and conquest. The heroic slain carried from battle by the Valkyrie to rise again, victor and vanquished to feast and carouse. Valkyrie, she lay in the bay below. My hands shook. This dank hole now surrounding me, the hallowed ground of departed spirits; I stood in a Viking Holy of Holies, The Ship of the Dead.

I rested against the walls of my digging, no wider than a coffin. Wet earth clung to my hands. Predictions invaded the grave, unbidden they surrounded me, curse like; transcendent mysteries of the fearsome Viking, the brave, the rapacious, the charitable. Odin, their Raven shouldered God who hung nine nights on a windswept tree and gave his eye to gain, not wealth nor worldly tribute, but the power of ultimate knowledge. The sun will grow dark, stars fall from the sky, the sea will invade the land; pursuing wolves will swallow Sun and Moon, Earth's bonds will crack, the mountains fall. And overwhelmed by the forces of chaos, Doom will be the Destiny of all Gods, their ship alone the symbol of a journey from death and rebirth.

The walking dead arose from the soil, the stones they murmured to me, those departed elements in an atmosphere which clung to this, the shrine of their corporeal existence. Their curse was on me. I shuddered with an inner cold, that dread of a soul which knows no way out. I stood spade in hand. Would I dig more? The western sky opened. Far out, on the tip of the Atlantic the sun made circles, yellow rings of light on a grey sea. Eachan's voice spoke in my head, strong as though he were beside me. I heard again the wish he'd imparted on the jetty of his croft. I would lift a last spade's depth, for him.

A slight jarring; something solid, though not rock. Dropping on my knees I scrabbled with my hands. Working carefully, I touched the outline of an object. Scraping a little and a little, finger tips only, slowly, faintly glowing, a tall narrow forehead emerged. Hemmed by the walls of a grave, dank and lifeless, my breathing rapid and fevered, I worked on. Two empty eye sockets, black hollows out of stained whiteness gazed through me, theirs no unseeing stare.

I stepped back, knew again the awful power which cast that headland to be the afterworld of fate. I looked into hollow sockets. Slowly they filled. Unblinking eyes shone from the cavities, eyes that understood that which consumes all life at the moment of death; not fear nor exaltation but the peace which slips before us as a sea fog will drift before a voyaging bow which awaits the rising sun.

Sunshine called from above. I hastened to leave, bent to replace the dark ground. Yet as mysterious powers guide a diviner to the precious, I was drawn. I delved. A bone, small and crooked, the segment of a finger appeared. I touched it, moved a little more ground.

The merest glint in the dimness of a coffin space; on hands and knees I'd dug, brushed away specs of earth with finger tips. More bones were scattered in the small hollow. Apprehensive at disturbing the sanctity of a skeleton I cleared particles of earth as delicately as trembling fingers would allow. In the diffuse light, a faint glow. I shrank against the wet earth. There, clasped by a skeletal hand, a small, golden, solar disc.

For long I'd stood, chilled by the fear of portentous horrors unfolding before me in that pit of Viking myth. I heard their saga, their poetry, 'Old forgotten far off things and battles long ago, the harp that once in Tara's Hall.' I looked out to the Hill of the Shroud, home of the raven; did I imagine their harsh croak? Was I the person the ancestral birds meant to find this token?

Tentatively I took the disc from the grasp of a Norseman. Gold, the indestructible metal, blood stained throughout human history, age old emblem of religions, halo of the gods, the mark of power. I rubbed it softly. Tiny etchings covered its face, a sliver of moon, tiny marks for stars, in my hand I held the golden talisman which carried life beyond an earthly grave. No promise of redemption, no priestly bribe of eternal bliss, nothing save an acceptance of the omnipotent sun.

Light from the windows of home emphasized the growing dark. A disconsolate sea boded winds of change. Fretting waves on the shore sounded lifeless, dull and ponderous, they reflected my thoughts. Those who tamper with the enigma of the eternal dust, I groaned inwardly, a line from a Norse saga, repeated itself over and over again, *'hang like rooks from a gallows.'*

Darkness closed over my brooding walk to the house. Eilidh waiting at the door, said nothing. She took the disc in her hand without surprise and both in solemn mood, we went into the kitchen. The candle had burnt low, a little smoke curled from its flame.

In the half light her golden hair had shades of a sunset. She turned over the disc. A strange desolation filled her eyes, the sorrow of a last farewell,. "After you went down to the jetty last night I slept for a little, a dream came to me, the sun, a huge circle, slowly shrank to a tiny disc until it disappeared into the western sea."

She sat at the table polishing the relic until the stains of soil gave way to gold.

And in the dying candlelight her hair outshone its glitter.

CHAPTER THIRTY-NINE

"A wee drap of the cratur."

The candles had burnt low when a soft knock came to the door. "Eachan?" I said quietly to Eilidh, instantly hopeful he was alive. She shook her head. Rising I opened the door. A shaft of candle light fell obliquely across a tall dark figure standing a little back, "Sorry to bother you, Mr. MacKenzie, ah just wanted to thank you properly for your help with my yacht." I relaxed, "Come in, come in, you're more than welcome." Into the dimness of the room the yachtsman stepped, shaking my hand again and from the other offering a bottle of malt, "This is in the way of thanks," he said, glancing past me to Eilidh. "Ach it didn't need this, but it's very good of you, Mr Anderson, it won't go to waste," and putting the bottle on the table, was aware he still looked at Eilidh.

This man, tall, rugged and not from a nursery of weaklings was the first stranger to whom I'd introduced Eilidh. His eyes sparkled and Eilidh blushed. I introduced him perhaps a mite too formally, a pang of jealousy in my tone perhaps reached her for she dropped her eyes, saying perhaps rather hastily to cover a little embarrassment, "You'll take a cup of tea, Mr. Anderson?" "Please lady, I'm Andy to my friends." Eilidh smiled and busied herself at the sink.

To ease the air of discomfort and out of courtesy I reached to the shelf, took down another bottle and two glasses. "You've rowed across, you'll be needing a wee toot of this." "Sure thing," and as I poured, "Mind if I call you Hector?" "No, no," and raising a glass, "here's to us." "You sure said it, Hector.

Say, did I see a solar panel on your roof?" I laughed, and not yet ready to open up a conversation beyond pleasantries, "You did indeed."

The American swivelled in his chair taking in the whole room, "I kinda like the pad you've got yourselves, kinda reminds me of what my grandfather told me about," and knocking back his dram, "His father was a Shetlander, had a little farm someplace up there, I aim to find it, got the charts and when I do, I'm gonna build a solar village, maybe start a fish farm. I've an idea for producing power using the osmotic pressure which builds when saltwater passes into fresh water through a membrane. Back home in the States ah saw a model, it really works, scaled up it'll drive a turbine; who in the name of hell needs nuclear energy?" At once I understood, first form science, shell an egg, stick it in salt water overnight and by morning when you make a pin hole a jet of water shoots out. The man wasn't ranting, he was right, harness the pressure from osmosis.

Eilidh set down a plate of oatcake and cheese on the table, "I cook for myself mostly, sure nice to get something from a woman's hand," and patting her hand, "thanks Eilidh." A very different style, up front, garrulous and immediately friendly, the Highland nature, reticent, far from disposed to communicate thoughts and feelings; how difficult for cultures to be comfortable together and still, in spite of his forwardness, my first instinct to like the man remained, with reservations. Eilidh seemed less inclined, "You boys will manage the tea, hope you don't think I'm rude," I noticed she baulked at saying 'Andy', and squeezing my shoulder, "I'm away to bed." Anderson rose to his feet and bowing, with a sweep of his arm, "Goodnight, Eilidh."

Reaching for the bottle he poured out three fingers, a man desperate for company and, I surmised, anxious to unload his problems. After gulping at his drink he surprised me by saying,

"America is a backward society, hooked on aimless trivia, fed the mindless anodyne of chat shows and inane movies. It's a society sleep walking towards dystopia on an underbelly of black poverty and a widening wealth gap. The country's run by an unholy amalgam of bonus hungry money lenders screwing the punter and hollering born again Christians keen on military muscle. Stuff international law and the United Nations, to smite is right and you bet it's good for business."

I paid attention. His words were not common parlance. "Hector, we're seeing the death throws of democracy, it's now a cover for the centralising of power and the hands of financial despots, a hierarchy of power with global tentacles which, by using puppet politicians, aim at total control of the world's diminishing resources, the mining of mineral wealth in particular. Nothing stands in their way, least of all the indigenous people."

His glass was already empty, "Believe me I've been behind the scenes. Set up puppet governments, who got the Iraq oil industry? The folly of Afghanistan, its pipe lines out of the Caspian basin and another puppet President, as for bribing the Taliban war lords to stop fighting, sad I'd say, didn't the Anglo-Saxon kings of England tax their subjects to bribe the Vikings and hope they'd stay at home? It only worked so long, Danegeld didn't they call it? We tried Georgia, the same idea, pipelines, but it's a harder nut to crack, tailoring foreign policy to suit the financiers."

Privately agreeing I murmured approval but there was no stopping his vitriolic flow, "and I guess Hector, it'll be the same over here, it's a network of politicians on the board of banks and multinational corporations, all fiddling their expenses whilst the planet burns and at the top of the wealth pile, you've climate change deniers sitting on their fat asses. No sir -they ain't gonna give up their even fatter eight cylinder off road, air conditioned lifestyles."

I poured tea for him, "Thanks Hec, mind if we have another, what is it you folks say, a wee drap of the cratur?" I winced inwardly. Without waiting for a reply he tipped out half the bottle. The man was covering up some sort of trauma, I began to be concerned, "I tell you, Hector, this goddamn world is splitting along the fault lines of wealth and religious mania and sure as God made li'l ol' apples, when this global warming finally pulls them apart and anarchy breaks out, you'll see the poverty stricken masses strip the fields like locusts. It's then the big boys will emerge. New control methods are being developed by the US military, believe me I know; a lot of it based on mini nuclear technology." He swallowed half his copious measure in one draught.

How to handle this situation? Getting him back to his yacht looked improbable. Before I mustered a change of subject, he banged the table with his fist, "I'm on the side of solar power, but it won't win the fight. Wind power," he waved a hand, "not worth a fart, maintenance is too expensive anyway, but this nuclear," his face became deadly serious, "this nuclear business, it's evil, and believe me pardner, I know, like I really know!"

Thoughts of how to get him out vanished. The briefcase still lay in the bedroom, untouched. "Evil?" I repeated quietly, "Yeah, evil, truly evil, in a way you haven't thought of, yet." This chap knew more than I'd first suspected. I leant forward, "That's interesting, but evil?"

Swilling the last of his dram round and round, he threw it back with a flourish. Its last drops trickled down his beard, the voice a low growl, "These nuclear guys are planning to hold the world's energy supplies to ransom and have all major politicians by the throat," his red rimmed eyes glared with hatred, "an ah jest happen to know one side winding pig who means to do it."

It sounded so ridiculous. I was fascinated, "How is this possible?" Pouring out the remains of the bottle, Anderson swayed back in his chair, "Simple, this enriched stuff is so deadly, a thousand years and it's still a killer," his words were slowing and slurring, "simple, the man, the man, who controls its production and espeshally the waste storage calls the tune."

At the word storage I looked at him sharply. "Yeah, Hec-Hector, making the stuff is one thing, not too difficult, I can do that," he hiccupped loudly, "par, pardon me, production not a problem, but storing its leftovers, like crap it piles up, that don't go nowhere easy. A tricky job, Hec, Hector, that's li.. like, real tricky." Rocking back and forth, he looked at the door in a way which gave me the impression the man felt in some danger. He seemed to be choosing his words,

"Nuclear terrorists, cyber-security, key codes and all that jazz," another dismissive wave before speaking with care, "Iran, maybe Yemen, all on the drawing board; they call it stra-strategic planning. Pakistan, the big one, that's to be done a different way." He struck me as a man privy to more information than might be good for him, a chap who'd broken ranks from the cabal of vested interests and was seeing life from the bottom up with the bitterness of a loser.

His rambles wandered into a spell of cursing some woman. A clenched fist banged the table. That appeared to steady him and bleary eyed he picked up his previous thread. "Libya's a class... classic, jest you wait, I'm a telling you, it's heading thataway. Yah sells a tin god with a chest full of medals a pile of clapped out weapons, maybe a slow plane or two and a heap of tanks, the big boys get the contracts and the lovely black gold pays for a pile of last years weapons, nothing too fancy. Real sweet it is, and when the di..dic...tator steps over the line yah bomb the hell out of him, set up the next guy, sell 'em another load of pop guns, it sh... sure is a beautiful circle, do those finance wallas love it. But I tell yah, Huh...Hec...Hector you gotta keep the big toys tight at home, like real tight." The voice droned on, weary and resigned, "Politicians and the nuclear boys need wars to keep on top, great for the economy, don't tell me, I know, terrorists are standard requirement for the nuc...nuclear industry and the little tin soldier politicians, keeps the job going nicely,"

Poor Anderson put his head in his hands as he mumbled, "job going, keep going nicely until that meg.. mega.. megalo..maniac who holds the keys to an international waste dump which could blow the western world off the planet has the crin.. cringing, poli.. politicians by the balls."

I helped him to an easy chair and went for blankets. As I covered him he looked up, his face made haggard by the contortions which plagued his thoughts, "Thanks Hector," he reached and shook my hand, "you sure are a lucky guy, lovely girl. Not me, pardner, had my fill of that, me I'm on a mission, and it sure ain't a holy one." Turning his head, he went straight to sleep.

CHAPTER FORTY

Cobwebs

The croft house of Ach na Mara had an air of detachment. Lying in the porch, his nose on his paws, Rab the old collie looked up but didn't bark. Used dishes lay in the kitchen sink. Eilidh shook her head sadly. We tapped on the room door and after a moment entered gently. The curtains were drawn. We stood silently. Filtered light imparted a hallowed stillness to the room; the tick, tick of the old fashioned wall clock seemed loud and intrusive. There was no need of time. One lifespan had been measured by the seasons of sow and reap, and on a gathered crop the sun sets but once.

Outside on the croft we'd left the sunshine of an early spring which each year would have lifted a winter heart. That day walking up to the house, the land seemed cheerless. Perhaps it was just in ourselves but the fields were desolate. We were not alone in our bereavement, the land too sensed the loss. The love of a man for the soil of a lifetime's care must lie on the land, and who could prove it would not know their time of parting. In a holism which binds a man to the land, who should divide the quick and the dead?

Ella sat at the head of an open coffin, sunlight faint through the curtains rested on its plain wood and varnish. In those first brief minutes as we stood quietly beside Eachan's remains, the days, months, the years, each sadness of the past, a prisoner of happy times was released and they came to me in the immense ocean's cycle of grief. I placed a hand on Ella's shoulder. She rose without a word and I gathered both women to me. Their sorrows mingled. No tears; they would be for the days of privacy and memory.

As in life, so in death, Eachan's presence filled the room. I put my hands on the edge of the coffin, looked at those of a man who had become father and mentor, the man whose vigour of body and mind had set the pattern of my new life, saved me from mental wreckage, had given me the wisdom by which I'd come to understand the values that underpin human existence. I watched his face grow young and he walked the croft, and the fields, fresh and green were filled with lambs. I reached down and touched his cold forehead.

Eilidh beside me put an arm round my waist. Long, long was her gaze before, from a pocket, she took the golden disc and placed it in the hand which had known sun and storm alike, and bending she kissed his forehead and a tear glistened on his cheek. Ella stood quietly, "I knew you would know and come over," was all she said. The living and the dead were one.

I left the women together and went out to the byre. Neck chains jingled as I pushed open the door and lying cows got to their feet. Heads turned and big round eyes stared at a stranger. The cobbles had been swept and the dung cleaned out, I guessed by Eilidh's brother Iain. Loosing each chain, I let the cows out for water and taking the worn pitch fork, filled their hakes with the meadow hay of a summer past. In a little I heard them back at the door and one by one in they trouped. Reaching round each neck I retied the chains and gave each a scratch behind their shoulder. A line of heads lifted and long tongues pulled down their evening feed. The sweet scent of sun dried grass was in the air and the healthy smell of cattle on my hands.

I sat awhile on the milking stool looking up at the cobwebs on the rafters, dusty with age. Eachan was of the unhurried days, a fading lifestyle lost to the age of haste.

We hadn't asked how he'd died, Ella would tell in her own good time. That night in the kitchen after supper, three at the table instead of four, Ella, strong minded and composed, began to talk, "He went out about ten o'clock at the height of that gale to check the boat. Well, well I waited an hour and he wasn't coming. I took a torch and went down to the jetty, even in the shelter of the jetty it was wild." Her voice fell to a whisper, "he was sitting in the stern of Hilda, I shouted down and shone the torch, but he was," she looked up as though seeing Eachan coming in from the byre, "...he was dead." I took Ella's hand and she smiled though the mist.

The long silence was broken by a knock at the door and a "Hello". Iain and his wife were the first of callers, friends and neighbours. Each went through to the room for a few moments of thought. A crowded kitchen had Eilidh busy with tea and bannocks whilst I dispensed 'refreshments' to the men. Muted conversations gave way to reminiscences which soon became more cheerful, crofting days and escapades. It was late, late, before the house emptied.

By candle flame we sat the night away through in the room. Ella spoke of their young days together, the children always about the croft and now scattered to a' the airts as were so many island families. They would come home in the summer, there'd be a family reunion. In her soft musical voice she spoke as if Eachan were still alive and indeed in her heart, so he remained, "I know he died thinking of the poor Hilda girl," was the last thing she said, and with her own thoughts she went quietly to bed.

Early morning sunlight flitted into the room. I watched it stray from face to face, the man in the coffin to the dark framed print of his grandfather above the mantelpiece of an empty grate.

Eachan's fiddle lay on the piano.

'From the ranks of death the minstrel boy was calling'.

CHAPTER FORTY-ONE

"Weapons grade material."

Lime trees in full leaf shaded the white pine coffee table at which Sir Joshua Goldberg sat awaiting the Private Secretary to the US Chief of Staff. The constant cooing of turtle doves somewhere up in the top branches annoyed him intensely. What an abominable racket! Rather smart in a new cream suit and his old Etonian tie, Sir Joshua squinted apprehensively into the branches above his head. Too late, a splat hit the table at his elbow. He clapped his hands furiously, a pair of doves glided over to another tree. Glancing at his Rolex... he should not be kept waiting. Seething inwardly Sir Joshua vowed these official types would one day learn their place.

Flecks of pink and white cherry blossom drifted onto the verdant lawns. A small flock of bullfinches flitted from tree to tree feeding on the young buds, their glossy black heads and richly pink breasts alive with April sunshine. Destructive little blighters, thought Sir Joshua Goldberg as his eye caught the flash of colour. A pair of pied wagtails, flicking their long tails and gathering insects darted about the grass. Across from him on an artificial lake of reed beds and overhanging willow, brightly coloured ducks were bowing and squabbling. A wretched grey squirrel came hopping over the lawn. Blasted tree rats, they could bite. Goldberg heaved himself to his feet. These damned Pentagon gardens are a veritable haven for wild life, almost a zoo he reflected, ridiculous, very distracting. This had to be a hush-hush meeting, nothing written or recorded, no obvious top brass meeting, but surely somewhere inside the building would be more civilised.

A gangling figure crossed the garden towards him. The loping step and loose arms hanging just wide of his hips reminded Nuen's Chairman of the sheriff in a third rate Western movie. How preposterous he thought, anyway he instinctively disliked thin men. Ignoring the proffered hand, Sir Joshua remained seated, "I trust you realise I'm a very busy man," was his greeting. The Private Secretary, sour faced and snake eyed, ignored the comment, "Well, Mr. Goldberg, I guess you're in a hurry, I won't detain you, it just happens that my boss wants to know two things. When will the weapons grade material for our Indian Ocean base be delivered and secondly, have you started work on the UK deep waste depository? We need results, pronto."

"The name is Sir Joshua Goldberg" he began coolly. Knowing full well that a programme for dealing with the Iranian problem had reached the drawing board stage in the military HQ at their back, his firm intention was not to answer any questions directly but to extract substantially more profit from their current agreement, "The material will be delivered for flying abroad in due course but I have to inform you that as a result of certain technical difficulties, which you wouldn't understand, the arrangement at this stage registers a shortfall of something in the region of five million dollars, as you will see from these figures. I would point out this is contingency funding and covered by clause five of our minute of agreement and my company requires this further reimbursement before proceeding."

"O.K. I'll pass that on." He picked up the papers which Goldberg tossed over the table, "What about the waste dump? You've managed to bypass Westminster? You realise the dump is needed for other than the spent stuff, it's gotta cover for the storage of weapons grade material. We need that facility outside of the US, and real private," and he drawled the words, "my friend."

Goldberg held up his hand, the impudence of the man. "My dealings with Westminster are not your concern. A provision for weapons grade storage is already agreed between Nuen and yourselves and will be incorporated in our building programme. Please convey to your Chief that what is not yet agreed is the cost of this extra facility. A substantial monetary advancement will be required prior to commencing any work on the repository, or dump, as seems to be your preferred description. It so happens my surveyors are on site as we speak and construction of the repository will begin as soon as your financial response is forthcoming."

Nuen's Chairman rose to leave, "Those papers I gave you are carefully worded to cover my Company's position and in the interests of confidentiality, for both parties, please ensure that once assimilated, they will be made permanently unavailable to anyone. By which I mean destroyed. Now if you'll excuse me, I'm exceptionally busy; kindly arrange these additional payments for both operations be made to my preferred account and at your earliest convenience."

The American official hovered over Sir Joshua, a foot taller and brittle darting eyes, "Jest one small point, Mr. Goldberg- your past chairman at Nuen, Mr. Anderson."

Sir Joshua, on the point of stepping past the official, stopped short, why Andrew Anderson? His heart beat quickened. Had the method of his take over of the Nuen Company been leaked? Surely only finance trader Nicky Fellows knew. Insider dealing? If that surfaced it would take somebody at the highest possible level to launder it clean. He swallowed hard and said nothing.

The Private Secretary took a long pause, allowing Goldberg to dangle in acute discomfort. Finally in a deadly casual tone, "You sure pulled off a nice one at Nuen, didn't you just, but we ain't caring too much about that jest right now." More harshly he enquired, "How much is Mr. Anderson aware of the re-routing of weapons grade material, the stuff you and I know about?"

Fighting for composure Sir Joshua spoke huffily, "Whatever his past dealings may have been, as far as I'm concerned he knows nothing of our present arrangements. Now, if you don't mind, I have another meeting in twenty minutes"

"One moment Mr. Goldberg," the American's sharper tone checked Sir Joshua's hurried steps, "I should tell you our men have kept track on your Mr. Anderson. Incidentally, by our reckoning, he became your ex-chairman pretty darn fast," and waving the papers he'd been given, "We'll maybe look over your latest bill." "Please do," was all a flustered Goldberg could say before in a nonchalant manner, the man continued, "Hope ya don't mind me a- telling you, this guy's on a yacht, holed up on a Hebridean island."

Goldberg froze, "Hebridean island?" The man's tone softened, "Yeah, an island. He used to be a good friend of ours and we don't like to abandon a real friend, now do we?" and in mock innocence, "He wouldn't be the sort of guy to have a loose mouth by any chance, now would he?"

Sir Joshua flapped a hand in dismissal, his face a shade paler than his smart cream suite. He began to hurry across the lawns. At his elbow, a soft drawl, "If Mr. Anderson's mouth just did happen to get a little too loose, sure the boys might have to arrange a small operation to tighten it," and with a quiet laugh, "or any other mouth for that matter."

Goldberg's chest tightened, he quickened his pace.

CHAPTER FORTY-TWO

The Trance

In the freshness of a lambing morning over the Sound they sailed, relations, friends, island folk brought together in the closeness of a funeral. To each there would be a last journey, undreamt by the young, imagined by the old. We'd roped Eachan's coffin on the foredeck of a fishing boat as the sun rose upon a spring day peerless in its unblemished clarity. Near and far the islands of the Atlantic emerged from the sea to an intensity of light so pure that, in its transparency, I saw they too in the fullness of time were fragile.

Quietly we moored beside the Sandray jetty. A green tarpaulin covered the remains. Eachan would have approved, the more so it took six men with slings to hoist him ashore. In that gentle rocking the reflections of a varnished boat scattered on the still waters of an ebbing tide.

I stood at the jetty's edge. Little by little, each ruffle of water left wet and glistening razor shells, cockle shells broken and empty, bronzed scallops, the fruits of an ocean awaiting the grinding of tide upon tide. Slowly on a bed of mica sand they would dry in the sun, lose their lustre, be buried by the tumult of a storm to become the limestone richness of life out of death.

And the people of the islands came. Children at hand, the old with stick, their long line wound away from the jetty. A piper tramping the rough ground led the trackless journey out to the headland. Turn about the men folk took their place at the carrying poles. The cry of the birdlife was about the cliffs, echo of the pipes, plaintiff and calling.

Ella walked unbowed, the dignity of love and respect. Behind his remains, her steps made slowly to the headland which had claimed their daughter; was to be the resting place of her husband. Within the sorrow of parting lay an awakening to the fullness of summer. The abounding bird life that nested the headland sailing against the brightness, the seals and their cubs whose curiosity followed our arrival, they too lived its pattern. The day needed no pomp, a simple funeral, the island's peace granted her solace. She understood.

There was no bleakness on the gathered faces. Bare headed, we stood amongst the pondering stones. At our feet, the tranquillity of the Atlantic made tiny ringlets in the gullies. A soughing wind warm off the sea gave the promise of spring, made our prayers.

Eachan once had said, "These are the tunes that will see me across the Sound." He foresaw it all. And Eilidh at the foot of his grave played them, and the fiddle sang the psalms of space and wilderness. Mystical notes of trembling fingers carried beyond the cliffs to mingle with the pulse of the sea; and the island folk stood silently for the music and its meaning was of their thoughts.

I looked into the grave, smelt the fresh earth so recently dug, and gazing at the coffin I read his name. I too saw them, as Eachan had surely done. Out of the ground they arose, wraithlike, the generations that went before. Sailing, roving, out of mists that clung to memory they sailed, eagle eyed, rugged men, on the winds that drew them into the sunlight they sailed, Eachan at the helm cleaving the waves.

Bidden by a power from the graves of the past, I spoke the lines which had written themselves at this self same place, "Time lingered as the note that waits poised on the fingers of some plaintive air which guides the pain of beauty into trance. Ocean birdlife wheeled, their cry above the unfolding ripples sigh. The canvas filled, a raven croaked but once above the making tide. A dragon prow nodded to the swell, to a sun alone above the amber hills. Northward trailed the isles, their skyline pointed home, took living eyes to a land they saw in sleep beyond the sea, they sailed by day to a sea they hoped to cross, in the trance of death."

At the foot of the grave the piper played again. Cearcal a' Chuain, The Ocean's Cycle, Solus na Madainn, The Morning Light, the tunes reached out. At his final note I stepped forward, "Piper take your dram." He held up the glass a long moment, took a solemn draft. Onto the coffin he poured the remainder.

I dug a spade of soil. Ella stepped forward. I handed it to her. Surrounding faces blurred. She gazed down at their years together. In her eyes a man, sun tanned and young, strode up from a hay field. There was no coffin. She cast the first ground, it fell, a dull thud. Each in our turn we took a spade full; they thudded one by one, echoed on the lid, the drum beat of centuries before, a summons of those to come.

Across a gathering of bowed heads, the stillness of the ocean enhanced the clarity of light, singled out a day which bridged the ages, filtered away the superfluous; the flesh, the bones, nothing remained except the spectral lines of the elements which give us thought and bind us to the unending western horizon. Eilidh read my mind, she pressed my hand, here and now mattered. Lovely woman, her fleeting smile dissolved my brooding into the happiness of our being together.

Ferocious cawing broke the silence. Repeated alarm notes, harsh and distressed, reached us. Heads turned quickly, necks craned, hands shielded eyes. Above the Hill of the Shroud two ravens, flapping heavily were striving to gain height. Threshing the still air and calling anxiously they attempted to spiral; huge black wings beating against the mid-day sun.

A humming sound somewhere to the east took every attention. At first a low grumbling, louder and louder until swamping the stillness a large camouflaged helicopter appeared over the hilltop followed closely by a second and a third. The first machine hovered, preparing to land.

The raven stooped, attacking the 'chopper'. The draft off flailing blades threw the birds tumbling to the ground. Out from the cliff face two young ravens, just able to fly, abandoned their nest and, flopping off the ledge, landed spread winged on the lower slopes.

Distraught parents attacked the intruder again. One bird swooped too close. Flung into the air it fell to the ground, a feather rag. The second bird attempted to alight beside a fallen mate. The down draft swept it off the cliff. Over and over the bird tumbled down the slope until, with drooping wings, it stood cawing defiantly beside two crouching chicks. In the brilliant light we could watch it all.

'The raven will not nest again on the Hill of the Shroud.' Eachan's words rang in my head, Raised before me were his outstretched arms. He stared from his kitchen window in the throws of dismay. What had he foreseen that strange morning, the day of his death?

Utterly shocked nobody moved. A second machine landed. The third helicopter banked sharply and veered towards us. Ella stood beside the half covered grave. Murmurs of disgust were raised amongst the crowd. The racket became deafening. Terrified young children began to cry.

Tilting slightly, the 'chopper' circled above our heads. The thrusting air caused many of the crowd to crouch. Nesting birds fled the cliffs in alarm adding to the cacophony as they poured out to sea, a screeching white mass of twisting wings. Fulmar, gulls and kittiwake, many eggs would be scattered by their panic.

Faces studied us from the windows. The machine made two circuits before the pilot swung away churning the bay into a froth as he crossed over to pause above the Valkyrie who still lay at anchor. The slim little artic terns, newly arrived from their Antarctic wintering, fled the beach for the open sea. My fury mounted. Old heads shook in disbelief, nobody spoke. Finally the helicopter roared up the hillside to land beside its companions.

The sanctity of a day and the dignity of a silence remote from the modern world had been mauled, profoundly mauled. We pressed down the last of the earth and replaced the divots.

No wreaths were laid, nothing placed but the turf divots I'd cut. Already tiny purple violets, first of a summer's wild flowers showed amongst the greenness which had given resting to the north bound geese.

Of the raven there was no sign.

A cold realisation was dawning.

CHAPTER FORTY-THREE

The Shaft

The safety belt was chaffing Sir Joshua Goldberg's stomach. He thankfully loosened it the better to command a clearer view below, "What in the name of creation is that mob of people doing down there?" he shouted to the helicopter pilot, "out in the middle of an utter wasteland, most of them dressed in black? It's got to be some quack American religious gathering, idiotic bunch of zealots expecting the end of the world. It happens every few years." In excellent spirits, now work on Nuen's key project was getting underway, he condescended to attempt a little joke, "I saw one of them looking at his watch." The pilot failed to appreciate his wit.

A tall fellow amongst the supposed fanatics caused Goldberg to prod the pilot, "Circle them again pilot, if you don't mind." Even from a distance the style of the man was distinctive. He delved his memory, the confounded din of the 'chopper' was not conducive to thinking, it would come to him. "Head to that yacht, pilot." They swept across the bay, ignoring the fishing boat at the jetty. Their draft heeled the yacht. "Can you read her name?" he asked impatiently. "Valkyrie," the pilot informed him. "What a ridiculous name," Sir Joshua snapped. It didn't mean anything but his recent unpleasant conversation with that Pentagon official came instantly to mind. Could this be Anderson? A bearded man stood in the yacht's cockpit waving his fist, obviously cursing them. This must be checked, if necessary dealt with and very firmly indeed. Anderson knew too much, certainly for his own good.

Climbing towards the summit they flew above the island's sole house, "That hovel looks occupied!" he bawled across the cabin. The pilot nodded. "Somebody actually living there, that's absolutely ludicrous." He grabbed the pilot's binoculars, "and damned solar panels, it's monstrous." His private hate, anything connected to solar energy. Sir Joshua fumed inwardly. He'd been assured in London the place was uninhabited. Government owned- the fools should have known, "Confounded squatters," he said aloud. Getting them out, not a problem; keeping the media's nose out of this development, vital, both for Nuen and the Government. It might take a cash inducement to get them removed quietly; seldom failed, naturally a last resort and one which he found painful. As for those damned penguins perched on the headland. Goldberg's good humour evaporated.

The pilot landed skilfully on the hill top. Sir Joshua's personal assistant helped him descend the ladder. Already survey poles and levelling instruments were in use, the constructional engineers were busy, impressions count. Nuen's chief designer walked over to greet his new Chairman, reflecting to himself- 'Gone the easy going Anderson who seldom left New York and didn't attempt to screw down salaries or production bonuses'. "If you've time for a few words, Sir Joshua I'll explain the site's general layout." "Of course, MacDonald, that's why I'm here."

Together they stood on the summit. Goldberg zipped his leather kapok jacket to the neck and wiped his watering eyes. A panorama of interlocking islands reaching to the serrated line of mainland hills presented no appeal, none whatsoever, "This sort of topography is absolutely worthless," and allowing his aversion full rein, went on, "we shall revitalise these backward islands, bring in fresh population; they tell me the natives are highly inbred, no doubt that accounts for their excessive proportion of imbeciles."

He became aware the engineer glared at him, "now then MacDonald, explain to me your plans," the cool air caused him to wheeze, "and kindly, not in too much detail, I have studied your outline drawings. My main concerns are schedules and containing costs."

"Well Sir Joshua, we shall flatten fifteen hectares up here to the level of that cliff top, that will be the upper area- buildings, control units and helicopter pads. The tunnel entrance which leads to the main chamber will be three hundred metres down the east sloping face, we'll drive the shaft in at thirty degrees for two hundred metres and then excavate the main hall from which the bore holes will run vertically down through the solid rock for six hundred metres. The extracted spoil will serve as infill as we construct a road down to that eastern bay over there. There'll be something in excess of a million tons of rock which we'll use to infill the breakwater needed to protect the deep water installation required for berthing the vessels carrying waste."

The Nuen Chairman had heard enough; he merely nodded and had begun to walk back to the helicopter when it occurred to him to ask, "Where is the labourers' camp to be situated?" MacDonald pointed, "On that flat green ground beside the old house, we'll put in a service road up here to the operations. There'll be accommodation for up to four hundred men at the peak of construction. Their supplies will be brought in via that jetty, the bay's too shallow to be any use for the vessels which are to bring in the waste. Two years should see us ready to move in the high tech equipment and we'll be ready for waste shipments in another two years."

"Good, MacDonald," and turning sourly he faced the engineer, "I think I've told you before, we do not refer to waste and certainly not the word nuclear. This whole operation is a rock quarry for exporting road metal to England. Kindly don't forget, no matter to whom you speak," adding, "if you value your job that is, need I say more? Remember I shall visit from time to time."

Stumbling over the rough ground, Goldberg paused for breath. Looking round at the empty vastness served to reinforce his previous opinion, this was really the most odiously primitive area he'd ever had the misfortune to visit. The only consolation, every ton of rock would be a golden nugget in disguise and twenty-four carat gold at that he thought, mentally rubbing his hands.

An eddy of breeze ruffled a scatter of jet black feathers. The carcase of a bird, a bloody mangle of torn flesh with bones protruding, lay in his path. "One mangy crow less!" he boomed, kicking it aside. Its great beak opened, a pink tongue showed. It moved slightly. He stopped.

Unblinking eyes stared up, malevolent orbs they seemed to penetrate his thoughts. The loathing in their expression frightened him. He shook it off. Just a glutinous carrion crow and now a twisted heap of feathers, he smirked. And me a scientist! It couldn't possibly be alive. Could it?

Tentatively Goldberg stirred the mutilated body with his foot. The faintest croak emerged, the exhaling of dead lungs; the twitch of rigor mortis.

Aiming a kick at the carcase he fell heavily. The engineer lifted Nuen's Chairman to his feet, "Are you all right?"

No reply. Taking an elbow, he guided the trembling Chairman to the waiting helicopter.

A large brandy restored Sir Joshua's composure and, in spite of the engine noise, he slept.

Fingered wings, outstretched and flapping; a bird strutted towards him, jerking its head from side to side, cawing with greed. Black eyes of hatred pierced his being. The raven bent. A cruel beak opened. It began to peck out his eyes. Howling in terror he attempted to beat it off.

Rigid with shock an awakening Goldberg cried piteously for help.

The pilot paid no attention.

CHAPTER FORTY-FOUR

A legal Injunction

From the tints of an Atlantic sunset the stones of the old house took a rosy glow. By the time lights from its windows cast yellow lines towards the bay, more than the stonework had a rosy tinge. Youngsters and their mothers had been ferried to Castleton aboard the fishing boat, back she'd sailed with a few who'd missed the internment. Inside, outside, filling both tiny rooms, sitting on window ledges, leaning against the walls, some tramping over to inspect my 'lazy beds'. "You fairly bent your back, time to get the tatties planted," comment and encouragement, a wealth of folk who knew and understood, a laughing, talking crowd; when had our croft known the like?

As the man we'd buried that afternoon believed, it's a poor giver who measures the bottle, 'You'll just be having a wee, 'oh be joyful' he would say, pouring out one of his generous libations. I followed his style. Eilidh's brother Iain had brought over his accordion, "just in case" he winked. Before long I heard someone call, "Come away, MacLeod give us, "The Dark Island," That was all it needed, a neighbour with two kitchen knives drumming on an upturned biscuit tin set the timing. The crowd made room, Eilidh and I waltzed around the kitchen before she took up Eachan's fiddle. In the house, out on the grass, the folk danced, music and the lively steps which lightened the heart. I poured, never a glass left empty.

The songs flowed. Gaelic favourites that told of the natives' love of their island homes. 'The 'band' played a Highland

Scottische and I danced with Ella. We did his memory proud and as I held her hand, she said simply, "Eachan would have been the keenest to join us here tonight," and she smiled up at me through her first tears of the day.

The helicopters had flown out late that afternoon, perhaps out of most minds by that evening. For me their intrusion above the funeral and the killing of a raven embodied the encroaching threat of some unknown conflict. The bundle of feathers flung skywards floated to the ground again and again. The raven's tragic cawing wouldn't leave my thoughts, I heard it behind the music and laughter, the cries were those of a raven whose lineage matched that of the man we'd buried, the wise eyed raven of the Viking rovers whose cawing brought them to Sandray. The morning before his death Eachan saw in his mind the raven of his forebears, of that I have no doubt; for him the weavings of fact and fantasy were as one. For him, as for his Viking ancestors, visions of the imagination were the harbingers of the hand of fate; the shadow which stretched before them all.

At some point amidst the dancing, out of the darkness, Anderson appeared from his yacht, "Ah gee, you sure got some music going, I just couldn't not come across." A glass in hand, soon he made himself known to the gathering. Eventually the musicians drew breath and Ella had hot soup ready on our tiny two burner Calor gas stove. Tea, soup and sandwiches, the evening drew to a close in the friendship of an island community.

Some of Eachan's vintage joined me, struck up memories;friends and relations, they remembered his parents, how the island had once been, cultivated and fertile. Wistfully for their generation, behind our 'wake over' revels, the day had an underlying meaning, more than Eachan was being buried, their private lamentations were for a slowly dying culture.

One old man, a cousin of Eachan's, spoke gently to me, "When I was a boy I worked the sheep on this island with him that's gone; out on the hill at the lambing and the island for a friend. What are the young folk at today? No interest in the land, always a screen in front of their faces or playing with some phone gadget, website friends, if that's what they call them, lonely people talking on a dumb machine, making superficial friends in an artificial world."

The eyes of yesterday were sunken in regret. "Out on the hill that's above this house, what a workbench, sun on your face and the world turning at your feet; nobody puts a value on it today, all busy running past themselves. Money hunger eats a man's heart out; it's a sad craving, but you'll never buy all the peace that's here, away from computers and the like. It's a fine place for a home, a' bhailich; if I were young again and had a woman like Eilidh..... I'll tell you Hector boy, there was always a MacKenzie on Sanday," One by one they shook hands, wished us luck.

As the line of waving of torches and lanterns made down to the fishing boat, Anderson drew me aside, his voice low and guarded. Without any preamble he said abruptly, "I recognised one of the faces watching out of the helicopter." Anderson's sudden disclosure shattered that quality of which the old folk had spoken. "We'll be across on Halasay for a little time but as soon as we're back, if you're still anchored here..." It was all I could offer in reply. My words trailed off; the spectre of a world I'd blotted out arose before me. The value of its peace was at stake.

In the days that followed as Eachan had wished I signed the document which made me the official crofter of Ach na Mara. Ella, if she so desired, could stay, remain living in the house which had been home all their married days. Eilidh's brother

Iain happily agreed to run this croft along with his own. We would cross back and forth to help with the main jobs, tattie planting, peat cutting and the hay making. Our intentions remained keenly focused on making Sandray a crofting home, but for Ella's sake we stayed on, hoping to ease a little of the sadness.

She had gone back to helping with the cattle and had decided to handle the lambing. Without meals to make for a hungry man, her being busy helped fill the empty days. In quiet moments I would notice her looking from the kitchen window out to the fields. Was it all a dream? Eachan would come back, his easy stride and the sun on his back and she would waken. Each night we sat through in the room. Ella spoke of him as though he were present, had just gone to the byre and the stamping of feet in the porch would herald his return.

Days passed until one evening as we sat quietly before the room fire she said calmly to us, "You know, the third night after Eachan died, he spoke to me; it had to be a dream, but it was as real as I'm seeing you now. We were down together at the Hilda boat on a bright summer's evening and he climbed aboard and smiled to me, 'I'm away fishing Ella, but I'll be back, keep the place going Ella,' I watched his sail vanishing into a sunset just like the one on the day of his funeral" There were no tears to her telling, the manifestation was her strength, for she went on to say, "I know Eachan wants you to have the Hilda boat," and laughingly nodding towards Eilidh's expanding tummy, "for your island adventure."

At Ella's mention of the Hilda I sat again on the pier at Castleton, a physical and mental wreck, staring at a graceful boat as she lay in the harbour, a silhouette in the gloaming. A stranger put his hand on my shoulder. Now, as of that moment, the sudden awareness startled me. Eachan was at my side, with us in the room, I felt his grip. Slowly I turned, he stood looking down at me as he'd been that evening, tall and angular, his sea blue eyes alight with recognition. Maybe it was minutes, gradually he became fainter and fainter, drifting into the darkness of the farthest corner. Dropping my gaze, I hesitated before summoning courage to speak to Ella, only to realise she'd been watching. "Thank you both," I said. Looking past me, she smiled.

Eilidh was adamant, our child would be born on Sandray and Ella would come and stay as its time approached. The prospect of the birth involved the two women in endless conversation and much knitting. Not to be left out of preparations for our momentous event, I found suitable wood in the tool shed and set about making a crib. Iain, finding me at the finishing touches, managed a straight face, "You can't beat a wooden fish box for that job; if that's a baby's crib you're knocking together I'd drill a few holes in the bottom." Father of four, he knew about these things.

Early one morning with a spring tide setting us across the Sound, we sailed the Hilda back to Sandray. A boat to be proud of sharing, no finer gift could come our way. She would not lack care, I talked excitedly to Eilidh of my idea to build a rail track with a cradle and winch to haul her clear of the water for regular attention. Surprisingly, the Valkyrie still lay at anchor. Apprehension returned. I fought it off, the old house had the welcome of home. Bouncing with enthusiasm I offered to carry Eilidh across the threshold. She squeaked, I just hugged her instead.

Alone together, back in our own home, and a growing collie pup dancing at our heels waiting to be trained. Today I'd plant Eachan's seed tatties. Mild open weather, sunshine and showers, grass which needed sheep. We planned to ferry some of Eachan's ewes across once they had lambed. Wanting the place to ourselves, I resented the yacht. Tomorrow I would row out for a meeting with the chap.

"Valkyrie ahoy!" I hailed the yacht several times before Anderson appeared in the cockpit. "Come aboard!" he shouted. I shipped oars and tied alongside. The hand grip, though firm had a tremour. I looked into bloodshot eyes, red rimmed and dull. The smell of drink wafted to me as he spoke, "Glad to see you, Hector, come on below." Even from the companionway the sight was not reassuring. I clambered down.

The beautifully teak lined cabin, leather couches to either side of a mahogany table, lay in a shambles. Crumpled heaps of clothes were mixed up with oilskins, a variety of half used tins of food sat abandoned in the lockers, empty bottles rolled about on the cabin sole to the slight motion of the yacht. Central in the cabin's disorder, a case of whisky occupied the table. Sadly the man's appearance said it all, a beard bedraggled and speckled with food, his shirt equally so, the self neglect of a man fighting off black thoughts by uncorking a demon. I felt truly sorry for him.

"Have a tot with me," he rummaged in the galley, produced a glass and had two large measures poured before I got round to saying it was a bit early for me. Taking his own glass in both hands, with a "Cheers, good to see you again," he swallowed a large mouthful and fell coughing onto his bunk. This was dangerous, a yacht and a man alone heading towards the D.T's

Eyes closed, he remained motionless. Had the man choked? Suddenly sitting upright, he buried his face in his hands. Finally looking up through sentences poured out in a disjointed manner, "Ah gee, that bloody fat faced spy.. spying crook, out of the helicopter, nobody knows, how in hell's name. Nobody knows where I am," he gulped more drink, muttering incoherently, "A criminal, criminal, sure as I'm Andrew, Androo, An." He began to shout, "They shafted me, stole off a multi-million dollar company. Banks, banks, thieving criminals!" Raising his glass, "To my bitch of a wife, good bye my darling bitch." By now his glass was empty. A shaking hand refilled it. He drank more and rambled on without apparently noticing me. I sat on the edge of a littered bunk.

"Yeah, I have a job to do, he'll find out," more mumbling threats continued. I got up to leave. At that point, he seemed to notice my presence, squaring up I was fixed by his watery eyes. His mind cleared a little, "That man, that treacherous underhand spy, he sure swindled me, yeah, defrauded me, now though, the company he controls, he's selling nuclear weapons grade uranium, illegally, it's top secret, but I know, I know, who better than me knows, my friend. His buddies in the middle-east, the ones with the nuclear arsenal that don't admit they have it; yeah, primed to hit Iran, a pre-emptive strike, just wait my friend. Washington turns a blind eye, it's top secret, sure thing, don't think I don't know, I know, I.. I.. have a mission, dangerous, a very, very..." his mind shut down and as he slouched back on his couch, I thought him about to pass out.

If his assertions were fact, not idle guesswork, then he indeed possessed alarmingly lethal information. Before it would drop and smash, I tried to ease the empty glass from his hand. At this he roused. Bloodshot eyes glared wildly about the cabin. He began tugging his beard quite frantically, the agitations grew almost convulsive. Drink and the tendentious statements allied to menacing threats could be unhinging his sanity.

A murderous hate obviously directed at some apparently unsavoury person was consuming the man. Curling lips formed a snarl, "Gold, gold, you love your gold don't you, but I'll turn it to dross. You ain't gonna like it, no sir, not one dime. I have a job to do, nice little job, just wait, be patient." Sneering words gurgled in his throat, I strained to hear him. "Wait, Sir Joshua, my gold loving, uranium dealing, Mr. Goldberg." A groaning Andrew Anderson attempted to rise but staggering, he fell senseless on the couch. The agitated spasm had passed. Lifting his oilskin legs and using cushions, I propped him on his side, nothing else I could do for a paralytic drunk.

A quick glance round the cabin, the name Sir Joshua Goldberg had immediately prompted memories of the U.K.'s Chief Scientist, his slippery eyes and evasive manner. My imagination played with sickening possibilities, I needed air.

Many months had passed without it entering my thoughts, now from the far corner of our bedroom in the evening light, the briefcase stared at me. Not since the day of my meeting with Goldberg and the ex-Prime Minister had it been opened. I'd always realised my research on nuclear waste disposal could make the expansion of the nuclear industry highly contentious. Events crowded about me, the supposed archaeologist who'd attempted to kill me. His contorted grimace reappeared. He pointed a pistol at my head. I succumbed to uncontrollable shuddering.

Entering the bedroom I awakened Eilidh, "You're shaking Hector," she looked startled. I took her hand and without speaking, bent over and kissed her lightly, "Something to do with Anderson and those helicopters has alarmed you." Walking to the window, I nodded. As myths will surface from deep within the sub-conscious, the dying rays on darkened waters picked out the white form of the Valkyrie. She floated as an apparition might appear in the fevered wanderings of a delirium.

I gripped the window ledge, listening over and over to the sinister ramblings of her skipper towards a scientist whom I'd met and instinctively distrusted; a top scientist whom I'd defied by the contents of that cursed briefcase; that this very man should have been here on Sandray; irreconcilable happenings reached beyond the sphere of coincidence. The cawing raven circled again, black feathers of a dismembered bird fell sinister upon a twilit bay.

Turning sharply from the window I lay on the bad without taking my clothes off, not least in case that drunken creature might somehow find his way across. I loathed worrying Eilidh. We neither of us spoke and presently her steady breathing came as a relief. Sharing thoughts of the possibilities which might unfold left me inwardly wretched.

I lay thinking. Starlight crept into the bedroom, reflected on the mirror. Sleepless eyes watched planets giving stars the illusion of immobility. Speed, acceleration, spin and density, equation built upon equation floated on a mirror of the heavens and my mind wrote again the equations which predicted the behaviour of sub-atomic particles, as had the calculations tucked away in my briefcase.

Ten years ago we physicists decreed, no particle accelerator in the foreseeable future would have the power to create a black hole. Two years later we weren't quite so definite. Equations showed that should extra dimensions of space-time exist then the Large Hadron Collider might produce mini black holes, three years later we agreed they would instantly evaporate. Much relief ensued until six years on came a safety warning based upon astrophysical arguments and the observations of the immensely hot and dense stars, the so-called White Dwarfs.

Serious allegations were made- our experiments on the Hadron Collider, 'particle race track' could create a black hole sufficient to devour this planet and beyond. These valid concerns became the subject of a number of lawsuits from various countries hoping to achieve a court injunction which on safety grounds would order the closing down of the Collider.

Just how many judges were capable of understanding the complex equations involved? None! Therefore the experts called in to explain and advise had to be the scientists themselves, who else? Given the shifting sands of scientific reasoning and the interests of public safety being intimately connected to that of the planet, might not a judge come down on the side of caution?

Suddenly I sat up. The answers were in my briefcase. It contained sufficiently damning evidence on the dangers connected to the storage of enhanced radioactive waste. Any major breakdown entailing radio active emissions and ....not for days or weeks but for centuries, public health was in jeopardy. Much as the British and American Governments played down the risks and denied connections, the case against radiation exposure stood up. Thoughts raged on, I knew the strength of the nuclear lobby behind the scenes to be impressive with personal contacts to the very top.

Eilidh's pregnancy prompted me to think of the babies born in parts of Iraq with horrific birth defects. Following the invasion and the use of depleted uranium shells, the rise in the number of deformities had been so dramatic that women were advised against having children. It brought back my meeting in Number 10. Utter revulsion towards the politicians I'd met was rekindled; the establishment's 'softly, softly, don't tell the public more than you have to' approach stank of corruption.

The correct legal frame must be found for bringing forward an injunction to prevent any nuclear company proceeding with the unproven method of deep underground waste disposal. Purely on grounds of public safety, an injunction, a decree to stop any work going ahead.

The harmful effects of radioactive emissions must be fully exposed in court, from the vomiting of radiation sickness to genetic damage resulting in birth defects, from leukaemia to the development of other forms of cancer; this criminal madness of putting the public at risk must be halted, the insanity of taking chances with radiation must be stopped.

Challenge the nuclear industry? It could prove dangerous. Young men from this island 'went over the top' and faced the machine guns for a cause not of their making. They did not come back. I vowed it. No man who carried their name would be a coward. The island would live again.

I'd disturbed Eilidh, she stirred and pulling back the blankets quietly took my hand and placed it on her tummy. I felt the hefty kicks from her inside, the big round dome bulged here and there, quite alarmingly. Eilidh whispered, "You've wakened him, now he's playing a game of football with his father." She didn't doubt the baby was a boy.

I felt another mighty kick, "No, no," I laughed, "he's rugby player," another thump, "there's a flying tackle," and at that I hugged them both back to sleep.

CHAPTER FORTY-FIVE

Sheep and Men

"The Valkyrie must have weighed anchor before daylight." No doubt I sounded pleased. Eilidh rose and stood beside me at the bedroom window. A week had passed without Anderson venturing across to see us, nor did I risk another visit to him. The yacht had sailed and her destination was of no matter. The whole episode, from his outlandish arrival to this abrupt departure, contained elements which made me uneasy. The threats which a drunken man had levelled at Goldberg couldn't possible involve us here on Sandray, could it? What ever might be the nature of 'the job' Anderson threatened to carry out, it seemed he intended to deal in some way with an eminent scientist whose appearance on the island I found extremely disturbing.

"I'm glad the bay is empty again, the seals need peace," her relief matched my own. The misgivings which I tried to hide gave way to a quiet euphoria, the quality of a peace without people. Eilidh put her arm round me. I looked down at a body made lovelier by the fullness of expectancy. Every curve of womanhood touchable, I caressed her back and believed there could be nothing more beautiful than the radiance of this woman awaiting the birth of our child.

She smiled at up me in the way of that first fleeting contact, the same unfathomable, ocean blue eyes which had transmitted such a compelling vision, created the pivotal moment that drew me to find her in these islands of sea -washed light; and now in this translucent haven, to attempt to live the echo of an illusion.

The consummate happiness at our being alone dispelled such thoughts, the will to make an island home redoubled, and yet, who is not a little afraid of happiness?

Using our two boats I ferried across fencing material, farm gates, posts, wire and tools, all I needed was the know how. Studying the fences which Eachan had built over the years on Ach na Mara provided the theory. Forty hectares of Sandray's pastures awaited a sheep proof fence, not to mention the hectare already dug and soon to begin growing our supply of potatoes and vegetables. A week into building fences, I discovered that mastering the tricks of a computer were more easily acquired than gaining the knack of doing a job which to the layman looked simple.

Strip to the waist weather, swinging a fourteen pound mell round and round, smack on the top of each post, driving them down, inches at a blow, it opened the shoulders and sent a trickle of sweat down the back. Straight runs, corners, tightening and knotting the wires, twelve days and a few mistakes, our first field was fenced. Long days and Muille my companion, simple tools were all I had, and the luxury of time. Rest a hand on a post and watch a skylark alighting after its carefree song, stroll to the tussock hideaway they'd chosen to shelter their grass weavings. My fondness was for the little brown meadow pipits. Tramp the fence line hammering in staples and they'd flutter up from my feet. Their squeaky song had the charm of modesty.

May had given me the bracing days when the sea's reflection seemed brighter than the sky. Each morning and afternoon Eilidh brought out oatcakes and a kettle of tea. We'd sit quietly sharing something of a working picnic. Cup in hand, I rested on an elbow, a calmness that was on the Atlantic gave it a breadth I hadn't seen before, "I never weary of watching the sea, the ocean looks bigger today than I've ever seen it."

Turning to me from gazing seawards, "No nor I," and her smile shone through eyes, bright as the sparkle that bounced off the sea. "I was counting the different shades of blue from here to the horizon. Eachan always said the ocean has a mind and a soul. If he's blowing smoke from the wave tops his temper's up and he's better left alone, but on a day like this when he's stretched out flat Eachan would say, the old man's happy sunning himself." Our happiness seemed boundless as the ocean we watched, and in the warmth of the day I pulled her down beside me; my brown arms hugged her growing body and face to face, we too lay in the sun.

Ella had put her heart into the lambing of Eachan's ewes, we guessed it brought them together. Early and late round the croft, Rab the old collie helped her to catch any ewe in trouble and gradually the drawn lines of bereavement became the rosy face of recovery. A batch of twenty ewes with twin ewe lambs at foot awaited our collection. At dawn before the sea wakened I brought the Hilda alongside the Halasay pier. Iain and Ella already had the bleating bunch penned on the end of the jetty. A full tide raised the Hida's gunnel almost level with its edge.

Milling ewes terrified at the sight of water, lambs springing onto mother's backs, how to load such a scrum? No hesitation -Iain caught a lamb in each hand and dangled them down to me by their forelegs, "Wait, I'll give you another pair," another two lambs dangled down, "hold them by the front legs, keep them in the bow and don't let them go," Four legs in each hand and four lots of bleating, I clambered up to the bow.

Quick as he'd given me the lambs, two ewes were caught and manhandled into the boat, more lambs caught and dropped onto the bottom boards, half a dozen ewes were bundled after them and the rest began to jump aboard. "Let your lambs go!" he called. I jumped ashore to help Iain force aboard the remaining few. My introduction to sheep handling, a boat full of large frightened eyes and the Hilda low in the water with a living cargo.

Iain was already untying ropes, "They'll settle once you're on the move." I wasted no time. "Run the boat on the beach, get a hold of a couple of lambs and draw them along the ground by the front legs up to your field and the ewes will jump out of the boat and follow." Swinging the Hilda away from the jetty, I heard Iain's final advice above the roar of my outboard engine, "Keep your young dog on a string!" Ella waved, "Take care." Eachan's sheep heading for Sandray, what would be in her thoughts?

We were making a slow crossing. Overloaded? To my surprise the sheep were uncannily silent, not a bleat. More surprising, water was sloshing over the bottom boards. A deeply laden Hilda had begun taking in water between her upper planking. I steered and pumped, jets of water shot over the side. Eilidh out on the headland and the young dog prancing at her heel, I couldn't wave. A sharp morning breeze from the east came with the sunrise.

Wavelets appeared, slopping against the hull. Sheep around the edge of the boat shook their ears, they didn't like it, and for a vastly different reason, neither did I. Glancing ahead again, Eilidh had vanished. Approaching the headland, still pumping hard, how badly were we leaking, difficult to tell. The water sloshing at my feet became slightly deeper, the pump hardly copping. I leaned over the gunnel, ten inches of freeboard. I throttled back.

Guessing Eilidh's intention, I willed her to appear. Thank the lord, up ahead a shower of spray and the bow of Eilidh's boat. Cutting speed abruptly, she swung in astern. I worried for the sheep and the boat we'd been given. Half waterlogged, she moved sluggishly. I eased round the point, close as I dared. Some sheep might get ashore if the worst happened.

Edging us into the bay, out of the wind, a water- borne
shepherd with a very tired arm steered for the sandy beach
below the house. Barely moving, twenty yards out, a gentle
crunch and the Hilda grounded. Over the side, waist deep,
grabbing the bow rope I waded ashore.

Eilidh hurried round from the jetty, "Woman, was I glad to see
you crewing the lifeboat." The laugh of relief sounded in her
voice, "I could see water spouting over the side, no need to let
him get any wetter than you are now." Such impudence got her
a wee smack on the bottom.I emptied my wellies and seriously,
"no looking," I stripped off and wrung out my trousers.

The sheep seemed to know their transport was safely aground,
ewes heads went up and the bleating started. "Tomorrow to
fresh fields and pastures new," I wagged a scholarly finger, "for
you lot it's today." The young Muille dog fixed her eye on her
future charges. She and I would need to start training for
shepherding duties. "Eilidh, keep her on a rope!" we all three
were excited.

Twenty minutes of falling tide and the Hilda lay over in a few
inches of water. Not as deft as Iain, I pulled a couple of
lambs from amongst what sounded a mutiny. Going by his
instruction, I trailed the squirming creatures a little way up the
beach. A duet of loud bleating brought anxious replies from the
boat. Sure as Iain's prediction, two ewes scrambled over the
side, splashed through the shallow water and cautiously
approached to sniff their lambs. Mothering instinct did the
trick. Keeping hold of the lambs, I walked a few steps at a time.
The mothers followed, a shade suspicious, until, as if by a
signal, the boat emptied in one noisy stampede.

Pied Piper style, I drew our flock up through the dunes and
onto the machair. Eilidh kept behind them, not too close, the
trainee sheep dog firmly on a rope. Still carrying the two lambs

by their front legs, very quietly I drew their mothers through my new gateway and set the decoys on their feet. Off they bounded, no ways the worse. The remainder eyed the gateway, their flock mates were already grazing. We stood, not a move. Would they make a break and head for the open hill? Is this another con? First, one vaulted over some suspected booby trap into the field, a moment's study and the rest, judging it safe, entered with same precautionary leap.

Immediately every ewe's head bent down and muffled bleats from mouths full of grass called lambs to their sides. We stood at the gate watching them mother up until they became pairs of white dots spreading over the sweet grass of early summer. "The first sheep on Sandray in nearly a hundred years," Eilidh sounded just a wee bit emotional. "Soon they'll be checking my fences," I said with mock concern, and at that we laughed for the sheer pleasure of it all.

"If the bottom line is a healthy lifestyle then a hill shepherd must be on a top salary," my lightsome comment came as we climbed to the top of the field, neither of us out of breath. Eilidh patted her bump, "And the boy and I are getting all the exercise that's needed." Our dawn round of the ewes and lambs, drinking hill air, clean and fresh, as June light pulled islands out of the horizon; if happiness was in a casket, life in the hills held the key.

Still, amidst the contentment I fell to staring down at the old home we were renovating, it can only have been transitory, there was smoke at the lum, people busy scything hay and children ran about, until they faded into nothing and the house crumbled into nettles. Lines written beneath the white Australian sun went through my head, 'At the shieling was their happiness, only tears remain, and the generations live on song, and doors creak for their return and happiness clings to the winds of their going.'

I became aware Eilidh watched me. Muille stayed at my heel. Bending, I pulled her ear and got a wagging tail in return. Tips on her training were being supplied by Eilidh's childhood memories of her father's collies. "Iain will bring his dogs over to gather the ewes for the clipping," and speaking to the dog, "then Muille you'll see how it's done." My learning curve had to be just as steep, "Don't suppose there's a manual on sheep clipping," catching Eilidh's hand I grinned, "and next the baby will be born." Swinging my hand as children will do, she tossed unruly hair, golden as early light on hill pastures and in the fragrance of summer growth we walked down to the house.

I was busy, extremly busy converting the old byre into a bathroom. Outside drains were dug, plumbing parts scattered a concrete floor I'd laid, bath, wash hand basin, pipes and a shower unit leant against the wall. I had an electricity supply to arrange before the next winter. Luckily the old stone walls were dry and sound, I'd strapped and packed them with insulation and was cutting plywood when Eilidh came from the kitchen, "I see a launch at the jetty, I think it's a Castleton boat, hope nothing's wrong with Ella," and after a pause, knowing I'd thrown mine away, "You know Hector, perhaps we should have the mobile phone, in case she needs help." A shade glumly I nodded. "You're right, until I get power supply fixed up we can always get it charged when we're across on the mainland," as we jokingly called Halasay.

"Whoever it is will come to the house," I said as Eilidh went back to the kitchen. In the midst of cutting a large sheet of ply I was unwilling to stop. A man's voice at the door startled me. "Hector Mackenzie?" Caught unawares, I spun round. Disbelief turned to shock; filling the only doorway as though to prevent escape, I stared at two uniformed policemen.

Neither moved from the door, the one whom I recognised as the Castleton police sergant repeated my name although he knew it perfectly well. Bristling slightly at the questioning tone

I replied, "Is there any way I can help?" His counter was blunt, "Well now, Mr. Mackenzie, I hope this won't be difficult," a little pause, "for your sake." I hadn't ever bothered to go along to the station over the drowning of that supposed archaeologist. My God, surely not arrest?

Eilidh's flushed face appeared behind them, she spoke to them in the Gaelic, "The kettles boiling, you'll be needing a srupach after coming over the Sound." It broke a mounting tension, "Well now Eilidh, we'll be in shortly," he too spoke in the Gaelic. I understood their brief exchange and awaited their next move. The Halasay policeman reached into his tunic and held out an envelope towards me, "You'd better read it, Mr MacKenzie." I eyed him straight. I was trapped. The urge to fight coursed red and blazing; about to spring at them animal like, I was on the edge of going berserk. They must have spotted my ready fists. The younger man stepped forward. I tipped onto the balls of my feet. "For sake of Eilidh, Mr. Mackenzie, just cool it," the sharp words of the older Halasay man stopped me. Ashamed and not a little stupid, "I'm sorry gentlemen," I said and taking the envelope, "Come on into the old kitchen and see the changes we've made, I'll read this when you're at your tea." I admired the old bobby's tactic.

Through we went to the smell of flour and Eilidh busy at the stove. Of course she knew the local policeman, "Now MacNeil, I never heard you say no to a pancake straight off the girdle." Sergeant MacNeil put his peaked hat on the table and sat down, "Yes, you have me there." The young Constable remained sullen, saying nothing, his eye not leaving me.

Mugs of tea steamed before us. "You'll have to make do with powder milk," cautioned Eilidh, "don't worry we'll have a cow to milk before the winter." I forced a smile. The Sergeant looked uncomfortable. None the less he and Eilidh blethered away, sometimes lapsing into Gaelic. I understood enough to learn Ella was well. The atmosphere relaxed to a degree. The envelope lay at my elbow, unopened. Rather pointedly, the Constable clearing his throat, pushed back his chair and stood up. MacNeil ignored him and continued telling Eilidh a story about her grandfather falling into the harbour, "and I'm keeping an eye on your brother, Iain," he finished with a wink at me. In spite of the occasion, I warmed to the man. The old Highland style is difficult to gainsay. He won, in his own way.

Running a finger along the flap I opened the envelope. Thick official paper, folded in three, stark black lettering,

Unauthorised Occupation Property Act revised 1973.

Warrant by Order of the Lochmaddy Sheriff Court this the Twenty-first day of June in the year two thousand and ten.

Island of Sandray.

I hereby give notice to the removal forthwith from the above island of any person or persons and all chattels thereby pertaining to them, and whatever livestock, alive or dead as may be integral and any further encumbrance as may form any part of the occupancy and be deemed prejudicial to a total clearance of the aforesaid Island of Sandray in the Parish of Halasay, Outer Hebrides.

Legal jargon poured down the page. Unbelieving of the words I read the bottom lines,

I hereby receive this warrant and agree to abide by the order.

Name and Signature, --------------- Signature of two witnesses - ------------------ Date

Signed, Brian Shuttleworth, Sheriff Officer, Lochmaddy, North Uist.

The document fell on the table. I watched it curl back to its three original creases. The trap was closing. Two silent policemen; a smirking young constable and a thoughtful Sergeant, merely tools of the system, carrying out their duty. I stood up and went to the window. My eye followed the sweep of white sand into what had seemed an unending blueness, an existence that needed no requiem; in its simplicity I had glimpsed a reality that needed no lamentation. As the carving of an unrelenting sea will do, the surge of change beats a yawning cavern of desolation, grinding cliffs, consuming land, devouring peace and planet, forcing the tramping mass towards an airless chamber.

The sky faded. Sunless streets pointed to domes of arrogance, concrete leered down at me; I read the flashing neon sign, you fools there is no escape. Light filtered through the shutters of a modern world, its unending clank, the curling fumes unnoticed, halogen blue and wailing siren, you fools there is no escape, no escape from the growing walls of artificiality, the entrance to a tunnel of darkness. There is no escape.

I spun abruptly. The two men rose sharply, "And what if I don't sign this warrant?" my voice was low. Sergeant MacNeil met my eye without flinching, he said nothing. The silence lengthened. Without taking my eye from MacNeil, I heard the Constable say with a barely suppressed snigger, "Don't worry Mr. MacKenzie, we'll be back with the Sheriff Officers." The sergeant quelled him with a savage look and going to the door, "I'll leave it with you Mackenzie. In your own interests, come across to the station."

Without my realising, as I'd stood at the window, Eilidh had been handed the document to read. Her face drained of colour. Its whiteness emphasised the intense blueness of her eyes, proudly fierce in their defiance, "Make no mistake, Roddy MacNeil, our child will be born on this island, as were the generations of his forebears."

CHAPTER FORTY-SIX

A mouth too wide

"Yeah, and this ain't no bullshit I'm a telling you ma friends," Anderson's American accent cut across the rumble of local voices which formed a background to an early Friday evening in the Castleton bar. Weeks had passed since the Valkyrie had anchored in the harbour below the hotel and her skipper became the daily fixture on a bar stool. Sometimes he talked to the locals in riddles, wild talk of financial crash and nuclear war; they listened politely until his ranting became incoherent. Finally he would succumb to staring fixedly at pages of The Ocean Navigators Handbook which he always carried, before proceeding to drink morosely until last orders. Although Hotelier MacLeod had long since tired of hearing Anderson rambling about thieving banks, faulty nuclear installations and the sabre rattling Pentagon, he realised that the man seemed privy to information which in some quarters might be deemed highly sensitive.

That particular Friday as MacLeod took over from the barman it pleased him to note the bottle of twelve year old Highland Park, pride of his the line of optics at four pounds a nip, had been half emptied; with less pleasure he observed that, thanks to the generosity of two hotel guests, it appeared most had gone towards fuelling the paranoia of a now loquacious Andrew Anderson.

Two fellow countrymen sat to either side of the yachtsman on a bench in the farthest corner; the American couple who appeared to have befriended the tiresome Anderson had booked in that afternoon. Homer MacDonald and Bart MacDougal, New York, looked stylish on his hotel register and Angus MacLeod made them welcome, "You'll have relations in the islands Mr. MacDonald?" The man beamed, "Sure thing, two hundred years back, ma folks hailed from a li'l ol' farm on the Isle of Wight. My mom told me they called it Cowes and say, guessing by the horns on your bovine critters, sounds like it must be some place hereabouts; ah jest have to see it."

Always the genial host, MacLeod let the gentleman's stab at the map poster with a friendly smile, "Now, now isn't that strange. Cowes, yes Cowes, oh well I'll tell you there's plenty locals in the bar will give you directions; the ruins are there to this very day," and pursing his lips as though deep in thought, "Was your great, great grandfather a Donald MacDonald by any chance?" The descendent of the once mighty Clan Donald appeared thrilled, "Sure was, gee it's unbelievable you would know that." "Not at all, not at all, Mr MacDonald, your name gave me a clue," screwing his eyes and looking to the ceiling, "I think your ancestor was a first cousin of the Clan Chief- he was killed at the world famous battle of Culloden." "Stone the crows, you don't say," and grabbing the hotelier's hand, "shake on that, pardner." MacLeod kept his counsel and the peculiar trio passed the evening under the curious eye of an off- the -cuff historian.

Regular trips to the bar counter, "Barman, a large malt whisky and two cokes," were paid for by the chap calling himself MacDonald. The loudness of Anderson's voice ensured that much of his comment also crossed the bar, "You two guys ever heard of Diego Garcia?" The pair of tourists sipped their cokes and looked mildly interested. Common to those gaining an audience, the yachtsman launched into to his story, and given the diminishing contents of the bottle on the optic, with a surprising lucidity.

Swilling his fourth large one, "Yeah, I guessed not, well my friends, it was a paradise island, paradise, near as you get it on this goddamn planet, in the Indian Ocean, sun and surf. Y'see in nineteen seventy-one the Brits booted out its natives and their dug out canoes, exported them by force to the Seychelles; some little faceless wonder behind a desk in Whitehall let our military bulldoze the palm trees and their woven huts. Sure did trash a paradise, covered it in concrete to make a refuelling base for our nuclear submarines."

Although drink flushed the man's face, it failed to hide empty cheeks haggard from lack of food, "They built a big base, and oh boy I mean big, runways, stealth bombers, I've been there, yeah too right I've been there. Weapons, warheads, the real nasty stuff, shipped out from California. Believe me I owned the company involved, working for the good ol' Pentagon, we provided the real hot stuff for their nuclear submarine fleet. An' don't you forget these weapons are on instant alert, fired by computer. Ever heard of cyber terrorists? I just happen to know certain hackers have got into the US military already, lifting secret documents." His two listeners exchanged eyebrow lifting glances, "Now Andrew, that sure is a mite interesting."

Anderson twiddled his empty glass. A nod to the bar by the MacDonald chap brought Macleod over with another round. "Diego Garcia," the yachtsman returned to his theme, "yeah it's just a dot in the ocean but pivotal to Uncle Sam's control of the Middle East; climate change and water wars will go hand in hand, maybe nuclear," and throwing back half his dram, "Diego Garcia," he repeated slowly, "such a nice quiet corner to play with a computer, handy right now for relocating the terrorists to some quiet place where they get a board to lie on for their tongue- loosening splash of water, and believe me chum, for them that's the easy stuff."

Regardless of who might overhear and be offended, Anderson spoke loudly, "Y'see, you can't depend on the Israelis, might cut up rough, lose the plot, take over the Holy Hilltop, Temple Mount; it's the crux of their fight with Islam. Sure Israel's got the bomb, we gave it to them, my company fixed it some time back, but Iran, now that's real tricky, we've got to know when to go in; or do we let the Israelis do the job? Di.. Diego Gar... Gar, I'm a gonna sail down there, pretty mighty soon, pretty mighty sss...oon, when I.. when I get clear of this place."

The trembling yachtsman staggered to his feet, a man destroying body and soul with a hatred aflame in hollow eye sockets. The horrors of delirium assailed him, he began shouting and pointing, "I'll wait, you'll come alright, it's your real big spinner, make you a billionaire, but I'm a gonna blow this whole goddamn game apart, and one asshole, one almighty bastard, you ain't gonna like it, no not one tiny little bit, not one."

MacLeod catching a banned word and the sudden movement looked over sharply. The outburst seemed to exhaust Anderson and he slumped back onto the bench. Rapid strides across the bar and the hotelier stood over his semi-conscious client. The matter was immediately resolved, "OK barman, we'll take care of our friend." Before Macleod could object the two American compatriots holding a legless man between them helped Andrew Anderson through the swing door of the Castleton bar and out into the crystal starlight of a mid summer's night.

"He sure is heavy," the man called MacDonald grunted. The pair of them struggled with an inert Anderson, "This'll be his dingy, you go down first and catch him." The second American clambered down the jetty steps. "If he goes over maybe the water will do the job." "No, no, get him aboard, do it my way, this has gotta be a sure thing."

For a second Anderson realised he was aboard his beloved Valkyrie. Relief swept his mind, thank God. He felt safe. Tomorrow he'd sail, head for Shetland, find the croft his grandfather left and then, the Indian Oc...... The prospect of getting back to sea thrilled his every nerve. Tomorrow, "Valkyrie," he muttered, "just you and me, I'll take you home my lovely." His head fell to one side and he drifted in a haze between shouting and dreaming.

Faces grinned from a boardroom table, his screaming wife bent over him, the warm Caribbean became a great curling wave of chaotic motion, he struggled to grip the tiller; in a frenzy, his hands couldn't move, the wave was crushing him, he fought for enough air to shout, fought to breathe.

In a smothering darkness his aching chest was collapsing under an immovable weight.

A light burnt his eyes, became a receding halo.

Out of it grew the leering face of Joshua Goldberg.

CHAPTER FORTY-SEVEN

Salvage

Squatters, we've just been made into squatters, told to get out, and there's force waiting in the wings if we don't," My voice sounded remote, oddly detached from the significance of our eviction order. Rage gave way to despair. The island was threatened, its environment about to be sacrificed to progress. The blow to our aspirations left me mentally numb. Uncertainty overshadowed all the inspiration which had grown from the roots of belonging. Our flight to the sanctum of yesterday's ideals no more than a nostalgic ploy, a childish whim hoping to evade the reality of a shrinking world and encroaching human stupidity?

Stupidity? Not for the first time these thoughts plagued me. Was I not guilty of the folly of idealism, imagining we could stand apart and watch others despoiling the planet, believe as some great work of lasting art we could weave a tapestry of living which would leave an imprint of the simple old values now being crushed by today's blind stampede? Perhaps all golden ages are pretend and happiness always yesterday. Had we aimed at an illusion? Outside the sunshine became dull, how easy its desecration.

The Sheriff Warrant remained on the table. Since confronting the police sergeant, Eilidh hadn't spoken. We stood at the window, a long time silent. Two uniformed figures sauntered to the jetty. Perhaps because they appeared alien to the relationship we hoped to foster by living side by side with the islands abounding wild life, I saw them in a wider context;

indeed they became insignificant by comparison to the uncomprehending minds of those in higher authority who lacked any hands on experience of the momentous power of change sweeping the planet at its most fundamental level for many living creatures.

How many of the soft handed career politicians understood the implications for world food production engendered by the phenomenon of 'colony collapse' which affected frogs, bee stocks and now bats. Did the insect control afforded to crops by frogs and bats or the vital role of bee pollination come into their economic calculations? And again whilst they concentrate on putting financial incentives into cutting carbon emissions, did they comprehend that our abuse of the nitrogen cycle has already passed the danger point.

Eighty million tonnes of nitrogen, more than twice a safe level, is fixed industrially from the atmosphere each year and spread worldwide on the earth's soil; a proportion returns to the air as the greenhouse enhancing nitrous oxide, two hundred times more potent than carbon dioxide. Never mind that the acidification, death to vulnerable species and a reduction in the ability of the soil's delicate ecosystem to recycle excess nitrogen to the atmosphere, leads directly to aquatic blooms sucking oxygen from the water and creates massive dead zones in lakes and oceans. Add together the tonnage of nitrogen fixed by nature to that fixed by the industrial process and we exceed by four times the sustainable cycle. Plunder the atmosphere, degrade the world's soil to feed an expanding species and increasingly the planet becomes an artificial unit at the mercy of man's macro-management.

Eilidh, an expert on environmental issues had sown her views onto a receptive mind. They fitted my train of thought as I watched the two policemen board a waiting launch. Governments and their industrial cabals were fixated on a blinkered attempt to subjugate the elements, bend the planetary forces to the comfort and wellbeing of one species; still to register was an over riding probability their efforts would trigger 'colony collapse' amongst the increasingly crowded ranks of the common man.

Suddenly Eilidh spun round, no tears, her eyes aflame with fighting spirit. Grabbing the warrant she tore it into shreds, threw them into the air and turning back to the window with a fierce gesture, "Let them come and get us, I'll go in handcuffs and the nation will know why."

Bitterness showed, perhaps because her expertise had an emotional base, "the fool politicians are leaving it too late to tackle the approaching catastrophes of climate change, I happen to know scientists will be gathered this week in California making plans for geo-engineering, solar radiation management as they call it, space based reflectors, stratospheric sun shades, ocean fertilisation, all high risk, last resort tricks when the cheapest, most effective and certainly the safest would be to re-afforest the planet," and pointing to the sky, "This is what must be saved; this is the balance we must protect."

The cerulean majesty of mid-summer's day had a purity of light which outlined the puff edged cumulus clouds towering above the still Atlantic. White crinkles and the shaded grey valleys, they gave us the warm showers to grow our first hay crop. Clouds that travelled as shadows on the sea, parted to allow the sun to make ringlets on its surface. They were our friends, as much a part of the whole as were the seals nursing their pups out on the rocks or the confetti of yellow primroses strewn across a verdant machair.

My thoughts during our silent minutes perfectly matched her defiance. In a flash my despondency evaporated, I took her by the waist and we danced round the room, "That's my girl, it'll have to be a tranquilising dart into me before they get chance to put the handcuffs on you."

Out in what had once been the byre and was set to become our bathroom, I'd unearthed lengths of wood which by their shape and staining had been the planks of a boat. That afternoon without telling the mother to be I'd fashioned a baby's crib. Through to the bedroom I sneaked and whilst Eilidh busied with supper, put it beside the bed.

I heard the squeaks of surprise as she got undressed for bed, "Hector, it's exactly what I wanted." and she came bouncing back to the kitchen and hugged me as best the bump would allow. "It's made from an old boat," I explained seriously, "that's why the sides have a slight curve, perhaps I should have fitted a drain hole." Knowing my fondness for teasing and not to be beaten, "Maybe you could fit a mast and sail," she laughed, "it's our boy's first boat."

And that night the warrant forgotten, we talked babies.

At first light the following morning the Hilda rounded Sandray headland and into that serenity which awaits the sunrise. Darkness was leaving mainland hills, a crimson sky cast the Sound into deep mauve; and tiny whorls across its surface marked the tideway. Stealthily, the great orange tip sent fangs of new light into the clouds so the edge of each little whirlpool for a fleeting moment became its own bright cosmos; and in the beauty of their fragility I saw the mirror of all universes caught in an endless tide of change.

We were Castleton bound, me to face the police, Eilidh to make plans with Ella for the baby's birth. Up ahead, much to our surprise, we sighted a yacht. Not under sail, there was no wind, but not under power either for she drifted beam on to the tide. Maybe engine trouble, surely not abandoned? Eilidh lifted her binoculars, "It's the Valkyrie." Her tone as shocked as were my thoughts, I commented, "Would the Anderson man be fit to be at sea?"

Out in the centre channel the yacht drifted across our course and with the current under us we were closing fast. It would be against the common decency of the seaman's code to sail past if there appeared a problem. I hesitated. We would pass her at half a cable. Should we leave well alone? No, do the time honoured thing, I swung over and hailed, "Valkyrie ahoy!" Twice I called and waited. She rocked gently to the gathering tide. Soon it would sweep the yacht past Castleton and into the Minch. "I'm going alongside." Eilidh nodded, getting fenders and rope at the ready.

We lay moored to her. I knocked loudly on the hull. Nothing, was she unmanned? It struck me, had Anderson gone over the side? Drowned? Her rigging was slack, it tap, tapped against the mast. Had he been trying to make sail? I didn't like it, an empty yacht, drifting. The sunlight glancing off the wavelets, rippled along her white hull. The last of our wake caught up. The yacht rolled slightly. Bang, her cabin door banged loosely, a disturbing enough sound. A group of gulls alighted close by and began their hungry wailing. The whole thing was becoming sinister.

One swing and I was aboard. Into the cockpit; I fastened back the cabin door and looked below. Sunlight stabbed the cabin, flitting across the table onto the starboard bunk. Wellington boots were towards me. "Dead drunk," I breathed to myself.

What now? Step by step I backed down the companion ladder. The cabin reeked of drink. A length of cord lay on the floor, a feather pillow, soundless, only the tap, tap of ropes out on deck. In the chill of early morning it felt morgue- like. I was about to experience something vile. I knew before even daring to look, Anderson was dead. My nostrils caught the first whiff of its sweet smell.

Round the table I moved, looked down on an ashen face. Huge eyes, wide open, bulbous with terror. A red and swollen tongue lolled out of the side of his mouth onto an unkempt beard matted with froth. His shirt was badly ripped, an arm hung over the edge of the bunk, a swollen wrist marked with a massive crimson weal. Physically sickened, I backed away, touched nothing. Anderson had met a violent end.

I hurried on deck breathing deeply and much shaken. "Are you all right, Hector?" Eilidh at the helm of Hilda called up. It took a minute to speak, "The man's alone, and I'm afraid he's dead." Her eyes widened but otherwise she remained calm, "I knew as much when we saw his yacht adrift."

"Woman, you never fail to surprise me," and gathering myself together, "We'll have to tow her into Castleton. Will you handle Hilda if I stay aboard here?" "Yes, but it's calm enough and if we stay lashed alongside, it might be easier when we reach the harbour." She was right. I quickly secured the yacht's tiller and jumped into the Hilda. Once under way, the two boats in tandem moved easily. I spared Eilidh any description of Anderson, except to say, "It could be murder." Shock spread over her face, she said nothing. In half an hour we laid the Valkyrie beside Castleton pier without a bump.

Our unusual arrival had not gone unnoticed. I threw up the yacht's mooring line. It was caught and made fast by an impassively waiting Sergeant MacNeil. "Good morning, MacKenzie," at least he'd dropped the formal Mr. Without replying I motioned him to the pier's iron ladder. Rung by rung, once on deck he smiled down at Eilidh before addressing me in an official tone, "I take it when you went aboard this yacht, presumably as salvage, she'd been abandoned," and a shade suspiciously, "by her owner?" "Only abandoned in a manner of speaking, officer," and not wishing to go below again, "as you'll see," I said pointing to the cabin.

Eilidh, sitting in the Hilda, looked tired. I joined her, "Perhaps we shouldn't take the boat round to the Ach na Mara jetty today, give Ella a phone, I'm sure she'll come and collect you," and indicating the problem moored beside us, "I'll deal with this lot." To my relief she agreed but speaking carefully and quietly, "You know Hector, by the rules of salvage at sea, we might now legally own the Valkyrie."

Before I could muster a reply, MacNeil appeared from the cabin. Only the extreme pallor of his cheeks marked the shock of discovering a body, "This is a serious matter, Mr. MacKenzie, you'll kindly accompany me to the station, immediately. Anything you say may be taken down as evidence and used if required."

It needed not the gravity of his voice to emphasise my critical situation. I helped Eilidh onto the pier and waited as she phoned Ella. Apart from a rapid mobile phone call the sergeant remained silent and didn't leave my side. No attempt at handcuffing but in effect I was under arrest. Within minutes a police car drew up beside us. Hasty instruction sent the constable to stand guard over the Valkyrie. "Don't worry, Eilidh," I left her waiting for Ella as MacNeil marched me in silence to the police station.

Locking the door and seating himself at his desk, he began taking particulars. On giving the Sandray house as my address, he pinned me with a sharp eye, "This is the second dead body in which you appear to have been involved. I would advise you not be flippant, you may find that eviction warrant is now surplus to the whole matter," and in a far from easy Highland style he added, "You're not obliged to say anything, but I'm arresting you pending further enquiries."

I said nothing. Crossing the room, he held open a door. A curt, "This way." I walked the length of a corridor under fluorescent lighting. The concrete floor stank of disinfectant. Careful not to be too close behind me, he indicated a door to the left. Without option I entered.

Quicker than I could turn, the door slammed. I swung round sharply. No inside handle, the metallic click of a lock, a loud sound in an empty cell. A mattress on the floor, a slit of window too high to reach, and suspected of two murders.

I leant against the concrete wall, dropped my head into my hands. The sun that meant freedom grew black in the shadow of an eclipse, until only plumes of fire marked its disc

Lying at my feet against the cell wall, the crumpled briefcase from beside our bed swam into my unfocused eyes.

The lift attendant's smart salute drew a brusque nod from Sir Joshua Goldberg. Swiftly and silently it descended to the labyrinth of reinforced control rooms deep below the Pentagon. A heavily carpeted corridor led him to a private meeting with two top US officials.

Coffee and pleasantries were brief, the Chief Scientific Officer to the US Ministry of Internal Affairs spoke freely in a Texan gun- slinging style, "Bore a hole half a metre wide and five kilometres deep into hard crystalline rock, drop in the canisters of spent fuel, stack 'em up two kilometres high, cap the little lot with clay, asphalt and concrete and sure thing the geological barrier has only to last a million years for the waste to decay and become as harmless as putty, yup, that's the method the big boss would very much like your company to adopt here in the US. Simple, keep the stuff close to the site of production and safe as houses; ah wouldn't mind one in ma own back garden." A sullen Sir Joshua sat quietly without comment.

Nuen's Chairman was under pressure, not least from the White House for his company's extensive nuclear operations to adopt this cheap and easy form of waste storage. Apart from the method involved, Goldberg found the whole proposal entirely contrary to his strictly private ambition. Monumental influence and wealth would be in the hands of an international controller of nuclear waste, he intended those hands to be his own.

Perhaps in an attempt to expose their clients thinking, perhaps to add an element of persuasion, the Chief of Weapons Procurement in the Pentagon broke the embarrassing lack of comment on the part of an aloof Goldberg by changing the subject, "You've no need Sir Joshua to let today's agreement between our boss and the Russian President worry you. A thirty percent reduction in nuclear weapon stocks, yeah, it's high level window dressing but still leaves us and the Bolshevik's with ninety percent of the world's big toys."

After a deliberate pause the Weapons Procurement official drew himself up, "With Iran's nuclear programme coming into the cross wires we needed to tame the Trots, which brings me to the point," he placed the tips of his fingers together. "The arrangement we have with you for the re-fuelling of nuclear submarines at our Indian Ocean base at Diego Garcia is under surveillance,"

"And?" by sounding a little aggressive Sir Joshua attempted to maintain the strength of his position. Should Iran require subduing, he knew it would not follow another Iraq debacle, hence the importance of this strategic base, but under surveillance? Surely Nuen's lucrative contract for supplying nuclear fuel and fissile material to the oceanic base hadn't a problem? Surveillance? It was common knowledge that sufficient enriched plutonium to make several nuclear bombs had gone missing. Could his company be suspected? The palms of Goldberg's hands became sticky.

Less than friendly, the Pentagon Official sought to force an agreement. "It sure would be helpful to get an understanding on waste management before we discuss more delicate issues." and wishing to keep an edge over the meeting, he continued, a shade threatening, "Nobody outside these walls must know anything, this is top mouth shutting business." Letting the implication hang in the air, he spoke quietly, "We know fissile material may have fallen into the wrong hands, possibly stolen," another carefully weighted pause, "or maybe dealt, and you know better than most Sir Joshua, this ain't the stuff to carry away in a plastic bag."

The hint of a possible collusion between technical expertise and criminal elements was left boring into the mind of a frightened listener. Looking over the rim of his glasses the Official continued slowly, "Stolen, maybe a deal, whatever way this stuff went off account, the result could be real serious, might give fanatical terrorists a chance to pull off nuclear suicide right here. Maybe a rogue State is involved, it might not be Iran, Pakistan is one helluva close to Afghanistan, then again, just who do you think would want us to take our eye off the Middle East to follow their own private agenda?" He looked keenly at Goldberg, "Missing material, yeah, it's a specialist job," and almost in a whisper, "I hope Sir Joshua there's not any others privy to these shipments to Diego Garcia, or any other place?"

"Certainly not," Goldberg snapped back, shaking internally, any other place? Couldn't possibly be the material which Nuen had supplied very privately to a country not admitting a nuclear arsenal? It had had the blind eye treatment from the White House many years ago. Stolen or dealt, his mind raced to Anderson, he might have to implicate him in the missing plutonium. Veiled eyes fastened on Goldberg. Perhaps to catch him off guard, the Texan drawl of the Scientific Officer broke into the Nuen Chairman's acute concern, "Excuse me for being a mite curious Sir Joshua, how's that UK deep bunker storage programme of yours coming along?"

Realising this sudden diversion was part of their intention to get his international UK facility abandoned, Sir Joshua responded sharply, "Work is in hand. Under our existing contract I shall be ready for the first shipment of your high level waste in eighteen months time." Unable to contain his sickening worry, he forced an artificial smile.

Stolen or dealt, shifting the burden of any suspicion now uppermost in his thoughts, Goldberg enquired in a casual manner, "Ever hear of my company's ex-chairman Anderson these days? I'd just love to keep in touch with him, such a fine chap, the very life and soul of a party, knowledgeable too, but then on the other hand perhaps not all that, ermm..." and hinting a broad note of condemnation, he tapped his lips.

The eyes of two Pentagon civil servants met, "You don't say," again the slow Texan speech, "Well now Sir Joshua, ah heard it said a little knowledge can be a dangerous thing. Nope, we don't know his whereabouts but my guess is we ain't likely to hear of him no more."

"I see. Oh I'm so disappointed, he must really have gone to ground, such a pity." Attempting to appear genuinely saddened, Goldberg felt a surge of relief.

Should Anderson have met with an accident, he became the ideal, what was that cheap Americanism, the ideal fall guy.

CHAPTER FORTY- EIGHT

A Squatter's Rights

Claustrophobia, perhaps the stench of disinfectant but as a patch of yellow light slanted obliquely across the cell wall- a concrete wall, white and barren- I watched its pattern become narrow and slowly narrower until just a slit, it moved across the counterpane on a bed in a hospital ward. Skyscraper horizons deprived me of sunlight; the beleaguered days returned and with them again the hunger I'd known.

That same hunger which had driven me to work in the open,to heed a call which had become ever more insistent until the sun in some way embraced my every day. Health, vigour, the plants I nurtured, the seals I watched basking on the rocks, its light on the bay when I lifted my head, the colours which excited me, from rising to setting its presence wrought an inseparable bond. The plight of a captive, native of the outdoors would die of longing; the slit of a window, a sun that went away, the eye that looked in, the torture of separation. The pallor of such victims, filled my prison wall, white and blank and I understood.

Two hours passed, time to rap on the door. Its viewing hatch slid open, the unpleasant eyes of the constable looked in. "Kindly open this door." He said nothing, the hatch closed. More hammering would be futile. High above me a fluorescent strip light replaced the shaft of sunlight. Demanding a solicitor would be pointless, the nearest had to be on the mainland. Given my lack of co-operation so far maybe a different approach might ease the situation. I lay on the mattress thinking and worrying about Eilidh. She should not be part of this ridiculous travesty.

A metallic click and the cell door opened. "Now Mackenzie we'll have a word in my office." The Sergeant stood back and motioned me to go ahead of him. Our footsteps echoed down the corridor, I found it amusing to think he must reckon me dangerous. Eilidh sat at the back of the police station. In mutual relief we laughed as she came across and gave the criminal a hug. "I came round to spring you but they caught me with the ladder." "No, no, not a ladder," although in poor taste, given a man's death, being pleased to see each other made us silly, "the window's too small. If I'm booked in tonight, get gunpowder, not too much, the accommodation's a bit cramped."

"When you two have finished, I'll maybe get a word." Just an impression, but Sergeant MacNeil could be a different man without a sneering constable in the background. He sat down to study his notes, "Subsequent to our first meeting when you claimed an assassination attempt, you failed to come forward. An identification of the corpse revealed it to be that of a Londoner, the body went south and so far the case remains open. Have you anything to add?" I shook my head.

"This second body has still to be identified, but it now seems clear you weren't involved in," he eyed me closely judging my reaction, "...in what may have been murder. Two Americans helped this yachtsman from the Castleton bar last night but didn't return to the hotel. I understand you'd met the deceased when he arrived at Sandray" Briefly I told the Sergeant what little I knew of Anderson. He wrote without comment, closed his note book and adopting a puzzled tone, "Why in the world would two Americans kill a drunken yachtsman, if they did?" then casually, "and why would some stranger come all the way to Sandray and attempt to kill you?" I shrugged, aware of being watched. "You say you didn't know your attacker, mmm, that suggests his actions could have been premeditated?" His easy style masked an edge, "Any idea why that might have been?" I preferred not to mention my briefcase or the London experience. "No, it's a mystery to me."

Small communities have a knack of divining more of a person's affairs than might seem possible and doubtless the sergeant wasn't behind the times. He began to probe, "You appear from nowhere, there's an assassination attempt, now a murder; who knew you'd come out here?" Not wishing to divulge a suspicion that somehow the two incidents were linked, "Nobody had any prior knowledge, my decision to travel north happened to be entirely a spur of the moment whim." "Is that so," one eyebrows rose, I hoped not in disbelief, "Well now, a whim; perhaps you're just a photo in a Post Office window that reads' missing person'," the tone almost smacked of teasing. I guessed he knew plenty about me. "That suits me fine," I grinned.

After a lull, fresh thoughts prompted the sergeant to lapse into his natural manner, "Look here, there's the question of this man's boat." In a roundabout way of telling me he spoke to Eilidh, "You know salvage can be claimed by the first person aboard any vessel found abandoned on the high seas," and as if hinting at our course of action, "I suppose the yacht wasn't exactly abandoned, just drifting with a corpse on board, anyway the pier master's the official Receiver of Wrecks." Wearily he returned to shuffling notes, "This boat and its owner is some complication."

We awaited his next move. Eventually glancing from Eilidh to me, he framed a question almost as if hoping my reply would be evasive, "You'll have signed that Sheriff Warrant?" Eager to get outside, this was not the moment to tell him it lay in shreds, "No, not yet Sergeant, I'm thinking about it." His stare took time to pass. "Whilst you're busy thinking young man, you'll be wise not to leave Halasay, that eviction order meant what it said."

Directing us to the door and once out of earshot of a glowering constable, he spoke to me in a friendly manner, "See you look after that woman MacKenzie, her folks were good friends of mine," adding in to no one in particular, "I believe there's something called squatters' rights."

Down at the harbour the masts of Valkyrie and the Hilda swayed above the lip of the pier. A fluttering strip of blue and white tape hung on poles. "I dare say they may be waiting for detectives but if I can get past MacNeil's cordon, I'll sail Hilda round to Ach na Mara this evening." Eilidh squeezed my hand, "Don't worry, he's one of us."

Driving back to the croft, Eilidh was in high spirits, "Iain's busy clipping, I told MacNeil to stop his nonsense and let you out." Bonnie girl, she laughed and laughed. The bleating of ewes and lambs greeted us. Newly clipped sheep free of their heavy fleeces sprang up from the clippers of the shearer. Fresh white coats, smelling differently, had puzzled lambs running away from equally mystified mothers. Iain, head down, his back bent and sweating in the heat, stopped the clack of his shears long enough to welcome me, "Come on MacKenzie, this isn't the day to be passing time in the cooler, I've just started and there's a new sharpened pair of shears awaiting you."

Iain made the work look easy, a sheep against his knees, a sweep of the arm, rhythm, flow and the steady clack of metal amongst creamy new wool; in minutes the fleece would be a neat heap and four pounds lighter, shorn and white, the ewe would bound away. Bending was not for Eilidh, but Ella, deft for her years gathered each fleece and rolled it into a tight bundle for Iain's willing children to carry and stack on the growing mountain of wool. Given a few tips by the expert, "Don't hold the sheep too tightly, keep the blades flat against its skin and mind your fingers." I picked up the shears- they were razor sharp. After a couple of hours of struggling and finding their fleeces fell into pieces instead of coming off like a rug, I realised that learning which button to press on a computer was child's play compared to clipping sheep.

Eilidh brought out tea and pancakes warm off the girdle. We sat against the stack of wool and smelt like the animals now happily back to their grazing. The ones I'd dealt with stood out, going by the neatness, I realised Iain had clipped six to my one and thinking I'd have learned the skill more quickly, I shook my head. "Don't worry, it'll take at least five hundred ewes before you get the idea, but you're coming on Hector boy, some never get the way of it." All afternoon we'd clipped away under a hot sun, sweat dripping and the morning forgotten, I was happy again. The last clipped sheep bounded off to find her lambs, supper arrived and a needful dram.

Iain dropped me at Castleton pier and thinking of the five hundred sheep before I learnt the skill, "I'll be over to give a hand with your own clipping tomorrow." "That'll be great," and over his shoulder, "if your back isn't too stiff." He was right, my back ached.

The mainland steamer had sailed hours ago. A deserted pier, no coloured police tape to prevent me from boarding Valkyrie. A quick look about, nimbly down the iron rung ladder and I stood on the yacht's teak laid decks admiring her lines. Truly she was a beauty, the elegance of a sweeping bow matched the curve of her stern, strength and grace. Would I pursue a salvage claim?

I looked at her cabin door and felt impelled. Heavy brass hinges and mahogany panels, it opened smoothly. Evening shadow

405

darkened an empty bunk. A faint smell hung about the cabin, a sweet sour odour, the lingering stench of a corpse. My skin prickled. The body had gone, but the contorted face of dead Anderson stared out of the bunk, the lolling tongue, frothing saliva trickling down a cheek faintly blue in the first stage of decomposition. Huge eyes bulged from their sockets, burst blood vessels flared red. No longer starting eyes of terror but imploring, abjectly pleading, turning slowly. I followed their gaze. The navigation table; I looked down and on it, unfolded, a chart of the Indian Ocean. A pencil line circled a group of islands. I bent to read their name, a corner of the chart lifted, ever so gently. The cabin door swung softly.

I leapt back. Instantly the eyes vanished. I was staring again into an empty bunk; in my nostrils the wafting sweet rancid odour. Sickness welled up. Bolting up the companionway, I was out in three steps. Gulping the clear air, I hurriedly cast off mooring lines and swinging over the rail, dropped aboard the waiting Hilda.

Standing out on the yacht's bow, there above my head, her black lettered name, 'Valkyrie', now a yacht cursed by some dastardly murder. So a boat is the animation of the elements, so too their spirit is in her, in her name. Would the maidens of Viking belief carry aloft a dead man's soul in their arms? Are all souls in the arms of a myth, a myth within a myth? I made haste to sail.

The day's waning heat brought a breeze, and light though it was, coming out of the south west it put a curve into the Hilda's old brown canvas and a ripple at her bow. Often on a fine evening, just as I was doing, Eachan had chosen the aloneness of sailing round to Castleton and home again. A gentle night settled on the ocean, and as it would have done for him, the course for home on its glittering surface was lit by stars. Unheeding of a complexity which smothers the voice of simplicity, the sea spoke to me, the island slipped past, and the beaches of the gloaming awaited a moonlit hour when grains of silver would become treasure and emptiness their reassurance that all was not yet within the cell of man's ingenuity.

The haunting tune, Lassie with the Golden Hair, sang in my thoughts, and in the gloam of a summer's night it brought me to the jetty of Ach na Mara, and Eilidh.

Ignoring warrant and warning, ten days later we were back to our Sandray home. Another week and I had the conversion of byre to bathroom finished. Eilidh, calm and content, busied herself with baby clothes and bedding for the crib I'd made. Out on the croft Muille and I learnt a little of the art which passes between a shepherd and his dog. A mixture of luck and us both running, finally drove our small flock into the pens I'd built. By late afternoon the ewes were clipped and their fleeces spread over the loft space I created above our two rooms and the bathroom, "What better insulation. Do we need a new mattress?" Eilidh thought me half serious, and on reflection it wasn't a bad idea.

A hot day, copious sweat and pleased I'd managed to clip our sheep without too much struggle, down to the bay I ran and splashed headlong into the sea. Eilidh followed down more sedately, the baby was due anytime. She undressed slowly, waded in and attempted to float alongside me. "I'm front heavy!" she called, turning over after the third try. I swam across and lifting her in my arms let her float face up. Wavelets circled the mounds of her body as I gently let her rock up and down. An intimacy that harks to the primitive surrounded us, and naturally as the setting sun is wedded to the long horizon, we belonged. Pressing her tummy Eilidh whispered up to me in a little excited voice, "I think the baby might come tonight," and the blueness of her eyes glowed from the depths of a great happiness.

After supper I sensed Eilidh grew uncomfortable and ventured to enquire, "Should I go across for Ella?" She reached out and took my hand, "No Hector, it'll be all right, I want it to be just us both," she held her stomach for a moment, "so don't leave me; that's the first wee pain." We'd talked about the birth often enough, now the baby was on its way. I fought to stay calm, "Would you like to lie down?" She smiled, "No thanks I'll just walk about outside, don't worry I'm fine." Shaking inwardly I nodded and taking her hand, we walked round and round the house.

Every so often Eilidh would pause. Her contractions were becoming stronger, more frequent. We leant together on the gable of the old house. No shroud that night to cover the hill of its saying, for as at fullness of a golden harvest, an orb arose, wide, close and watching. Orange beams pierced splintered crags, the hill reached out, a black shadow at our feet. Haunted stone and fallen slab, amidst the breathless air, the solitary tread of a last journey, "A blue eyed boy, born beside the sea, his talisman a raven in a cage, it brought him here a thousand times ago," Eilidh tilted her head, moonlight fell across her face, "The raven is gone, his severance from the coming of the sea kings is complete," and in the hushed voice of reverence, "yet we are here."

A woman was soon to add a generation to those from whom we came; time and place, wherefore its mystery? Words formed, extemporal and unbidden, "The hill too will vanish, the moon wander from its orbit, sun and planets be dragged into a blackness from which there is no escape, but for us there is no severance, no parting from the birth of light or from its ultimate future; we are entangled in an endless cycle, and to each other." We went into a house that stone upon stone was built of the Hill of the Shroud.

In our bed by the light of the Tilley lamp, the baby appeared. A dark head of hair, Eilidh whimpered softly. I helped with the shoulders and a child slid into my hands, a boy. I lifted him and cleared his mouth with my finger. The umbilical cord, two pieces of thread knotted tight, my hands shook; scissors; I cut swiftly between the knots. The boy began to cry.

At the sound, Eilidh half sat up, and dragging pillows in behind her she cried quiet tears of elation. I put the slippery bundle into her arms. She bent over him and quietly licked his face. The crying stopped and stretching his arms he pursed hungry lips. After a little time stroking the boy, touching his long limbs, spreading out toes and opening his hands, Eilidh tenderly gave him her full red nipple. She looked up, tired but smiling. I smoothed her hair and out of a heartfelt joy, we laughed and rubbed noses.

The boy settled on his mother's chest and they both fell asleep. A harvest moon had journeyed the heavens, a baby had been born. In the moon's dying glimmer before the dawn, I slipped outside to bury the afterbirth, a part of us had returned to the island soil.

Mother and child wakened as early light flooded over Sandray. Covering our shoulders with a blanket, I took Eilidh on my arm and carrying the boy in the crook of my other, we walked barefoot to the beach. Wet sand, salt air fresh and heady, glittering pools blue and abandoned, two sets of footprints followed us into the sea, into the mirage of beginnings; there was none other to watch or gainsay; we were the last of a world grown weary of mankind.

We waded knee deep, nothing disturbed the emptiness. Eilidh splashed droplets over the child, a saltwater christening, "We'll call him Eachan," she announced. Equally certain, I agreed, "A fine boy and worthy of a name that's handed down."

I held the dangling new born creature aloft, his face to the sunrise, and then gently in the tide, we washed away the blood of his birth.

And his blue eyes were those of a son of the sea.

CHAPTER FORTY-NINE

Containers

The shock of waking revealed two masked faces framed against the ceiling, white eyes, black heads, a glint of steel. Fingers closed around his throat thumbs crushing his windpipe, a light blazed into his eyes. Arms dragged him naked to his feet. The slow drawing of cold metal crossed his neck.Terror seized him, he was about to be killed, a slit throat spurting blood. In abject fear his knees crumpled. They let him fall. Sprawling before them on the carpet was the gross frame of Sir Joshua Goldberg. An acid stench of urine filled the bedroom.

Behind the masks a snigger, no words, they knelt on the arms of a trembling heap of flesh. The torch rendered him blind. Unable to rise, Sir Joshua broke into hysterical pleading, "Don't, don't, please, mercy in god's name, oh pleeese, pleeese, anything, I'll do anything..." gradually his total abasement reduced to a blubbering whine.

A voice from the back of the bedroom spoke easily in a deliberately casual manner, the accent being that of a gentleman schooled at Eton, "My dear Goldberg, do calm yourself. I must apologise for this impromptu call at such a late hour, and I see we've upset you a trifle, most unfortunate, but then it does seem you've avoided contacting me these past few months, not the way to treat such a generous friend, now is it old chap?"

Instantly Goldberg recognised the voice, an influential businessman with Middle East connections. Into his fear contorted mind flashed the transaction to which he'd been drawn by the huge sums involved; the deal, the money, now this horrific nightmare, in the hands of remorseless martyrs, they'd detonate a mini nuclear explosion, trigger a mass conflagration, life had no meaning, but they'd kill him for pleasure, maybe torture first. The numbness in his arms acutely painful, the stinking wetness of the carpet, "Please, I don't want to die." he lay whimpering.

The tone from the far side of the room sounded cool, a little impatient, "Let me remind you of our deal, four million dollars a kilo, thirty kilos in three consignments, and frankly gentleman to gentleman, believing you'd honour this arrangement, our first payment for a ten kilo container was placed with Midas Holdings in the Cayman Islands some months ago. Naturally a man of your undoubted means won't concern yourself with paltry amounts of petty cash and I'm sure the container is in transit, but in case not, just thought I'd call, as one might say, to jog your memory."

A squirming Nuen Chairman blabbered incoherently, "Please, yes, it has, it will, please, they watch... I... I... time, a little more, it'll be taken off our next shipment to.. to.." he began crying.

"Your next shipment to?" the voice queried. Petrified of revealing top secret US military affairs, Sir Joshua's crying rose to piteous wails. "Come, come, Goldberg, less tantrums. You were saying, a shipment to?" Threshing his legs on the carpet the cries became a fever of pleading. Cold and insinuating the voice said smoothly, "Stop making a fool of yourself; I hate to be unkind at this juncture but perhaps a little rehearsal of our special treatment might help your powers of recall."

A gloved hand caught Goldberg's chin, crashed the back of his head on the floor, stretched out his neck. He felt the first sharp nick, heard the voice flat and emotionless, "Please gentlemen, let us save his windpipe a moment longer. Now Sir Joshua, you were saying, a shipment to? "

The knife remained pressed on his throat. Warm blood ran into his ear. His bowels became water. Saliva left his mouth, gurgling its last drops; barely audible, he gasped out, "Diego Garcia."

CHAPTER FIFTY

Cages

Several days passed before Eilidh would put Eachan into his crib and come outside with me to admire the kitchen garden. "Never in my life have I grown any food and to see this lot appear," I waved a hand towards our crop of potatoes filling the 'lazy beds', the long drills of carrots I'd painstakingly thinned which we were eating raw straight out of the ground. Green topped rows of curly kale, fat purple swedes, the strong scent of the parsnip, never mind the taste and colour, they should keep us in vegetables through to the spring. "A plate of soup each day, that's fair exchange for the sweat of hauling seaweed, better value than playing the stock market," I said gravely, but unable to keep a straight face, "Next year I'll grow you and the boy a prize marrow."

Many the demands of a self sufficient home in the making, Muille at heel and a round of the sheep, a look to the boats, more fencing and building until the evening light finished my work for the day. Into the softness of candlelit kitchen and Eilidh would be feeding the boy. She'd look up smiling and her sea blue eyes would unveil the tenderness of our unspoken betrothal.

At two days old the child was put to sleep in his crib beside our bed. During the hours of darkness a snuffling wakened me. Eilidh had lifted a hungry boy and as she fed him mother and child fell asleep together. I put my arms around them. Busy days and broken nights, Thursday or Friday? We'd lost track, a week passed, maybe two. Summer's light into autumn night and as the old folk must have done, I felt the apprehension of the coming months of spindrift and gale. The sun no longer set midway across the bay, that evening its angry tip fell behind the line of tooth like rocks which sheltered the seal's roosting haven. A southerly swell was running, columns of spray burst on them in rainbow plumes that hung uncertain, and then fell back.

"The winds gone round to the south, tomorrow the Sound will be flat," was all I said, a trace of sadness behind the words. Eilidh reached into the crib, somehow equally downcast. I stroked her hair. The intimacy of these days and months, as private as we could have wished had given us this fragile beginning to the circle of another life, and it seemed we couldn't bring ourselves to break the spell. Eilidh shook away a tear, "Hector," she murmured, "this is beyond happiness; it's the happiness that becomes a suffering." Rocking the boy in her arms, she looked from him to me, "tomorrow we must take young Eachan to see Ella." Quietly we went to bed.

Crack, the air splitting snap of a rifle, another shot rang out, several more, reverberating on the window. At the first shot I was out of bed and at the door. The sickly yellow light of a dawn before the rain met me. In a trice Eilidh was at my shoulder, the boy in her arms. Dressed in seconds I ran for the jetty, a fusillade bouncing over the water echoed from the headland.

Two large inflatable dinghies slowly manoeuvred about the bay- kneeling in each bow, a man aiming a rifle. They were shooting the seals. Obviously the first shots had been at the colony lying hauled out on the rocks. Instant panic would have sent the animals crashing into the water. Now as they swam for the open sea each black head surfacing for air became the target. More snap shots. Bullets ricocheted off the water, thankfully not all found their mark. Throwing on shirt and trousers, I was at the jetty in minutes.

Leaping into Eilidh's small dinghy, one pull of the starter cord and I roared out towards the nearest inflatable, bellowing at the top of my voice, "Stop, stop that bloody slaughter!" Before I reached them, a seals head broke the surface fifty yards off my bow. I heard the smack. A bullet found its mark. The head sank. I powered on. My bow wave shone red, the wake astern churned blood. A smell of cordite stung my nostrils.

I pulled alongside their inflatable, rouring at the two men, "What the bloody hell are you doing?" Equally furious they shouted back "Who the hell are you? Get out of our way!" the snarling voice certainly wasn't local. Another seal came up for air. The rifleman took aim. Opening throttle, I rammed them. His shot went wild. "You damn fool!" he screamed at me, turning his rifle in my direction.

The second inflatable sped over, the man at their helm shouting at me, "Clear off, you've interfering with a licensed cull!" I took him to be in charge of the slaughter. "Get out of the way, get back to that jetty, I'm reporting this straight away." He fiddled with a mobile phone.

I must drive the seals out to sea, get them out of range. Ignoring shouting and waving, I swung away from their boat and began circling the bay. Risky tactic, they continued firing. Eilidh appeared on the shore carrying Eachan. The possibility of a bullet spinning off the water greatly alarmed me. I steered rapidly for the beach.

Obviously this attracted their attention. Firing stopped and the boats drew side by side. Loud voices carried across the water, there seemed to be some arguing, presumably a thwarted operation had had to be abandoned. In a flurry of spray both inflatables disappeared round the headland. I made straight for the jetty, moored our dinghy and ran round to meet Eilidh and the boy. Poor woman, she knew too well what had happened, looking across to the empty rocks, her face glistened with tears, "Oh Hector, the seals won't come back."

Silence, and with it an air which had smelt of rain gave way to waves of drizzle that advanced from the sea. Folds of grey curtain closed about us hiding the seal rocks from our view. We walked back without speaking to a house surrounded by the first threat of winter.

An incoming tide and eight bodies washed back and fore in its swell. Three were of seal pups born that spring, their blood on the sand. One by one I dragged them up the beach and buried them beneath the dunes.

Violent shuddering overcame Sir Joshua, he remained sprawling naked beside the bed in a deep state of shock. Petrified by the belief his throat was about to be slit, creases of fat quivered in an uncontrollable reaction. Congealed blood filled an ear, his arms felt useless. For whatever time might have elapsed he lay, a groaning, prostrate mound of flesh on a carpet, soiled by his own defecations. Sunrise attempted to pierce the heavy damask curtains of Goldberg's bedroom in a luxury suite of Qatar's finest waterfront hotel. The stench surrounding him brought his numb mind to bear upon the ghastly nightmare. Finally he realised the men had left as silently as they'd arrived. Unsteadily he got to his feet and fell onto the bed sheets.

The service phone wakened him. He reached over, "I wish to be left in peace, do not ring again," and banged down the receiver. This automatic form of addressing hotel staff bolstered his self esteem. The total humiliation he had suffered, both mental and physical, began to fade. Completely ignoring the filth smeared beside the bed, he showered, dressed, slammed the door, paid his bill and still inwardly shaking, stepped into a taxi. "Airport!" he rapped at the driver.

A car swung in behind them. Fear returned. Were they being followed? He slouched down, desperate to reach the safety of the Emir's private airport lounge. Lift the phone and one of His Highness's jets would be made available. Get out of this country; oh my God, hurry, hurry! Clasping hands to stop them shaking he fell to a silent importuning prayer, "Please good Lord, protect me from evil, from all who seek to cheat me. I have not buried or wasted your talents, truly I have multiplied them, not ten but a thousand fold. Lord, I am your humble servant, trust me," his supplicatory rambling brought them to the airport and he felt strangely uplifted. Directing the taxi driver to carry his valise, Sir Joshua made rapidly strides to the Emir's private lounge. With a salute of recognition the security guard ushered him in immediately. How useful to have influential friends he thought as the plane took off, so admirably wealthy, one day I shall...... he dozed off amidst the oriental cushions of the aircraft's lounge deck.

Careful scrutiny in the bathroom mirror of his Hyde Park penthouse reassured Chairman Goldberg, it's nothing more than a shaving nick. A good night's sleep and time to think. Rage built by the minute. Compromised by a common arms dealer and his murderous thugs he might have been, and OK, the wretched man had graded up from supplying Kalashnikovs to Somalia, but to imagine that they could influence the deal in enriched uranium by brute force was laughable.

A consignment of this material would now be heading secretly to Diego Garcia. Goldberg worried mightily over his conversation with the US military; one mistake and -so far as they were concerned- he didn't care to speculate. High time to weigh up the risks, Mr Dealer should understand containers didn't just fall off a lorry. Time indeed, and critically short, Sir Joshua poured a coffee. Risk detection or renege on the deal and lose forty million? Renege, maybe, but how to avoid these criminals in future- hand the dealer's name to the FBI? The man wouldn't be seen again but he might squeal in the process. Goldberg cursed, the loss would be unbearable, fifty million. Agitated fingers drummed his head, maybe wisest to abort the deal.

If he did, security would be paramount. Sir Joshua looked nervously at his own door. How had those thugs gained entry to a bedroom in Qatar's most expensive hotel? Bribery, it wasn't a break in, pure bribery, nobody's trustworthy, anything for money. How much had it taken he wondered-five hundred dollars, surely not? Security, yes, as from today he'd hire bodyguards from that reputable London agent with experience in Iraq. Yes, ten million in his Midas account, courtesy of that upstart of an arms dealer, it should cover safety fees nicely, and a little to spare. Goldberg smiled, why not use Mr Clever Dealer's dollars to protect himself from another visit?

Payback time, the idea appealed. Mind made up, he dashed off a text to Nuen's Chief Technical Director, the one man with knowledge of the transaction and in full charge of the current shipment. 'Ensure safety first and foremost.' A prearranged message, it would immediately alert his director that the deal was off. No exchanging containers during the flight, but of course the dealer would receive a consignment. Unfortunately the particular canister selected for him to innocently pass on would contain ten kilos of lead.

Capital thinking, problem solved, the weapons grade uranium stayed safely at Diego Garcia, no duping the US military, the dealer would escort the container he'd collected to its final destination. At this point Goldberg's thoughts broke into gleeful laughter, "And he'll carry the can when it's opened. How awfully annoyed the recipients will be, they'll certainly arrange a little farewell party for Mr. Big Dealer." Though seldom finding other people's jokes amusing, Sir Joshua was not averse to laughing at his own.

And back on top form, he barked a stream of instructions down the phone. The international consortium dealing with the nuclear waste project in Scotland received an ultimatum, "Unless you commence stage one construction within a month, I shall regard this as breach of contract and instruct my lawyers to begin proceedings accordingly."

To witness the pride with which Eilidh handed over the baby for Ella to inspect and nurse was a pure delight, two women happily sharing their motherly instincts. For Ella it must have been the reawakening of a succession of children bathed in the kitchen sink, children creeping down the stairs in the dark when she and Eachan sat at the fire, the sound of her family playing in the fields, one day to be scattered abroad. No reproof followed for our not calling on her to aid the birth, only admiration in Ella's tone as she asked a few womanly questions.

I noticed she carefully refrained from enquiring his name. Finally Eilidh could hold back no longer. The old lady's face at once solemn, "I knew you would give him the good Gaelic name." The memory of old Eachan showed in her eyes and she hugged the boy to hide her emotion.

Leaving the women to their talk, I pushed open the steading door and sat on the front wheel of Eachan's little grey tractor. Hammers and saw bench, fencing tools and hay rakes, all the hand held implements which kept a working croft alive were much as he had left them. His scythe hung from a rafter, its worn sharpening stone on the window ledge, a spade propped against the wall, their idleness added to an air of disuse which brooded over the shed. I found it difficult to grasp that running this croft had fallen into my hands.

Looking thoughtfully to the far off fields I could see the cows and calves. Ella no longer milked a house cow. The calves would be sold, perhaps the cows? Iain, good friend and neighbour had made the season's hay crop, small stacks dotted the nearest field. Carting them to the barn would be the first of many day's work.

Three weeks since coming over to Ach na Mara and each day had counted. Our hay forked by hand onto the trailer and into the barn, Ella's lambs sent away to the mainland sheep sale, all the pleasantest of work and set to a purpose. Whilst down at the Castleton ferry loading the lambs, I noticed the Valkyrie had been moved out to a mooring in the harbour. Nose to the breeze, riding her chain amongst the local fishing boats, even from a distance she'd taken on a look of neglect.

In his unhurried manner the pier master leant on the rails of the sheep pens, "Your lambs are in great fettle, whatever the trade will be." He gave no indication that I was a total amateur with sheep and turning his back to look across the harbour, "We needed to move the yacht, MacKenzie." It was his way of opening the subject. Being equally slow to broach the matter, I stated the obvious, "I saw that." He turned slowly to face me, "There's papers in the office, if you're interested." Clearly in his capacity as Receiver of Wrecks, the question of salvage required attention. "Right, I'll be over in a little," I'd fallen into the easygoing island style.

Apparently from documents aboard Valkrie, Anderson's next of kin had been traced, a Mrs. Anderson did exist. She had no knowledge of her deceased husband ever owning a yacht of that name and nor did she wish to pay the cost of its salvage. Unrealistic as it sounded, legally I could claim the boat. The pier master come receiver sat at his desk aware of my hesitation, "You please yourself, MacKenzie," adding in a noncommittal way, "She's a fine yacht, never a better came into this harbour." Perhaps it was his way trying to help me make up my mind. Small wonder I had doubts, the sight of Anderson's brutal end remained unpleasantly sharp. "Don't be leaving it too long or she'll have to be sold." The yacht's tall mast took my attention, on an incoming swell it circled against the horizon. Two days later Eilidh and I sailed her round to the jetty at Ach na Mara, and young Eachan in his crib roped on a bunk.

Like myself, Eilidh wearied to be back in our Sandray home. To leave Ella alone made it difficult. Good woman, she guessed as much, though our feelings were never expressed. Would we sell the cattle? No, she wanted the work to help her pass the winter and Iain or his wife would be calling most days. Around the croft few things had changed, so too about the house little had been moved, in her own way Ella wanted to live with memories.

We'd spent the best part of the day loading supplies onto the Hilda and with Eilidh, the boy and the dog perched at the bow, it was late of the day before I steered away from the Ach na Mara jetty. A dark night, banks of cloud rested their burden on the grey Atlantic. Eilidh rocking with the boat's motion had fed Eachan before tucking a sleeping child into his crib. I'd lashed it to the thwart behind the mast and as Eilidh reached for an oilskin to put over the bed, I spotted Muille sneaking a lick at the leftovers on the boy's face, "She's got a taste for milk," I laughed the length of the boat. Eilidh called back, "Well the boy's taking all my supplies, he's got some appetite, another month and it'll be mince and tatties." The note of her voice told me of a happy, excited woman. We were a family unit again, including the dog.

A black ocean had no margin to offer a matrix devoid of starlight. The dead air held un-natural warmth. Given luck, we'd beat the approaching rain. In under the headland, I'd steered the track so often, each time with the thrill of a homecoming. Difficult to see, don't swing in too soon, I held course, open up the bay. The mass of headland passed astern. Instantly out of the blackness, a flashing light, a small orange light, another further inshore, both towards the south side of the bay, flashing every few seconds, certainly not a vessel, anchored or otherwise. "What the hell?"

Now I had my bearings. We were at the mouth of the bay. Over the tiller, hard a- port, "I'm going to run across to investigate," Eilidh stared, equally surprised. She nodded and put her hand onto the crib. Cold air struck the back of my neck. Behind us hissing began, rain on the sea.

I steered for the light, closing in. The first blast of rain hit us, large drops, stinging my ears, rattling on the canvas covering our supplies, beating a tattoo on the sea. Eilidh pulled an oilskin over the crib. Ahead the beacon flashed. Orange light spread on the water for a second, vanished for two. Dimly the seal rocks appeared at each pulse, owlish and yellow.

Close in we saw large objects undulating in the slight swell. Each garish flash outlined low angular frameworks, the hideously incongruous wood and metal struts of fish cages. Factory farming, fish fed to fish, the ocean plundered to turn cheap fish into expensive fish, and the bay an arena consigned to another environmental rip off.

The bleakness was not of the unceasing rain, nor the rising wind that swept numbing sheets across the jetty as we landed, that would pass; it was the inner desolation of knowing the advance of exploitation had sought and found another victim. The bay and the innocent would suffer.

I wrapped the boy in my jacket. We trudged the path through the dunes, both soaked. That meant nothing, tomorrow the driving rain would give way to sunshine. The desecrating of a natural world would yield only the sorrows of a barren waste.

The incessant buffeting pushed us on, the moan of a rising storm at our backs. We hurried, anxious for the shelter of home. Uneasiness grew at every step. The island had been broken into, robbed of its spiritual warmth, no feeling of welcome. Somebody's here? I became wary.

Without warning the storm broke. A jagged bolt of lightening split the heavens, the crackle of ionized air quenched its energy in the sea. A second's brilliance illuminated indigo waves, turned the underside of the clouds stark white. Lashing rain smelt of discharge. Darkness intensified. Thunder reverberated from the Hill of the Shroud. We felt the pressure.

Home, just fifty yards. Great black bellied clouds impounded the sky. Another mighty flash and ear shattering crackle. Through grey rain it lit dark objects.

Heaped before the walls of the house, our furniture, sparse as it was, chairs, table, bed and mattress, lamps, dishes, broken and scattered.

Eilidh gasped, stifling a cry she clasped her bedraggled hair. The boy began to whimper, I passed him to her.

Shaken by disbelief I ran to the door. Boards were nailed across it.

A sign stared me in the face.

NO ADMITTANCE.

CHAPTER FIFTY-ONE

A civilised shape

Fluorescent tubes illuminated the broad desk of a spacious planning office in the London headquarters of a multinational construction consortium. Three be-suited gentlemen turned sheet after sheet of plans. From an artist's overall impression to the intricacy of its computer control room, every aspect of the underground storage facility about to be built for Nuen required a final verification; its capacity, the safety back up system, security against nuclear attack, a maze of detail, all to the satisfaction of the energy giant's chairman.

Flanking Sir Joshua Goldberg were the consortium's chief designer and its executive director. Given that the gap between paper plans and practical reality often tended to diverge, it suited none of the trio to admit that the project would include an element of inspired guesswork on the part of the foreman and the 'brickies'.

A tiring session, Sir Joshua's varicose veins were aching, his elastic stocking were too tight. At last they came to glancing over maps which indicated the site for accommodating the labour force; not strictly a concern of Nuen's chairman but having another scheme in mind, he demanded to assign its location. "That is not where to erect your worker's huts. I suggest you make use of this area." Behind his back the consortium executives arched their eyebrows, however this being a major contract, they chorused, "Very suitable Sir Joshua."

"Of course it is," he snapped not wishing any interruption, and pointing a stubby finger, "demolish that ruined house, divert the stream and so forth and remember, I want the utmost care taken over this piece of land, no burying of any rubbish or dumping residue from the construction." The chief executive bristled slightly, "That is not our company policy, Sir Joshua." It brought a snide rejoinder, "Am I correct in recalling your company being fined two million dollars last year for a toxic spillage?"

The question was ignored. Cocking his head, the Nuen chairman expanded on his latest theme, "You see getting away from the packaged holiday throngs appeals to those with sensitivity, escapism if one wants to call it that, it's the in thing, and as my main contractor you should bear in mind that ultimately, once this place is carefully landscaped, I shall build a concourse of exclusive holiday bungalows, facilities to match, swimming pools, etcetera."

His hand swept over the plan, "and this flat area which at the present is a totally worthless expanse of grass and sand dunes, I shall lay out as a golf course. I shall call it, Oceanic Paradise. In years to come, once the place has been knocked into a civilised shape, I shall also incorporate a luxury timeshare complex."

"Naturally Sir Joshua, any future venture will receive our closest attention," the chief planner smiled ingratiatingly. "Our record in tasteful developments is second to none; you may be aware that we are the consultants involved in Dubai's visionary new city."

Goldberg merely grunted. Half a head shorter than the company executives, he drew himself up and turning from one to the other, "Gentlemen, I find myself reasonably satisfied with your final designs. I insist however on immediate action, move in your heavy equipment, the site clearance must begin at once, and kindly do not use adverse weather as an excuse for any delay."

Much civility escorted Sir Joshua from the consortium's top storey offices. Ticking over on their forecourt waited his personalised Bentley, SJG, 1. The newly engaged bodyguard held open a rear door, and taking an elbow, helped a wheezing Goldberg into his limousine. Behind darkened windows Goldberg settled himself deep into its leather upholstery, "Downing Street!" he ordered his chauffeur.

Oil spilling into the Gulf, financial meltdown, renewable energy mania, never had there been a better time to turn the screw on politicians and taxpayer alike; the initials, PFI had an appealing ring, music to his injured pride. The side of a red bus loomed over the Bentley. Goldberg leant forward, "Kindly remember driver you're not employed to give way to London Transport, my time is valuable."

Yes, he assured himself, Private Finance Initiative, how accommodating of the Chancellor to dream up such a clever wheeze for keeping some of the Nation's debt off his capital account, so helpful towards getting a handsome return on one's outlay. Let the taxpayer get a taste of the cost of borrowing, turn up the rate, this countrys' been living on handouts too long, everything on the cheap, NHS is a classic, turned UK into a troupe of malingerers, they require a smart lesson in paying for what they get, a Nation in need of his expertise must be taught a lesson in economics.

This surge of righteous indignation brought on an attack of panting. Sir Joshua glared at the wrought iron gates of the Nations political playpen, he was no longer a behind the scenes Scientific Advisor to an outfit of amatures. Soon they would know the strength of his financial muscle.

Taking an elbow the chauffeur helped him alight.

CHAPTER FIFTY-TWO

Scattered or taken

Darkness and driving rain, I wrenched frantically at the boarding nailed over the house door. 'No Admittance' jeered at me. I ripped the sign off, flung it to the wind. Berserk, in bare - handed fury, I beat and tugged. The nails held. Nothing came away. More frantic wrenching, blood ran down my arm. Unable to see clearly, I gave up for the moment. My heart pounded. Hurriedly I checked. Every window in the place and the byre door, nails and boards! A clap of thunder grumbled away south. Eilidh stood dripping, Eachan tucked beneath her oilskin. They needed shelter. I must get them some form of shelter.

Lifting the table I carried it round to the lee side of the house; still raining at least it was out of the wind. Furniture, books, clothes and all our possessions were heaped on top of each other to form a bonfire, obviously ready for burning. I dragged our sodden mattress from under the chairs, lugged it round and squeezed it in below the table, a tarpaulin covered the table top and down the sides. Nothing dry to lie on, I delved amongst the heap.

Bursts of heavy rain swishing in across the bay rattled on the kitchen utensils. In spite of my hurry I moved things carefully, searching for something which might just be dry. Our two easy chairs were near the bottom. I pulled one from the pile. Our bedroom mirror lay in pieces amongst some of Eilidh's clothes. Even in the blackness, drops of blood from my bleeding hand showed up on one of her white blouses. It needed a bandage.

I raked the jumble for a bed sheet to rip. My hand felt a piece of leather. Even in the dark I knew it, my cursed briefcase!

Plastered hair, rain dripping off the end of my nose I groped for a strap, jerked it free. Flap and lock hung open. I thrust inside. Empty. All my notes, the research papers on the dangers of nuclear waste storage, gone. Scattered or taken? I stood up, felt the rain run down my neck, my spine, for the first time that chilling night, I shivered.

More hasty delving, an old cupboard lay on its front. I dragged out dampish towels and blankets and hurried them round to the makeshift shelter. Handing the boy to me, Eildh took them and vanished under the table. Her head popped out a minute later, "That's the bed ready." I patted her soaking hair, "Won't be long, I'm away down to unload the boat." As so often before, I ran to the jetty, this time without a lightness of heart. By the orange flash of a fish farm beacon I washed my cut hand in the sea and after unloading the Hilda, pulled a tarpaulin over our pile of stores.

Heedless of the weather, I stood on the edge of the jetty watching the Hilda. Each tug on her mooring ropes shed amber droplets of rain. Streaks of orange reflection across the bay glistened on her varnished planking, timbers which had known the shores of a tree clad fiord. The long poem written by my great grandfather of the old women frozen beneath a larch tree, her sacrifice for a new born child, wandered through my head. The swish of gusting rain played on the water, first beside me, then somewhere far away. In its lulls and flurries the larches swayed, and autumn needles fell thick and auburn on a carpet of hidden memory.

Shaking the rain from my hair I jogged back to the house and stripping off, wrung the water out of shirt and trousers before crawling gladly beneath the table. Eilidh's warm body greeted me and with the boy snuggled between us, to the pelting of rain on the tarpaulin, we slept.

"Do you mind telling me where you found these papers?" "Found, Sir Joshua, found?" the blank expression on the face of a Downing Street Permanent under Secretary suggested he intended to be both evasive and strictly official, "We do not find such things. They were merely obtained." At the stiffness of tone Goldberg snorted, contempt filling the pools of his dark eyes. "And may I remind you, Sir Joshua," the Secretary showing just a trace of condescension, "they have been obtained partly at your request to the past P.M., quite some time ago as I recall."

Realising his question had been blocked by the last remark, Goldberg countered, "I take it you will have copies of them?" The man rose, height and hauteur looked down on his questioner. "I am not personally aware of that, Sir Joshua." At Goldberg's eye level his Adams apple yo-yoed up and down a scrawny throat. "Is there anything else you require?" Such an obvious and pre-emptory dismissal left the Nuen Chairman only capable of choking out, "I think not." Without further word he gathered the papers into his briefcase, turned his back on the official and stood waiting for the man to open the door.

That evening Sir Joshua sat alone to dinner. "Table for one!" he'd barked at the Head Waiter of London's top West End restaurant. "That one over there in the corner, if you please." "I'm sorry Sir, that table is reserved." "Nonsense," snapped Goldberg, "find whoever it is and move them elsewhere." Knowing from regular visits this customer's taste in expensive wines, though not noted for leaving any 'consideration', the waiter bowed, "as you wish sir."

Under the watchful eye of his personal bodyguard sitting out in the foyer Sir Joshua drew from his briefcase the papers which he suspected could prove critical, thoughts of which had thoroughly spoiled his dinner, so much so he'd called the Head Waiter to complain about the fish course. Now, flicking page over page, his face grew tense. He digested the salient projections of this confounded MacKenzie's research work.

As he'd feared at his only reading of its conclusions on the day of meeting this interfering fellow in Downing Street, these deductions must not ever, ever be seen by any other person. Momentarily the whereabouts of this scientist, if he still existed, clouded his mind. The answer he'd been given to a casual but highly discreet enquiry at top level in an office along the Thames, "the matter is in hand," was not altogether reassuring. Likewise his relaying of the location of ex-chairman Anderson to his US contact had drawn a non-committal response. However that was a totally different issue, mentally blanking it off, he gulped wine and read on.

The supremely agile mind of Nuen's chairman was alarmed. Below the table his knee twitched unnoticed and unstoppable. The utterly exhausting work of getting the waste storage plans over so many hurdles, he rested his forehead on a sweating palm. The calculations which MacKenzie had given on storage density of enriched waste and possible temperatures could not be contained comfortably within Nuen's design without reducing intake. Cut intake, cut profits, a bead of sweat fell on the papers. He thrust them savagely into his own brief case. "Tomorrow," he growled, "for this little lot, it's the incinerator."

Sitting back he took stock of his thoughts. Of course he'd sanctioned the cutting of corners, albeit by a tacit nod, never on record. Far too late to change anything now, go back to square one. 'Never, never!' screamed inside a bursting head, utterly impossible; his shares would crash, his chairmanship under threat, oh my God.

Safety and profit, forever a damn difficult mix, there was no such thing as a hundred percent safety, the totally unforeseeable, now that always made an excellent alibi; if this whole nuclear process had one factor built in, it was uncertainty.

An equally nimble minded bodyguard followed Goldberg out of the restaurant, "Shall I carry your briefcase, sir?" he enquired quietly touching its handle. His startled client jumped aside, "Certainly not."

To the bodyguard's ear Sir Joshua's voice seemed unnaturally shrill. "As you wish, sir," the man said softly.

CHAPTER FIFTY-THREE

Where life is young there's hope

Sometime during the early hours the storm had passed away to the east, and at first light we crawled from beneath our table shelter, to the scent of tangle freshly washed upon the beach. Pulling on wet clothes and leaving Eilidh sitting on the table top feeding the baby I rounded the gable with a marked reluctance. Soaking furniture met me, ruined books and clothes mixed amongst the sticks of what had made a home- all were heaped yards from the boarded doors and windows, but by whom? Presumably the Sheriff Officers had paid a visit, but who was behind our eviction? The fish could be owned by a multinational operator and they might well require an onshore base. Supposing we were in their way, even by the usual steamroller tactics which money and power was capable of adopting, this approach seemed drastic.

Last night's rage lapsed into a morning's bitterness. Standing in the grey before sunrise, I saw the shambles of our belongings in a wider perspective. Ruined furniture, the gutting of a house, it meant less than the loss of sanctity which existed on the island. We saw ourselves as guardians of an integrity which demanded respect of the land, its wildlife, the dead of generations to whom it was body and soul. Not for the first time I brooded, were we as outdated as flat earth believers, the dupes of an intangible nostalgia, back to nature sun worshippers via a solar panel?

Unwillingly I raised my head. Out on the bay, beyond the back of an upturned chair, the catwalks of three fish cages merged with an empty Atlantic. I gazed upon the purple horizon which comes with sunrise and wondered, join the morbidity of yesterday or be in the never, never land of tomorrow conversing to robots. What lost, what gained?

Poor Eilidh, she came round and leant against me, young Eachan in her arms. Could we pick up the pieces,begin again? Our conversation, such as it had been, did not touch on the possible abandoning of Sandray, I fancied the prospect would be difficult for us both to contemplate and left it unsaid. Eilidh straightening her shoulders, passed the boy to me and pulled his crib from under the chest of drawers, "It's hard to credit but this must be the work of the Sheriff Officers," her voice sounded matter of fact. "I never believed they would get round to doing anything, not once we were established," and viewing the fish cages her tone changed to one of defiance. "It's all part of a takeover."

I caught her mood, "Eildh, if you think yourself and the boy will manage, we'll take back the house." At once her eyes flashed with a fighting gleam and tossing back her hair, "Manage?" she echoed, "Hector as the old folks used to say, we've never died a winter yet," adding with a note of mischief, "What's more our tattie crop is ready for lifting."

Hammer and wrench, door first, windows next and we stepped inside, our footsteps hollow on bare boards. The house felt tainted, sullied by the attitude of those alien to things the old folks held dear. Marks on the wall showed where the dresser belonging to my great grandfather had stood. It was not so much the flinging out of dresser itself which saddened me, boxwood and the best they could afford, but rather that my ancestor and his family would have sat beside it. Poor folk in material terms, wealthy in a way which no longer finds expression.

The sink remained intact. I tried the tap. We had water. Whilst Eildh sat on the worktop feeding young Eachan, I began lugging in the vitals of living, gas cylinders and the cooker for a start. A quick trip to the jetty for a box of food, in no time I stirred oatmeal porridge and cracked eggs into a pan to give the boy his first taste of solid food. By mid morning the warm westerly breeze rippled through a line full of clothes and using the boarding which had barred the door, I got a fire going to dry our mattress. With due ceremony their No Admittance sign added to the flames. Laughter lifted our spirits, "Never realised we had so much furniture, wouldn't enjoy a shipwreck." Before evening I'd dug half a drill of tatties. That night laced with butter they could not have tasted better.

After supper we sat talking. Muille who'd spent an equally damp night curled at our feet beneath the table, stretched warm and dry on the wooden floor. The dunes blanked out any lights in the bay, only the natural darkness at the window and the odd bold star; we were a family unit, back home.

Days passed in bringing back some order to our living space. Ignoring the whine of the heavy outboard engines of the fish farm's inflatable boats proved more difficult, the more so for flocks of wading birds down from the north and crowding the beach to rest. Often their startled alarm notes amidst a cloud of wings rising above the dunes warned us an inflatable had rounded the headland. Nor did our seal colony venture back to their roost. Valuable salmon stocks required frequent inspection and their automatic feeders refilled with pellets.

Apart from checking on Hilda at the jetty we restricted our visits to the beach to when the bay happened to be clear. Knowing that sludge would gradually accumulate beneath the fish cages, swimming lost its appeal. Moreover that night of storm sweeping across the fish cages had washed several empty five gallon drums to the foot of the dunes. Their contents were not stated, perhaps chemicals for the treatment of sea lice. Burying them deep, I could only guess.

Short days gave the pleasure of sitting together each evening. An Atlantic high settled over the Minch and although the sun hid for a short part of the day behind the Hill of the Shroud, the air turned still and uncommonly mild. Such was Eilidh's enthusiasm for catching the good drying weather it required me to extend the clothes rope. The curve of washed blankets, not to mention a generous contribution of nappies enlivened the view from my sheep round. It pleased me to see a line of white squares flapping from the gable, I told myself where life is young there's hope.

Adjustment to the changes came not without regrets; most acutely we felt the disturbance to the wildlife. To offset bouts of pessimism, I modified my old rucksack and hoisting it onto my back with Eachan strapped to the frame we'd walk over the ridge to the east side of Sandray. The Viking landing, as I christened it, remained untouched. One afternoon when the sun dabbled on the ripples, we swam in the warmth of a sea heated all summer. Whilst I floated, Eilidh would hold the boy on my chest and without fear of the water his delight was obvious. There was none to hear our laughter and wrapped in towels, we sat amongst the rocks.

The seaweed rose and fell. An incoming tide swilled gently amongst the rock pools. The westering sun turned floating strands to golden tresses and unknowing of our presence, a family of otters twisted and played in the shallow waters; lithe dark bodies, they were in our thoughts as we walked back over the ridge to a sunset which spread deep crimson over the vast Atlantic ocean.

CHAPTER FIFTY-FOUR

"Bloody hell in this ruin?"

A distant whine rapidly swelled to deafening roar, slates on the roof reverberated. A plane about to crash? Mid morning coffee on the table three weeks after our island return, "Outside!" I bawled above the ear drumming racket bearing down on us. Eilidh grabbed a crying child and we fled from the house.

A helicopter hovered over the rooftop. Suspended beneath it a massive container, not fifty feet above our heads; the pilot appeared uncertain. He banked slightly before flying across to the flat machair ground. Hardly had he eased the container onto the ground before a second helicopter cleared the shoulder of the hill. Another container was followed by a third machine. We stood aghast, Eilidh trying to soothe a boy who had not heard noises other than the cry of sea birds.

Terrified sheep panicked. Whirring blades and an unholy racket, at first they'd scattered, running wildly into the fences, until finally they packed together at the top corner of the field. Poor brutes, should I let them out to the hill ground? Muille had vanished. Eventually I put my hand on the head of a shaking animal cowering under our bed. Nothing would coax her to come out. Moving the sheep without her help would be impossible. By evening the machair had sprung a crop of huge steel boxes.

I reasoned they must have been lifted from a ship on the east side of the island, its speed and efficiency resembled that of an army invasion. Early darkness halted their operation. Dismay filled our conversation. The oil lamp threw our shadows onto bare kitchen walls.

After supper I walked across the machair to the sound of the tide, nothing more, the bird life had fled. Rows of great oblong boxes, massive end doors heavily padlocked. I ventured amongst them, my mind searching for their purpose. Was this to be a base camp, part of a Nato exercise? I leant against cold metal.

Out of the darkness came a solitary whistle, high above me once again the creatures of the northlands were passing. I listened, alone with the starlight, feeling their kinship and hoping; no calling came, nothing to tell me, no sound save the breathing of the night.

I retraced my steps.

Sculptured crags reached down the hillside, long shadows, old in the moonlight.

Rows of containers, square in profile were behind me,

shadows of a coming age.

Ghastly newspaper headlines were the last thing Sir Joshua needed to jolt him horribly awake. In bed, propped on the pillows of a luxury hotel overlooking the River Clyde, he scanned the morning papers whilst awaiting his breakfast tray. Glasgow's Sunday Herald blazoned it, 'Dangers of nuclear waste disposal exposed.' The newspaper shook in trembling hands, his eye ran down the edge of each column, an increasing anger vented itself as he read. "Bastards, sneaking bloody journalists, it's all a plot, they've been put up to it," he ranted on, "Greenpeace or some such crowd of head- in -sands fools,"

Minus technical detail the article summed up much of the findings in the MacKenzie papers he'd been given just days previously.

How the bloody hell had this information surfaced? The whole business of developing a nuclear waste depositary had to be kept out of the public domain, at least until construction was well underway. That was vital. Everyone from the stupid anti nuclear lefties in the House of Commons to those Nuclear Disarmament activists, they'd all be braying like donkeys, encouraging these dangerous protester types, the rent a mob layabouts, marches, placards, hooligan campers. A vision of the possible disruptions raced through his mind, most especially the extra costs cutting into profit. "This is absolutely bloody well intolerable, this leak has to be plugged. Now!" his shouting reached a tearful crescendo, "Can't even trust the fucking Treasury, they might delay payments, haven't had a penny out of the bastards so far, they'll ruin me." The extent of his swearing, a measure of his exasperation.

Flinging bed sheets and newspaper to one side, Goldberg grabbed his calling device, pressed its emergency button and stumbled over to the hotel bedroom's security locker. Briefcase still there, the key, the key, yes, still in his wallet, feverishly he tried the lock. It refused to turn, the damn case was already open. I wouldn't have left it unlocked. He cursed, ripped back the flap. The papers remained inside. Had they been rifled? He began shuffling through them.

Seconds later the bedroom door opened, a man entered and quietly relocked the door behind him, "You all right Sir?" In his fright Goldberg dropped the briefcase and turned. "Perfectly," he managed to blurt out and staring at the man in alarm, "Who the hell are you?" Eyeing Sir Joshua carefully, "Your bodyguard sir?" he replied. Goldberg gathered himself together and realising the indignity of standing naked, "Pass my dressing gown!" he snapped, and draping it over his shoulders, "You're not my regular bodyguard." "No sir, your usual security cover has," the man's eyes flickered momentarily, "has decided to leave our employment."

How much had his previous bodyguard learnt? Always thought him a sly, cunning devil, hanging about within earshot. Had he gone through my briefcase? Alerted at once to the possibility of blackmail, an inwardly panicking Sir Joshua struggled to keep authority in his voice, "I want that man arrested, immediately." His new bodyguard frowned, "That will be difficult sir." "Why?" demanded Goldberg, his pitch rising. "He left the country yesterday." "What!" a frightened Chairman was now shouting, "I'll speak to, er, to London at once. Where's he gone?" "I'm not sure Sir, it could be anywhere," the bodyguard watched his client without blinking, "for all I know it might have been Tehran." An icicle of fear stabbed Goldberg, "Tehran," he echoed weakly.

A man wearing a safety jacket and yellow helmet confronted me at the door. "You live here, mate?" his question expressed a note of incredulity. I nodded. "Bloody hell, in this ruin?" he attempted to look past me. Eilidh, carrying the boy, appeared at my elbow. Astonishment registered on his face, "Pardon the language lady, but Christ Almighty you don't live with a nipper in this, this?" He considered his words, "Is it not a bit of an outlandish dump of an island?" The coldness in Eilidh's blue eyes seemed lost on the man. He shook his head in apparent amazement.

All day the airlift had continued. Heavy plant arrived, earth moving machinery, dump trucks, all manner of equipment was slung onto the machair. Teams of men landed. What appeared to be construction material was unloaded from the containers before helicopters whisked empty boxes aloft and disappeared back over the shoulder of the hill. We could only watch in disbelief. This was no army exercise. Our work about the croft halted. I'd been down checking the boat in the early morning and had sat awhile contemplating the fish cages and now a village of steel containers." It's final decision time," I'd said to Eilidh at breakfast. Equally despondent she'd agreed.

Whatever might be this man's authority in the fast developing scene, he stood on the doorstep as though attempting to come to terms with finding us here. "They gave me to understand the island was unoccupied." "Well it's certainly not," I spoke for the first time. The construction foreman, or whatever might be his role in this invasion, dropped his gaze and speaking deliberately, "You have a problem. My instructions are to site our workers camp kitchen right here, and pronto. This house has to go." "Go, go where?" harshness sharpened Eilidh's voice. The man swung round on his heel and speaking over his shoulder, "Into the ground lady, tomorrow. Sorry, but that's my orders. Please yourselves." Dumfounded though we were Eilidh reacted, "You'll need brute force to get us out," she called after him. Stopping at ten paces, he looked back, "We'll see."

Back in the kitchen I hugged the girl, waltzed them both round the room, desperate as our prospects had become, we laughed. Eilidh's eyes glinted, wild with fight, "They'll need to attack us with a bulldozer." The visitor's threat served to raise our fighting spirit. We'd sit it out, see what happened. Lunch was eaten to the drone of heavy diesel generators, by four in the afternoon gangs of halogen lights blazed over the machair. Last thing at night I stood on the doorstep. Headlights illuminated the hillside, diggers and earth moving machines were in operation. Talk, talk, and try to sleep, it's either some projected military base or a major wind farm we decided. Men on shifts worked round the clock and darkness pounded with engines.

First light, I came hurrying back indoors, "They've cut through our fences, there's yards of it ripped apart. The machines are starting to drive a road up the hillside, all the sheep are out on the hill." Eachan was getting his morning feed, her stoic comment surprised me. "There's plenty grazing for them, they'll be happy on the fresh ground and if we don't remove them," she smiled, "good luck to them, Sandray's their home."

Another two days passed. By choice we remained virtual prisoners at the house. Our initial cheer began to wane. Disgust was telling. The contents of the containers, to much hoisting and hammering, became accommodation units, squat prefabricated buildings. Vehicles roared about, tearing up centuries of wild flower grassland and nesting homes. Bulldozers skimming the turf pushed it and piled it onto the dunes, we presumed to create a windbreak for what was fast becoming a village of huts. The scale and speed of the operation left us dazed, not least by the loudness of its range of noises. Any sounds of the sea were lost. More astoundingly, by afternoon we could see machinery being landed on the Hill of the Shroud. A beacon of change, that night its plateau blazed under a gantry of ark lights which obliterated the stars.

Eilidh pleaded with me not to climb to the hill, but late the following morning I was determined. We were witnessing no ordinary development, this was something totally different. It demanded that I confirm my strong suspicions. In shepherd style, Muille trotting at heel, I strode off. A massive gouge in the land was already winding its way up the hillside. Ahead of us four machines were grinding and tearing. Steel screeched rock, huge blades flashing in the early sunlight heaved heather and boulder aside. One moment I could smell fresh earth, the next a billow of diesel fumes poured down on me. A dozer driver lifted his hand. I waved back, though chose not to walk on the scar they were creating.

Rounding the shoulder I climbed the last few hundred feet and onto the hill's broad summit. Machines were busy scraping its surface down to bare rock. Vast amounts of spoil had already been bulldozed over the ravens' crag to form a heap about its base. A thin carpet of moss and alpine plants hugging the ground to beat an Atlantic gale were no match for a steel blade and two hundred horsepower. I stood on the edge of a hilltop, torn and bleeding, aghast at the power of machines to destroy in a few hours ten thousand years of nature's moulding.

On the far side of the cleared area a group of men in yellow safety helmets seemed engrossed in conversation around a small fat man waving his arms, minus a helmet, I noticed. At a little distance from them a helicopter sat parked, its blades drooping as a dragon fly might alight on a summer pond, I thought wryly before walking a few steps to look down on our Viking bay of the swimming trips. Beyond where white sand and turquoise turned to the ultramarine of deeper water a large, wide decked freighter lay to her anchor, obviously the source of the containers and much else. Several landing craft driven onto the shelving beach had their ramps down on the sand. A wealth of activity, hurrying men and crawling machines.

I remembered my strange vision on the morning I first gazed upon this bay; the Viking galley who'd brought my forbears was drawn up, and the wading ashore of men, sword and helmet, and the Raven of the crags; all was locked in me, in my blood, my genes and my lips drew tight in sorrow. And all to come to this; another conquest, no bare hands to build and till the land, just biddable levers and their gaping mandibles ripping open the ground; already down on the beach, a huge caterpillar tractor crunching its way over the rock pools left a wide stain on the clear water. I thought of the starfish we'd seen, bright orange on the clean sand, the multitude of tiny creatures that lived by its pureness, and the otters playing.

Hard fingers caught my arm, "How did you get here? This island is totally out of bounds to anybody. You're trespassing. Anyway who the fuck are you?" engrossed in thoughts I'd been unaware of his approach. I shook him off fiercely. The snarling voice fitted the twisted mouth of a bullet headed brute of a fellow, cropped hair and flaring nostrils. We stood unmoving, breathing deeply, eye to eye. One false move, he would attack me. Tight beside me I heard Muille softly growling. Minutes passed. Attack him or defend myself? A fat little man waddled across and appeared at this thug's elbow.

Putty face, black hollow eyes and the squatness of a toad, in a split second I recognised him, "Goldberg!" his name breathed out of me in utter astonishment. A rotweiller awaiting his order to spring, the brute's eyes flicked down to his scientist master. The hooded eyes of this loathsome specimen was busy searching my face. Suddenly he staggered backwards, his pallid face, white and frightened in total shock. So extreme the reaction- was he seeing me as a ghost? His flabby mouth trembled, formed my name, "MacKenzie." A second later he began screaming, "Damn you, damn you, you bloody meddling scientist, you should be, should, should…!" His flow reduced to a stare.

"Should be, dead!" I barked the word, 'Dead!' It spiked the air, "Is that the word you missed saying, my friend?" Both must have seen my eyes aflame. A panicking Goldberg howled at the brute, "Arrest this man, arrest him!" The thug began reaching inside his jacket. Quick as a gun cleared its armpit holster, my fist was quicker, force and crunch, his jaw sagged, broken.

He lunged at me. Muille flew at his ankle. A moments distraction. I caught the upswing of wrist and gun. Crack, a bullet whistled into space. Twist and throw, the brute hit the ground, dropped his revolver, Goldberg screamed, "Get him, get him you useless bastard!" The man lay groaning, I'd snapped his wrist. Goldberg grovelled for the revolver. Nothing could stop me. One swift dive, I grabbed him. Killing madness, bare hands, I had Goldberg's throat. Grip, squeeze, squeeze, I was throttling him in the insane joy of killing. Shouting men were running across. Snake black eyes were bulging.

"Hector, Hector!" Eilidh's call reached me from far below. I flung Goldberg aside. A quaking heap, he sprawled at my feet, struggling for breath. Utter loathing blazed in his eyes, a furnace of hatred consumed him. In a voice croaking with pain he gasped, "This will finish you." The fallen revolver lay within reach. Still panting, he made a grab for it. Abruptly I became rational. Kicking the revolver out of his reach, I spoke loudly, the men were almost on me, "Self defence, pure and simple my dear Goldberg, here's my witnesses. Try it," and I swung back down the ridge. Eilidh carrying the boy climbed towards me.

Careless of the steepness I bounded towards to her. Spats of turf flung into the air at my heels. The sharp crack of a revolver sounded somewhere above. Madness, one of them was shooting. A puff of dust a yard at my back, another shot, splintered rock whined into the hillside. "Keep away, keep away!" I screamed at Eilidh, leaping zig-zag down the slope rock to rock.

Out of range I stopped. Chest and heart pounded. Shading my eyes I could see the squat Goldsmith surrounded by men standing defiantly on the rim of their hilltop operations. Eilidh hurried down by a different route. I ran over to her. Words jerked out, "Eilidh, Eilidh woman, you saved me from strangling someone." By her gasp of dismay I must have sounded insane.

The cold realisation I'd just committed a brutal assault led to a fit of uncontrollable shaking. My legs almost gave under me. Truly frightened Eilidh took my arm, supporting me, "You're wounded, where, where?" I shook my head, "No, no, I'm OK thanks, they're rotten shots." I felt far from joking, nor did Eilidh laugh. I straightened and taking her hand, "Eilidh you saved an unholy tragedy, I'll tell you everything in a little. Let's get home."

Rubbing the boy's head in fatherly affection, I took him on my back. Too much had happened for a conversation until our minds could settle. We retraced the morning's anxious steps. The sheep now were spread across the Hill of the Shroud in twos and threes, Muille eyed them, as collie dogs will, and waited my command. "Not today Muille," her dark quick eyes met mine and she gave a wag of her tail. What would be the fate of our flock? The first browns of winter tinged the hill, wild fescue had seeded and un-grazed these many years, it rustled at our feet.

As we walked spokes of afternoon sunlight were thrusting from a tiny blue window in a sky of great rolling clouds. Often on the shepherding days when time was as at my heel, I'd watch their moving pools of brightness glide across the sea. That afternoon of all days, above the western horizon, lines of ragged grey crept slowly amongst mighty white towers changing their shape and colour. One by one the streams of light, which had danced their brief moments on the sea, were driven behind the clouds.

Even before we crossed the last ridge the mechanical clanking reached us. The house roof came in sight, a few more steps brought us to a halt. The arm of a digger, pawing the ground at the back wall of our building, had already opened a massive hole. A sizeable bank of earth covered part of what had been my potato and turnip drills. Curling into air I could see a length of black piping. Our water supply was cut.

We tramped past the mound of earth. The machine operator lifted his hand, the hydraulic arm reached into a deepening hole. Here and there the white of a potato showed, cabbage which would have seen us through the winter topped the pile. Apart from the noise, round at the front of the house everything remained as we'd left it, unusual shells on the window ledges and drift wood which had taken our fancy, waiting to be carved, nothing of value, except in pleasure.

Not for the first time I studied the lintel above the doorway, rough dressed stone hand cut from the raven crag, dragged down the hillside. Find a shelter, survive and build a home for your family; that was the way of it. How easy to pull a lever, destroy in one hour's comfort a generation's work of callused hands.

Reluctant to enter the old house for what I knew would be the last time, I sat on the stone at the end of the gable, my thoughts dwelt on the visions it had brought to my folks. The day of my first visit with Eachan I'd noticed the stone. My slight knowledge of geology told me the stone wasn't of the local rock.

Almost as if impelled I studied the stones shape. Although weathered by unknown years of winters' gale and salt the faint marks on its surface suggested it had been cut to fit a purpose. The same prompting seemed to be telling me it had belonged to some ship's ballast. Certainty came me, the stone had arrived aboard the first longboat to beach on Sandray, the raven's boat of my great grandfather's story, a Viking stone.

Eachan stood at my side as I'd seen him at his crofthouse window looking in horror across to the island on the day he died. The remains of a burning sunset were quenched in an undulating sea of molten iron. Beneath it sank a black sun, and the lava like coagulation turned to the green of verdigris. All about me on its rotting surface the white fish floated, belly up.

Eilidh put her hand on my shoulder, "This is it, Hector," she said simply. The power of the vision had dazed me. Hardly back in our present grim situation, I followed Eilidh into the old house. There seemed little to gather. A few clothes were stuffed into bags, the odd book we'd saved, Hector's crib. My great grandparents' table and dresser, fashioned from shipwreck planks and worn by scrubbing, they were better to stay where they belonged.

One journey to the jetty took all our belongings barring the crib, which I placed on the stone. Eilidh busied getting the Hilda ready. Footsteps back to the house went unnoticed. I stood in the kitchen, the wounds of this day would not heal. Tigh na Cala, House of the Haven, a shelter to birth, a presence at death; love and sorrow entangled. Evening shone through the window, patterned light crossed the floor, fell bright upon the mellow walls of age. I stepped outside and closed the door; never a lock or key, always a welcome. The mechanical arm dug a grave.

Round to the yawning crater I walked, surely he must be near the final bucketful. I motioned to the digger driver. He stopped his machine and after an obvious hesitation climbed down. "Sorry about this lot," he appeared a trifle upset. "It's not your fault, but I'd like to show you something." He followed me to the gable end, "Please save that stone. Just put it to one side, I'll be really grateful," adding, "If its not too difficult, try and save that doorway lintel." The driver glanced anxiously to where a township of huts was taking shape, "OK mate I'll try, if the foreman doesn't show up, he's a hounding bastard." "Thanks," I had no cash to offer him; somehow he didn't seem that type.

Thinking him a decent chap, "This is some operation," I commented by way of a question. "Blimey, you've said it mate, it's all rush and hush with this outfit." He sounded a

Londoner. "You're far from home." "Too fucking far," he pulled a face, "the missus isn't well and I need the remoteness pay. I've worked in some corners but this bloody dump is the end of the earth." I swallowed his opinion, "What's going to be built?" "Ain't got a clue mate, nobody's been told and the buggers are just as tight with the money."

By now he'd become curious about me, "Hope this ain't your house." "You could say it is, that's why I'm hoping you'll save this stone, and maybe the doorway lintel." Shifting uneasily he shook his head in disbelief, "They're only old stones. Are you sure?" "Positive, please, if you can manage, I'll come for them soon, somehow." A bulldozer was rumbling towards the house, with a quick nod the digger driver hurried back to his cab. I lifted the Eachan boy's crib from the stone. No looking back, I joined Eilidh aboard the Hilda.

Enough noise already echoed round the bay. To the ripples of a south east breeze we left the jetty under sail. Before the headland put the house out of our sight, the arm of a digger appeared high above its ridge. Jaws opened and began ripping off the roof, lifting rafters aloft, dumping the broken bones of our home. The squeal of grating metal carried over the water. Eilidh put her head on the gunnel and cried.

A bulldozer soon would put its blade to the walls, ground levelled, job finished. The pace of the elements had passed away; the days of haste had arrived. A single hand by single day would bury a thousand years without remorse.

Only memories would remain unbroken,

in the graves of those who belonged.

CHAPTER FIFTY-FIVE

"Breached?"

Running men reached his side as a kneeling Sir Joshua took aim
for the third shot at a figure bounding down the steep hill face.
"Stop, stop shooting, there's a woman and child!" one of them
bellowed at him. "Give me the gun!" The sharp command was
enough to halt a vengeance bordering on madness. Turning
round, Goldberg, still on his knees, threw the weapon at his
bodyguard, "You useless bastard, you've let that criminal
escape, you useless, totally useless idiot."

Two of the team of engineers helped a white faced Sir Joshua to
his feet. The shrieking tirade went on unabated. Pointing to the
lurid red marks circling his throat, "That, that madman tried
to kill me, kill me. You saw him, you're my witnesses,
attempted murder, murder no less, he won't escape, I'll, I'll..."
his words stammered to a standstill.

The men glanced from one to another for several reasons, not
least the newspaper headlines which would draw attention to
operations on Sandray; none wanted to be drawn into the
fracas. His Chief Engineer spoke firmly, "I think, Sir Joshua, I,
er, indeed so far as we could see, a gun was pulled on the man
and he acted in self defence." Goldberg lashed out in a fury of
words, "Bloody traitors, loyalty, wait- wait, you'll see.." and
his words trailed into a babble of incoherence.

"Sir Joshua," the engineer waited for Goldberg to calm down
a little before saying very pointedly, "I think you should
consider the publicity angle before taking action." The quiet

remark effected a surprising change. Goldberg felt his bruised throat. Little dark eyes hid below their heavy lids and loathe to agree with other than his own opinion, he snapped at the engineer, "Help me to the helicopter. I'm going back to London immediately. Just carry on as I've instructed."

On hearing that transport was about to leave the island his bodyguard, clasping a broken wrist, spoke through the pain of his broken jaw, "Get me out of this place Goldberg, I need treatment," Glaring up into the man's face the Nuen Chairman reverted to his business tone, "As from this moment you are dismissed from my service. From now on you are free to make your own arrangements. Contact your company, just as I shall to doing to obtain redress for your obvious shortcomings. They, I presume, will cater for your travel."

"Look here," a hollow eyed Sir Joshua wearing an expensive silk cravat addressed the Chief of Britain's covert MI5 operations in a curt manner, "security has been breached at the site of our developement on a Hebridean island. I trust you are aware that the objective of our building programme must not on any account become public knowledge." The officer stood looking over the Thames, his back to a visitor who'd arrived without an appointment. "Breached?" he commented, aware it might sound offhand, "Kindly explain."

Annoyed at speaking to the back of a complacent civil servant, "I said breached!" Sir Joshua snapped, "The scientist MacKenzie whom I was assured some time ago would cause no further inconvenience has appeared at the site, no doubt as a result of the absence of adequate surveillance," he chose his words carefully, "Unfortunately we lacked the appropriate means to detain this intruder. It represents an act of wilful trespass on a top Government restricted area, all our workforce are carefully vetted, none except my leading engineers knows what is being built, but this damned MacKenzie is clever enough to guess and take steps to alert the anti-nuclear lobby. We shall have Greenpeace and their suicidal antics to cope with, think what that will cost."

The name MacKenzie instantly registered. Much to the senior officers regret one of his better agents had been lost on a failed mission to deal with this scientist. The MI5 chief frowned. Strangely his opposite number in the CIA recently alerted him to the case of a man, Anderson, also presumed drowned off the same Hebridean island. Later in the same conversation his American counterpart indicated they were following a lead on the smuggling of weapons grade uranium. He remained gazing thoughtfully towards the river. Should Goldberg be sounded out on the smuggling issue? Never forewarn any possible miscreant, no matter how unlikely they may appear. Say nothing.

The man's impertinent manner was testing Goldberg's patience, "I want all necessary steps taken to ensure there is no further intrusion. The safety of this repository and the deliveries of radio active material depend on your anti-terrorist security being one hundred percent." The Ministry Chief spun round to face Goldberg, "One hundred percent, Sir Joshua?" Nuen's Chairman found his supercilious attitude intensely annoying, the man appeared to have little concept of the extreme dangers involved in dealing with nuclear waste.

He may be chief of a clandestine organisation but the man must be brought to heel, "I said one hundred percent," Goldberg allowed the point stand alone before adding, "already certain unfortunate information relating to the storage of nuclear waste has reached the press." Calculating eyes studied Sir Joshua, "Reached the press, oh I see, by what means?"

Slightly flustered and not wishing to mention any possible connection to the briefcase documents Goldberg blustered,

"Should there be any further lapse in your security arrangements and my company's involvement again reach the media, then you will ensure that the various controllers of its outlets are suitably persuaded that we are building a relay station to cater for the electricity generated by the totally unnecessary and highly inefficient wind farms that will shortly devastate the scenery of these Hebridean islands."

The chief of UK's service walked to the door and holding it open, "I appreciate your comments, Sir Joshua," the sardonic smile was not lost on Goldberg and grossly affronted at being summarily dismissed, he paused only to say, "I shall be speaking to the Ministry of Defence later this morning by way of ensuring that the appropriate lines of communication between the two organisations are in place. I shall expect no further inefficiency regarding security."

Nothing more was said, two men parted, the one making a mental note to contact the CIA with regard to smuggling, the other suddenly concerned to be in touch with his man in charge of the last shipment of nuclear fuel to the American base on Diego Garcia.

Strange, not to say uncanny, are the wavelengths of unspoken thought.

CHAPTER FIFTY-SIX

Renewable

Outraged at being driven from home and objective, the deeper hurt of leaving Sandray had yet to come. Uppermost was our shock at flagrant disregard for irreplaceable habitats. Only crass ignorance could inflict such devastation, obliterate wild flower moorland and nesting sites without apparent concern. To those involved, Sandray must appear simply an insignificant island, remote and dispensable, ideal for some form of development, its uncontaminated state of no consequence, and what of those blameless dependent creatures? Not for us alone the hurt. We'd talked it through too often, coal, oil, wind, tide and nuclear, the more energy at man's elbow the greater his lever on global destruction.

An island taken over, no information issued, no warning given, secrecy paramount, the public fooled, kept in ignorance by political expediency? Eilidh's environmental work led her to suspect that the capital interests which dictate global destiny would soon engage in clandestine feats of geo-engineering. No consulting the masses before highly outlandish trials seeking to modify the upper atmosphere were undertaken. Deflect the power of the sun, hope to offset climate change, attempt the preservation of the unsustainable lifestyles of playtime planet. What future the young at the hands of the foolhardy in the reckless pursuit of elemental control?

A steady breeze, the headland cleared. Darkness and a winter crossing, we sailed from the liberty of self-determination and a lack of restriction. The love of nonconformity and free expression must have dominated the sea rovers who sought the edge of a known world. Wind and sea quivered though Hilda's timbers. Could we but sail on and on, find another empty island, begin again, build a home with bare hands, be free? I fought back the tears of great longing.

Eilidh and the boy crouched low before the mast, her hand white and cold on the gunnel, her arm around young Eachan. In the glimmer cast by each toss of spray from the bow her thin face shone pale and tired. Her's the intimate tears of song and poem that mirrored the grief of Highland folk severed by sheep and burning thatch from land and place; that listened to the lamentations which fed the stories of peat fire and sheiling and kept alive an affinity.

Blackness joined an island to the sky. The Hilda sailed an ocean dark as a path without a star. I looked astern, and in the tangle of our wake the specks of life which existed un-noticed by the day shed their light; the minutiae of the sea lived their few seconds of glory in the coils and eddies of our leaving; tiny phosphorous lamps, each had a moment's glow, and then no more. Yet they carried us from Sandray on a stream of golden particles, flecks of existence, powerless as a comet's tail ensnared in the warp of time and space without an edge. Each press of the breeze brought the slightest heel, we too were no more than particles in the flow of a greater ascendancy.

We sailed beyond the timescale of that night. To each pulse of conscious form is given a measure. Within the realm of particle decay and rebirth are the constructs of thought. To each particle is a lifespan entangled in a flow of energy, it binds the infinitesimal to an immeasurable. Two extremes bonded in the mystery of an unending change veiled by the swirls of cosmic dust which gave rise to a conscious being.

The golden specks trailed astern; out of the swell there rose an inexpressible calm. The sea around me seemed old and wise.

Late as we'd arrived, the table of Ach na Mara supper was laid for three. After Ella's tumultuous hugging of Eilidh and young Eachan, I teased her, "You're having guests tonight woman." "Yes, and it's yourselves," her face rosy with excitement, "I knew you would be here tonight." Although I'd always suspected Ella was gifted with an uncanny knack of perception, our unannounced appearance might just have been a shrewd guess. That was to change.

Supper over and although tired almost to the point of exhaustion, a little of the old treatment revived us and our talking took us into morning's hour. Eilidh and I agreed not to mention the shooting, enough was enough. Eventually we got round to describing the bulldozing of the old Sandray house. As its painful detail emerged she nodded without any sign of surprise, "I knew that would be the way of it," her eyes were downcast. "Eachan foresaw all the destruction," she leant from one to another, "I never wanted to tell it to you, it was the last thing he said to me before he went down to the Hilda that day," she took Eilidh's hand, and eventually she whispered the words, "that day he died." There was nothing to say. I sat swirling my glass, remembering the strangeness of my last day with him, our drams together and the depth of his thinking.

Silence pressed into the room, transposed the night. Even the sea was silent, nothing to break a penetrating stillness. I'd known it before, in this self same room, in this old house, by the edge of an ocean that ever murmured at its windows, built on the bones of those who'd wandered the beaches and lived by the riches of the tide. Built on the bones, the phrase repeated itself. The inner voice that speaks unbidden was guiding me through a hidden age. The people laid her in a grave amongst a ring of stones, a dark haired women, a necklace of gem stones around her neck. Sand blew, winnowing through the dunes, covering bones. I looked from the door to the fireplace, and in dread, up to the face above the mantelpiece.

Ella's whispering startled me, "Last night I saw old MacKenzie sitting on that stone at the corner of Sandray house," I realised Ella too was staring up at the sepia print. "He seemed to be looking into space," her wavering voice sounded frail, "I heard him speak," save the Viking stone," he said, "save it from a grave." Her words trailed out of existence, and slowly the Viking stone was on the ground before me. I could see the faint marks, the cuts which shaped it. I raised my eyes. A hunched figure sat, his back to me, immobile, transfixed by thought.

A sun was setting, thick, blood red. Gradually the figure grew transparent, his clothes fell away to dust, the sun's last rays passed through his form, only an image remained, a skeletal imprint of glowing bones on the indigo night.

An utterance surrounded me, as an echo in the darkness will fill the entombing walls of some ancient sepulchre, "You tamper with the force that binds the atoms of the universe. All stones set one above another will crumble, beyond the grave is life's false promise, into the cosmic abyss all will wander, roam as a wave of pure energy, destitute of hope until drawn spinning into the heart of an immutable blackness from which there is no escape, no escape." Stars shone through a rib cage. The spectre rose from the stone, turned to me. The face of the macabre image slowly became flesh. Salt stained wrinkles, the death mask of the old man. His eyes were alive.

My head spun, the world revolved, turning faster and faster, I watched the globe receding, until it seemed a faint dot amongst a whirling crescendo of golden specks. Without warning the heavens erupted, unleashing a blinding flare of cataclysmic destruction.

Horizon blue eyes, they drew me towards the brink of a swirling vortex. Around its rim spun a light of indescribable brilliance. His voice was gradually fading, "Life's purest emotion alone will survive. This is the whirlpool which devours all consciousness, the twist of an infinity through which this universe will pass, the ending which leads back to the beginning."

The words were stretching, becoming fainter and fainter, I fought to hear them, "in a flash of consummate knowledge there will be a universe reborn, strands of emotion, pure, sublime as the music of the spheres will emerge afresh, held together by the inseparable bonds of en....."

The final word receded, its ending syllables dissolved into the ripples beneath the Hilda's bow. She was heeling too far. I gripped her tiller. Pull her head into the wind. Golden specks of phosphorescence swirled around me. Only a blue intensity remained above the horizon.

Eilidh was shaking my elbow. Starting bolt upright I looked up, the same blueness was in her laughing eyes. "Hector," she smiling down at me, "you'll pull off the arm of that chair, anyway you're past sleeping, come on."

At the limits of physical and mental exhaustion, I remembered nothing more.

Next night was again without a moon as suited our purpose. Iain and I headed to Sandray. There was no need of a compass, we steered to a profile of an island created by floodlights. The summit of the Hill of the Shroud blazed like a beacon. Turning into the bay we lost the breeze. Iain at the mast had just lowered the sail when a resounding explosion shocked the atmosphere with the effect of broadside. He spoke in disbelief. "That's rock blasting, they must be knocking the top off the Shroud."

Neither of us moved. The Hilda drifted in. The slopes of the hill were totally blacked out by the gantries of arc lights ringing the summit. Giant earth moving equipment appeared to be operating in a silver void suspended between a black pit of nothingness and the darkness of the heavens. Machines made grotesque silhouettes; insects waving pincers whilst devouring their prey. We moored at the jetty to the toneless rumble of diesel generators; their fumes clung to the surface of the water on the calmness of damp night air.

"What about the sheep?" I'd worried about them since we'd left. "Sheep, they'll be away to the old village on the south side," and Iain being the typical crofter, "so long as their mouths are busy grazing just leave them alone till you see what happens. There'll be more when you come for them." Up from the shore, telescopic cranes and fork lift trucks were moving amongst the prefab huts, a night shift of working shadows. We clambered over the levelled dunes hardly able to get our bearings in the dazzle of overhead lighting. "Surely this is where the house was?" I kicked at the soil. Nothing remained, fresh earth rolled and flattened, not a trace of house, garden, fences, no stone or lintel saved, all levelled as over, a newly closed grave.

Though Iain had not asked me directly he must have wondered at my obsession with a stone. In fairness, the oddness of our mission prompted me to tell him of old MacKenzie's plea to Ella, 'Save the Viking stone from a grave.' "She might have dreamed it." I thought for a moment before revealing such personal happenings, "you know Iain I've had some strange experiences sitting under the old grandfather's photo late at night."

He laughed a little, "Eachan was always good with the drams," and then, maybe it was the incongruity ranged about us, he went on seriously, "Though I'm telling you I doubt if anyone else knows, maybe Ella herself." His manner surprised me. "When Eachan was digging the foundations for the extension he put on the back of their house at Ach na Mara, it was long since, when they first came there, before I was born, but he told me this one night," the lights shone on Iain's face. I saw he was wishing he hadn't started to tell me something of which perhaps only he knew.

"Well whatever, he was digging, it's sand of course and he went deep, looking for a foundation, though I'm telling you he came on stones, that surprised him and he dug carefully, Eachan never went past the school in Castleton but his knowledge was wide, anyway, bit by bit he uncovered a ring of stones, they'd all been placed carefully, so he recognised he was opening a prehistoric grave."

In the silence between us, the thump, thump of diesel engines beat tomorrow's excavation. "At one side of the grave, he was just scraping with his hands, he found an earthenware jar, a bell shaped pot with little slanted markings round the neck. Near it where the ground was stained he told me he'd found teeth and a few strands of dark hair and a circle of wee polished stones." I breathed deeply. All of this, before Iain's telling, I knew. Built over bones, I saw again the hair, the necklace of gem stones, the people, small dark figures, laid a woman within a circle of stones, on her side, her knees drawn up as a foetus lies in the womb. A tingle of static energy lifted the hair on my neck.

"Eachan reckoned maybe five thousand years ago, and he set to putting it back, near as he could the way he'd found it, and told nobody. You see, he didn't want teams of archaeologists swarming over the place, taking stuff away. He'd always a respect for things of the past. Anyway he'd no option, concrete founds went on top of the grave. That worried him for the rest of his life," and very quietly Iain remarked. "You know, he was given to, how will I say it, seeing things."

The house of the croft Ach na Mara built over an ancient burial site, a place of other worldly visions where spirits past and future communed with those receptive. I spoke for the first time, my words hesitant and stilted, "Iain, though I was never told this before, I knew." Garish lights flashed across the dark humps of an incoming tide which spread in yellow pools on the beach of an island carved by the ocean. Amongst the dunes, the noise of machinery made them soundless. I said nothing more; nor did Iain.

We cast about, searching wider and wider. Nothing. I'd failed to save the stone. Head back for the boat. "Hi there!" We stopped. I realised the approaching man carrying a spade was the digger driver, "You two looking for a stone?" he obviously recognised me, "Dig under that sand bank. I hid it there. Sorry about the lintel, that bugger of a foreman was watching." The driver had honoured his word. I shook his hand. "See here mate," the man sounded almost serious, "your bloody stone nearly got me the sack," and he pushed away the note I offered. Laughing with relief I informed him, "It's a Scottish bank note, worth twice as much." Eventually he accepted, "Thanks mate, I'll send it to the missus, it'll do as a souvenir of this hell hole."

Moving the stone taxed our combined strength. Two slings beneath it and we staggered down to the waiting Hilda. Below the bottom boards the stone fitted snugly across her ribs. It seemed with her new found ballast she sailed as effortless as a tiny petrel skims the waves.

In the chill early hours we placed the Viking stone at the gable of Tigh na Mara, the gable which looked to Tir nan Og, Land of the Young.

"Draw the sun blinds," Sir Joshua Goldberg snapped at his private secretary, without taking his eye off the screen. Sunshine on the Hudson River, how he cursed it, the more so when flicking through the early Wall Street trading. He'd noticed the share price of that upstart Sahara Solar Power had for the first time edged ahead of Nuen. Time for manipulation, banker friend Nicky was the man. "Wind farms, bloody sun farms," he muttered, "by God, the nuclear industry needs a war."

Since the days of Nuen's Chairman Anderson's departure their elaborate New York offices had been enlarged to include Goldberg's taste in works of fine art. Pride of place was given to a large, much admired example of Jackson Pollock's drip painting style; it occupied most of the wall opposite the room's main entrance. Rather than taking all his substantial annual bonus in cash or shares, the chairman opted for expensive oils. "Always a useful investment," he informed Nick Fellows, "nor so troublesome on the company balance sheets at the AGM."

Selecting his next acquisition was far from Goldberg's mind. The company's recent shipment of weapons grade uranium to the US base at Diego Garcia was the sole responsibility of Nuen's chief executive, the only other person privy to their strictly off the record deal. A coded message had reached Goldberg's computer early that day indicating some problem. From that moment on he became unapproachable, swearing fluently if disturbed. The fool must have cocked it up, the penalty would be diabolical. Sir Joshua re-read the message. Had their arrangements been leaked? This could mean personal ruin. He loathed digital systems, damned satellites and instant information, hacker's playground or government tool, one had nothing private any more.

Goldberg seethed inwardly, the last coded instructions to his chief executive were clear. If the nuclear arsenal of America's Middle Eastern ally discovered the switched container held lead rather than weapons grade uranium then let the middleman take the flack, the man wouldn't trouble them again. Sir Joshua paced his office. Ten million down payment on the agreement was already in his offshore account. It must be moved immediately to avoid trace. Screwing the deal, losing the outstanding forty million dollars, oh God, the acid stress burnt his stomach.

Little dark eyes slid under heavy lids. Maybe all was not yet lost. Should he play the innocent upright citizen. Expose this 'on the side' deal to the C.I.A. Speak to the Pentagon, they'd turn a blind eye, mutual interests in Middle East affairs and all that; more interestingly they might be persuaded to contribute quite a sum for his help in tracking this dastardly piece of uranium smuggling. It could be one way to claw back at least part of the forty million and absolve himself from suspicion. Goldberg warmed to the idea of revealing the deal.

There had to be a 'fall guy', so be it. If Nuen's Chief Executive had created any hitch, let him fend for himself, my word against his; as for the middleman, he was disposable. Goldberg sat down to think. This might be the wisest plan, ditch this bungler in the interests of safeguarding the great Uncle Sam and plaudits would flow. Sir Joshua toyed with the idea, after all one had to believe in exposing international criminals.

"There's a gentleman in the outer office who is insisting on seeing you, sir," the secretary sounded nervous, his employer had been in a foul mood all morning. Sir Joshua swivelled round, "Tell him, who ever he is, to go to hell." A respectful cough, his secretary hovered at the door. "What is it now?" Goldberg growled. "The gentleman gave me his card." "Bugger cards, get out!" "I think, sir," from a safe distance his secretary held out the card. Squinting over his half spectacles Goldberg could just read, Criminal Investigation Authority. His patience cracked, "CIA., Give to it me." He snatched the card. The next line read, Chief Inspecting Office, U.S.A. Security. Twinges of indigestion title gave way to a sickening jab of pain.

Avoiding further announcement a man strode into the office. Sir Joshua rose to greet him with an ingratiating smile, "Good morning. Have we met before?" The greeting drew neither answer nor handshake. Instead the tall, cold eyed visitor replied, "You got my card. I need a strictly private word with you on a matter concerning my agency." Goldberg hesitated, the card might be a fake. Nervous of a sudden attack, he avoided being alone if at all possible. Casually placing his large desk and its panic button between himself and this unexpected caller Sir Joshua briefly scrutinized the man before dismissing his secretary with a significant nod.

Instinct suggested a friendly tone, "Do sit down. Care for a coffee?" Sir Joshua smiled, always a model of gracious manners if the situation hinted problems. "No thanks, I'm here on an issue which might have serious international repercussions."

"Ah, I see. How may I help?" Still careful to remain affable, Goldberg looked concerned, and not without good reason. The officer's face showed nothing, "You are directly responsible for your company's top secret supply and movement of weapons grade fissile material, are you not?" The directness of the query sent a sickening twist of apprehension through Nuen's Chairman; he fought to appear matter of fact, "You could say so, that is the case up to a point. I'm extremely busy, I have a multifaceted business."

"Quite," the inflection implied some suspicion lay behind the comment. It was not lost on Goldberg, he clasped his hands to stop them trembling. Glancing over the office before locking Sir Joshua in a penetrating stare, the investigator used words calculated for their effect, "A quantity of weapons grade uranium is unaccounted for. We have reason to believe it has been smuggled into the Middle East, by somebody," his stare intensified, "or persons, in Nuen."

The final, 'or persons' mentally paralysed Nuen's chairman. His ashen cheeks sagged. His mouth opened as though to speak. It hung open, a glittering display of gold fillings. Recovery took many minutes. Appalled at the implications, finally he stammered, "This is, is very serious, extremely serious indeed." The CIA official remained silent, waiting, poised.

"Theft or smuggling, it's impossible, I'll have to, to.." words failed. Sir Joshua needed no excuse to manifest his total alarm. The appealing thought, not twenty minutes previous, remained uppermost. Instantly Goldberg decided. Survival, him or me, no question; the fate of Nuen's Chief Executive, sealed. There was no other means of escape. "The only person, and I truly hesitate to say this, but I find your suggestion so grave, in all honesty, though I can barely believe it, the only person who might be involved if your statement has any possible validity, is my Chief Executive."

"I see," the investigator's eye had not left Goldberg's face. "You know this man's whereabouts?" "I'm not altogether certain," Sir Joshua was regaining mental equilibrium, "his day to day movements are not my concern. He carries out his work entirely at his own discretion." Flipping a hand towards his desk, "Naturally I can easily find out."

The CIA officer stepped smartly to the door, "That won't be necessary." His last words as insidious as his parting glare, "He's not Diego Garcia by any chance?"

The door closed without Goldberg noticing. His secretary entered quietly and stood watching a man who by appearance could be gravely ill. Should he call a doctor? "Are you feeling all right sir?" His employer ignored the question, instead he barked, "I'm flying out immediately, get my plane organised!" The secretary fled the room.

Sir Joshua sat on the edge of his desk talking inwardly to himself; this needs clear thinking, if that fool chief executive hadn't totally erased their communications; that would be the only link the CIA could find. The stupid man might have kept them, safeguard himself, double cross me, blackmail. If this thing leaks, I'll need friends' right at the top, fucking politicians- the most untrustworthy of the lot, but they have their uses. Thank God the banker has sense, first job, see him face to face, shift that cash; there must be no trace, no phones or coded messages, face to face, there's nothing safe in this bloody sneaky world. Never had he felt more in need of caviar and Caribbean sunshine, nor the more in need of an emergency meeting with his banker.

"Your plane is waiting on the tarmac, sir."

Of an evening when skies were clear, I'd step from the byre and for a little time watch the southwest horizon; the pleasure derived from my first glimpse of the evening star, a lone outpost in the twilight mauve, poignant and unfailing. Did beauty exist apart and beyond us, a dimension in the cradle of creation awaiting the gift of seeing? I turned away. Venus no longer graced our southern sky, the blind arc of lights over Sandray claimed the horizon.

Both of us had abandoned scientific careers to chase an ideal. Much was to be decided, the ruination of our aspirations made us unsettled. Should we return to academic work? The guilt of having completely abandoned my team at the Hadron Collider in Geneva still surfaced at times of indecision. Likewise Eilidh was plagued by the feeling that her experience in highlighting some aspects of climate change required her drive and common sense approach. We remained ambivalent. Even if we could pick up the threads, back to the city? I'd often remarked to Eilidh, 'The first mark of intelligence is a healthy lifestyle.'

One evening as we walked the croft and summer's warmth lingered in the soil, a thin mist settled the undulating hollows of grasslands which stretched towards the night. Beyond us the dunes floated on an opaque white cloak of mist, hunched backs moulded by the dying light. From the far north a skein of geese flew in, the beating of their strong pinions brushed cool air on our faces. Splayed feet at the ready, wings angling to hit the flight path, they coasted in to land with a chatter of voices and burst of flapping to slow their descent. We laughed together. The birds, happy in their own world of chance, lifted the gloom of weeks.

I took Eilidh's hand and drew her to me, "They're home for the winter." Gently she rubbed her lips along my bare arm, "Yes, and so are we." I clasped my fingers amidst the thickness of her unruly hair, in the scent of her nearness there was peace. We had young Eachan, we had each other, and the land would sustain us.

Crofting Ach na Mara it was to be, and in the ways of Eachan. Little had changed, cows, calves, ewes and lambs, Ella, with help from Eilidh's brother Iain, managed to keep together the livestock of which the old boy was so proud. Following his footsteps would be a privilege, simple, wholesome and unhurried; fresh air by day and last thing each evening the warmth of a winter byre to fill the hay racks above each cow's head and give a scratch to their necks. Finishing for the day I'd step into starlight, snib the door and stand listening to the sea;

so to a supper grown on the croft and the long nights of knitting, reading and music.

Winter slipped into spring, the horrors of our last days on Sandray were fading. Down in Castleton we heard of tunnelling into the Hill of the Shroud and the building of a vast breakwater on the east side of the island. We didn't wish to be reminded. Reports from the local fishermen spoke of an island covered in activity and an atmosphere of secrecy. Landing was strictly forbidden. Several journalists manning a hired inflatable sped off intent on breaching the island security, only to reappear at the Castleton bar later that day with soggy note books--- buzzed by a patrol boat whose curve of spray had the wetting affect of sleet in a force eight gale. Value to the locals from story hungry journalists ran to many drams and beads of sweat on the brow of MacLeod the publican. Even an assault by Greenpeace could not provide more entertainment.

Although I joined in the fun at the bar counter, Goldberg's involvement confirmed my suspicions that Sandray was destined to be an underground receptacle for nuclear waste. This was less amusing for if this information proved correct it represented the backup for what my researches warned me was mankind's ultimate stupidity. Anger flared from time to time. I should be fighting its building, climbing their towers shoulder to shoulder with the true activists, creating maximum disruption, sacrificing my insular security in the interest of humanity. And yet here I was a chattering objector, torn between a hankering for things past and the morbid fatalism of things to come. Indecision equates with weakness, and I did nothing.

Instead of resolute action, I ranted to the ever patient Eilidh. The most deadly force known to the universe placed in the hands of greed and religious violence. Set that folly against burgeoning energy usage and the stresses of climate change, add in the escalating race towards control of global resources, and then rest fully assured no safeguard exists against human error, political insanity or the forces of nature. Succeeding generations were being handed a lethal inheritance from which there would be no reprieve. On that note my diatribes invariably ended; Eilidh would take my hand and hope the creaking old stairs didn't waken Ella.

Young Eachan was beginning to crawl about the house and pull things out of cupboards. By the following year he'd follow me about the croft and at summer haymaking, dungarees and bare feet, he'd play amongst the coilacks with his pal Muille. The house could not contain him, beach or field- the boy was happiest in the open. Modern living rumbled on without us, a tumbrel beyond our horizon. We were able to feed ourselves at small expense, our needs were few, the 'have everything ' ethos had yet to permeate Halasay living. Little did we appreciate the difficulties of those who faced the concerns of a society grappling with unemployment and the financial chaos driven by greed; to us it appeared in turmoil. Only the breaking into unscarred landscape across on Sandray and the smashing of natural systems by brute force brought us face to face with the unmasked hunger of a single species under pressure.

The years were to bring about dramatic change. Vested interests of planners and Government agencies fanned the wind of economic forces blowing from the south. A new housing estate built outside Castleton saw the precious arable of several crofts planted with eighty homes. Population was on the move, mostly from the industrial conurbations and fuelled by a property boom. Furniture vans from far a field struggled with single track roads whilst house prices soared out of reach of local pockets.

Strange names, different customs and manners, Iain and I noted the change, especially at the bar counter of the Castleton

Hotel on a sale day. Due to complaints sheep had been barred from wandering through the village, cattle kept off the roads; we, along with the few crofters who'd stuck with it, provided photograph opportunities for passing tourists as we unloaded sheep from trailers at the local auction mart. After the auctioneer's hammer fell to a dealers last nod and the livestock sold and loaded aboard the steamer, we stood at the counter enjoying a dram and admiring the cheque for a year's work. As oilskin oddities smelling of sheep we were ignored by a congregation at one end of the bar, symbolic of two cultures drawing apart.

One escalating aspect of the crofting scene I had not considered, until an avalanche of brown envelopes and swarms of visiting inspectors became a regular feature. They arrived from the mainland, spent a pleasant night on expenses at the Castleton Hotel and by coffee time an expenses fuelled car would arrive at Ach na Mara. Many of the old timers packed up in disgust, and the islands livestock number fell in step with the increase in form filling. The big picture on the mainland was the rapid advance of factory farming, we still milked a house cow and Eilidh made butter; by contrast the consumers' sugar pops enjoyed milk from the eight thousand head dairy herds of cloned indoor cattle. Price pressure from multinational operations and an avalanche of regulation- the family farmer's role would soon be that of servant to a bureaucratic control. Sadly we faced the reality that our dash for freedom on Sandray had little chance of long term success. Remote as the island seemed to us, it could not hold out against the escalation of deleterious human activity.

In day to day life at Ach na Mara, Ella lacked her old vigour, she seemed happy to be sitting all day, when of old she would be up and busy. In evenings through in the room, young Eachan sat at her knee and listened to stories of her youth. A doctor was out of the question and any hint that she might be tired was brushed off with a flurry of activity. Beneath her cheerful self we knew she missed her own Eachan and although we had no TV maybe the news filtered through. The radio reports would leave her in no doubt we were headed into a world of which she wanted no part.

The following summer witnessed the building of pylons. The blades of one- legged giants captured the winds which swept hill and peatland on islands far to the north of Halasay. The same breezes which dried our hay became the energy to light an office and power the factory; a green disguise for the footprints of economic development. By the time I had the hayfields cleared and another winter's feed safe in the barn, across the land which bordered Ach na Mara, loops of cable drooped between gangling steeples. Scenery made way for saving the planet, maybe a small price to pay in an attempt to defeat a two degree temperature rise and protect western consumerism.

Tallest of these *monuments to progress* was being erected on the south side of Halasay where the Sound of Sandray lay at its narrowest. From our kitchen window it towered above the horizon. "Atlantic gales will soon power the island, we left too soon," Eilidh didn't laugh, my cynicism wasn't funny. Presently another gigantic structure built on Sandray became a feature of the skyline, legs akimbo, wide arms of steel struts, its massive cables conquered the Sound. Its feet straddled the headland, the Viking grave of Eachan's resting lay ominously under concrete, so too the grave which he himself had covered those many years past beneath the walls of Tigh na Mara.

Ella viewed this scenic intrusion with considerable misgivings, perhaps with hidden fear. Its outline pierced the Hill of the Shroud and she would gaze from the window at the colossal triangle of girders and braces without speaking for long spells at a time. Each night when a dazzling brightness illuminated the hilltop it stood with arms outstretched, a skeleton cross against the faded starlight.

Not long after the pylon took over our southern view, we sat through in the room one evening as was our fashion. The boy had been told his bedtime story by Eilidh and I sat reading, to the click of knitting needles. Ella broke the quietness, her mind far from stitches, "I was with Eachan last night, on Sandray, just as we used to be." I lifted my eyes from the page, Eilidh glanced at me. Ella's words took us completely by surprise. She spoke with a dream like abstraction, "We talked and talked." Her eyes were closed. Poor Ella, her heart had broken. "That steel statue was over us, over the stones, above everything, pointing at the sky," she caught her breath, "and Eachan stood at the foot of that hideous cross, and looked up, 'This will be the end,' her voice broke down, "and he turned and stepped into a galley and sailed with the Raven,"

She looked down at her lap, "He gave me this golden disk," and her knitting fell to the floor from empty hands.

There was no illness. On a night when the rain filled a solstice gale and the wild Atlantic beat its drum upon the shore, Ella died peacefully, her hands clasping the gift of her dream.

The headland that took her daughter had been her wish, beside the man whom she loved. It could not be. The community gathered, many joined by the bond of blood, and we laid her amidst the leaning crosses of her forebears, and the burying ground above the wide beaches at the edge of the Sound of Sandray looked to the island of their youth.

The people sang, but to me the psalm was in the voice of the sea, and the sky drew its lament from a cloud that darkened the sun.

For these were the unknown days.

CHAPTER FIFTY-SEVEN

'I have a job to do'

"We understand that several years ago, Mr. MacKenzie you claimed salvage of an American registered yacht called 'Valkyrie' and she's presently in your hands. Is that correct?" Two ordinary looking men stood at the croft house door, smart tweed jackets but unremarkable apart from the American accent and the nature of their query. "Come in, come in," no stranger was ever left on the doorstep. "No thank kindly sir, we'd rather not," replied the spokesman of the pair. I could see the other chap studying me. "If it's OK with you, we'd like to look over the boat."

Last thing I wanted was any trouble over the yacht. Apart from sailing her round to the jetty here at Ach na Mara, I'd done no more than a little superficial maintenance. "By all means, whom I speaking to, please?" The spokesman passed me his card. I read first the name, Allan Cunningham, followed by a string of degrees, and then in complete disbelief, Chief Executive, Nuen, New York, USA.; a company I knew from research days in Geneva to be the biggest worldwide name in nuclear generation. The silent fellow chose not to reveal his particulars but I had an idea he was the reason behind whatever might be the purpose of the call.

During our walk to the jetty they both seemed markedly preoccupied, my bland comments went unheeded. I had heard sounds of a helicopter but the constant activity in connection with Sandray meant I'd paid little attention. However, crossing the dunes revealed their transport parked on the beach, they'd flown in. The executive chap hurried ahead to the chopper and rejoined us on the deck of the yacht carrying a small instrument, "Mind if we go below?"

I followed them down into the cabin and sat at the navigating table. A chart of the Indian Ocean remained spread out, just as Anderson had left it. I hadn't needed nor indeed cared to go below decks since bringing Valkyrie round to the Ach na Mara jetty. Graceful yacht though she was, many times I'd wished her elsewhere. Something about the boat, no more than a nagging unease, lacking any rational explanation. I'd passed it off as superstition rather than face the possibility that, lurking in subconscious memories, Anderson's corpse, throttled and gaping, haunted me.

The cabin smelt damp. Mould had grown over the bunks and bedding. The yacht listed slightly, the merest stir as an incoming tide crept around her keel. The air had the mustiness of decay. I shuddered. This yacht was cursed. She'd already led to a strangled corpse. My eye rested on the chart and a circle drawn around Diego Garcia, an American base, I knew the reports of alleged rendition of terror suspects. What else? Anderson's drunken threat and its menacing, 'I have a job to do' was somewhere here.

The Nuen executive swept his monitor carefully across the bulkheads, the cabin sole, into the fo'c'sle. The gadget hovered over each surface, a sentient robot delighting in profound evil. It emitted a faint ticking. A louder click, click, I recognised the sound, my flesh prickled. The Chief Executive piped in a shrill voice, "I told you, now d'you believe me?" He held the sensor poised over a section of the fo'c'sle flooring. Totally ignoring me, two heads intent on reading the dial bumped together. The rate of ticking warned me, a high level of radiation, tick, tick, tick, the clicking of a dice which only fools throw.

I stood on the jetty in the midday light of early June, glad of sunshine. They offered no explanation and, a shade flustered, Nuen's man confronted me," We've established that the owner of this yacht was a past chairman of my company, she will require to be returned to his dependents." I almost laughed in his face, he might have thought up a more convincing excuse.

Privately relief was overwhelming, "By all means, today if you wish." The silent man gave me a curious look. "Thanks for your help," and with an easy style which hardly disguised a threat, he added, "Maybe you recall your experience when you found this yacht. You won't be recalling this visit to anyone, that sure would be an unhealthy memory." They left abruptly.

I jumped aboard the Hilda and moved her clear of the Valkyrie. The pair walked smartly back to their helicopter unaware that voices carry over water. The Nuen Chief sounded to be almost pleading, "Believe me it was entirely Anderson's own arrangement, you saw the chart, Diego Garcia circled. I'd no part in it, no more part than I've had in any of J.G.'s schemes, I always follow his instructions, I'm only responsible for overseeing the handling of the material." I heard the second man grunt, but didn't catch what he'd said as they climbed aboard. A sand cloud lifted from the dunes and the chopper headed towards Sandray. I repeated the initials aloud, "J.G." and then slowly, "Joshua Goldberg."

Screeching terns had divebombed me early that morning on my visit to check the boats. A shingle area along the beach from the jetty was the bird's communal nesting site and they returned each April to the scrape of pebbles amongst which they were born, the bay where they fished. More people now strolled the beach; holiday makers came with tents, teams of kayakers swarmed into the bay, all innocent folk not realising that for the birdlife it was home. Over the years the numbers of terns dwindled and on my daily visits I took care to avoid disturbing their pebble nest in which they laid three olive eggs.

As the racket of the helicopter died away, I walked home across a beach devoid of bird life. No sharp high pitched alarm cries, the bay was eerily silent. The helicopter had landed amidst the terns breeding site. I picked my way carefully over to the shingle. Several birds who'd sat their eggs to the last moment were pulp. Scattered about were the yellow splashes of smashed eggs where the parent bird had risen in panic. Here and there a few hatched chicks crouched in the pebble hollows as my shadow fell on them. Most fledglings had been blown about the stones to their death. Other chicks far from their nests lay panting, their newly feathered wings spread out in the heat. Hoping to catch sight of the parents return, I stood for a long time looking out to sea, and an empty horizon.

Another summer and winter passed and so far as we could tell the major construction work on Sandray appeared to be finished. It was no longer such a cloak and dagger operation. Enquiries under the Freedom of Information Act as to its purpose were initially met with a blank refusal, National Security being the standard block; however thanks to internal leaks and a press campaign by the Glasgow Herald the nation now knew that a Scottish island had been developed by an American conglomerate as an international underground storage facility for highly radioactive nuclear waste. Few in the population at large had any idea of Sandray's whereabouts; anyway it was suitable remote and the news passed with little adverse comment except on the part of environmental groups and a scattering of green MP's.

Attempts to discover which politicians and government agencies had been involved in slipping decision making past the Scottish Parliament and various official planning bodies, proved difficult to unearth. Parallels were drawn with the sleight of hand which produced the Iraq war. Greenpeace called for a public enquiry but that was turned down. Tracks had been well covered.

Their imprint on Halasay life however was more obvious. Paramount to the running of the base was maximum security. Sandray Sound and the waters around the island were closed to any type of shipping. Local fishing boats, yachts, even inflatable dinghies were warned off by patrol vessels. On the hill several radar towers' scanning arms revolved continuously. Local gossip assumed the huge listening cups pointing at the sky formed some part of the facilities' protection from air attack.

The Castleton bar became a hot bed of conjecture. Heads were shaken over drams, what safety existed from an incoming missile? Archie at the end of the counter looked into his whisky, "It might even be an incoming drone." Seamus ordered another round, "Whatever that is, it couldn't be worse than that droning bugger of a politician in the hall last night."

To a catalogue of prospective disasters the troop of Halasay worthies gloomily drained their glasses. A gentleman new to the island, who perhaps considered himself better informed on the latest forms of terrorism, elaborated on the impact of an outbreak of cyber warfare. Even those listeners unfamiliar with the word 'cyber', nodded none the less when he informed them in solemn tones, "A deadly virus could infect the phalanx of computers which run the Sandray complex. That would dislocate all their programmes, the effect would be calamitous."

To allow his message to sink in he looked from one to another. They stared back in silence, until, "A virus, you mean a sort of 'flu in the wiring?" remarked Seamus feigning innocence.

"Exactly, absolutely," replied the disciple of doom, unaware the circle of locals buried their faces in pint glasses. A wide eyed Seamus broke the silence, "Well now, I'll tell you, Mr. er, er.." "Montague Cholmondly," the man interjected his name. Seamus swallowed hard, "You can't better a wee toddy for the 'flu, unless it's another one."

Much barstool debate speculated on various earth shattering possibilities, in fact almost to the exclusion of the ruinous sheep prices on the mainland. A desire to 'get my hands' on the waste dump operators frequently curtailed the deliberations at closing time. Few however of the hotel regulars had met or even set eyes on Sandray's latest occupiers; from nuclear technicians to chefs, the islands workforce operated as a closed community, at least so far as it reflected their lack of attendance at the bar counter.

Perhaps just as well. To describe as hostile the attitude of Halasay locals to the takeover of Sandray without any form of consultation, would be risible. Meetings had packed the village hall to hear celebrity environmentalists warn of the dangers lurking next door, an alarming reality which served to fuel the anger of an island community who knew they'd been duped, made victims of the 'not in my backyard' syndrome.

Attending another gathering, Eilidh and I sat through a Westminster MP's attempt to justify government action. He'd spoken boldly about job creation, moving towards sustainable low carbon lifestyles, and finally emphasising the safe role of nuclear power in cutting harmful emissions had ended by making the case for a wise mix of all options in the overall National energy policy. More mouth than man, we exchanged looks but kept silent. One old crofter at the back of the hall got the only applause when he stood up and addressed the platform, "It seems to me, and you can talk about being wise, Mr. Politician," he'd forgotten the chap's name, "the peat fire has done my day without harming anyone, apart from giving my wife a bad back." We all laughed until he said quietly, "But last year my grandson was killed in Afghanistan."

It came about that one day, a shade reluctantly, the three of us set off to climb the hill above Castleton. An excited Eachan scrambled up ahead and stood waving down from his perch on the summit cairn. Eventually we reached him, to find the clarity of light exceptional. Island upon island blended into each other until slender tips, they became images on the blueness of a day that marbled the tall white clouds of June on an unruffled ocean. The hilltop air in its stillness floated tranquil as the sea.

We sat quietly. First it was near, and then somewhere far away. Was it out on the ridge? There was no telling. A lone whistle, soft and elusive, plaintive as the calling of what once had been. "That's a golden plover," I whispered to Eachan. "It's the shyest of all the hill birds." The boy listened in fascination. I looked across to Sandray flushed by summer grass, green and inviting to those of a shepherding mind.

A vast breakwater complete with a sizeable navigating beacon curved out from the east side of the island, an immense structure. A huge quantity of jagged rock, blasted from tunnel and hilltop, had been bulldozed into the deeper water, ton by ton dumped and levelled. I visualised a modest sized ship sheltering in the bay unloading steel containers of radioactive waste. Sitting on a sizeable pier a couple of hefty looking cranes reached over the water; they'd be for lifting the consignments onto a track way which, beneath a series of concrete pillars dotting their way up the hillside, led to a tunnel mouth and into the storage chamber.

An array of turrets and antennae spiked the flattened top of the Hill of the Shroud suggesting some of the incoming material might arrive by helicopter. Even to the naked eye the level of activity was staggering. Huge trucks and land rovers crawled along a road zigzagging up the hill and down to the east bay. Obviously building work continued apace. The scale of it all alarmed me. This was no small home- based requirement; at the very least it smacked of American, if not international involvement.

The headland, made conspicuous by its singularly tall pylon, hid the site of our old house. Cables dangling above the Sound continued in a line of pylons striding over the hilltop, carrying the supply of electricity which I knew to be vital to maintaining a critically cold temperature in the storage tubes. Leaning against the cairn I shaded my eyes, groups of sheep grazed the hillside unconcerned by the roar of an incoming helicopter. Another took off, heading east. A moment's glint of light caught large letters along its side. They read, Nuen.

The sound of a departing helicopter followed us down the hill. Quietness returned as we sauntered down the lower slopes to where the wild fescue grew tallest and the warmth of an afternoon sun brought out the scent of bog-myrtle.

CHAPTER FIFTY-EIGHT

"A flash on TV."

Six years old, Eachan walked the two miles over to Castleton Primary School and always keen to help if he thought there was work with the animals, he'd run home. "Do you need a hand Dad?" The abandoned satchel hung on the gate, to the sound of his mother shouting from the door in Gaelic, "Come in and change your clothes." Eilidh ensured the boy was bi-lingual, even I found myself fluent enough during our supper time conversations to talk sheep, cattle and the weather.

Weeks of unbroken sunshine baked ground and grass alike. It had been the easiest summer for hay making. Even the old worthies for whom the weather had always been better in their school days, complained of sunburnt bald heads and admitted that never before did such a spell of heat settle itself over the islands. Pastures and bodies alike were tea brown. A relentless sun favoured the appearance of bikinis, sometimes even less. The tourist migration to Halasay's wide open beaches added a fresh dimension to bar counter comments on global warming. Towards closing time, often tempered with a little wisecrack, the stories of an older generation tended to reflect the changing seasons, rather than the earthy observations of the more concupiscent.

"There was no school bus when I ran barefoot to the school and home again at the double to go fishing or whatever was doing," my crofting neighbour, Roddy MacDougal, a man who'd gained his Master's Ticket at twenty-five and sailed the world, had just topped ninety. "You see my father used to graze the cattle on Eilean Fada, you know where I mean," he nodded over his shoulder, "out there on the west side. I wouldn't be in school even, but many's the time I drove them across the strand, no problem, when the tide was out, the channel was dry. About May time it would be; what grazing, what a shine it put on them. You could pull a chair under them and eat your dinner off their back, it would be like a table. When the geese came back in October we took the cattle home, but in the old days the young women, my granny was one of them, would go over and milk them and make cheese, and stay for a month or more in a turf hut, and sometimes the boys would go across," he winked at me," and on an occasion more than cheese would be made."

Whatever story lay behind his wink, Captain Roddy gazed into the mirror behind the optics. Thoughtful eyes saw childhood days, a sheet of water, thin and bright as glass covering the sand and his father's cattle splashing their way across the ford. I waited until he looked back to me, "You see as the years went by it got more difficult, you had to wait a half moon and drive the cattle over at the neap tide. That was fine, but you'll know yourself, Eachan," I'd long since become used to answering to the Gaelic of Hector, "that north-west gale we had two winters ago, I never saw a bigger sea running, the breakers were eating the dunes by the yard. There'll be no more cattle grazing on Eilean Fada, nor the geese either. The sea level is rising, and nothing will halt it now. The island just about covers at high water, and Eachan you'll see it yourself at Ach na Mara, those dunes at the far end of your croft are getting washed away." "Yes, the marram grass isn't holding them stable now and when it goes." there was no point in my stating the obvious.

A look to MacLeod and the ever attentive hotelier served another round. "The old granny used to say when I'd come home from sea and be telling about Atlantic gales, 'Don't be speaking, it'll all be the same in a hundred years,' but you tell me, I'm not so sure. They talk about climate change, storms follow heat, I tell you, the whole western seaboard of these islands is threatened; when Greenland gets back its colour these crofts will need more than a seawall."

Sweltering heat indeed, Eilidh and I had made the most of it. A hay crop stacked in good order yielded a feeling all that mattered in our little insular world remained secure. We passed an unhurried afternoon raking up the last wisps of hay. Weeks of sunshine had lightened the shade of Eilidh's hair; it fell flaxen gold over her tanned shoulders, feminine and luxurious. A little ahead of me she gathered the scattered grass into lines. I watched the easy flow of her body.

Perhaps she knew, perhaps the sunshine betrayed my thoughts. With a laugh, I caught her by the waist. She spun around. The hay rake fell to the ground unnoticed and gently she curled her arms about my neck. Her eyes held in their light the blueness of our every tomorrow, "Eilidh, if only you could realise how much I..." She drew my lips to hers. My eyes closed. In the sun that would not let us part, time was for another day, another place, nothing could change. She trembled ever so lightly, "I know, I know how much," her words, deep and tender, broke the silence, "it's the same for me, always," and amidst the fragrance of summer we lay together in the hay.

"Here's the helper," his mother spotted Eachan on the road, school bag bouncing on his back as he ran, "there's some hurry on him today." Red cheeked and panting he flopped onto a coil of hay. This wasn't his normal happy canter home. Adult like in its expression of alarm, his young face looked up to us, tense and serious. I glanced questioningly to Eilidh.

"There's a war started." The abruptness of his outburst startled us both, not least the effect of the horror in his voice. Blue eyes, deep set like his mothers, overflowed with worry. Eilidh spoke first, "Who was telling you this?" Words poured out, "I heard the teachers talking, they were all speaking, there's been a flash on the T.V., I don't know, they weren't telling us, they just seemed frightened."

The strained look on his small face carried to me the plight of so many children bewildered by the world of grownups that threatened the shelter of childhood; a world in which for the first time a fear of death came to haunt their growing minds. "Will it come here, Dad?" "Don't worry Eachan," I spoke with a reassurance which I hoped covered my own dismay, "it's not happening here," and with forced cheerfulness, "what about giving us a hand? We'll need a help to gather these rakings, it'll be the last stack we'll make this year." The boy looked relieved. Eilidh searched my eyes, "Supper will ready when I give you a wave." Although the pitch fork was too big for him, Eachan set about lifting the lines of hay. We worked side by side, man and boy.

Old ways are hard to better. Supper started with a plate of porridge and most evenings for a short time the headlines of BBC's six 'o' clock news overlaid our conversation. Out of choice we had no T.V. and didn't miss it, nor did Eachan seem to feel deprived. Whether about the animals, down to check the boat, or roaming Halasay with his pals, he spent most of his time outside. But there could be no hiding that night's serious concentration on the broadcast.

In spite of the BBC's customary avoidance of any emotion on the part of their newscasters, the sombre tones in carefully measured words conveyed more than a hint of grimness. An overnight pre-emptive strike, deployed from a US station in the Indian Ocean and from bases in Israel had destroyed nuclear installations throughout Iran. Several major fires were burning, including one in Tehran. Heavy radioactive fallout carried by a strong south westerly wind was spreading across Pakistan and up into the mountains of Afghanistan. No reports of Iranian casualties were available. A small number of retaliatory rockets had struck Tel Aviv but did not carry nuclear warheads. Israeli casualties were put at eighty-two dead and over two hundred injured. Our heads bowed in rapt attention. The boy looked from one to another.

Westminster MP's had been recalled from their summer holidays. The Prime Minister would make a statement to the House tomorrow. The United Nations Security Council in New York were meeting in an emergency session. All flights in and out of the Middle East cancelled. Total condemnation in the strongest terms had come immediately from Russia, India, China, and North Korea. Germany, France, the whole of the EU, apart from Britain, had issued warnings. Already people on the streets of Paris and Berlin were massing in protest. Given the gravity of the situation in terms of an international conflagration, the terseness of the report fully amplified the extreme nervousness of the UK Government's position in being America's staunchest ally.

Radiation casualties, an escalation of the conflict; as best we could, we kept our dread of all out nuclear war away from Eachan. He lay in bed that night asking his mother, "Why are they bombing Iran? What will happen to us?" Difficult questions to answer without creating feats of imagination and fear in a young mind. Eilidh finally got him settled down to his bedtime story, a children's tale of adventure about a stowaway on the last windjammer.

I sat alone through in the room. Almost in a state of shock my thoughts wandered over the ramifications of such precipitous action. At least those instantly vaporised at the nuclear sites wouldn't suffer the terminal vomiting of radiation sickness nor endure waiting the months or years before being picked off by the misery of some form of cancer. More insidiously, the land

and water supplies upon which millions of some of the worlds poorest depended could remain contaminated for many generations.

I shivered with a feeling of helplessness. Democracy reduced to a capitalist dictatorship. There seemed no way out, the trap was closing, inexorably closing, for the planet's billions the actions of a handful, sane or otherwise, determined the fate of countless innocents. Globally, lethal weapons concentrated in so few trigger happy fingers begged the possibility of unilateral retaliation on the part of some autocrat. TV spin or torture chambers, megalomaniacs on the grandstand of extremism, thriving on the mirage of their own self-belief and the curse of religious rivalry. A planet destroyed by the hand of human ingenuity and the myth of religious truth.

Sanguinary images paraded through my head in a tapestry of carnage. The features of a drunken Anderson persisted in appearing. Again I saw a circle on his chart surrounding the island of Diego Garcia, America's launch pad for this strike. 'I have a job to do.' Had his vicious rant any significance? No, impossible, pure fantasy, anyway what job? Why was Valkyrie and her hidden cargo radio active, Sandray ----Nuen's major involvement? My temples thumped.

The room faded, Twilight encroached. A fever of uncontrolled thoughts challenged any basis for reality. An idyllic day for us, a cataclysmic end for so many; in the flash of the tube train explosion, I stood on the lip of a precipice, assailed by the dizziness of vertigo.I was falling, swirling into the blackness of an unknown dimension.

Creaking boards dragged me from the edge. Eilidh tiptoed down the stairs. "He's sleeping at last, it wasn't easy to get his mind off war." I rose and pulled her to me. I needed to look into her eyes, see beyond the darkness. "I can believe you," was all I could say. Not wanting to cast the shadow of a hopelessness that drained me, I went over to the piano.

Eilidh put her hands on my shoulders and gently rubbed my neck. Softly, I began to play some of our favourites, 'Bonnie Mary of Argyll, The Rowan Tree, My Ain Folk', the tunes of old Scotia that would not die.

CHAPTER FIFTY-NINE

"As Britain's finest Prime Minister once said."

Fragrant steam drifted upwards the elaborate stucco mouldings which corniced his bathroom ceiling. Ingeniously concealed lighting enhanced their delicate filigree. A special commission, they were the work of a much sought after Italian master plasterer of classical taste. A bald head lay back on the cushioned rim of a pool- sized marble and alabaster Jacuzzi. The dilettantish Sir Joshua Goldberg relaxed. How fittingly the whole magnificent effect reflected his appreciation of life's finer aspects.

Nuen's concerns during the gloom and doom days following that nuclear fiasco at Fukushima were no more than the little curls of fragrance lifting off the warmth. These matters are always best left to experts he reflected. How very sensible of these Japanese chappies to take my advice on the PR, what's a drop of radioactive coolant in a pond as big as the Pacific, and really that tsunami, nothing which couldn't be rebuilt, Iraq proved it, godsend to his friends in the construction industry, such a windfall. But, he cautioned himself, one mustn't be envious. The grey hairs on his chest and corpulent midriff winnowed in the swirling waters, already his back felt easier.

In jocular mood he flipped a little water over his bathing companion and confidante, Nick Fellows. "I have to say, Nicky, I wasn't taken by surprise, knew this exciting little Iranian tea party was about to be pulled orf. Pentagon chaps told me as much after our last shipment went out to Diego

Garcia. Job well done; only way to deal with these extreme types. No occasion to worry, bit of fallout, it'll soon blow over, mercifully in the right direction," Goldberg's frame shook with laughter sending ripples round the pool. "By the way, hope you understood my clever little hint the other month. One shouldn't hold back, excuse the pun, it was a golden opportunity to stock up the vaults. Perhaps you did the same?" he enquired innocently, reaching out a hand for his glass of Chateaux Noir, 1993 Special Reserve.

Banker Fellows wriggled his toes, surreptitiously tickling those of Sir Joshua, "I couldn't be more pleased, Joshy, brilliant timing, you must have seen the market today, bedlam in there, billions lost in minutes; suicidal, out of the window stuff. You're such a friend, yes- I improved my position in gold, immeasurably." Beneath the bubbles, he patted Sir Joshua's chubby thigh, "Up forty percent on the day, maybe another ten at first trading, a little profit- taking then up, up, just lovely. Run on the dollar today, it was pure dysentery."

Goldberg sipped his wine and whilst fending off Nicky's straying hand he allowed their toes to mingle a little more. "Good boy, how simply divine of you, but please don't be so coarse." The slight admonishment gave Nuen's Chairman the edge he needed. "Look here Nick, I may require your help," he squeezed the banker's hand. Fellows moved a little closer. "Not just now, Nicky dear." No distractions, for the moment. "It is most useful to have an ex- prime minister on one's board, I have it on the highest authority that Britain's nuclear submarine station and weapons storage base is to be privatised."

Sir Joshua flapped a petulant hand, "Unfortunately it happens to be located on the river Clyde in Scotland. I can't stand the Scots, always poncing around in kilts reciting incoherent nonsense from some philandering poet of theirs." He patted his friend's hand, "More to the point, the whole of this base is to be sold orf, supposedly to the highest bidder. Naturally I happen know the right people so it's the least problem, easily handled." Instantly reading the Chairman's intention, a 'friend' of course, but a banker's evasive mentality first, "How interesting," he trilled.

Goldberg sniffed, "As you know our last accounts show that I, or rather I should say my company has made a highly rewarding investment with our waste facility on that God forsaken island, turnover's up twenty-five percent so far this year, material's just pouring in. Obviously with our new build reactors in England going ahead, acquiring this naval base is a logical step, it's only half an hour's helicopter away from our island operations. Pentagon is pressing our case within the MOD. The US submarine fleet have used the place for years. It really should be under our control. We're talking large sums, very, and that's where you come in, Nicky dear," Sir Joshua gripped the banker's hand. "When this deal goes through I need enough finance available for a majority holding. Vertical integration, always wise you know, and I want control."

Fellows smiled through the steam. Bubbles jetted up from below lifting their two bodies. Thighs touching, they floated side by side. "Joshy, I don't see any difficulty, you have masses of collateral. Dollars sinking like a pricked balloon, the Chinese Government's huge holding of US treasury bonds is such a disappointment to them, and they just love gold. All the Arab States, even Israel, are dumping dollars and buying gold. This smart operation in Iran is such a God send to us, we have plenty of the lovely yellow metal, it could double in value in the next week. Financing your take over will be easy, there's been plenty heat over Iran since yesterday; I always say, make gold whilst the sun shines."

Goldberg perked up, "Heat, I so glad you mentioned heat, Nicky, Perhaps I haven't told you, but under Nuen's wing," the turn of phrase pleased him, so clever. He repeated it, "under Nuen's wing, on a world wide basis of course, I'm launching a company which supplies air conditioning systems, houses, factories, whole cities if you like. It's really energy greedy and guess who'll supply the juice? You see Nicky dear, before long, many cities, Houston is one, will become so unbearably hot and sticky the vulnerable, old, sick and what have you, will be swatted like flies. Uptake of my systems will be exponential, for those who can afford it,"

Sir Joshua added with a smirk, "This global warming lark definitely has its plus side. As a scientist myself I can assure you Nicky, it's a lot of hot air," his reams of fat quaked with laughter. "Heat waves dear boy, everything rises with heat, especially shares in my latest venture, got to put this climate guff to good effect you know." He smiled at his friend, "Just another of my wheezes to turn an honest coin as they say. I shall call the company, Air Con. Amusing name don't you think? Want me to let you in? "

Nicky wasn't listening. His hand began to wander, excitedly. Sir Joshua didn't object, his mind floated as freely as his body. No wonder the CIA lost interest in that off the record dealing in weapons grade uranium. Nuen's ex-chief executive was safely behind bars and the investigation closed.

This latest strategy lifted Goldberg into paroxysms of delight. Already Nuen enjoyed controlling shares in uranium mining, the control of a major section of the world's nuclear energy production, control of waste storage and soon the overseeing of a US, British and French weapons base. Presidents and Prime Ministers had no option but to consult him on any major international issue. No more waiting in the anti-room, some menial informing him, 'The President will see you now.' So demeaning.

He sipped more wine and gazed up at the classical mouldings. Ancient civilisations afforded due deference to power and greatness. The colossus of Rhodes, that giant statue of Apollo had stood astride their harbour. He, Sir Joshua Goldberg, would straddle the most powerful force known to man. "You know Nicky dear, this spot of punishment had to be inflicted, the Iranians needed to know where their true interests lie," and waxing philosophical for a moment, "There's no profit without pain, for someone," he added.

Today all had gone well. Gold was moving nicely, Nicky would fix the finance for his Scottish nuclear base, dear Nicky. Goldberg slipped an arm under his friend's waist. The pair rocked gently together. The warmth, the alluring scent, the soporific warmth, Nuen's chairman saw himself on a white marble plinth, busts of the great and good lined the stairs of his mind. "You know Nicky," he drooled, "we need a mini war from time to time, keeps the system topped up. As one of Britain's finest Prime Ministers once said on a successful day, 'Rejoice, rejoice.'

Sensual lighting from the masterly ceiling reflected upon two white bodies, and in its caressing glow the whirlpool of bubbles sparkled. A responsive Sir Joshua was beginning to enjoy his friend's attentions.

It was play time.

CHAPTER SIXTY

Asleep

Smashing fundamental particles together as they accelerated round a circuit within an intense magnetic field had been my job. All those years I'd spent working at the Hadron Collider outside Geneva, staring into a screen crunching data through my computer now a seemed world divorced from a creative thinking which saw more artistically into the origins and future of the universe. I didn't belittle my scientific background. It yielded the raw material to fire my imagination, and imagination is the fuel of science. Simple life at Ach na Mara was the catalyst of fresh ideas; as with Sandray, I had time and space.

Regarding Einstein to have been mistaken was heresy but I'd come to believe that any measurement, no matter how large or small, could only be an approximation. I saw the universe as an immense evolving system without any constant factor and therefore no fixed point. Were there even one constant, such as a finite speed for the photons of light, I believed the universe would not exist in the form we presently observe it, or indeed even exist at all. The introduction of a cosmic constant into calculations was a mathematical trick. The aim of my research in Switzerland had been to find the fundamental particle by which energy transformed to matter. Now, contemplating the nature of the universal driver of eternal change stirred my imagination.

The trigger for these thoughts came about through young Eachan's need for a computer as part of his schooling. We both had doubts as to its function in promoting learning and least of all for encouraging common sense or advancing an order of priorities which might aid future survival. The internet communications it opened up, such as Twitter and Facebook appeared to us pointless and time wasting by comparison to reading or playing games in the fresh air. Its role in providing children with violent games and virtual reality stunts left us disgusted.

Our concern however went far beyond the classroom. Highly vulnerable areas of modern civilisation were serviced by computers. Banking to accounting, aircraft to weapon systems, satellites and power lines, down to mundane usage, we were falling victim to IT domination and its vulnerability. Recently we'd learnt that the perimeter of the nuclear submarine and weapons base on the Clyde was patrolled by autonomous robot vehicles operating independent of human control.

Apparently they were able to engage an intruder using a laser weapon if necessary and return lethal shots if fired upon. "Safeguarding nuclear weapon dumps could be trickier than just deploying intelligent surveillance machines," We talked seriously one evening after the boy was in bed, "How long before robots are out on the city streets?" I commented and Eilidh extended the theme, "How long before the mega-wealthy have them running around the outside of their exclusive compounds?" I ended the conversation rather grimly, "Autonomous killing by robots is just round the corner, and if you want gloom and doom I'm your man." We laughed in spite of the thought.

The attack on Iran stepped up the level of security on Sandray. The round the clock drone of helicopter activity drowned out our natural world. Naval vessels appeared over the horizon escorting incoming ships. Castleton School overlooked the

Minch and on one occasion, Eachan, his eyes bright with excitement, came bursting through the door to tell us, "An aircraft carrier was in the Sound today, we could see the fighter planes on the deck."

In many ways the danger of an attack on Sandray by external forces worried me less than the knowledge gleaned from visiting other nuclear installations many years ago. Experience told me that the Sandray underground dump would be a maze of computer and robotic controls. From working in Geneva I understood and feared the unpredictable nature of complex systems.

Producing food rather than commuting to an office emphasised a change in weather patterns. Weeks of dry terminated in endless spells of rain. When storms hit, the wind speeds had no problem reaching ninety. Livestock and crofter alike, in our simple way of farming we were struggling; it was far from factory farming- all under a roof converting oil into food. Most obvious to me working outside, was a quite distinctive shift in the type of rain which fell. Not so much the thin soft drizzle, a cross between fog and rain drifting in off the sea to settle on my woollen jersey like a silver mould; more frequently the droplets were large and heavy, pounding the ground, causing me to turn up my coat collar.

Record droughts in Australia, followed by torrential rain and floods, melting glaciers in other parts of the world, mud slides engulfing remote Brazilian villages and tragic flooding on the plains of Pakistan; mystic soothsayers of the sandwich board variety quoted Nostradamus, *the end is nigh*. More scientifically minded pundits blamed the extremes of weather on the sun's current quiescent state. Astrophysicists informed us that the normal eleven year sun spot cycle had stretched. The period of minimal activity on the sun's surface did appear to be unusually extended.

Historians quoted the mammoth disruption to the world's fledgling communication network of 1859. The spectacle of the northern aurora was witnessed over Rome, the sky blazed with shooting colours and people flocked to church. Apart from Quebec's entire power supply being knocked out 1989, well, history was history... what's on tonight's telly?

In America, scientists at NASA's Space Flight Centre were becoming increasingly concerned. The sun was sleeping, and they sure didn't like it.

Sir Joshua arrived unannounced on the summit pad of Sandray. He preferred his visits to be a complete surprise. It kept the staff on duty in a state of unease. His personal helicopter flew out from Nuen's nuclear weapons base on the Clyde, ostensibly heading for London. Once airborne he shouted into the intercom, "Head for Sandray!" The pilot nodded and banked northwest. Fully aware this change of course should immediately be notified to the Traffic Controller at Glasgow airport, he remained silent. Goldberg preferred it that way.

A flurry of courtesy greeted their Chairman. Would he care for lunch, coffee in the central operating gallery? "Not at the moment, I shall go straight down to inspect the storage chamber." Goldberg had no wish to allow any delaying tactic which might enable possible shortcomings to be rectified.

The Chief Technician, alerted from the switchboard, made a hurried appearance, "Good afternoon, sir." Goldberg inclined his head, "You'll kindly accompany me. Firstly I want a full inspection of the underground area." "Of course, of course, sir," the technician ushered his employer to the main lift shaft and the pair descended into the bowels of a storage centre designed to hold enriched uranium with a half life varying from a few hundred to tens of thousands of years.

Five hundred feet below the summit of the Hill of the Shroud, Goldberg stepped out of the passenger lift into the halogen whiteness of a huge concrete lined chamber. The couple stood on the stainless steel platform looking down on a series of massive lead covers securing the top of an extensive line of boreholes. To their left, a track way running alongside them disappeared down a narrower tunnel which led to the unloading jetty on the shore. A large container of waste on a low loading trolley moved silently, inch at a time, up the track. Robotic machines, their green security lights flashing, slid into place. Clawing arms waved towards the cylinder. Another massive robot positioned itself over the mighty lead cap. Operators in the central control module regulated the whole slow motion dance on 3D screens.

Man, robot and remote control. No humans ever entered this subterranean hall without express permission, nor without wearing heavy lead lined clothing. Ignoring his own regulation Sir Joshua stood before a majestic display of human endeavour. In the Halls of Valhalla, amidst cloud and thunder, lived the Viking Gods of the sea rover's belief, omnipotent in their power over the life or death of humankind. Under the hill of their island sanctuary, the Hill of the Shroud was built. A chamber of echoes, hallowed alone by its power to obliterate human life. In the funereal hollow, before moving arms which knew no feeling except the pulse of circuits, Goldberg deemed himself at the apex of his life; supreme control, answerable to none, other than his own free will.

"Where is that consignment from?" Sir Joshua watched the canister's deliberate trundle towards its burial vault, "France, sir." "Excellent. How close are we to capacity?" "Only twenty-five percent storage left, sir." Goldberg smiled inwardly. The inestimable value of what he controlled, the sheer unadulterated, fabulous wealth, his cultured mind whispered; a fortune beyond even the fabled riches of Babylon.

"Follow me." Sir Joshua spoke over his shoulder, "I shall examine the far end of the unit. We shall widen this tunnel, drill some deeper bore holes, double the present capacity."

Along the wide steel gantry flanked by monitoring dials and lights, Goldberg marched.

His footsteps rang out, hollow and metallic...

CHAPTER SIXTY-ONE

Awake

Ninety-three million miles and twenty-five days to each rotation, the furnace at our solar heart turns slow. Six thousand degrees are on its face, a roaring fusion is within. Five billion years remain to drink our power house dry. Crunched by gravity's brutal jaw, a shrunken dwarf, it's girth no bigger than this earth. Electrons jostle protons, pack so dense and tight a spoonful of its matter weighs three tonnes or more. No planets left, away it spins, its light a guttering flicker. Our once proud sun and fifty billion dwarfs which too were suns are companions in the galaxy. There, inert and feeble they await the day when the great Andromeda spiral will crash into our Milky Way; and Dark Energy begins its fight to oust the power of Gravity; and deal the final hand of fate.

Three hundred million years is one rotation of our galaxy, a dot amidst the denizens of space where a hundred thousand million systems swirl. Can we contemplate such span of time? Death will banish time. For at the centre of this Universe, gargantuan and supreme, there spins the black dark hole through which all things are drawn; a single point that turns infinity to eternity. And in the brightness of one creative flash all posibilties awake to fields of Universes new. Will consciousness endure, be born again? Become some form which owes survival to imagination's strength? Will entangled waves of this self same energy feast on knowledge, posses the power to build a Universe?

Each eleven years is the ebb and flow of sunspot cycles, pulse of our miniscule cosmic presence. It slowed. Twelve years passed. The white hot surface of the sun remained almost free from the dark pock marks of cooler gas which block the coronal emissions. A maelstrom of particles in the blast furnace of plasma at the sun's magnetic heart were churning, smashing, annihilating; energised beyond the strength of gravity.

A bubble swelled on the surface of the sun; swelling on a molten face which revolved towards the earth. Gigantic pressure built.

It burst; twenty billion tonnes of matter hurled in leaping fangs of glowing plasma, flicking tongues of energy whipping into space at near the speed of light.

Particles, highly charged, their destructive power a billion atom bombs surged earthwards. Unleashed energy smashed through the earth's magnetic shield.

The skies blazed. An aurora of terrifying brilliance unseen before; a solar outburst of extreme violence enveloped the planet, a vast geomagnetic storm all powerful in its fury.

Satellites veered wildly out of orbit. Global navigation failed. Weapon systems crashed, computer networks crashed. Power cables criss crossing the globe became the giant storms antennae. Worldwide communication ceased. The arteries of civilisation were paralysed. Fires and multi explosions ripped through city and homestead alike. Ripples of panic spread, waves of chaos engulfed the masses at their phalanx screens, the herdsmen on his empty plains.

Terror turned to anarchy. Fear swept all before it!

People gazed towards the sun.

Was this the time to pray?

Sir Joshua Goldberg and his Chief Technician walk slowly along the steel gantry towards the end of the huge underground storage chamber. Beneath them is the line of installations which cover the actual bore holes. Down three hundred feet into the solid rock beneath the hill, are the stacks of containers. Massive lead caps seal their tops. Seemingly unending pipes carry the vital cooling liquid. Banks of lights indicate every aspect of the state of the nuclear waste, the various pressures involved and of paramount importance, the material's critical temperature.

The couple stand at the end of the long steel gantry. Nuen's Chairman looks proudly back along the chamber. Bright green lights shine from each control point, the plant was working extremely efficiently, all was as he'd planned it. Entirely satisfied Goldberg smiles, and waving his arm towards the dead end of the chamber he speaks expansively to his Chief Technician, "This is where I shall build my next phase of the expansion on this Goddamn island. This facility has solved the problem. My Company is the saving of the whole nuclear industry."

Instantly they are in total blackness, primal, complete and without sound, a density of blackness without point of reference, an absence of all else but the sickness of claustrophobia. Such its suddenness neither speaks. Their shallow frightened breathing quickens. Goldberg moves. His foot strikes something soft. He reaches down. His hand contacts a prone body. "You bastard, you've fainted. You foul bastard, get up, get up, get me out of here, get me to the lift." There is no move, no breathing. "You fool, you blithering fool, are you dead?" Goldberg kicks the inert form, finds its face and kicks again and again.

Horror- struck Goldberg stumbles, falls against the handrail. Which way, which way? This way? Inch by inch he shuffles. Both sweating hands slide along the rail. The lift, the lift, I must reach the lift. I must reach the... is this the main platform? Only blackness, the underground blackness is a creeping phantom, untouchable, yet a presence that moves with his every shuffling step. Another yard, another, another, the rail turns. He follows. Yes, the lift door. He runs trembling hands over the control buttons.... must find the control, his hand paws, his fingers feel.

These must be the buttons. They won't press. No power, the lift is without power. A screaming Goldberg beats the unyielding door, "Get me out, get me out pleeese!!!" A hollow voice echoes out of the black silence. "Get me out, pleeeeese!" The scream fades, stretches into the void, the wail of torment entering the tunnel of dread.

He listens to the echo, is there someone? His bare hand has struck some object, he feels blood. His sagging legs give, he sinks down, leans his back against the closed door and stops the futile screams. There is nobody to hear, nobody.

His broken voice trails into sobbing. "Please, please God get me out of here," he clasps beseeching hands. Now there is no echo. The trap of utter blackness swallows his whimpering voice.

How long passes? There is no telling, only darkness. His mind is emptied of rational thought. His heart pounds with fear. He leans to one side and vomits.

He closes his eyes, and prays.

Upstairs in the central control room the on duty team sitting before a bank of winking consoles relax. Goldberg and the boss are safely below inspecting the storage chamber. They swivel their chairs and chat. Ordinary, mundane comment, last night's dart match in the centre. No mention is made of the arrival of Sir Joshua. Their whole work area is under continuous surveillance by camera and microphone, every word and move is recorded and computer analysed. During the past month a number of alerts have been relayed to them, mostly unidentified aircraft. Unknown to Goldberg his helicopter pilot had checked in their flight to avoid another such incident. Since the Iran attack a completely revised set of security rules applies. Neither ship nor plane or any person allowed near Sandray without double verification. The terrorist threat is at red, its highest level.

The safety door's light is flashing. "It's Jim," comes over the intercom. He's in the outer vetting compartment. The foreman checks him on the screen and punches in a code. The door opens allowing an off duty colleague to hurry in. The door automatically closes behind him.

"Hell chaps! There's something bloody funny happening in the sky, its turning green, great stabs of light are streaking across it." The panic in the eyes is not lost on the group. They swivel off their seats and surround the man, "Back to your stations!" barks the foreman, equally alarmed. "This might be an attack."

Suddenly complete darkness. Every screen, every panel light, cut out. The foreman technician is first to react. "Emergency, emergency drill," he shouts, "switch to number one base generation." The team leaves their seats. They fumble about feeling their way, bumping into each other. "No response, no response," shouts the first back to his control web.

Frantically each man on reaching his desk presses buttons. Dead, the system is dead. The leading technician reaches the emergency door, "Hell's teeth it won't open!" Voices begin to babble, try this, try that, the first wave of panic is setting in. The air already feels sticky. No vents, no air conditioning.

"Christ boys, we'll be cooked alive in here!" a shrill voice above the rest. "Shut your mouth!" the foreman barks out of the black dark. "Stay at your desks."

Nobody yet dares mention the thoughts upper most in every mind. Has the cooling systems surrounding each waste filled bore hole has been cut off? Each man knows the consequence.

Meltdown. The prospect of death stalks through the control room.

Goldberg stirs, lifts his head, opens his eyes. The faintest green glow suffuses the chamber. Only too aware of what is happening he groans, on and on, the low groaning of total abandonment to abject terror. He screams again, "God of my people, please, please." He slumps back exhausted.

The green radiance intensifies. He looks round the chamber, flickering light is playing a ghostly hand on its vaulted ceiling. His crazed mind flashes back to his treasured bathroom, the beauty of its mouldings. This can't be happening; it's a dream, a horror of a drug induced nightmare. I must waken, must waken.

The heat is making his breathing difficult. He stares down stupidly. The nearest lead cap is melting into a green fluid. Without warning his platform begins to tilt, slowly to buckle. "No, no, no!" his voice is broken from screaming. He grabs at stanchions, hangs on. The tilt increases in slow motion. His hands are burning; the stench of a sacrifice on the altar of mammon.

A plume of fluid spurts out of the bore hole. Blazing droplets fall on his legs. The pain is beyond feeling. He watches his flesh melting, running down the sloping platform. His legs are dripping. Tiny flames of tallow course down the ribbed steel. The heat is searing his lungs at every breath. Goldberg throws his head back.

In a cracked shrieking he pleads, "God, God, save me, I give you all my money, God of the ten talents, pleeeese, pleeese hear me, I'm your servant, I made it for you, all my money is yours, millions, milli......" To those that have shalt be given.

The heat cuts off his breath. His burning hands release their grip. The acrid fumes of his burning flesh choke his lungs. The green glare burns his eyelids.

Unable to close his eyes, Sir Joshua Goldberg slithers gradually, imperceptibly down the platform. His closing anthem approaches.

Radiation, a requiem for all mankind.

The white hot furnace waits.

White hot as the erupting sun.

CHAPTER SIXTY-TWO

"As a whisper that will pass in the larch."

The fact that my inheritance vanished during the banking crash into somebody else's pocket didn't give me the slightest cause to grieve, nor could I find any reason to envy the lifestyle enjoyed by financial tycoons afflicted by the disease of making money. Our needs were slender, the income from the croft paid the bills and healthy living filled the bank. Eachan stretched into a tall, strong boy,able both at school and on the croft. Cows and ewes by their yearly offspring supported our family unit, just as we fed and cared for them, a mutual arrangement with much affection on our part, and if I read the animals minds correctly they viewed us with friendliness, especially when hay appeared. Given the sorry state afflicting many of the world's poor we were fortunate. Not without a twinge of conscience- there seemed little missing in our lives, and yet....

That morning I walked about the croft talking to the cows, "Well girls, you'll be glad the weather has taken a turn for the better." Day after day of unseasonable weather had forced our cattle to stand heads down and backs to driving rain and gale. The calmness which followed possessed an unusual quality. Maybe the passing of the storm heightened the sombre nature of its tranquility. The atmosphere struck me as odd. The sun had long risen to a sky without mist or cloud and yet the land and sea were imbued with a sickly paleness that lacked the animated colours which peopled my memories.

The sun appeared extraordinarily white, its serenity the evanescent calm which precedes the unforeseen. Perhaps it created my mood. No measure of time will erase the silent weeping for a loved one, deep emotion is an ebb and flow, sometimes a recall unbidden, and so the hurt of losing Sandray. I gazed into past happiness. Only the piping of the shore birds to waken us, their rippling calls at the edge of dawn. My arms around Eilidh at the door of the old house, we listened, and I would kiss her neck. Island mornings, I longed for their loveliness and the innocence of not knowing.

But who would unpick the threads of destruction? Knowledge without understanding is dangerous, the fate that had befallen our island, a web spun without wisdom.

Before going in for breakfast I studied the Atlantic. Shoals of herring might be running the coast, I needed action to lift my humour. "Isn't it time I was out casting a net over the side, get the salt barrels filled again?" Eilidh didn't reply immediately. "Maybe it is," she agreed, pausing some moments to look out of the kitchen window. "The barrels are empty right enough, and I think Iain's free tomorrow." Her brother often went fishing with me, but I knew, whatever the reason, she didn't want me to go to sea. Not that she put doubts into words, they showed in her eyes. There appeared no obvious reason not to set out and though it wasn't my nature to go against her feelings, almost doggedly I gathered up the gear needed.

Eachan was at school. I didn't wait his homecoming. Eilidh made up a thermos and mutton sandwiches. She insisted on coming to the jetty with me and I began to regret my decision. We walked quietly, their seemed little to say. A peculiar lull rested upon the sea. Along the beach huge semi-circles of white froth lay in the sand ripples. Somehow the unbelievable quiet of the day lacked peace. No sound carried from the ocean, its oppressive silence broken only by the cry of a solitary redshank. The beach was empty, deserted, as if all life had fled.

Due to the restrictions surrounding Sandray the Hilda hadn't been used for some weeks. Today I would flaunt the blockade. Windless conditions meant a trip using the outboard. I tried to reassure Eildh, "They'll never spot me without a sail up." In spite of looking miserable, she laughed, "A cormorant out fishing would come up on their screens." Together we loaded the nets, floats, outboard engine and fuel.

I stowed the gear. Should I go? My misgivings over putting to sea were more to do with concerns for Eilidh. I jumped back onto the jetty, "Don't worry Eilidh, I'll be home before dark, herring or no herring." I'd done it a thousand times. I wrapped her in my arms. "Eilidh I, I..." the words wouldn't come. I could only tell her with my eyes and crush her to me.

"Hector," so faint my name, I bent my head to hers, "I love you, Hector." Her eyes were pools of blue light, her voice hushed as a whisper that will pass in the larches, "from ice capped hills the milk blue melt of spring put longboats back to sea." I was unable to speak. Nor did I understand.

Eilidh cast off the ropes. I looked up. Her liquid eyes held me. Southwards reared the headland of Sandray, so often our chosen bearing, and I turned the Hilda northwards. Just before the land was to part us from sight, I saw Eilidh still on the jetty, waving. I stood in the stern of the boat and returned her wave.

The walk back to the house went unnoticed. The emptiness of the bay meant nothing, if her tears could only fill it again. Eilidh stared at the spot where the Viking stone had been placed the night Hector and her brother took it from Sandray. In her wretchedness she wished above all the stone back beside the gable of Tigh na Mara, looking over the Atlantic. It had gone with Hector. The stone was back aboard the Hilda. They'd said she'd sailed so effortlessly. Her last words between them returned, spoken, not knowing why. She repeated them again and again. 'Put longboats back to sea'. A breath stirred in the larches, and she understood.

From the window of the kitchen Eilidh watched the sky. An unnerving stillness grew on the day, no wind, and the sun, cloud free, became a strange nebulous of intense white. Alone in the house, Hector gone, the fear which she had carried privately to the boat that morning, that had burst free into tears as she waved, now held her in a desolate mourning, the anguish of knowing. Unable to stand the silent house, she rushed outside and stood against the gable.

Green light filled the sky, reflected on the Atlantic. Flashes of red and white seared the heavens. The sea lay as she never before had seen it, a mirror of unnatural calm shining with a deepest violet intensity.

Young Eachan hurried home from school to find his mother standing at the end of the house. "All the power has gone, why is the sky so green? They sent us home, there's no phones working or anything else. Where's Dad?" Eilidh rested a hand on his tousled golden head, "He's away to the herring fishing. He'll be back before dark. In a little we'll go to the jetty and watch for him."

The boy looked from the lurid sky to the purple sea, and gently into his mother's face.

Brave boy, he put his arm round her waist and fought back the tears of childhood.

The Hill of the Shroud and a tip of land out from the bay of Ach na Mara was my transit, my bearing for returning home. I wondered at the day's unusual calm, it reached across an ocean flat as the eye could see. The greatest area on earth devoid of any movement, it stirred a deepening apprehension. I viewed the sea with a tinge of fear.

The suggestion of a breeze lifted off Halasay, no more than a cat's paw on all the immensity of the Atlantic. To resist my unease, I cut the outboard and hoisted sail. Rarely had the Hilda headed northwards. Maybe it was in myself, maybe fancy, only a breath in her sail and she came alive. I felt it. Beyond any horizon I'd ever crossed, she sailed for a land of phantoms where men who'd bent larch into boats believed the spirit of the wind was in their ships. And on that faintest breath, driving Hilda onwards I heard Eilidh's ghostly voice, "put longboats back to sea."

The longing for Eilidh became an exquisite pain, borne only for the joy of holding her again. 'Believe in beauty,' my father spoke from his deathbed, 'its melody is the key to eternity. If ever you find the key, guard it with your life.' Should I turn back?

I sailed on, stood at the mast, scanning the sea for the ripple which would tell me of a shoal. The hill of Sandray was just in sight. I'd sailed further than intended. I reached for the rope which would bring Hilda's sail across and set us running for home. I let the rope go. There, some distance ahead a jabble on the water broke the surface. Gannets speared their prey. Herring, swimming north, excitement carried me on, I must cross their heading. I tightened sail. The Hilda sprang to action, she heeled and bore away.

Make sure of my return bearing; I glanced aft, could still see land. For a moment I barely recognised the sun. A glaring silver blob daubed on a tight canvas now glowing with a greenish pallor. Hurry, the sky warned me. Gannets were still diving, someway astern. Bellies full, they headed west with Saint Kilda in their sights. We'd forged away beyond the shoal. I'd sailed such a distance, one cast and haul, then home.

Over the side went the large end float, now the net, small cork floats. I swung Hilda across what should be the fishes' track. A shoal of herring swims slowly. The net, shot and secured, I sat amidships on the Viking stone and waited.

The work of setting the net had taken my eye off the horizon. Not since that night of the great aurora on the Sandray headland had I witnessed such a spectacle. The northerly heavens were swathed in a green radiance; its shade flickered, light to dark. Dynamic barbs of white light of blinding intensity stabbed into the earth's magnetic field. A purple sea cowered in the reflected image of unleashed swords. The Gods of Valhalla surged towards us.

Planet earth was fighting a solar storm, the manifest power of the sun to destroy us. I was frightened. The fate of mankind danced with the Sun.

Haul the net, haul it fast. Feet braced on the gunnel I gripped the securing rope. Heavy, but it came aboard. Herring tumbled into the boat, flapping bellies silver as the sun. No warning, a sudden blast of air. Hilda's sail cracked over, hit me in the back. No hold, save the net. Water closed over me.

I surfaced. Hilda sailed on. I'd lashed her tiller. The net paid out, yard by yard. It jerked taut. Snap! It parted from the boat. A floating mass tangled my thrashing legs.

Head above water, I tried to swim. The net was dragging me. A streak of red shone on the water. The tip of the Hill of the Shroud blazed into the sky. I watched. Slowly it sank.

The moon was on the bay, and I stood beside the gables of memory.

Red into a green world, and slowly, so slowly, it became the blue of Eilidh's eyes

The Hilda sailed on, a lone empty boat crossing an ocean. She headed home.

And I sailed with her.

They stood together on the jetty of Ach na Mara waiting for a boat to come sailing in. The afternoon drew on, still he wasn't coming home. The greenness of the sky shone on the bay. Flashes of white light ripped across the heavens.

Eilidh trembled. Eachan clung to her, "Is it all right mum? When will Dad come home?" Eilidh stroked his head. "Soon," she murmured, her eyes searching, willing him.

But she knew, she knew, "Oh, my Hector."

The roar split the air, the blast threw them against the jetty wall. There they crouched. Flames poured into the sky. The Hill of the Shroud blazed. Another deafening explosion, its violence flung rock skyward. Glowing rock fell shattered into the Sound.

Hot ash filled the atmosphere, the miasma of mankind's making.

It floated down. Mother and son struggled to breathe, it filled their lungs.

Slowly, so slowly it settled.

Grey and choking, it covered land and sea.

Gently it fell upon two golden heads.

My boat crunched on the sand, white sand, beautiful and crystalline in the secret light that awaits the dawn. The air of the mountains floated down to me and I breathed again its freshness. Tall mountains, ice capped and glinting, they towered skywards over the narrow inlet of my landing.

I climbed the hill. Amongst the sweeping larch branches, their fallen needles golden in the winter light, I climbed and climbed. Her voice reached me, calling, calling. Calling as I'd heard it so often when morning crept across a sleeping ocean.

I ran, breathless and stumbling. Beneath the great larch I found her, my Eilidh, my golden haired Eilidh. We clung together. I held her as I had when time would lose its meaning.

I lifted her head. At last I was able to tell her, "Eilidh, I love you."

The first shafts of sunrise broke free. Their radiance surrounded us. "Hector, I knew you would find us here, just as I found you, long ago." She spoke, gently and wistfully. I saw her again in that first moment of longing, on a day far away, on the pathway of fate.

We looked down. Kneeling beside a willow cage our young boy talked to his raven. Black eyes sparkled up, the eyes of an ancient wisdom. In its beak the Raven carried a small disc, golden with sunlit memories.

Eilidh smiled, and her breath drew me as the breeze that lives on hill and sea.

I touched her hair.

And her eyes, blue and loving, held us entangled,

for all the time there will ever be.

Epilogue

Entanglement.

The braids of space, dimensions splice
Are threads of possibilities infinite,
And life a throw of chaos' dice.

All that has ever been, that may ever be,
The matter, time and space of this present universe,
Is crushed to a single eye, its spin beyond
the speed of light,
A density, the sum of all reality,
In the grip of gravity.

Magnetic frictions grow, matter melts to energy,
Atoms heat to unguessed degree,
A particle flux that fills the cusp,
A coiling hissing pit.

One inst, a nano-seconds flash, imbalance strikes,
Blinds the eye of singularity,
Its matrix bursts, electrons flee,
A fresh universe is born,
The ghostly hologram of all eternity.

One force survives, undiminished throught the eye,
By some strange ethereal affinity,
An echo, universe to universe,
Entangled photons fly.

Speed nor distance, nor any realm of space
can separate their bond,
Each particle of existence has a partner mate,
And the mystery of entanglement
Is our circled fate.

For life in whatever form is but a wavelength drawn,
Consciousness, its path without a bound,
And imagination's journey
A dance before the sun.